PRAISE FOR RICHARD B. SCHWARTZ

Proof of Purchase

It's like this guy is just channeling Raymond Chandler on every page. . . . The ending . . . would make Mike Hammer proud.
— Jochem Steen, *Sons of Spade*

In this engaging hard-boiled mystery, one of three in Schwartz's Jack Grant series (Frozen Stare; The Last Voice You Hear), the seasoned California PI looks into the disappearance of an ex-girlfriend at the request of the woman's husband. When her mutilated body turns up in the woods, Grant makes it his mission to track down her murderer. With the assistance of Lt. Diana Craig, an attractive fast-riser in the San Bernardino police department, Grant follows leads that point to his client, as well as to a consortium of underworld bosses who are branching out into a mega-real estate project. The pair find time, between car chases and gun battles, to begin a relationship. . . . Fans of Robert Parker will enjoy encountering Grant . . . .
— *Publishers Weekly*

The Last Voice You Hear

It's not often that an author's second book is as good as the first, and even less frequent are the instances when an author . . . top[s] it with an extraordinary second . . . deliver[ing] a walloping good tale as well. Richard B. Schwartz has done just that. In *The Last Voice You Hear*, Mr. Schwartz places himself on par with our finest contemporary murder-mystery writers. This is a book you won't want to miss. . . .
— Alan Paul Curtis in *Who Dunnit*

The author . . . writes vividly, putting the reader right into the scene. Schwartz explores the meaning of right and wrong, crime and justice.
— Mary Helen Becker in *Mystery News*

The story rockets along . . . a fast-moving, well-told story with a surprising conclusion that blurs the line between crime and justice.
— Joseph Scarpato, Jr. in *Mystery Scene*

Jack Grant, the Vietnam vet and Pasadena-based PI who debuted in Frozen Stare (1989), returns in this engrossing sequel by Schwartz, author of several scholarly studies of Samuel Johnson. Schwartz knows his London, but surprisingly he evokes California with equal ease, mainly with vividly etched strokes. An apparently maniacal killer is on the loose in London, someone strong and very practiced at impalement. So far, so nasty. But when a victim is dispatched in similar fashion in Disneyland, of all places, Jack Grant is called in. He discovers the killer's identity, but there's a problem: there's a method to the killer's madness. Moreover, Grant has an ethical problem of his own: he's plagued by his conscience, since he understands and even sympathizes with the murderer's cause. The cinematic climax takes place high above the floor of the California desert, and Schwartz squeezes every last drop of suspense from his setting. . . . The result is a high-tension thriller awash in sanguinary detail. Paper towels, anyone?
— *Publishers Weekly*

Frozen Stare

I welcome Richard Schwartz to the club. It's been a long time since I've seen two more engaging characters entering the series scene.
— Sandra Scoppettone

Grant and White play nicely off each other and the switch-on-a-switch works well.
— *Kirkus Reviews*

This tale, in the California private eye tradition, has a rousing finish and is an enjoyable read.
— *Publishers Weekly*

A new author devoted to the hard-boiled tradition. . . . Schwartz has the hard-boiled formula down pat. . . . Schwartz does not break any rules in Frozen Stare. . . . He writes crisply. The narrative moves at a slam-bang pace as bodies pile up. . . . As a dedicated student of the hard-boiled school of detective fiction [Schwartz] has learned his lessons well.
— *The Washington Post Book World*

Gives a whole new meaning to the phrase 'cold-blooded murder'. . . . This is a quick read with plenty of action. Schwartz's first novel is a winner!
— *Sarasota, FL Herald Tribune*

This is a delightful tale, full of amusing touches, and the relationship between Grant and his good cop friend, black Frank White, is a joy. I hope that Schwartz can keep this standard up for a long time to come.
— *The Armchair Detective*

Nice and Noir: Contemporary American Crime Fiction

Opinionated but always fascinating, shrewd and smart, but always readable. . . .
— *The Thrilling Detective*

BOOKS BY RICHARD B. SCHWARTZ
FICTION

The Jack Grant Novels

Frozen Stare
The Last Voice You Hear
Proof of Purchase

The Tom Deaton Novels

Into the Dark
The Survivor's Song
Nightmare Man
Death Whispers

CRITICISM

Samuel Johnson and the New Science
Samuel Johnson and the Problem of Evil
Boswell's Johnson: A Preface to the Life
Daily Life in Johnson's London
After the Death of Literature
Nice and Noir: Contemporary American Crime Fiction
The Wounds that Heal: Heroism and Human Development
(with Judith A. Schwartz)
ed. The Plays of Arthur Murphy, 4 vols.
ed. Theory and Tradition in Eighteenth-Century Studies

MEMOIRS

The Biggest City in America: A Fifties Boyhood in Ohio
Accidental Soldier: A Reserve Officer at West Point in the Vietnam Era
Postwar Higher Education in America: Just Yesterday

EBOOK

Is a College Education Still Worth the Price? A Dean's Sobering Perspective

A TOM DEATON NOVEL

DEATH WHISPERS

RICHARD B. SCHWARTZ

DARK HARBOR BOOKS

DEATH WHISPERS

Published by Dark Harbor Books
First Edition 2022

Copyright © 2022 by Richard B. Schwartz

All rights reserved. No part of this book may be reproduced or utilized in any form or by any means, electronic or mechanical, including photocopying, recording or by any information storage and retrieval system, without permission in writing from the publisher. Inquiries should be addressed to the author.

This is a work of fiction. Names, characters, places and incidents are either products of the author's imagination or are used fictitiously. Any resemblance to actual events, locales or persons, living or dead, is entirely coincidental.

Cover design: Jana Rade

ISBN: 978-1-7374748-9-0 Paperback Edition
          979-8-9855721-0-0 Hardcover Edition
          979-8-9855721-1-7 Digital Edition

Library of Congress Control Number: 2022900755

Author services by Pedernales Publishing, LLC
www.pedernalespublishing.com

10 9 8 7 6 5 4 3 2 1

Printed in the United States of America

xx-v5

For Judith—wife, partner, best friend

Who will rise up for me against the evildoers?
Or who will stand up for me against the workers of iniquity?

Psalm 94, A Prayer for Vengeance

I

ABOVE LAKE ELSINORE

ONE

I turned my left cheek across the creases of my top pillow and focused on the array of red dots that formed the numbers announcing the time on my clock/radio. It's one of those old cube-shaped things, inexpensive and reliable, the kind that's easy to program. It read **4:18**. The right side of my body was suddenly chilled. I had given up the blue comforter, which had felt too heavy and confining and substituted a single sheet. A flat sheet; who uses those anymore? I bought it on sale in the spring--part of a package deal--and I had promptly stuck it away in the back of the linen closet; last night I found a use for it. Now it felt like a narrow strip of simple, wrinkled cotton—a child's security blanket--caught between my knees, the point of its corner held in the fingers of my right hand. I had pulled it over my face and ear, wanting to muffle the noises of the world so that I could rest, but suddenly I could hear everything . . . the sound of the wooden mattress supports creaking against their steel frame, the sound of the wind blowing through the California black oak beyond my bedroom window . . . the air conditioner compressor at the opposite corner of the house . . . the refrigerator motor . . . the water softener cycling.

The water softener was my father's favorite, that and the stone shower stall that had replaced its molded plastic predecessor. I was spending most of my time in his house now; since the death of my mother he's been living at the marina, sleeping on the boat that carries her name. As a child I had always slept well in this house, but since my surgery my nights have sometimes been unsettled. I had resisted my internist's repeated offers of a prescription for Ambien. A man in his thirties who does a full day of honest work shouldn't need pills to calm his nerves or help him sleep (so my father and grandfather would have said), but neither should he awake several times each night, concerned about his health and when it might next be disrupted or lost.

A profound sense of relief and release generally accompanies a positive medical report, but when that report comes five years after the diagnosis and treatment of a brain tumor there remains the realization that there are no ultimate guarantees and that a report of 'clear' is no more than a statement attesting to the fact that you happen to be clear for the moment. For me, probably for everyone in this situation, any hint later of the smallest discomfort or even the tiniest indication of a change in sensation was accompanied by doubt, suspicion and the fear that what had once appeared unexpectedly and without warning could be reappearing again in that very same fashion. Headaches, blinks, twitches . . . seeing floaters across my field of vision, seeing that sudden flash of light at the far edge of the eye . . . even something as slight as blurred vision upon awakening or the echoing of sound or change of voice that accompanies a simple head cold . . . it didn't take much to bring on sober thoughts and fears.

I had developed a set of defensive responses for these situations— testing my memory by calling up specific forms of information, repeating mnemonics--sometimes aloud, sometimes silently; humming complex melodies, blinking my eyes and refocusing them, turning in my bed or rising from my chair, clearing my throat, running my fingertips across my head . . . the process was personal, obsessive and completely unscientific. I hadn't even mentioned it to my internist or surgeon.

Jeff Hanley, the neurosurgeon, told me to be alert but not overly concerned. "Even if they haven't had a previous incident I'd tell all my patients to stay alert for warning signs. In your case you're likely to be hyper-vigilant. Just remember—the healthiest person on the planet still gets headaches and twitches and memory lapses. Be attentive but don't drive yourself crazy."

The *previous incident*--like a brake failure or a minor burglary, except that I was hit by a grade I astrocytoma. It made its presence known when I began having seizures and developed vertigo. These tumors arise in the star-shaped cells that form the supportive tissue of the brain. The astrocytes are a form of glial cells and the tumors are often called gliomas. Grade I isn't really bad; it's actually classified as benign, but yet . . . it's there, somewhere it's not supposed to be, and that raises questions. Grade I's are more common in children and adolescents; the more aggressive astrocytomas tend to appear in adults over 45. I asked Jeff why *I* was blessed with one and he just shook his head.

This morning, just after I returned to sleep for the third time, I experienced the feeling of falling. It's called a *hypnagogic myoclonic twitch* or *hypnic jerk*. Nobody knows what causes it. It may be that as you relax and your muscles go slack your brain gets confused. It misinterprets the relaxation signals and thinks you've lost control and are falling, so it jerks you upright, trying to protect you and set things right.

I got up and read about it on my computer. Years ago I would never have done that. This time I just wanted to be sure. Plus, I thought it would help me get back to sleep. It didn't, but the thought was there at least. The whole experience has made me think about human fragility or, at least, my own. My brain is my principal weapon. My job depends on it. I suppose everyone's does, but when you work homicide cases it's your first and often last line of defense. The guns-and-car-chases part happens, of course, but most of the work is mental—trying to sort through what you've learned, trying to sort through what people have told you, squaring their accounts, finding the gaps and the lies, trying to counter strategies and ploys, reacting to changed circumstances, to blind alleys and stone walls, to hints and glimmers.

Sometimes I think that the cases have kept me whole--preserving the instrument by strengthening it, as one strengthens muscles and lungs through sweat and exercise. The losses of others become my remedy, my nostrum. At a deeper level I know that the cases will come, whether I need them, want them or not and when they do, I, or someone, must be prepared to deal with them.

It was 4:35 when I returned to bed, straightened the sheet, took some deep breaths, stretched my legs, flexed my ankles, extended my toes and tried to think restful thoughts. The next time I looked at the clock I was in the shadow zone, not really asleep and not yet fully awake. The clock read **5:12**. Turning on my other side and doing my best to clear my head I must have finally fallen asleep, because when the call came the clock read **6:13**. The wind had subsided; the room was quiet. It was that time in the early morning when you could finally sleep.

It was Chris Dietrich, my chief. "Tom," he said, "we've got a situation."

TWO

"I'll pick you up," he said. "I'm about fifteen minutes away."

With the small force that we have in Laguna there are few days that go according to schedule. A year before I made lieutenant I started to shave at night rather than in the morning. I put a small refrigerator between the corner of the wall and the bed and stocked it with things that could be eaten on the fly. Fifteen minutes' notice is an eternity. I was fully dressed after twelve and a half, eating some grapes and a second piece of string cheese and sipping a bottle of cranberry juice, thinking about the antioxidants and other good things therein and wondering if they were really working.

"Sorry for the early wakeup," he said. "Looks like a murder/suicide. Just across the county line. Off the Ortega Highway, outside of Lake Elsinore."

He was wearing the same plaid shirt and black jacket that he had been wearing yesterday evening when I left the station. There was either nothing fresh in his closet or he was short on time. There was a paper sack on the divider between the front seats. I could see coffee spills along the side.

"Picked up some high test on the way," he said, opening the bag with his right hand and handing me a cup.

"Thanks, Chief," I said, reading the checked box on the side of the cup. "Is *vente* the standard large or the large large?"

"Large large," he said. "Actually the largest large."

"You *know* me," I said.

"Right. Enjoy. I passed on the 600 calorie-a-pop muffins. Figured it was just as well."

"Do we have any names yet on the decedents?"

"No. I got a call from my counterpart there; he said he'd fill us in when we arrived."

"Chief . . . Alfiori?"

"Right. Lou Alfiori. We worked together in the LAPD. I came to Laguna; he went to Lake Elsinore."

"That area is really growing," I said.

"Still affordable," Chief Dietrich said. "Unlike here. A lot of the day workers live there. The work's here, but the cheap housing is there. You know how much your dad's place is worth now?"

"The place across the street just sold for $650,000 and that's after the downturn. It's got 1300 square feet. Dad's has almost 1400. The market's crazy."

"Sometimes I think that prosperity keeps the crime rate down; sometimes I'm not so sure," the chief said.

"More wealth means more to steal," I said.

"Yes, there's always someone wanting to do that."

Chief Alfiori's black and white was parked on a gravel road just off the Ortega Highway. The light bar was turned off. Behind it was an unmarked sedan. We could see him standing on top of the hill above the road, but couldn't see the bodies of the victims. We could also see the backs of his techs who were bending over, working the site. He waved toward us as we pulled up. We carried our coffees with us. Chief Dietrich had a cup for him as well.

"Here you go, Lou," he said. "How have you been?"

"Good, Chris, thanks. And thanks for the coffee. Hi, Tom."

"Good morning, Chief," I answered.

"Just i.d.'d them," he said. "He left his wallet in his truck . . . down there." He pointed to a late model Ford F-150 that was parked in the burn about forty yards past the turnout for the gravel road. "Don't know why he didn't just drive up here. And I don't know why he'd leave his wallet in the truck. I checked his driver's license. The picture was recent. It's him. Terrence Randall. Caucasian, age 34, 5'11", 185 pounds, black/blue. Uncommon. Probably Irish or Scottish. And he's one of yours, Chris."

"From Laguna?"

"Hills."

"Tom's neighborhood."

"Came up here to Lake Elsinore to die . . . wonder why he took his wife with him."

"Was there i.d. for the wife in the truck?" I asked.

"No, there was a picture of the two of them in his wallet. The mole there, beneath her left ear, was clearly apparent. The heights work out also. She's about 5'5" and the height difference is noticeable on the picture. Her name was Susan. It's on his health insurance card."

"So he drove her up here to kill her and then killed himself?" Chief Dietrich asked.

"The shotgun is at his feet and the exit wound is through his cheek. I figure he shot her and then put the barrel of the shotgun in his mouth."

Chief Dietrich shook his head. I took a few steps closer in order to get a better look.

"Why would he have blown off her hand?" I asked.

Chief Dietrich turned to me and nodded. "It wasn't a rhetorical question," I said. "I don't understand it."

THREE

"We've been talking about that," Alfiori said. "At first I figured she might have put her hand up for protection, but the average person puts his or her hand in front of their face and there are no facial, neck or shoulder wounds. Her hand would have had to have been at her side, maybe even extended slightly from her body."

"And where did what was left of it go?" I asked. "Local predator?"

"Probably," Alfiori said. "It's not beyond the realm of possibility that a predator gnawed it off to begin with. She was shot in the stomach. God, it practically put a tunnel through her. She would have bled out quickly."

"So he wasn't aiming at her heart," Chief Dietrich said.

"No, not as far as I can tell," Alfiori answered. "I didn't get in and root around; she could have caught some of the shot there also. As you can see, there's a great deal of blood . . . with the winds around here, the scent would have drawn insects, birds and larger animals right away."

"What do you think," Chris asked, "sometime yesterday?"

"That's a good guess," Alfiori said. "Late yesterday, probably. There's not much dust on his truck. If it had been there for awhile it would have been stripped or hauled away. From the lividity . . . maybe ten to twelve hours. That's just an estimate."

"Who found them?" Chris asked.

"Off duty guy from our shop," Alfiori answered. "He was driving to Laguna this morning with his family. Just before first light. They were going to rent a boat, go out and try their luck fishing. He saw the truck and heard some birds at the top of the hill."

"The wife was thrown backward by the blast," I said. "That's why the blood and tissue splatter is slightly lower than the wound site."

"Right," Alfiori said.

"But where's the spray from her hand?" I asked, "assuming that it was blown off by the shotgun."

"Can't answer that," Alfiori said. "We only found four casings. We'll know more when the techs finish up. They'll try to find any stray pellets that missed the shooter's target and scattered in the dirt."

That shouldn't be too difficult, I thought to myself. The hill against which the wife had fallen was little more than dust and gravel. The ground cover was thicker in the distance and the morning mist had helped to turn part of it a light green, with the moisture reflecting from the cobwebbing in the individual plants. When the rain falls in a desert garden you can feel the movement around you, as the plants burst and flower. The desert where the two bodies lay was stark and gritty. No flowers, just distant scrub. The metal of the shotgun and the polished wood of its stock stood out like steel statuary or expensive sculpture against gray and yellow sand.

"A guy killing his wife like that . . . I don't get it," Alfiori said. "Usually that's a crime of passion or something calculated over time. A man finds his wife in the sack with somebody else … or discovers evidence to that effect … they start screaming, take some swings at one another, have a knock-down/drag-out and she loses … it happens all the time … or maybe there's another cause altogether, maybe just the endless effect of some day-to-day habit she has or expression she uses … finally he snaps and reaches for her throat or whatever blunt instrument happens to be handy at the time. That's after the shouting match and the food on the wall and broken china on the floor. Or maybe he's the more cautious type. He discovers something or comes to some conclusion and decides instead to bide his time. He plans something that looks like an accident … maybe in someplace remote … he thinks through his story … thinks about how the police will pick it apart … then he executes it … very carefully … and when he hears the cruiser sirens he calls up the shakes and the crocodile tears on cue. Most of the time it doesn't reach that point. The husband just starts sequestering his money and shopping for lawyers, preparing for the divorce. The only clue the wife has is that he's starting to lose weight, sprucing himself up a little, getting ready to go on the market again. But this … it makes no sense … none at all. 'Want to go for a ride, honey? Oh, and don't let me forget my 12-gauge.'"

"I see where you're going with that, Lou, but what about the fact that he killed himself after he killed her," Chris asked. "Somebody ready to do that … he may not be thinking very clearly. He's on the edge; he does something that's completely out of character. I mean … temporary insanity … it *does* happen. Maybe he's the sensitive sort; he felt that he couldn't do it in their house. Maybe he didn't want to get blood all over the walls and furniture. He feels for the kids or his parents or the housekeeper; he doesn't want them to have to clean up after him. Maybe it was a spur of the minute thing. The shotgun was already in the truck, but she didn't know it. She had no idea what he was planning to do. Maybe he wasn't planning to do it at all, but something happened and he snapped. You find a thousand people; you get a thousand different explanations. It's very hard to say. What do you think, Tom?"

"I don't know," I said. "I think you both could be right. Too early to tell. I figure we do what we always do—work the facts, talk to the people who knew them, try to see what kind of picture emerges."

"It's all yours, Tom. Where do you want to start?" Chris asked.

"I'll check on parents and relatives," I said.

"Good," he answered. "I'll touch base with our Medical Examiner. OK with you, Lou?"

"Go for it," Alfiori said. "Yours is much better than ours anyway."

FOUR

Chris dropped me off at home; I got in my cruiser and followed him to the station. I talked briefly with the desk sergeant, Bill Jensen, grabbed a second cup of coffee, checked to make sure there was no oil slick on top of it, went into my office, turned on my new computer and made my way through the series of security protocols that Chris had had installed on the station network. Then I started checking on the Randall family.

Terrence and Susan Randall had lived on Hillside Terrace, a pipestem behind Hillside Drive. It's about a mile and a quarter from my dad's place. Their parents were more difficult to find. Walter and Caroline Randall lived in L.A., actually in Altadena. Susan was born Susan Burkett. Her mother Elise lived in an apartment in Oceanside; her father, James Burkett, was deceased.

I called Elise Burkett first. There was no answer; I left a message, asking her to call me at her earliest convenience. Then I called the Randalls. Terrence's father answered. I identified myself and told him that I needed to talk to them. "Yes, yes, I know," he said. "Hurry." Before I could say anything else he had hung up the phone. I rechecked their address and got in my car, heading north. Mapquest had said that the 60+ miles would take me an hour and eleven minutes. Even at the edge of rush hour traffic I figured I'd be lucky if I got there in two hours. It took two hours and eighteen minutes.

They lived on a quiet, shady street, west of North Allen, above the smog line. Property values vary dramatically in Altadena. Being near the golf course is a good thing. Being in a classic craftsman is a good thing. Being farther south, closer to the freeway and the gangs, is not a good thing. Being above the smog line is a very good thing, but it's more expensive and it makes for a longer commute. The houses on the Randalls' street were relatively modest, but they were nicely landscaped and scrupulously maintained. There was a nice row of fan palms on either side of the street and some citrus trees visible in several of the backyards. One had lemons on it the size of oranges. As I checked the numbers painted along the curb and got closer to the Randalls' house I realized why Terrence's father had asked me to hurry.

The street was dense with vans with satellite links and the Randalls' front yard was filled with reporters. Some were speaking into camera lenses; some were standing outside the front door, clutching cell phones and trying to look in windows. I looked at my watch. It was 11:57. Two of the vans were from independent stations in Orange County.

I backed up, parked my cruiser about 75 yards from the Randalls' house, checked my service automatic and got out of the car. I didn't intend to shoot anybody; checking it is a reflex action. Whenever I enter a crime scene or approach a crowd of people who look hostile or combative, I do it. I try not to let them see me do it.

Halfway between my cruiser and the Randalls' front door I was met by a young woman with an earpiece, a portable microphone in her right hand and a cameraman at her side. He was balancing the station's hand-held camera carefully, high-stepping backwards and trying not to trip on the ground cover that outlined the Randalls' lot. I doubted that they'd be pleased by the fact that he and his reporter friend were walking through it.

"Lieutenant Deaton … " she said, "Lieutenant Deaton … Melanie Patterson, KABC Eyewitness News … "

"Yes?" I said, wondering how someone based in Los Angeles would know the name of a police lieutenant from a small force in Orange County.

"What can you tell us about the murder/suicide of Captain Randall and his wife Susan?" she asked, extending the microphone to a point just below my chin. The red light was illuminated on the hand-held camera.

"I can't tell you anything at this point," I said. "Two decedents were found this morning outside of Lake Elsinore. They have been tentatively identified as residents of Laguna Hills. Their deaths are under active investigation."

"Why would Captain Randall kill his wife, Lieutenant?"

"As I said, Ms. Patterson, the deaths are being investigated. I don't have any further information at this time."

"What about his mental state, Lieutenant? Is there any evidence to suggest that his service in the Middle East somehow led to the murder of his wife and his own suicide?"

"I can't answer that, Ms. Patterson. If you'll excuse me, I need to speak with his parents."

"What are you going to tell them?" she asked, as I walked past her.

FIVE

Both sides of the brick walkway were lined with Birds of Paradise rooted beneath dark mulch; the flowers were bright orange and blue and open to the midday sun but not yet dried by its heat. As I stepped onto the porch the reporters there came closer. I had hoped they would part and make way for me, but they anticipated that the Randalls might open the door when I knocked and they wanted to be close enough to get shots of their faces and hear anything that I might say to them. They jostled one another a bit, but became silent and began to aim their cameras as I lifted my hand to knock.

I said nothing, but held up my shield with my left hand so that whoever was on the other side of the door might see it through the tiny window at its center. When I knocked, the sheet of dark paper covering the window was lifted. I could see eyes and a man's brow. The knob on the dead bolt was turned and the door opened slightly. The reporters pushed forward. "Please!" I said, in a command voice. They were taken aback by the tone of my voice and before they could recover and react I slipped through the door. Its edge brushed my jacket as Walter Randall slammed and bolted it.

"You OK?" he asked.

"Yes, sir," I said. "Have they been harassing you?"

"They've tried," he said, without finishing the thought. "Come on in."

The house was decorated in vague Spanish-revival style with carved archways and warm earth colors. There were freshly-cut lilies and yellow roses in glass vases on a number of the tables. One corner of the living room opened onto the back and side yard and the wraparound garden there was impressive in its size, in the variety of its plants and the manner in which it had been maintained.

"This is my wife Caroline," he said.

"Tom Deaton, ma'am," I said. "You have my deepest sympathy."

"Thank you," she said. "This is all horrible … it's just … so horrible."

"I understand," I said. "I actually came here to break the news to you. It's obvious that it's too late for that now. I'm truly, truly sorry."

"It was on the television … probably while you were driving here from Laguna. They made reference to you and your chief … "

"Chris Dietrich."

"Yes, Dietrich," she said. "They said you were in charge of the case."

"That's very interesting," I said. "We were at the scene and then returned to the station. I checked for your address and your daughter-in-law's mother's address on the internet and then I left. I wasn't there much more than a half an hour. I haven't spoken to any members of the press and neither did Chief Dietrich."

"There was a leak," her husband said. "Somebody at the station probably has a standing arrangement with the press."

"Possibly at Lake Elsinore," I said. "The only person I talked to at our station was the desk sergeant and I didn't give him any details." For a moment we all just stared at one another. "Anyway, it's too late now to worry about it. I'll let the chief know and we can try to insure that this doesn't happen to anyone else in the future. I'm very sorry that it happened to you."

"You have to find out sooner or later," Walter Randall said. "It bothers me that it happened this way, but it doesn't bother me half as much as the lies they're telling about our son."

"Yes, sir … " I said, pausing to let him finish.

"There's absolutely no way in hell that Terry would have killed Sue. He loved her more than anyone else in the world. Terry would have died for her; he never would have killed her. Never."

I paused before speaking again, letting his statement sink in. "The press seems to know a great deal," I said. "They called your son 'Captain' and said he had been serving in the Middle East."

"California Guard," his father said. "He actually served two tours there, the last one in Iraq. The Guard's been asked to do a lot. They did it well. Terry did it well. They're talking as if he was shell-shocked or something, like he was out of his mind and somehow turned on his family. That never happened," he said. "Couldn't have. It simply … never … happened."

"What was his job there?" I asked.

"The first time over he was in Afghanistan. He was a senior first lieutenant, serving as the XO of an infantry company. The last time he was in a support unit. He was in a combat zone, of course, but he wasn't in direct contact. He spent most of his time with a clipboard and pencil, supervising technicians and filing reports. He got promoted to captain at the end of his tour. They're acting as if he was commanding a rifle company, taking enemy fire, and dodging IED's. He's done that sort of thing, of course, but not recently. With things winding down in Baghdad … well, it was almost routine duty, nothing that would drive a man like Terry over the edge. I'm telling you, Lieutenant. This could *not* have happened."

"My husband's right," Mrs. Randall said. "Terry was very strong and very grounded. He and Susan were extremely close. We don't know what to make of any of this. It's like a nightmare that people are claiming is real. We were up early this morning. It was cool; I was working in the garden. Walt was making some coffee, grinding the beans, making it fresh … it's so much better that way … we just bought the beans, yesterday … suddenly this reporter appears at the door and asks Walt for a comment on why our son killed his wife. Everything here was beautiful. A nice Tuesday morning. I came in a minute or two later, to have some coffee with Walt. When I came in he was standing inside the door. All of the color had drained from his face. He looked like somebody who had just had surgery. I asked him what was wrong and he told me that Terry and Sue were gone, that the press said that he had killed her. It was as if everything we loved and hoped for and believed in had been broken into pieces and thrown across our kitchen floor."

SIX

"And the reporter said that your son had some form of post-traumatic stress disorder?" I asked.

"Not that one, another one," she said. "The one from the L.A. Times."

"Did he give you any indication of why he would say that?" I asked.

"She," Walter Randall said. "Her name's Carmichael."

"Karyn Carmichael?" I asked.

"Yes," he answered. "She left us her card. And she didn't say anything about why she was asking that question. She acted as if we should have already been aware of the fact that he had a problem."

"And you weren't," I said.

"Of course not."

"I have to ask this … " I said.

"Go ahead and ask, Lieutenant," he answered.

"Yes, Lieutenant," his wife added. "We want to help you in any way that we can."

"Your son was not being treated for any psychological or psychiatric problems?"

"None," he answered. "No," she said simultaneously.

"You're certain?"

"He would have said something to me; he would certainly have said something to his mother," the father said. "He was a very mature young man, not some macho type who wouldn't talk about a problem if he was having one. Sue would have said something to us too. We were all very close." His wife was nodding her approval as he spoke.

"And he wasn't on any special medication?"

"He took pills for allergies," his father said.

"Allegra," his mother added. "The same thing that I take."

"Do you know his doctor's name?" I asked.

"Gilby or Gilbert, something like that," his mother answered. "His office is by Saddleback Memorial. I was with Terry one day when he had an appointment there."

"How about his personal behavior?" I asked.

"In what respect, Lieutenant?" his mother responded.

"Have you noticed any changes in his moods? Has he seemed aloof or withdrawn? Has he been depressed? Has his wife said anything to you that might indicate he was troubled in some way?"

"No," his father said. "I haven't noticed anything out of the ordinary. We haven't seen him lately though."

"When was the last time you saw him?" I asked.

"Just about five weeks ago," his wife said. "We've been away, visiting my sister and her family back in Ohio. We were on vacation and then we stopped off to see them on the way back. When we were here we tried to see Terry and Sue every other week at least. They were scheduled to visit us right before we left, but then something came up and they were unable to come by."

"Did he say what had happened?" I asked.

"Something to do with work," she answered. "He said they'd drive up as soon as we returned. We got back on Wednesday. We were going to get together the day after tomorrow. We had the whole day planned. We were going to drive up to Mt. Wilson. There's a lodge up there that has hummingbird feeders hanging from every corner of the building. Each one of them is covered with birds. There are dozens of them. Terry loved them. We used to take him up there when he was a boy. I was going to make some lunch. Sue was going to bake something nice. We planned it all before we left."

"Did you talk to him since you returned?" I asked.

"Yes … well actually, no," she said. "I left a message on his answering machine."

"But he didn't return it?"

"No," she said. "I've been waiting to hear from him."

SEVEN

"I have to go," I said. "I promise you that I'll stay in touch. Also ... I'd like you to be aware of something ... "

"What's that, Lieutenant Deaton?" Terry's mother asked.

"I'm going to continue investigating," I said, "and I don't want you to think that I don't believe what you've told me. I'll follow our standard procedures. I'll talk to your son's doctor; I'll talk to his wife's mother; I'll talk to everyone I can. I'll ask them about his marriage and about his personality and mental state (assuming they can help me in that regard). It's not a reflection on you. It's simply the best way to proceed."

"I was in the Army," Walt Randall said. "Whenever there was a violation of military law one of the officers could be tapped to defend the accused. I defended several young men, usually successfully. I began by asking all of those involved to tell their stories. Sometimes there were discrepancies from one person to another. Sometimes there were discrepancies within one individual's multiple accounts of what happened. It's very much as you see it on television. They talk and you learn. The only difference is that there's more dead space and fewer dramatic moments. The first step is always the same ... to get them talking. Then you follow up on what they say and see where that takes you. Don't worry about hurting our feelings, Lieutenant. I understand what it is you're trying to do. Just find out who killed Terry and Sue."

"I'll do my best," I said. "Were you in Vietnam, Mr. Randall?"

"Yes, the Central Highlands," he said.

"And you saw significant action?"

"Yes," he said.

"So you understand the kind of situation in which your son found himself."

"I do," he said.

"And it's something that's hard to forget," I said.

"You can block it out for a time," he said, "but you never completely forget. There's an occasional nightmare. For me at least, the steady ones started to end about seven years after the events themselves. That kind of experience affects different people in different ways. It's very real, Lieutenant, but it's also something that you simply have to deal with. My father was on Tarawa and Saipan. My uncle was in the Ardennes in 1944. My grandfather was with the marines in Belleau Wood. The Randalls have had the complete tour. Fortunately they all survived. My grandfather was gassed; my uncle lost part of his left foot … but they all made it back home. None of them killed themselves … or their wives. Our son Terry … "

"Yes, sir?"

"He was tougher than most; he was tougher than me."

"I'll stay in touch," I said.

I exited by the back door and walked through some adjoining yards before returning to my car. One of the reporters was waiting for me there, along with her cameraman. I walked toward them, pivoted and headed to the driver's side of the car. The reporter jumped in front of me, extending her microphone. The cameraman was trying to position himself for a closeup shot.

"What did the Randalls say, Lieutenant?" she asked.

"I'm not at liberty to discuss that," I said, taking out my keys.

"Did they tell you why he killed himself and his wife?"

"As I said, I'm not at liberty to discuss my conversation with the Randalls."

"But you *did* ask them why he might have done it, didn't you?" she said.

"I can't discuss what I may or may not have asked them," I said. "Now if you'll excuse me … "

"We *will* find out, you know," she said. "It's only a matter of time."

I gave her a look that was half cordiality, half contempt. My mother always advised me to be guarded with regard to my feelings. "Be especially careful about revealing anger," she would say. "It's a form of intimacy. You're giving them a part of yourself, something they shouldn't have."

When she offered advice like that, my father usually sat silently. Sometimes he would say, "Listen to your mother." I had the feeling that he was learning too. His own first response would have been to utter some strong curse or to break a nose or cheek bone, maybe blacken some eyes, but he had softened over the years, probably as a result of my mother's wisdom. The only time she began to show temper was when one of us was directly threatened. Most of the time she presented a front that was all strength and control. Like Walter Randall. "Save the anger," she would say. "You may need it later."

When I got into the flow of traffic on the 210 I called Chris Dietrich. I told him that the press was ahead of us on this one. He agreed with Walter Randall; it had to be somebody in the force; he said he'd talk to Lou Alfiori about a possible leak at his end.

"I'll be diplomatic," he said, "but firm. I don't begrudge the press the opportunity to do their job. I just don't want them doing ours and I particularly don't want them doing ours in a public and sloppy way."

I told him about the Randalls, about the military history in the father's family, and about their assurances that their son could not have killed himself or his wife.

"Could be denial," he said. "It's a natural response. They're too close at this point. On the other hand, nobody was closer to their son than them, except for his wife. At this point at least, they're our best witnesses."

I told him that I wanted to contact Elise Burkett. "If the press is swarming over the Randalls they're probably waiting to swarm over her.

When I called her earlier she wouldn't or couldn't come to the phone."

"You drive; I'll check on her," he said. "I'll try to have something for you when you get here."

"Thanks, Chief," I said. "I'm sure she'd appreciate any help that we could give her."

EIGHT

Fifty minutes later Chief Dietrich called back. "Where are you, Tom?"

"I just got on the 5," I said. "I'm heading toward the 133."

"Stay on the 5," he said. "I've located Elise Burkett."

"Is she at home, Chief?"

"No. She was actually in transit when everything hit the media desks. She was driving to Del Mar to pick up something at one of the stores there. Apparently she heard a report on the radio and ran into a parked car. An officer from the San Diego County Sheriff's Department caught the call, realized that the media would be trying to besiege her, and arranged for her to be temporarily sequestered."

"Where did they take her, Chief, Encinitas?"

"Yes. To the sheriff's office there, on El Camino Real."

"I know where you mean," I said. "I was there for a liaison meeting last fall."

"I talked to the Captain; you've probably met him—Dan Foley—he's expecting you."

Elise Burkett was huddled in the corner of the captain's office, sitting on a small leather couch opposite his desk. She looked like another transplanted Midwesterner: comfortable clothes, a slightly outdated hairstyle, a sweet smile. She was sipping from a styrofoam cup of coffee, which she was holding in both hands. When she wasn't drinking it she was blowing on the wisps of steam at its surface. They had offered me some as well. She said hello when I entered the room. Tear lines had formed around her eyes and there was a rectangular bandage on her forehead. She was composed, but she looked very fragile.

"I was thrown forward," she said. "The airbag prevented anything serious, but I still got a little bump. I don't even remember it happening. The report came on the radio and I just shut down. The next thing I knew there was a lot of traffic driving around me and an officer tapping on my window. At first I couldn't even focus on what he was saying. I was thinking about Sue and Terry. I was also thinking about my Jim. This would have really thrown him."

"Your late husband?"

"Yes. In some ways it's a blessing that he was taken first, but I could really use him now."

"I had hoped to be able to meet with you and break the news," I said. "The media got there first. I'm very sorry."

"There's no good time for news like that, is there?" she responded.

"No, ma'am, there certainly isn't."

"And they're saying that Terry killed Sue and then killed himself?"

"The media is saying that, but it's far too early to tell," I said.

"I can't believe that," she said, "not that I would be expected to. It's a terrible thing to believe about your son-in-law, but really, it's not the sort of thing that Terry would ever do. It's … it's *inconceivable*, Lieutenant."

"I've spoken to his parents and they share your opinion," I said.

"They're back, then."

"Yes."

"They were on vacation. I think they were also going to visit some of Caroline's relatives … "

"Yes, ma'am, in Ohio," I said.

"They're nice people," she said. "Walter was a soldier too. He made a career of it. Then they settled in southern California. He works at the Jet Propulsion Laboratory up in Pasadena. I believe he's some sort of senior administrator. He's an engineer; I do know that. My Jim was an engineer also."

"Did you relocate here as well, Mrs. Burkett?"

"Yes. From Virginia. That's where Jim was working. We're both from St. Louis originally."

"What did Terry do?" I asked. "I know that he was in the California Guard but I haven't had a chance yet to talk about what he did as a civilian."

"Originally he managed a bank in Irvine, a branch bank actually. It was a part of one of those large banks with smaller banks throughout the county. It was called AmeriCal Savings. The one that Terry managed was on Jamboree Boulevard, in a nice little mini-mall there. The parent company had problems and was eventually sold. They had made a lot of loans that they shouldn't have and they were forced to sell out. I don't know all of the details, but I gather that they were then reduced in size. The branch that Terry managed was closed. The new owner offered him another job, but it was in Long Beach and it was an assistant manager position in a larger bank. The fact that his Guard unit was about to be called up gave him something to do in the meantime. When he returned he began looking for a new civilian position. I know that he had some prospects. He was looking for just the right thing--a 'good fit' he said. He was very good with numbers, Lieutenant. And a wonderful young man. People felt comfortable with him."

"Did he seem depressed in any way? Withdrawn, perhaps?"

"No, Lieutenant. Terry was Terry. He was always upbeat and outgoing. I hadn't seen them for a couple of weeks, but he'd been back from Iraq for several months and every time I saw them he was fine. Sometimes they come back with diseases, you know. The heat . . . the diet . . . the hours . . . the stress. They have diseases there that we don't see over here. But Terry was fine. His biggest problem was that he missed Sue so much. It *is* different though now ... "

"In what way, ma'am?"

"Well, they have cell phones and they have email. It's not like the other wars. Jim was in Vietnam, like Walter. We'd get letters. Most of the time that was all. Now they have cameras hooked up to their computers. He and Sue were in contact nearly every day and they could actually see one another and hear one another's voices. That helps, Lieutenant. That helps a lot."

"What did your daughter do, Mrs. Burkett?"

"Sue was a nurse, Lieutenant."

"I have a friend who's a nurse. I wonder if she knew your daughter."

"It's possible. You know, they move around all the time. They're always in demand. It's a good job in that respect. They can work long hours but only a few days a week. A few on and a few off. They're like pilots. Sue was an emergency room nurse. I mean, she had done other things ... obstetrics ... intensive care ... but she liked the emergency room. It's not for everybody, I guess. She was thinking about studying to be a nurse anesthetist ... "

There was a knock at the door and a young officer asked if he could bring us some more coffee. "That would be very nice," she said. When he left to get it, she said, "They've been very kind to me here. And I appreciate your coming to see me, Lieutenant. I have to ask you this ... I know it's very early and you're just beginning, but ... who could possibly have killed my daughter and her husband?"

NINE

"I don't know, ma'am. I'll do everything that I can to find out. Can I ask you another question?"

"Of course, Lieutenant."

"I have to ask this … "

"Go ahead … "

"Do you know whether or not Terry owned a shotgun?"

"I'm sorry, I don't. Don't shotguns and rifles have to be registered, Lieutenant?"

"No, ma'am, not in California."

"I know that he had a handgun that he carried as an Army officer. They're allowed to have their own, you know. It had been his father's. Walter gave it to him for luck, I think. I can't say that I ever saw a shotgun. I don't believe that he had a rifle either. At least I never saw one. Terry wasn't a hunter, Lieutenant. He and his father went fishing sometimes, but not all that often. They were both very busy. Terry worked on Saturdays a lot. Some of the customers can only come in then. Terry was the manager and he had to look after the assistant managers and tellers. Some weeks the only time he had off was Saturday afternoon and Sunday. I know that he really valued his time with Sue. They were working different schedules and hers were sometimes irregular. The weekends were special for them."

"That's very helpful, ma'am," I said. "Let me ask you one last question. It's personal."

"That's all right, Lieutenant."

"Do you know if Terry and Sue had any plans to start a family?"

"It's not something that we pressed them on; parents want to become grandparents and we were no exception … you know, Lieutenant, that they were in their early thirties … "

"Yes, ma'am … "

"It's not that there was a great deal of urgency, but we were all aware of their ages. I had Sue when I was 22 and I think Caroline was about that age when she had Terry. They wait longer now. And they don't want to be asked about it. Sue told me that they were going to wait until their lives stabilized a little. But I know my daughter, Lieutenant … I suppose now I should say that I *knew* her … she wasn't saying that they were going to wait for years. What she meant, I believe, is that they were waiting for Terry to get a new job after he got back from Iraq. Then they could make plans. They were also talking about putting an addition on the back of their house. It's a lovely little place, Lieutenant, but it's very small … "

"So you believe that they were thinking about doing that … soon."

"Yes, Lieutenant. I'm sure that they were."

I paused before responding.

"It's not the sort of thing that you think about or talk about if you intend to kill your spouse and then yourself, is it?" she asked.

"No, ma'am; it certainly isn't."

I thanked Captain Foley for providing security and privacy for Mrs. Burkett; he said that under the circumstances no one was likely to press charges against her for driving into the parked car. "Finding out that your daughter has been murdered and that the prime suspect is your now-dead son-in-law is a pretty big shock, wouldn't you say?"

"Yes, sir," I answered. "A very big shock."

"Anybody come up with a motive yet?"

"No, sir. It's still too early."

"I understand. It's hard to know why people do the things that they do. Most of the time—on our end—the cause is alcohol or drugs. You've got all the usual things … jealousy, lust, greed … the drinks and the drugs just make it all worse. They multiply the effects--reduce inhibitions … stir up the blood … make it easier to reach for a kitchen knife … the bills in an open cash drawer … somebody else's wife … but this case you've got … it's different. I heard about some of it on the radio. Professional people. A military officer. An emergency room nurse. Not like the kind we usually see—drunks, tweakers, bar fighters. I guess sometimes that people with a larger view of life can also have larger problems, but still, something like this … it's rare."

"Yes, sir. Very rare."

"Anyway, if we can be of any help, just give us a call."

"I appreciate that, sir, and I know that Chief Dietrich will as well."

"Be careful out there, son. The roads are filled with dangerous people. Some are on drugs; some are on medication. It doesn't make a lot of difference in the results … "

"Will do, sir."

Chris was off on another case when I returned to the station. I got on my computer and did some checking. Walter Randall had filed the proper paperwork on his intra-familial handgun transfer and had paid the $19 fee to the DOJ. There were no other records of firearms registered to him or to his wife and none besides the single handgun to his son and daughter-in-law.

Susan Randall had mostly been working at Irvine Regional for the last year and a half. Prior to that she had been employed by St. Joseph's; more recently she had worked at Saddleback. There was no record of current employment for Terry. His work at AmeriCal Savings had terminated just prior to his departure with his Guard unit for Iraq. He had probably been temping. I wrote down the address and some simple directions to their home in Laguna Hills. Though it was close to my dad's house I had never been on the street—Hillside Terrace—before.

I called Chief Dietrich's cell number. He was in Mission Viejo when

I reached him. I asked him if there were keys available for the Randall house.

"Probably," he said. "The keys to his truck were on a chain that had several others as well. They're in the evidence room; I told Dave Hendrix you'd be needing them."

"Thanks, Chief. Where is the truck now?"

"It's at the impound facility; we're checking it for evidence. I haven't received any reports yet. No one really expects to find anything, but it doesn't hurt to check, at least for a little while."

"I thought I'd see if Hector's free. The two of us could go over to the Randall house … check things out. We'll be careful not to disturb anything."

"Sounds good," Chief Dietrich responded. "Remember, Tom … we do have other things on our plate."

"I understand," I said. "I just want to do a quick look, see if anything obvious jumps out at us."

"OK," he said. "Go for it."

I checked Hector's cubicle. He was out, but there was a note saying that he'd return in approximately forty-five minutes. I left him a note, asking him to check in with me when he returned. Then I got myself a cup of coffee and walked down to the evidence room.

"Looking for these, Lieutenant?" Dave Hendrix asked. He was holding a set of keys with his right index finger.

"Randall's?"

"Yes, Lieutenant. The chief said you'd probably want them."

"Thanks, Dave," I said.

"Good luck," he said. "I'd hate to believe that a guy like that would kill his wife and then himself. It happens, I guess. Well, let's be honest; we all *know* that it does, but I still hate to see it."

TEN

Before Hector returned I called Terry Randall's primary care physician. As Mrs. Randall remembered, his name was Gilbert. I talked to his receptionist; she put me on hold and a few minutes later he came on the line.

"Dr. Gilbert," he said. I identified myself. He said that he had heard about Terry Randall on the news and that he was shocked and surprised. He said some nice things about him and his wife. "She was an ER nurse," he said, "and a very good one."

I asked him about Terry's general health.

"It was excellent," he said, "except for some allergies. Just a second …" He picked up Terry's file and got back on the phone; I could hear him turn the pages. "Good numbers all around," he said. "Blood work … height/weight … b.p. … I saw him a few months ago. It was soon after he returned from Iraq. He had a virus, upper-respiratory. No big deal; it ran its course and he was fine. His general health was just what you'd expect in an active young man."

"How about his mental health?" I asked.

"I know … they're suggesting he had some kind of PTSD. In my opinion that's nonsense. Terry was a healthy and stable young man. Of course, it's not my role to provide psychiatric care, but if there had been a problem I think that I would have known. He was very open with me and also very cognizant of health issues. Officers receive some basic instruction in such matters; I suppose you probably did too, Lieutenant."

"Very basic," I said.

"Yes, well, I can't swear an oath that he was *unaffected* by his experiences; none of us would be. I *can* say that I did not perceive any significant *problems* in that regard. When we discussed his health he was always very specific. He had some tendonitis in his left shoulder, for example. And he had a little dermatitis for awhile, in his scalp. This was after his first tour in the Middle East. Neither was really significant, not even worth a referral to a specialist. The first was cured with some stretch exercises, the second with some cortisone cream.

"When patients are having psychiatric problems, Lieutenant, they often talk about them circuitously. In some cases they're not aware that their problems are psychiatric; in other cases they believe that they are but they're having trouble accepting that fact. They'll say that they're having difficulty sleeping, for example, or that they've had problems with diet or digestion. They'll say that they feel 'out of sorts' or 'distracted'. They'll talk about a general malaise. They're talking about *symptoms*. You ask a few more questions and you find out that their bodies are reacting to something beyond the purely physical.

"With Terry it was always *purely physical*—a sprain or a muscle pull, something treatable, something simple."

"That's very helpful," I said. "Did he ever say anything to you about wanting to start a family?"

"No, but I wouldn't expect him to. If they had been trying, unsuccessfully, he might have, but he had just returned from overseas. And as I said, his general health was excellent. Men can be sensitive about such things, of course, but he was young and vigorous and, as I said, very forthcoming. He was never shy or reticent. If he had questions he would have raised them and if he was simply thinking about starting a family he wouldn't have cleared it with me first, not at his age."

"Thanks, again," I said.

"You can see his records if you wish," the doctor said. "But I can tell you … there's not much there."

I thanked him, made some notes, and checked Hector's office. He was still out.

Detective Hector Campo had long commanded respect within the department, but Chris Dietrich registered some reservations when I recommended him for his recent promotion. He now functions as my partner of choice whenever I'm in need of one. In the best of times my Spanish is halting and awkward and I'm grateful for his fluency, particularly in extreme situations. I'm also grateful for his personal courage, which verges on utter fearlessness. He doesn't speak about it much; it's a sensitive subject. The unspoken assumption is that the anglo officers have lived lives of privilege and relative safety and have not been exposed to the kinds of experiences which they consider brutal and extreme and he considers commonplace.

Prior to his decision to seek a career in law enforcement he had spent most of his life on the other side. He grew up in east L.A. and then moved to Santa Ana. He had been a member of a prominent Orange County youth gang. We sometimes use euphemisms to describe them and we're trained to avoid calling a specific gang by name. The theory is that the more publicity we give them, the more likely they are to be successful in recruiting new members. Hector doesn't follow that policy and he seldom uses euphemisms. He said he decided to leave his gang-- the Barrio Boys or Bboys--when they became less involved in self-defense and, occasionally, property crime, and more involved with narcotics. Car theft and burglary were one thing, particularly when some of the stolen goods made their way back to the families in his neighborhood, but he drew the line at drugs.

It had come on slowly. Initially the Bboys wouldn't sell drugs at all; they convinced themselves that they were neighborhood robin hoods, defending their own and redistributing some of the wealth their way. Eventually, however, they decided that the potential profits were too attractive to resist. They began to sell drugs on other bangers' turf, but the dealers in those neighborhoods refused to stand by and watch from the sidelines. The Bboys soon faced armed competition and they started to find their members in Dempster Dumpsters and the trunks of burned-out cars. They found two hanging from a Costa Mesa freeway overpass in Tustin. Eventually they started working closer to home. Early in the process Hector decided to leave.

He studied at Cal State, Dominguez Hills before applying for a place at the Golden West police academy in Huntington Beach. Chief Dietrich took a chance and hired him as a uniformed officer and he's been impressed with his work, but his prior gang associations continue to affect the chief's judgment and he remains concerned that Hector might be inclined to follow questionable practices and use unauthorized weapons. "We're in a resort community," he would say, "with people of wealth and prominence. They want the highest degree of professionalism from their police and … well … they never want to feel that they've walked into a … culture of violence."

"I understand, Chief," I would answer. "And Hector understands. But sometimes the violence comes to us and we need to protect ourselves from it."

"Understood," the chief usually said. "And you need people who are 'mission-oriented'."

"Exactly," I said.

"Just try to keep the violence under wraps."

"I will," I said, "and so will Hector."

I was putting in a request for the Randalls' landline phone records when he knocked on my door. "I'm back, Lieutenant," he said, "and at your disposal." I've told him to call me 'lieutenant' or 'sir' at the station, 'Tom' when we're alone together in the field.

"I take it you've heard about the Randall case," I said.

"Yes, sir," he responded. "I take it you've got doubts … "

"I do," I said, "and so do the respective parents."

"Not a surprise," he said, "but honestly, Lieutenant, I've got some doubts too and I haven't even met any of the individuals involved."

"It doesn't ring true to me, Hector," I said.

"No, it doesn't. So why don't we dig a little deeper … maybe start by checking out the decedents' house."

I held up the key chain, shaking it gently.

We arrived at the Randall home on Hillside Terrace in a little more than ten minutes. The street was quiet. Except for a gardener weeding some dusty ivy and pachysandra ground cover in the late afternoon sun and a FedEx driver making a delivery at the other end of the street, the neighborhood was deserted. The house itself was modest but attractive—a small ranch with yellow siding, a shake roof and a spray of red bougainvillea along the edge of the driveway and car port. At the corner of the small slab porch was a row of terracotta pots filled with red, pink, and purple impatiens. Each had been watered recently.

We parked a door away, not wishing to attract any attention to the property itself, and walked up the driveway to the door at the rear corner of the house.

"Probably the kitchen," I said, reading the word **Schlage** on the lock and looking on the chain for the corresponding key. There were two; the second one turned easily and I opened the door. We entered the kitchen and closed the door behind us quietly.

The room was tidy but slightly dated, with dark tile on the floor, hardwood cabinetry with brass pulls, solid countertops and a vintage, brown wall phone. "No twists in the phone cord," Hector said. "Orderly people."

"Yes," I said, opening some cabinet drawers. There was a pad of post-it notes on the counter beneath the phone, but no indentation marks on the top sheet. "No reminders on the refrigerator door," I said, "and everything in its place."

"In a small house you either learn to be neat or you become buried in **stuff**," Hector said. "A military man and a nurse … they're not always neat at home. It's what home is for; it's what home is about … no need to keep everything sterile and in nice, evenly-spaced rows … no need to line up things in your foot locker or check your gig line … but these people … it looks as if they brought their work home with them."

Beneath the sink was a turntable filled with cleanser and cleaning pads, an aging jar of silver polish, Soft Scrub, Windex and dish and dishwasher detergent. I opened the dishwasher. It was filled, but the dishes, glasses and silverware had all been washed. The milk and O.J. in the refrigerator were still a few days short of their sell-by dates and everything else looked fresh. In the freezer there was some ice cream, frozen vegetables and two sealed containers of leftovers, each with post-it notes and recent dates. On the counter next to the refrigerator were two avocados and a plastic packet of fresh basil leaves. The avocados were not yet soft and the basil leaves were fresh and green. "These things turn black after a few days," I said. "They must have just shopped."

The pantry was narrow but had deep shelves. One of the shelves contained sugar, brown sugar, confectioners' sugar, rice, flour, baking powder, baking soda and an array of spices on a set of turntables. There were cans of vegetables sealed in 12-pack flats, boxes of pasta, some miscellaneous items from *Trader Joe's*, the usual liquids—white vinegar, wine vinegar, olive oil—some pretzels and taco chips, brownie and cornbread mix, table wine and two eight-packs of diet cola. Someone in the family liked tea. There were boxes of green teas, mint and other herbal teas, English Breakfast tea and Darjeeling.

"I don't see much dust anywhere," Hector said. "Hard to keep it down with the heavy traffic and the strong winds."

"He hadn't found a regular job yet, at least none we could find," I said. "They were living on her income and whatever he could bring in on a temporary basis. I doubt that they could afford a housekeeper."

"They were naturally neat," Hector said. "It was important to them.

But look here … " He pointed at a loose stack of magazines in the powder room off the kitchen. "They weren't pathological about it."

He opened the medicine cabinet above the sink. "Just a brush and comb, some aspirin and mouthwash. The prescription meds are probably in the master bath."

The living room and dining L were also neat. The heavily-upholstered furniture was slightly out of date--maybe some hand-me-downs from the parents--but the carpet had been vacuumed recently and the side tables dusted. There were books stacked on each of the side tables: one on quilts, another on desert gardens, a best-selling thriller and one by a guy who spent a year with his wife in a small hill town in southern Italy.

"No self-help books on saving your marriage and nothing on the trials and tribulations of shell shock," Hector commented. "I'm seeing flags and smelling apple pie. Could have been planted, I guess, but that's doubtful, not if he wanted to surprise her and he really did kill her. He didn't come back from the desert and tidy up first before returning."

"Too remote of a possibility," I said, "and why would he bother? If he was that desperate, why would he care what other people thought? Once you decide to put the barrel of a shotgun in your mouth, everything else is secondary. Let's check the bedrooms."

There was a small utility room off the central hallway. At one end was a sewing machine on a formica table. "Hobby or necessity?" Hector asked. On the opposite wall was a small table with a laptop computer and printer. "Let's take this with us," I said.

The guest room had two single beds on one wall. Their bedspreads matched; neither had a headboard. There was a small, pine chest of drawers that had been repainted several times. There were fabrics and some sewing materials stored in the bottom drawers. The top two were empty. The closet in the guest room had some open shelf space and some empty hangers for anyone visiting; the rest of the space was used for storage. There were some Christmas tree lights and ornaments in a box on the floor, some household tools in a plastic tray with a handle, a box with Terry Randall's military insignia and several plastic bags containing uniforms and desert fatigues which had been freshly dry-cleaned and laundered.

The master bedroom had a queen-size bed, a chest of drawers, two nightstands with books (another thriller and a book on wines) and a large cupboard. Two-thirds of it contained Sue's clothes and uniforms; the remaining third contained Terry's. The master bath adjoined their bedroom but it also opened onto the hallway, for the convenience of their guests. It was an old-fashioned bathroom—no soaking tub, no separate shower, no twin sinks. No marble or granite anywhere. The medicine chest contained tooth brushes and paste, eye drops, Advil, mouthwash and prescription medications. There was a package of adhesive pads containing Tiger Balm for sore muscles and joints. As his mother had told me, Terry took Allegra for allergies. Sue had some birth control pills and a bottle of lotion for poison oak. The latter was nearly empty. The birth control prescription had been refilled recently.

I opened the linen closet. The top shelves contained towels and wash cloths, the bottom ones sheets and pillow cases. The shelf in the middle contained Sue's cosmetics. She had one of those squisher things that women use to put curl in their eyelashes and a collection of scissors and nail files. There was also a box with a heating pad and—in the back—a humidifier that looked as if it hadn't been used for awhile.

"Very generic," Hector said.

"Suspiciously so?" I asked.

"Not in small space like this," he answered. "Like I said earlier, you either live simply or you get buried in **stuff**."

"One thing I've noticed," I said, "there's no space for a shotgun anywhere."

"Let's grab the laptop and check the locked storage box in the car port," Hector said.

ELEVEN

The pine storage box had been painted a dark terracotta color that matched the frame for the car port. Hector had to get the bolt cutters from the trunk of the cruiser to remove its small steel and brass combination lock.

"Close quarters for a shotgun," he said, "but maybe we'll find something interesting inside." The lid opened easily. "He used this thing," he added. "It's not wedged shut with cobwebs and mold and grit … "

"Let's see here … " he said, removing items and setting them on the pavement. "Hedge clippers … garden shears … work gloves … a trowel … a small bag of sakrete … miscellaneous gardening tools … a watering can … some insecticide … some herbicide … one of those pour spouts for oil cans … an old set of jumper cables … an army entrenching tool and one of those neat hoses that curls up into a small space and can be stored in a plastic case."

"And no firearms," I said. "Or shotgun shells. Or firearm cleaning equipment … "

"And no .45 automatic," Hector said. "Didn't you say he had his own?"

"Yes. Maybe he kept it at the armory."

"Maybe it was in his truck," Hector said.

"Could be. That would be very interesting--if he had his .45 but decided to use a shotgun instead. I don't quite get the shotgun thing to begin with, but if he had another weapon, one that was far easier to conceal, that makes the shotgun even more problematic."

"The shotgun makes a bigger mess," Hector said. "I can think of reasons why you'd prefer it and reasons why you'd avoid it."

"Right. We've got to get to know him much better than we do now. The house isn't telling us very much; at least it isn't telling us very much about why an apparently decent family man with a solid work record and impressive military record would suddenly decide to kill himself and his wife ... with a shotgun."

We set up the laptop back at the station and fired it up. "That's interesting," I said, leaning over Hector's shoulder. "It's not passworded."

"There was only the two of them," Hector said. "It's not as if they had a house full of teenage kids sharing the machine. Passwording it would be ... a kind of ... what ... a violation of trust?"

"Right. It's like you're saying that you've got something to hide ... maybe a lot of things to hide. On the other hand, if he had any confidential bank information or confidential email traffic, I could see how he would want to protect it. He and his wife could share their passwords with one another, but keep the computer secure from other people who might want to pry."

"People like us," Hector said, smiling. "Let's see here," he said. "They couldn't have been too impoverished if they bought a Mac ... "

"It's got the built-in camera," I said, "what do they call the app— *Photo Booth*? Easier to send pictures to one another when he was away."

"Right. And the whole thing's simple to use," Hector said, checking the icons on the dock. "Looks like a standard setup. It's got all the usual software packages. Let me check to see what kind of music they liked ... that's interesting ... it doesn't appear that they used the iTunes thingie. Let's have a look at the iPhoto files ... OK, they *did* use that ... lots of photos of Terry in the Middle East ... a file with pictures of Susan ... probably sent him copies when he was overseas.

"The desktop stickies documents are mostly household things ... lists of plumbers, electricians, a/c repairmen, a file on city services … heat and light, water, that sort of thing … emergency numbers for outages … nothing out of the ordinary. They used Safari as their default browser, not Chrome or Firefox. Their home page for the browser is … USAToday. Let's check their bookmarks. The Orange County Register … ESPN … EWTN … Weather Underground, with the primary site being … Laguna Beach, California. Surprise: the high today should be 81. Tomorrow, 79. They've also got a currency converter site bookmarked, a page on time zones … the kinds of things you need to know if you're being shuttled between California and different foreign countries. That's about it … a local theatre times site and the TV guide site. Where was the TV, in the living room?"

"Yes, on the table in the corner. A small flat screen. The kind you can pick up at Wal-Mart or Sam's Club for a few hundred dollars."

"Let me check the folder for their monthly bills," Hector said. "See who they were paying online … let's see … mortgage to Wells Fargo … utility bills … water and sewer, electric, natural gas … cable TV … VISA … State Farm insurance monthly pay plan … cell phones … no landline or internet service (probably bundled with the cable TV) … wait, here's something interesting—a storage facility in Laguna Hills. A hundred and twenty nine dollars a month."

"Standard fee for a mini-garage. We'll check it out," I said. "How about their bank?"

"Wells Fargo … on Ocean."

"Easy enough; that's my bank," I said. "We'll see who else they may have been paying and who was paying them. Make a note of their cell phone carrier."

"OK, no big surprise there--AT&T. Let's check the email … each of them had their own … here, I'll start with hers … some new spam … a book order from Amazon … some stuff from her supervisory nurse … nothing much. She emptied her trash regularly. All that the screen shows is the stuff from the last few weeks. His email is … let's see … a little fuller but basically same old same old. He's kept some old emails from army buddies … his father … easier to write to them later; he wouldn't have to look up their addresses. Well, Lieutenant, sir," Hector said, "all in all it's as generic as their house. It doesn't look as if someone has fabricated their lives; it's just that their lives were pretty simple and straightforward."

"Maybe we shouldn't be surprised," I said. "The medical profession is quasi-military and the military is all-military. They each boil things down to essentials, try to keep things uncluttered, focus on top priorities, home in on them, get the job done."

"What was his father's place like?"

"Pretty much the same as this."

"Let's check out that storage facility; maybe we'll find some secrets there."

TWELVE

The clerk at the storage facility checked our credentials and asked us to fill out a form. Her name was Rhonda Henson and she wore simple earrings, rings on each hand and a crisply-pressed brown uniform. In addition to managing the storage rental operation, she was operating a handful of related businesses: selling boxes, packing material and tape to movers; renting dollies, vans and trailers, selling padlocks and plastic storage containers and renting lot space within their grounds for people parking boats, trailers and recreational vehicles. She told us that the Randalls had begun renting the space more than three years ago.

"I have the combination to the Randalls' lock," she said. "We wouldn't usually have that information, but I had the lock available and offered to let them borrow it. Only certain kinds of locks fit on our garages. People are disappointed when they find out they have to buy a new one, so whenever I have one available I let them use it. That way you won't have to cut it off. When you're finished inspecting the locker I'll put the lock back on and secure the goods for their estate. I just need you to sign that form, authorizing me to open the locker."

"No problem, ma'am," I said.

"There's a space there for your badge number," she said. "This sort of thing happens from time to time … actually more often than you might expect … and we have to protect ourselves."

"I understand, ma'am," I said. "We appreciate your help and I'm sure that the Randalls' family will appreciate your protecting their possessions."

She smiled, checked a book in a drawer beneath the cash register, jotted down the combination, put a 'back in five minutes' card in the window and led us to the facility. "It's way in the back," she said. "I'll ride up there with you and punch in the code for you at the security gate."

"Thanks," Hector said. "You've been very helpful."

The lock was actually turned on its side, perhaps to protect it from rain and roof condensation. Rhonda leaned her head against the side of the door, turned the dial three times in opposite directions and opened it easily.

"We can replace the lock if you'd like us to, ma'am," I said. "That way you won't have to stand around waiting for us to finish. I'll put it on sideways, the way it was."

"That'll be fine," she said. "You can let yourselves out. The gate will open when you roll up toward it. You don't need the code from this side."

We thanked her again and Hector opened the door. It moved reluctantly, the cobwebs and grit in the tracks contrasting with the car port storage container which Terry and Sue Randall had obviously been using recently.

"Want a little help there?" I asked.

"I've got it now," Hector said. "This hasn't been opened in a long time."

The unit was 5' x 10', with an 8' ceiling. It was more of a walk-in closet than a small garage. There were three shelving units, one spanning the rear of the space and two smaller ones on either side. The shelves were filled with plastic boxes, the vast majority of which contained clothes.

"Look," Hector said. "This is just like those things you see advertised on late night TV. You put the clothes in the bag thingies and then pump the air out of them—put a room full of clothes in each box. I like the way the boxes are transparent. You can find what you're looking for without opening up half of them first."

"There's the pump," I said, pointing to the lowest corner of the shelving unit on the right.

"This is very interesting," Hector said, removing another box and lifting the plastic lid. "Baby clothes."

"Probably hand-me-downs from a friend or relative," I said. "What's interesting is that they kept them here, in reserve, as it were."

"Yes. My sister-in-law gave us a whole closet full. And you're grateful for them," Hector said. "Every few months the babies change sizes and you move on to the next set. Then you send the ones you're finished with to the next relative."

"Keeping them here, ready like this … it means they were looking to the future," I said.

"I wonder what's in here," Hector said, opening one of the cardboard boxes stacked on the floor in front of the shelves. "Whatever it is, they were trying to protect it. Look … "

He pointed to a series of plastic skids beneath the row of boxes. "Keeps the moisture out. Not that that should be a problem … " We had each noticed the fact that the storage facility was built on a small cement platform that rose above a drainage line that ran around the perimeter of the steel structure. "You can't really keep the spiders out," he said, "but moisture shouldn't be a concern. Whatever's in the boxes must have been important enough to them to install a backup system."

Hector took out a pocket knife and carefully cut through the tape running across the top of the first box. He opened the box and exposed another set of boxes, wedged into place by some crumpled, brown paper.

"Board games," he said, pulling out the paper and moving the boxes around inside. "Monopoly, Stratego, Clue … and something called Star Reporter. It looks like an antique."

"It's a collector's item," I said. "My father used to play it when he was a kid. We've got one stored in the crawl space above our garage. You travel around the world, scooping other reporters. The cool thing is that you don't use tokens; you use pins."

"Like on a situation room board."

"Yes, exactly. You moved from point to point and literally stuck your pin in the board. The home base became basically illegible after awhile—just a mass of gray from all the pinpricks."

I took the box from Hector and set it outside the storage compartment, while he opened the second box in the stack.

"Girls' toys," he said. "Dolls, doll clothes, a doll's house. Little mirrors. Tiny plastic shoes. A doll's umbrella … "

"Check out the next one," I said, taking the previous box from him and putting it with the box of board games. "You've got the best spot, Tom," he said. "It's getting hot in here."

"I'll try to redirect the breeze your way," I said.

"OK," he said, "box number three … boys' action figures. Translation: dolls. Also some miniatures—Star Wars … and something I don't recognize. Battlestar Gallactica, maybe?"

"Any pro wrestlers?"

"No, but here's Wonder Woman and Captain America."

"Try another box," I said.

"Athletic equipment. Kids' stuff. A small baseball glove, a softball, some swimming goggles … "

Twenty-five minutes later we had opened all of the boxes. Most of them contained toys. One contained a set of training wheels for a small bicycle. Another contained childrens' books: *Make Way for Ducklings, Where the Wild Things Are, Curious George, Madeline, Crow Boy, McElligot's Pool, Abel's Island* and *Sylvester and the Magic Pebble.* In one smaller box were two stuffed Teddy bears. Each was well-worn. The first had button eyes, one of which had been resewn with slightly mismatched thread. The second had a wrinkled pink ribbon tied around its neck.

"I guess that makes it female," Hector said, as he lifted it into view.

"The first was probably Terry's, the second Susan's," I said. "Either way, it's the same pattern—saving things from the past and looking to the future. The clothes, the toys, the board games … they're all here for their kids, kids their grandparents will never see."

"And one other thing … " Hector added.

"You don't have to say it," I said. "There's no shotgun rack, no cleaning oil, tools or patches. No firearms. No weapons at all."

THIRTEEN

We returned to the station; my in-box was filled with call slips from reporters; one of them—Melanie Patterson from KABC—had found my email address and left a message for me there. I told all of them that the investigation was ongoing and that I could not disclose any details at this time. Patterson emailed me back immediately and thanked me for responding. I then reported on the contents of the Randalls' storage locker to Chief Dietrich.

"Interesting," he said. "Of course, if the rental clerk's memory is accurate they would have put all that stuff in storage before his tours in the Middle East. A lot can change in a short period of time, particularly when you're in a combat zone."

"Right, Chief," I said, "but he was serving in a support capacity during the last tour. I realize that nowhere is really safe there, but it's not as if he had just been on the front lines, dodging sniper fire and dismantling IED's."

"I understand," he said. "It's interesting that you didn't find any shotgun rack or shells or cleaning equipment. Of course, he could have bought it all recently. For that matter, if he was only going to use the weapon once, he wouldn't need any cleaning equipment."

"He had a .45," I said. "That will make you as dead as a shotgun will."

"It was in his truck," Chief Dietrich said. "I just got a call. He had a lock box bolted in the back of his glove compartment. The box had a key lock and the weapon itself had a combination lock on the trigger guard. All very secure. There was also a magazine of ammunition. We hadn't seen it during our initial inspection. The lock box was black and there were some maps and things in front of it."

"Had it been fired recently?" I asked.

"No," he said, "it hadn't. There was also a LoJack device on the truck."

"Possibly to insure that the .45 could be recovered before it fell into the wrong hands as well as to protect the truck."

"Possibly," the Chief said.

"Funny," I said. "Most people would probably keep a personal weapon in their home rather than in their motor vehicle."

"And they didn't have a home security system," Chief Dietrich said.

"No, but they didn't have that much to steal," I said. "He may have felt that he could protect himself from any intruders without using a firearm."

"Possibly. But like you said, Tom … it's not what most people would do. Maybe the shotgun was in the bedroom cupboard, leaning against the wall, ready for use."

"Did they find anything else in the truck, Chief?" I asked.

"No, not really. The gas tank had just been filled."

"Not the sort of thing you'd do if you were planning to kill yourself," I said.

"Not usually, but remember—it's an irrational act, Tom. Also, if he was trying to keep his wife off guard it would have been in his interest to act as if everything was normal. Besides (not to be ghoulish about it), he wouldn't have to pay off his credit card balance anyway."

"True, Chief, but that line of thought and behavior would be very rational, wouldn't it?"

"Yes, it would, Tom."

"Has the M.E. made any progress?"

"He's still working on the autopsies. I talked to him about twenty minutes ago. He said he'd meet with us first thing in the morning. Why don't we go there together, say about 8:30?"

"Sounds good, Chief," I said. "I'll drive in and meet you here first."

I checked my watch. It was nearly 7:00 and I had planned to meet my dad for dinner at a new restaurant near the marina. There had been a seafood restaurant once in the same location on the West Coast Highway, a restaurant with a sister operation in Honolulu. For some reason or other its success had run its course in Newport Beach. The new place was Italian. I touched base with my dad; we were still on for 7:30. I would have liked to have had the chance to shower and change, but there wasn't enough time. Instead, I threw some water in my face, cleaned my nails and washed my hands, ran a comb through my hair and drove up the coast.

He was waiting for me when I arrived, sitting at a table overlooking the harbor.

"I waited for you to order," he said. "I haven't even had a drink."

"We can probably fix that," I said. "How are you, Dad?"

"I'm good, Tom, good."

The waiter approached and we each ordered Italian beer. When he returned with them he also brought us some bread, butter and olive oil. "Whichever you prefer," he said.

My father ordered wedding soup and veal; I ordered minestrone and chicken. I told him about the Randalls.

"It was on the news," he said. "Terrible, just terrible."

"I'm not sure that it actually happened the way it's being reported," I said. "There's no hard evidence either way."

"It must be awful for their parents."

"Her dad's dead; I met her mom and her husband's parents. None of them believe that he could have killed her and then killed himself."

"They *couldn't* believe that, could they?" he said.

"No, but if something *had* happened, something that would lead them to suspect that there had been a problem, I think they would have said something. His father's ex-military. They're usually not shy about things. They all said that they were certain. And it wasn't just that there was no evidence to the contrary. They said that the two of them were devoted to one another."

"He had just returned from Iraq, hadn't he?" my dad asked.

"A couple months ago."

"Maybe he found out she'd been cheating on him."

"Always possible," I said, "but we went through their house pretty carefully. There was nothing to suggest that she had been leading a separate life. She had some birth control pills, but the date on them was recent—just about the time when he was scheduled to return."

"Don't they get refilled month by month?"

"Yes, but there's a date on the vial that marks the time at which the prescription was filled. It also says how many refills remain on that prescription. From the number of those remaining it appears that this particular script had either just been written or an earlier one had just been renewed."

"Her doctor should be able to tell."

"Right, and as I said, if she had another doctor and another prescription somewhere, there was no evidence of it."

"And if he found out that she was involved with someone else she was either open about it or careless."

"Right."

"There is another possibility," my dad said.

"A female lover."

"Yes. It happens, Tom."

"I know, Dad, but even if something like that happened, it's an extreme reaction … "

"Killing your wife and killing yourself."

"Yes."

"And the parents knew nothing about anything like that or at least they didn't say anything."

"Right."

The waiter asked us if we wanted a second beer. I felt a little lightheaded and passed. My dad did as well. A few minutes later a second waiter brought our soups.

"A little generic," my dad said, "but it tastes pretty good."

"So does mine," I said.

The first waiter returned later with our entrées and also brought us each a small side dish of spaghetti. "On the house," he said. "You have to have a little pasta with your meal." We both thanked him.

"Nice touch," my dad said, as the waiter walked away. "He'll get it back in the tip. Sure you don't want another beer?"

"Thanks, but I think I'll pass," I said.

"Wine?"

"No. Maybe a little espresso later."

"That sounds good," my dad said. "Your mother never developed a taste for it, even with the lemon peel or the lump of sugar. She'd go for the cappuccino though. We used to like that place down the coast, in San Clemente. It was Trent- something."

"Trentino's," I said.

"Right. Nice place. The owner's name was Dominic. It wasn't Trentino though. That was the original owner. It was Dominic … Arezza."

"Tall man, very nicely dressed always."

"Meticulous. With every hair in place and always a flower in his lapel. Usually red. Sometimes a rose, sometimes a carnation. He was very nice to us. He always called us by name. It was one of your mother's favorite places."

I got home a little past 10:30, took the shower I had wanted earlier and went over my notes a couple times before refilling the refrigerator by my bed with fresh bottled water and some fruit cups. I slept well, even after the espresso. The next morning I got up earlier than usual, picked up some decent coffee on the way to the office, went over my notes again, told Hector I'd be with the chief for awhile and then drove with him to Saddleback Memorial to meet with the M.E.

FOURTEEN

Dr. Leonard Barnes served as the part-time M.E. for Laguna Beach. An Irvine Surgeon, he had morgue- and examining room space in the lower level of Saddleback. He had removed his lab coat and was drinking coffee when we arrived. Sally Cornell was sitting next to him. She was drinking tea.

"Chris, Tom, how are you?"

"We're good," we said. "Good to see you."

"You both know Sally."

We said that we did and greeted her. Sally Cornell is a forensic anthropologist from UCSD. A few years younger than Len, she consults with him on cases. She's usually not there that early in the morning. I wondered if there was some development in the case that required her presence or if their relationship had moved to a different level.

"I don't have any big surprises for you," he said. Susan Randall died of a gunshot wound to the torso. You already knew that. The pellets blew out most of her stomach and thoracic aorta; one or two of the pellets at the top of the shot group reached her heart. It's possible that there were two separate shots. She had also lost her right hand. It's not clear whether the hand was blown off by a shotgun blast or removed by predatory animals. It could have been a combination of the two. There were no remaining pieces of shot in her forearm, so if the hand was shot off it was a very precise shot at close range. I also did a full autopsy. She was not pregnant. There was no indication of rape or sexual assault. There were no life-threatening medical conditions. Her heart was tilted slightly;

that's no big deal. From what remained of her stomach—which wasn't much--she had eaten about six hours prior to her death. High fibre, high carb. Probably granola bars with some nuts, chocolate and dried fruit. Not much of a meal, but maybe she had been out walking or maybe this was more of a heavy snack than an actual meal.

"Her husband bled out from the gunshot wound to the face. The shot exited through his cheek. You already knew that as well. The exit angle is odd. Self-inflicted gunshot wounds are commonly done in several ways. Some people swallow the barrel. Some put it to their temple. Some put it under their chin. The latter is becoming more common. In his case several things might have happened. He might have had uneven footing. He was standing on an irregular surface of sand and gravel. My guess is that his hands were shaking. Killing your wife—assuming for the sake of argument that he *did* kill his wife—is an unsettling thing. With a shotgun with a full barrel the position is awkward. He had to extend his arm to pull the trigger. He may have slipped; he may have shook. Either way, he blew out the side of his face and bled profusely."

"Could he have had second thoughts?" I asked.

"You mean that he might have suddenly decided to remove the shotgun barrel but had already committed with his trigger finger?"

"Yes, something like that," I said.

"It's possible," he said. "This is not what I would consider a natural or normal action to begin with. Spousal murders are usually the result of passion, passion resulting from rage, rage that is often precipitated by jealousy or frustration and fueled by drugs or alcohol … often drugs *and* alcohol. Bludgeoning is common; strangulation is common; knifings and shootings are common. What is not common is premeditation involving this degree of planning and preparation. You see things like poisonings, but more often in English mystery stories than in real life. Driving out to the desert … using a shotgun … it's not the usual way of doing this. But then you already knew that.

"I autopsied him as well. No life-threatening medical conditions.

He had some previous war injuries. Nothing too serious. Light shrapnel wounds. More nicks and scrapes than anything else. He had broken his left arm, probably many years ago. He had eaten relatively recently. Junk food, high carbs. Doughnuts probably, maybe some other form of pastry. The sort of thing you eat on the run. And that's about it, gentlemen. I'll give you the full written reports, probably first thing tomorrow."

"Did you look at his brain?" I asked.

"Yes, I did."

"Was there anything out of the ordinary?"

"No tumors or lesions. What are you thinking, Tom?"

"The press is claiming that he was suffering from post-traumatic stress disorder and that that may be why he killed his wife. Is there any way that you can determine whether or not he *was* suffering in that way?"

"I think I'll let Sally take that one," he said. "Then I'll follow up."

She took a sip of her tea, put the cup down and folded her hands in her lap. "It's a very interesting question," she said. "To begin with, you have to be careful about your terms. There is, for example, something called 'combat stress reaction'. This was sometimes called 'shell shock'. The notion is that the stress of battle eventually took a toll on individual soldiers and reduced their ability to fight. They became fatigued; their reaction times slowed; they became indecisive and unable to set priorities and, in some cases, they even became disconnected from their surroundings. The deeper the intensity of the conflict and the higher the likelihood that one could become a casualty, the greater the likelihood that an individual could exhibit combat stress reaction.

"Post-traumatic stress disorder is something far more severe. It usually results from exposure to terrifying events that threatened or caused grievous bodily harm. The psychological trauma is ongoing, since the psychological defenses that one normally employs in everyday life have been completely overwhelmed by the experiences that caused the disorder. This situation can also be precipitated by psychological or emotional trauma, not just the threat or experience of *physical* harm. In many cases, though, these two are actually combined.

"One result can be borderline personality disorder or BPD. This is a form of mental illness in which one's moods, behaviors, self-image and personal relationships become chronically unstable. We talk a lot about schizophrenia but BPD is actually more common, though it tends to affect young women more often than young men. Suicide, suicide attempts and self-injury without suicidal intent are all seen. BPD accounts for about twenty percent of psychiatric hospitalizations.

"Now for your question … post-traumatic stress disorder *does* display biochemical changes in the body and in the brain. For example, most PTSD victims show a low secretion of cortisol and a high secretion of catecholamine in their urine. Cortisol is the so-called stress hormone and catecholamines are substances derived from the amino acid tyrosine. They include things like epinephrine and dopamine. Interestingly, combat veterans with PTSD can show a reduction in the actual volume of the hippocampus, a reduction of approximately twenty percent. We know that the amygdala is involved in the formation of emotional memories, especially those related to fear. Some believe that PTSD is associated with the hyperarousal of the amygdala and insufficient control by the hippocampus and the medial prefrontal cortex."

"Your question," Barnes interjected, "is whether or not Terry Randall exhibited any of these kinds of physical phenomena associated with PTSD."

"Yes," I said.

"The answer, Tom, is no, but I hasten to add that that does not mean—to an absolute certainty--that he did not suffer from PTSD."

"But if he *was* suffering from PTSD his parents would surely have noticed a change in his actions and attitude. And if he had something milder--combat stress reaction or shell shock or soldier's heart or whatever you want to call it--it too would have manifested itself in observable behaviors."

"Yes," Sally said, "but combat stress reaction is transitory. PTSD is more persistent."

"Right. So if one suffered from something more severe than combat stress reaction, something sufficiently severe to make you kill your wife and yourself, people should notice that fact, particularly people close to the person suffering it."

"Yes," she said, "but that doesn't mean that an individual couldn't do a good job of suppressing and hiding it. This is not something as explicit as a broken limb or an impairment such as deafness or blindness."

"I understand," I said, "but we're not talking about occasional melancholy or depression . . . take a couple of St. John's Wort pills and put on a happy face."

"No," Sally said, "we're not."

"I take it that you've spoken to the decedents' parents," Barnes said.

"Yes, to his parents and her mother; the father is dead."

"And they had not noticed anything out of the ordinary."

"No, they hadn't," I said. "They told me that they could not conceive of the fact that their son or son-in-law was capable of an action such as this."

"And you would expect that," Sally said. "On the other hand, except for his wife, who would have known him better?"

"That's why we're going to continue the investigation," Chris said, "at least for a little while."

FIFTEEN

"Where are you off to now, Tom?" Chris asked.

"The Wells Fargo branch on Ocean," I said. "I want to check out the Randalls' accounts."

"Good. Let me know if anything jumps out at you." He paused a second before asking his next question. "What do you make of Sally being there this morning?"

"I'm not sure," I said. "If she was driving up from La Jolla he'd probably have arranged for a later meeting time. Maybe she had business in Orange County yesterday."

"Or maybe they've become an item."

"That's always a possibility," I said.

"I wish them well," Chris said. "They make a good team. I don't know much about Sally's past. Len lost his wife about five years ago and it hit him very hard."

"I don't think she's ever been married," I said. "At least I've never heard her mention an ex."

"Listen to us," Chris said. "We sound like the women in the back corner at Starbucks, nibbling on their muffins and scones and speculating on the romantic status of everyone who didn't make it to the table that morning."

"Like you said, Chief, they're a good team. She's helped us in the past. The more we see of her and hear from her, the better."

"That was interesting, what she said about PTSD. You don't think he had it, do you?"

"I think we've all had trauma that we've had to get over. It's a standard part of being human. Soldiers have more than most, but they're also trained to expect it. I'm not sure they're trained to get over it. This generation … it's different … different than it was in the past … back when we had a draft and a lot of people served. Now the soldiers are spread out. It's not like the World War II generation. We were surrounded by veterans … in business … in the colleges. If *they* had all come down with PTSD the country would have ceased to function."

"And by and large they managed to make it through," Chris said. "Our grandfathers and great uncles … some of them were in combat for years. And neither the war in Europe nor in the Pacific was any cake walk."

"No, they weren't," I said. "Now the veterans may be more isolated within our society, but not all of them … Terry Randall was still in the Guard. He was still meeting with people who had shared his experiences. I never knew him, of course, but from what people are saying about him, I'm just not seeing a person on the edge, a person lost and confused and dying inside, a person capable of shooting his wife with a shotgun (twice, perhaps) and then killing himself."

"Let me know if you learn anything interesting at the bank," Chris said. "I've got a confab with the mayor and the city council. No big items on our agenda, but they're all looking forward to their bagels and juice and they'll be collectively disappointed if I'm not there."

The manager of the Ocean Avenue branch of Wells Fargo was a young woman named Caroline Farley. We overlapped at UC-Irvine; she was studying economics and I was studying general humanities. We didn't know each other at the time, but we've talked about our experiences there from time to time. This morning she was wearing a dark business suit. Her brown hair was up, off her neck, and her glasses were stylish but simple—the narrow rectangular kind that so many are wearing. She had a small red handkerchief in the top pocket of her jacket and a flag pin on her lapel.

"How are you, Tom?" she said, extending her hand.

"I'm fine, Caroline. I haven't seen you in awhile."

"The company bigwigs love to huddle," she said. "I'm in meetings with district managers almost constantly and we have regular meetings in San Francisco with the top muck a mucks. Apparently it helps when we all wring our hands together."

"I understand," I said.

"What can I do for you, Tom? Let me guess … the Randalls' accounts … "

"Have the esteemed members of the press corps been hounding you?"

"No more than fifteen or twenty of them," she said, "fifteen or twenty times each."

"They must have gotten to someone on the Randalls' list for monthly payments, probably one of the utilities or their cable TV provider."

"Yes. No secrets anymore, Tom. Something to think about, right?"

"I'm always on *my* best behavior," I said.

"So am I," she said, "though neither of us probably has much time to get into any trouble."

"Not as pillars of the establishment," I said--both of us smiling now.

"Why don't you come into the conference room," she said. "There's a computer in there. I can pull up their accounts for you and you can study them privately. I'd prefer that you not print anything out, but there's a pad in there if you want to take some notes. You can also come back and recheck them, any time you need to."

I told her how much I appreciated her help and followed her down the hallway past the safe and safety deposit boxes to the room they called the conference room. It contained a small table and six chairs. The computer was on a side table with wheels that could be positioned anywhere within the room. After I got comfortable and began to work she brought me a cup of coffee. "Black, right?" she said.

"Yes, thanks Caroline. You didn't have to do that."

"We aim to please, Lieutenant. At Wells Fargo we are happy to offer a full range of financial services and some days the black coffee is more important than anything else in the bank."

SIXTEEN

The program offered an initial screen with a list of options: savings accounts, checking accounts, money market accounts, certificates of deposit, mortgage accounts, VISA accounts, personal loan accounts, safety deposit boxes and *other*. I started with the mortgage account. Monthly payment: just under $3,000, probably a stretch for them, particularly when Terry was between jobs.

There was no safety deposit box, no personal loan or loans, no certificates of deposit and no money market account. There was a modest checking account balance of $823.00 and a conventional savings account containing $4,235.00. The Randalls were getting by, if not in grand style. They had a debit card which enabled them to draw money from ATM's and make purchases by debiting their checking account. There was relatively little activity on this account. It appeared that, unless they had other credit cards, they were keeping their debit card available for emergencies and making the vast majority of their purchases by cash or hard-copy check.

When I checked *other* I found a copy of the documents filed when their original accounts were established. There were no other credit cards listed as part of their mini- credit history. I returned to their checking and savings accounts and drilled down to examine details. Susan's checks had been direct-deposited by the hospital which employed her, the checks varying in amount based on the hours she worked. It appeared that she had increased her hours in recent weeks, no doubt to compensate for the reduction in Terry's Guard income.

Terry had received some checks from an organization known as FirstGrowth, but they were not direct-deposited. He had endorsed hard-copy checks and then put them in their joint checking account. The vast majority of debits from their checking account were online payments for their mortgage, utilities and repeating household expenses. Both Susan and Terry did grocery shopping, sometimes at Vons, sometimes at Pavilions, but mostly at Ralphs. They bought gas with their check card. Their savings account was mostly intact, but withdrawals of $275 and $300 were made at the end of two recent monthly periods and transferred to their checking account. They were apparently stretching to make ends meet, just prior to and during the time when Terry began receiving payments from FirstGrowth.

I used Wells Fargo's computer to access the internet and checked on FirstGrowth. It sounded like a financial institution of some sort. That would have squared with Terry's banking experience, but the only listing I was able to locate was in the white pages of the Irvine directory. I made a note of their 800 number and returned to the Randalls' Wells Fargo account screens. I jotted down some dates and some amounts, thanked Caroline for all of her help, told her that I would take her up on her offer to recheck the accounts, as necessary, at some future time, thanked her again for the coffee and walked out to my car.

The sun was very bright now. The marine layer was gone and the inside of the car was warm. I turned on the ignition, lowered the windows, blew out the heat with the a/c and made some arrangements to check the Randalls' phone records. Then I drove back to my office. Hector was standing in the doorway when I arrived.

"Guess who's here," he said, "your biggest fan."

"Maria?"

She came around and joined Hector in the doorway.

"Hello, Lieutenant Tom," she said.

Maria is Hector's niece, a precocious three-year old with a heartbreaking smile and the fashion sense of a runway model.

"My mother says that you are looking after my Uncle Hector," she said, "that you keep him from being naughty and getting into trouble."

"That's true," I said, "and that's a very big job."

"That's what my mother said," she answered. "She's going to pick me up soon. We're going to go shopping."

"Where are you going, Maria, to the mall?"

"No, Lieutenant Tom, we're going to the grocery. We need bananas and a whole lot of other things. Like cereal. And milk. I like bananas the most though. My mother says that they're good for you."

"They *are* good for you," I answered.

"They have po'tassum in them," she said.

"Yes, they do and you need that."

"I like grapes too," she said. "And chocolate milk. And peanut butter."

"Some people eat peanut butter and bananas on sandwiches," I said.

"I would try that," she said. "At least I would try it *once*. My mother says that you should be willing to try everything once."

"Your mother is a very smart lady," I said.

"She's pretty too," Maria said. "She says that she got all the beauty in the family, but I think she says that just to tease Uncle Hector."

"He's not as pretty as your mother," I said.

"No, but he is very good at fixing things. He is very smart. He helps my mother with our car sometimes."

"He is *very* smart," I said. "He helps me with a lot of things."

"Like catching criminals," she said. "That's very important. Criminals are bad people, Lieutenant Tom."

"Yes, they are, honey, and he helps in protecting and helping good people also."

"That's nice," she said. "That's important too … well, I have to go now, Lieutenant Tom. It was nice to see you again."

"Good bye, Maria. Say hi to your mother."

"She's just there … see?" She smiled and gave me a tiny wave that was like a mini-salute. Hector ushered her out to the lot and returned a few minutes later.

"She's a sweetheart," I said.

"She's three going on thirty-five," he said.

I briefed him on the Randalls' banking records. We each had a cup of coffee and some packaged sandwiches from the vending machines. "No peanut butter and bananas," Hector said. "Just the stuff that looks vaguely like meat and cheese, in unidentifiable combinations."

He brought me up to date on a stolen vehicle case he was working and he reaffirmed his desire to help with the Randall case whenever I needed him. I thanked him, finished my sandwich, and returned to my computer, first working my way through the security protocols and then settling in to check the Randalls' phone records.

SEVENTEEN

At first they seemed innocuous enough. There was the expected cell-phone traffic between Terry and his wife and that between the two of them and their parents. They seldom used their landline, relying on their cells for unlimited calling between themselves and the members of their calling circle. They checked the time from their landline and, less often, the temperature, and occasionally called utility companies, grocers and local merchants. Terry had recently used his cell to call FirstGrowth. I assumed, at least, that he was calling FirstGrowth, because the number that he was calling—with the exception of the final digit--corresponded to the 800 number for the company which I had gotten from the Irvine white pages on the internet. I figured that he was calling the number of his supervisor rather than the general corporate number in the phone directory.

Susan made more calls than Terry, the bulk of the recent ones being to Saddleback Memorial, probably to her supervisor there. We could follow up on those calls later. For now there was only one set of calls which elicited any immediate interest: a series of calls from Terry to two specific numbers, one a cell phone and the other a landline. The calls were made at all hours of the day and night, a number made at the time during which most families would be eating dinner, some as late as the early morning hours after midnight. The landline was in Santa Ana—an apartment building on North Flower, near the **5**. It took me a few minutes to check the cell records, but I eventually determined that the billing address for the cell service corresponded to the address of the landline. The person Terry was calling at all hours was named Jeffrey Bandar.

I checked on Bandar in a number of our data bases and saw that he was a man in his early thirties, most recently employed by a trucking company in Tustin. He had served in the California Guard, but had been recently separated from them. There was no criminal record on him, no involvement in litigation and no stories, favorable or unfavorable, in any of the archives of the local newspapers. He had been married, briefly, to a woman named Jennifer Hester, but they had divorced three years ago.

I called his landline number and let the phone ring fifteen times; there was no answering machine. I tried his cell phone number and got a voice mailbox. I left a message, identifying myself as an acquaintance of Terry Randall and requesting that he call me back on my cell line. An hour and a half later there was still no call back. I turned off my computer, checked on Chris (he was out for a late meeting) then Hector (he was on a stolen vehicle case, checking on a chop shop and gone for the day). I looked at the time, closed my office door and went out to my car.

After five minutes in the car my cell phone rang. I put it on speaker to keep my hands free. It was Jeffrey Bandar. His voice sounded as if it was coming from the other end of a muffled pipe. He said he was at home and gave me the address. Before he could say anything else the signal started breaking up. I got on the 133 and headed toward the 5.

I caught the scent of the burned coffee from the parking lot below his third-floor walkup and followed it to his door. I knocked and heard a voice saying that it was already open. The living room was spartan in its decor: a couch with orange, cloth fabric, an overstuffed side chair, a small formica coffee table with wrought iron legs, a TV on a metal stand, a carpet remnant in the center of the floor and some small boxes stacked in distant corners. Jeffrey Bandar was stretched out on the couch, huddled beneath a cotton throw, his head wedged against a miniature, square pillow. He looked tense and he looked tired.

"I'm Jeff," he said, eking out the words.

"Tom Deaton," I responded. "Are you OK?" It was at least 80 degrees in the room; I wondered why he needed to cover himself with the throw.

"I feel like homemade crap," he said, "but I can talk. It's about Terry, isn't it?"

"Yes," I said. "I'm a lieutenant with the Laguna Beach PD. I'm investigating his death and the death of his wife."

"He didn't kill himself," Bandar said. "And he didn't kill his wife. I guess you know that already."

"I can't really comment on the investigation," I said, "but we routinely follow up on all possibilities."

"You've got your doubts," he said. "You'd have to. It's too pat. Too easy. And he was too good a man. Guys like Terry … they don't do things like that."

"What was your relationship with Terry Randall, Mr. Bandar?" I asked.

"My *relationship*? That's a long story, Lieutenant."

"I've got plenty of time," I said.

"So do I," he answered. "Could you do me a favor?"

"What's that?"

"In the refrigerator there's some bottled water. It's not really fresh . . . it was once … but after I drank it I just kept filling up the bottle with tap water. I like it cold and, besides, it tastes about the same as it did when it was fresh, so why bother?"

"Sure," I said.

"If there's anything in there that looks good to you, help yourself," he said.

There was some milk a couple days past the sell-by date and some generic cola. I passed on both and brought him the bottle of water. He drank it as if it was his first drink in a long while.

"Sorry about the coffee smell," he said. "Once it starts to bake against the bottom of the pot it takes days to get rid of it. I had the windows open for awhile, but I felt chilled and had to close them."

I wondered if he had the flu. His body was quivering and the half circles beneath his eyes were deeply etched. Before I could ask him a question he began to speak.

"Terry was ... I guess I'd say ... my *coach*. I think they usually call it a *sponsor*, but a sponsor is somebody who's been where you've been and come out successfully on the other side. Terry was never there--never where *I* was--but he understood what I was up against and he tried to help me. He was my First John back in the Middle East, back when I was in the Guard. I was a Spec/4 working on light armored vehicles. Nothing fancy, mostly routine maintenance. And I was doing OK. More or less, at least. Most of the problems I had I took there to begin with. Terry kept me straight and he kept me sober. When I got back here they started up again. It all probably goes back to the fact that my wife and I had split. She was my other anchor.

"I never did anything hardcore. It's just that when I started to drink I had trouble stopping. I came back here and started working for a trucking company over in Tustin. It wasn't good for me. I'd have stretches on the road and then stretches back here. Too much time on my hands. Too much time to think. Terry said to call him anytime. I did, and it really helped. Sometimes I'd leave a message, not always at the best of times. He'd always call me back, no matter what day it was and no matter what time it was." He paused before adding a final thought. "Now he's gone too.

"It's probably hard for you to believe it, Lieutenant, but I haven't had a drink in six days. I basically changed addictions, switching to coffee and cigarettes. I haven't had a cigarette in three days. My throat got so sore I couldn't tolerate them. I ran out of coffee yesterday and got on the couch. I've got a cold or flu or something and I couldn't hold anything down anyway, so I'm trying to wait it out, to beat it, I guess. So far, so good ... I'm trying to stay hydrated. I probably should eat something. My mother used to say you should feed a cold and starve a fever. Maybe it was the other way around. It doesn't matter either way, because I don't have any appetite. Anyway, I'm just trying to rest up now, get a little strength back, work my way through this."

"How long did you work with Terry Randall, Mr. Bandar?"

"Please, call me Jeff, Lieutenant. He was my CO for ten months, but we stayed in touch after that."

"When was the last time you talked to him?"

"A couple of days before he died. I was going out on the road for a few days and he told me to stay straight … keep to my mileage quota but not try to extend it … stick with the rules … get my proper rest … shave, shower … eat decent foods … just hold things together."

"How did he sound?"

"The way he always did."

"There was nothing different in his voice?"

"You mean like anger or tension?"

"Yes, anything out of the ordinary."

"Not that I could tell. He was a very … measured … man, Lieutenant. Very grounded. Very stable. Cool in a crisis … the person that everybody else turned to for answers. What can I say? He was pure class, Lieutenant. He held me together when no one else could and he stood by me when everybody else left."

"Did you know his wife?"

"I met her a couple of times. She was a nurse, you know. She told me to follow her husband's advice and she told me that whenever I had a medical problem I should see somebody about it, that I shouldn't be afraid or ashamed, that I should check in and make sure everything was OK with me. People in combat zones … they bring things back with them … I'm not talking about mental stuff; I'm talking about bugs and diseases, things we don't see over here, things we've never developed an immunity for, things that our docs aren't used to seeing regularly. You wouldn't believe the steps we had to take with the vehicles, Lieutenant. It was as if we were detoxing them. You move them from country to country … bring them back here … you want to make sure you're not bringing something nasty along with them. Maybe that's what happened to me. Maybe I've got something now, something that was like, dormant, for awhile and finally decided to bite me in the ass."

"Her advice was good," I said.

"I know. I'm gonna give this another day or so and if it doesn't clear I'm going in and get checked out. If it's something exotic, something other people brought back with them ... the people at the VA will have a handle on it. I *will*, Lieutenant. Don't worry. I'm not gonna lay here and live with the chills indefinitely."

"Tell me, Jeff," I said. "Did Terry say anything to you, anything at all that would suggest that he was in trouble, that there was something wrong in his life or his marriage?"

"Like I said, Lieutenant, he wasn't that kind of guy. He was the one with the big shoulders. He didn't burden other people with his problems; he helped them with theirs."

"So you were surprised when you heard the story of his and his wife's death."

"Surprised? I was fucking flabbergasted. That's not the guy I knew. Not at all. Jesus, Lieutenant, when the reports came in ... when the reporters were spouting all that garbage ... I was talking back to the television set. You know ... as if they could actually hear me or something. And it wasn't just that I had lost a good friend. It was the bullshit that he had some sort of battle fatigue or shell shock. The guy was a rock, Lieutenant. I'd bet money that his wife was standup also. I only met her a couple times, like I said, but she was the sort that you'd want standing next to your bed when things were tight. She'd seen a lot ... you could tell that right away. She had this kind of warmth, but she was also firm, if you know what I mean. She'd take care of you and she'd stay with you until the job was done. We saw nurses like that in the Middle East. Trust me; I know them when I see them. The two of them ... they were a team, Lieutenant. He'd never kill her, but my guess is that he'd kill to save her."

"Why do you say that?"

"You could tell when you saw them together. There was a bond. They were like athletes who had seen adversity and come out of it, together."

"Did he ever say anything to you about the work that he was doing?"

"You mean job-type work?"

"Yes."

"Not really. I think he was like, temping or something. He didn't have anything permanent. He was looking, I think. Doing something temporary to tide him over."

"Did he ever mention a company called FirstGrowth?"

"No, not that I remember. I'm sorry, Lieutenant. It's like I said … he was helping me … he wasn't asking me to help him."

"I understand, and I really appreciate your talking to me, Jeff," I said. "Are you going to be all right?"

"I think so," he said. "I *want* to be all right. I'm going to do what I have to do to be all right. What else can I say?"

I gave him one of my cards. "Call me if I can do anything. I've also got a friend who's a nurse. She would know where to direct you if you needed that kind of help."

"Thanks," he said. "Could you do something for me now?"

"What's that?" I asked.

"Fill up my water bottle and put it back in the refrigerator."

"Sure," I said. "I'm happy to."

EIGHTEEN

As I drove home I had the radio on for a minute or two but then I turned it off. I didn't want to hear any more voices and I didn't want to hear any popular music. I didn't have much of an appetite myself, but I called my dad and asked him if he'd eaten yet. He hadn't, so I picked up some sandwiches and drove to the marina. When I got there he was sitting in the stern of his boat on a deckchair, looking at the lights reflecting on the ripples in the harbor.

"How are you, Tom?" he asked.

"I'm OK, Dad; how about yourself?"

"I'm OK," he said. "It's a nice night. Not too cool. I thought I'd sit up here and look at the harbor. I never get tired of the lights and the motion of the water. You know … some people come here and never leave the marina. They sleep on their boats; they lay on the beds in their staterooms and feel the movement. They watch the lights and the shadows as they shift. It's like being rocked in a cradle; it comforts them. Some of them think it's a better investment that way, never leaving the slip. When they sell their boats the buyers want to know how many hours are on the engines. They can say, 'hell, almost none' and get a better price. Then they buy a bigger boat, rent a bigger slip, and just sit there, never taking it out. It's funny … but on nights like this … it's easy to understand why they do it."

"I know," I said. "People buy houses with nice kitchens; then they never cook. It's a place to stand around in … to drink wine … eat finger food made by a caterer. You see multi-million dollar homes with half-million dollar kitchens and only a single oven. Mom wouldn't have understood it."

"No, she wanted three—one for the roast, one for the cake, one to keep the pie warm in. I miss her cooking, son … almost as much as I miss her."

"Me too, Dad. Every day." I put the sack of carryout on the table next to his deck chair. "How about a sandwich?"

"Sure, what's the choice?" he asked.

"Ham and cheese on rye and ham and cheese on rye. I can also rearrange things so you can have all ham or all cheese."

"Ham and cheese sounds good," he said. "How about a beer? I've also got soda."

"I'll take a soda," I said. "I was starting to get a little tired in the car. A little caffeine will pick me up."

"Pepsi or Pepsi?" he asked.

"Pepsi, I think," I said.

He also got out a tube of Pringles. "I like these things," he said. "The ones with no fat. They don't taste like the originals, but they're low-cal and they don't blow my guts apart like some people warned they would. Once you put it on … at my age … it's harder to take it off. Plus the tubes fit in the little compartments in the galley. I stack them like wine bottles sometimes. Your mother wouldn't touch these things, of course."

He paused after the small talk and said, "How's the case going—the one with the soldier and his wife?"

"Nobody thinks he did it," I said. "I just met with one of his old Spec/4's, a guy with a drinking problem. He said that Terry Randall was his sponsor … he called him his *coach* … said that Terry kept him sober. He said he was a standup guy and so was his wife … that they were very close … like a set of teammates who had seen a lot of adversity together and stayed tight throughout it all."

"And you've been checking records, I guess … " he said, "bank, phone … that sort of thing."

"Yes."

"And nothing jumped out at you."

"Just the Spec/4," I said.

"So what's next?"

"Their workplaces. She was a nurse at Saddleback; he was working for some place called FirstGrowth."

"Sounds like an old savings and loan or something like that."

"Yes. I've got a phone number. I think I'll check on her first."

"You could talk to Sarah," he said. "I'm sure she would know her."

"Yes. I figured I'd start with Sarah." He was always trying to promote my relationship with Sarah, both when it was on and when it was off. Lately it was more on than off. Some warmth, not a whole lot of fire.

"How's the sandwich?" I asked.

"Great. How about a Pringle?"

"I'll pass, I think."

"They won't hurt you," he said.

"I know. The Pepsi tastes good."

"If you change your mind, there's plenty of beer down there."

"Thanks."

"Excuse me a second, Tom. I'm going to hit the head. You could call Sarah if you wanted to, set up a time to talk with her ... "

"Thanks, Dad," I said.

He got up and I called her on my cell. I got her voicemail; she was probably working. I told her I'd call her tomorrow and took another sip of the soda and a bite of the sandwich. I heard some bells at the outer edge of the marina and some voices from a distant slip. Life was going on, as it always does.

When he returned I told him I had called Sarah and left a message for her. He just nodded approvingly and took a bite of his sandwich and a drink of his beer before he spoke. "You know, son," he said, "I was just thinking about somebody from the old days. Back before your time. Practically before my time, for that matter. His name was Howard Carter. This was back in Kentucky, long before we moved here. Howard was a quiet and decent man; he was famous in western Kentucky and some people even thought he should run for congress. He owned a hotel. This was back before the Holiday Inns and other chains. Back before the mom and pop motels that you'd see on the roads into town. There were boarding houses, that sort of thing, and usually one real hotel in a decent-sized town.

"Howard Carter was not the person you'd expect to own one. Back then … you'd think of someone with a dark coat, a vest and a watch fob, pressed pants, a cigar, mustache and probably a stiff hat. He wasn't like that at all. Usually he wore a brown sweater over his white shirt and tie and he didn't carry a cigar in his hand because he lost his hand in the great war.

"He was also an orphan. He was found, abandoned, on the steps of a local church and he was actually raised at St. Joseph's Orphanage, across the river, up in Ohio. He learned a trade. Concrete work at first, but then he went into carpentry. After the war and the loss of his hand, he became a building inspector. The men in the construction trade admired him greatly and he eventually became a partner in some building projects. After a few years he made enough money to build a hotel.

"He never married. People said that the town was his family. When there were floods or mine closings he would look after the locals, put them up for awhile, give them some work, help them get back on their feet. He never asked for anything in return. He was just a fine man, the kind they used to make movies about, only Howard Carter was real.

"The point is … are you sure I can't get you one of those beers?"

"No Dad, thanks. I'm fine."

"Tell me if you change your mind."

"I will."

"Anyway, the point about Howard Carter is that there are some people out there in the world who are just *good*. No matter what kind of hand is dealt them, no matter what advantages they have or problems they face, they're just fundamentally good. I know there are psychologists and such who try to figure out how much of the way we are is based on upbringing and how much of the way we are is based on our genetics. The point is that there's some mystery there. You see kids who grow up in the same family with the same house, the same parents, the same food, the same schools, the same neighborhood and somehow they're very, very different. You see a quiet guy who lives alone, keeps to himself, nods his head when you pass, maybe tips his hat to the ladies … and one day you find out he's got bodies in his basement or murder trophies in his refrigerator. They make movies about those kind of people because the movies like mystery. They like to stir up your imagination and, of course, make money by titillating the paying public. Nevertheless, there are some Howard Carters out there. They never had much themselves but somehow they managed to give back much more than they received. Good people. They *do* exist. What I'm saying, son, is that this young man and his wife who got killed … "

"Yes, Dad … "

"It *is* possible that they could have been good. It's possible that something terrible was done to them, something they never deserved."

"I know that, Dad."

"And I know you'll find out, either way."

"I'll certainly try."

"One other thing, son. I want you to do me a favor."

"What's that, Dad?"

"When you see Sarah … when you talk to her … tell her I'm thinking about her and I look forward to seeing her again."

NINETEEN

When I got home the message light was blinking on my answering machine. I hit the *play* button: "Hi, Tom. It's me. I was in and out of the ER tonight and didn't want to play telephone tag. I figured you'd get home eventually and I could leave a message there. I'm on tomorrow from 4:00 until 12:00. How about lunch? Just leave a message on my voicemail and I'll see you then."

We met at one of the hotels at Dana Point. This one does nice salads and serves lunch on a terrace that overlooks the Pacific. She was wearing her nurse's uniform. The nametag read: **Sarah Ritter, R.N.** When she met me at the table she kissed me lightly.

"I hope it's OK that I'm dressed like this," she said.

"It won't be a problem," I said. "People are comforted by a medical presence. How are you?"

"I'm fine. Busy, of course. We had a wild night last night. There must have been a lot of parties that got out of hand. When they move on from the appetizers and the cocktails to the knives and broken beer bottles we're their next stop. We also had a full array of conventional problems—broken limbs, burns … the aftermath of a three-car accident on the **5** … anyway, we all survived. How are you?"

"I'm fine. My dad says hi and that he looks forward to seeing you again soon."

"He's a sweetie. How's the case coming?"

"I've talked to some people. No breathroughs yet. It's one of the reasons I wanted to talk to you now."

"Because I knew her?"

"Yes."

"I didn't really know her very well. I haven't been working the ER until recently. Mostly (as you know) I was working the ICU. Occasionally there'd be a shortage and I'd be assigned to the ER temporarily. We overlapped on a couple of occasions; that's all."

"What was she like?"

"Excellent. Highly professional. She had the perfect temperament for the ER. It's what I would describe as a tightrope job. You have to be able to deliver care quickly and efficiently and you have to be technically precise. At the same time you've got people who are overwrought and often in great pain. It's not like they knew they were coming in for a checkup or test or procedure that had been scheduled and anticipated for days or weeks. Something sudden and unexpected happened to them and that's always upsetting, whether the cause is medical or not. You add some blood, some edema, some bruising, a child that's crying and can't be comforted … a general feeling of desperation … you know what I mean. You've been there yourself, many times. Anyway, you have to solve the problem but first you have to calm everybody down. Usually you can't do the former until you've done the latter. You can't just hit them with a needle and sedate or paralyze them the way they do on television.

"Anyway, Susan could do both. She was very smart and very skilled but she was also excellent with people. One night I remember in particular. There were the usual cases—lots of blood and gore, but with people who'd been there before and knew the drill. (We get a lot of repeat business, you know.) All of a sudden a Latino couple come in with a small child, maybe 3 years old. He wasn't desperately ill, but he was obviously frightened. He was covered with hives (probably a simple allergic reaction), and he knew what was waiting for him."

"A sharp needle that he thought would be about a foot and a half long," I said.

"Exactly, and he didn't know that 'sharp' was a good thing. Anyway, the more he thought about the shot and the more terrified he became, the more adrenalin his body released and the more the hives continued to disappear. And they were nasty … he was covered with them and it was going to be hard to find space in between them to insert the needle. As soon as they receded he got excited and told his parents he was cured. When they left the waiting room and got back in their car the little boy relaxed, the adrenalin subsided and the hives returned. He tried to hide the fact but eventually he couldn't and a few minutes later they were back in the waiting room. Susan had to calm him down, explain to him and his parents what was happening and assure him that she'd be very gentle in giving him the medicine.

"And you know, Tom, a lot of the regular visitors to the ER are filled with booze or drugs, often both, and as bad as they might look they've at least already had some anesthesia. The only thing that the little boy had going for him was the assurance offered by the nurse and his parents. In the larger scheme of things, of course, it wasn't a big deal. It wasn't as if he was in excruciating pain or anything, but to him the fear was very real and Susan handled it all perfectly. By the time the family left the ER they were inviting her over for Sunday dinner."

"Did you ever meet her husband?"

"I was never formally introduced. He came by one night. I think he was just dropping something off for her. They seemed fine together."

"Did you ever hear her talk about him?"

"Not at any length. Remember, we only overlapped occasionally. There was certainly nothing negative. I remember her saying something once or twice about the experiences he had had in the Guard. She seemed proud of him, interested in what he had done … that sort of thing."

The waiter brought our salads. Sarah had gone for the full veggie deal; I had some chicken on mine and some avocado. We sipped our iced tea and enjoyed the sun.

"One other thing," Sarah said. "Although I didn't see her that many times, she never seemed preoccupied. If a couple are having problems they might not talk about it directly, but you can sometimes sense that they're distracted. They're looking over their shoulders, futzing with things in their purse or wallet, checking phone numbers, times, appointments. Their lives are … I don't know … somehow *out of joint* and you sense it in their behavior. I never got that with Susan. She was always *there* and focused."

"That's very helpful," I said. "It confirms what a lot of people have been saying."

"But it's not helpful in the sense that it doesn't explain why he would have killed her and then killed himself."

"Right, but it's consistent with what others are saying. No one I've talked to can understand how this could possibly have happened."

"Then it must have happened for some reason you haven't yet discovered."

"That's right."

"Then that's what you have to find out."

II

FIRSTGROWTH

TWENTY

Hector hurriedly left me a note concerning a Canadian company called FirstGrowth. It provided exploratory services for gas, oil and mineral deposits. I figured that Terry could not be freelancing as a petroleum geologist and that a company of that size would not be paying southern California part-timers with hard copy checks. I wasn't sure of the degree to which you could copyright a company title, but I figured that there could be a FirstGrowth Inc., a FirstGrowth Partners, a Mr. FirstGrowth and other possible permutations. Absent any other items on the internet, I called the directory 800 number I had secured earlier.

I got an answering machine, telling me that I had reached a specific number and inviting me to leave a message. That was odd. Most businesses that wish to thrive do not conceal their names from the general public. Using a line that wouldn't pop up on a caller i.d., I called the number in Terry's cellphone records, the one that was different from the corporate number by a single, final digit.

A man's voice answered, offering nothing beyond a simple 'hello'. I didn't identify myself but simply said, "FirstGrowth?"

"Who is calling, please?" the voice responded.

"I'm calling with regard to one of FirstGrowth's previous employees, Mr. Terrence Randall," I said.

"If you leave your number I'll ask his supervisor to call you," the man said.

I gave him the number of an unregistered cell phone that I use for purposes such as this.

"Can I give Mr. Randall's supervisor your name?"

"It's a confidential matter," I said. "I'd prefer to speak to him or her directly."

Sooner or later I'd have to identify myself, but in the meantime I thought I'd keep them off balance. It was clearly what *they* preferred to do with me, so I decided to follow suit. Their secretiveness and evasiveness appeared to be part of their standard operating procedure and that in itself was interesting. It was also interesting that the voice at the other end of the phone said nothing to me about Terry's 'branch', his 'division', his 'office', his 'department' or his 'section'. The company was apparently very small; perhaps (my overheated imagination suggested) it was a front for some secretive government operation or possibly criminal enterprise. Either way, that was interesting as well. Most organizations use 800 numbers to make it easy for potential clients to contact them. Such organizations tend to be large or communication-intensive, like mail order businesses. I wondered why FirstGrowth would use such a number if it didn't welcome that number's use.

The prior question, however, was how would Terry have known of FirstGrowth's existence? Either they advertised publicly and he responded to the ad or he was referred to them by someone with whom I had not yet spoken. While I waited for the call back, I checked the local newspaper archives and the online job services. The job sites that I found didn't archive past entries and there were no current entries for FirstGrowth, but I found an old notice in the *Orange County Register* that may have been the ad to which Terry had responded:

Mature, discreet individual required for part-time employment. We are an upscale vendor with a select client base and require an individual capable of serving as an interface between central management and those clients. Generous compensation and benefits. The ideal candidate will be an individual with a record of responsible service in an organization requiring both high levels of security and high expectations with regard to professional values and efficient performance.

I wasn't quite sure what that meant, but it sounded like the kind of ad which might have drawn Terry's attention. The contact number was a P.O. box in Newport Beach. I checked with the branch in question and was told that the box had been rented by the month for a period of ninety days. The renter was a company called FirstGrowth **Distributors**.

Two hours later I received a call on my unregistered cell. The voice was deep and polished.

"Good afternoon," the man said. "My organization received a call concerning one of our employees."

"That was me," I said. "I was calling concerning Terrence Randall."

"And are you with the press?" the man asked.

"No, I'm with the Laguna Beach Police Department," I said. "This is Lieutenant Tom Deaton."

"William Richland, Lieutenant. You'll forgive my asking about the press, but Terry's death is, as you surely know, a tragedy to all of us who knew him. Personally, I'd prefer to keep the vultures at a distance as long as possible."

"I understand," I said.

"I believe you've already had your exchanges with them," he said. "On the news … "

"Yes," I said. "We've had some discussions."

"Well, I'll be more than happy to speak with you, Lieutenant. I don't know what I can add, but I suppose any information may be of potential use. Terry worked for us for a brief time. His loss is a great shock and it's a professional loss to us as well as a personal one. He was an exceptional individual and an exceptional representative of the company."

"Can you tell me the nature of your business, Mr. Richland?"

"Of course. We're a wine distributorship. Actually, a highly specialized one. I would not describe us as unorthodox, because our organization is structured specifically for the goods and services that we provide. We are, however, a bit out of the ordinary. Our warehouse is in Irvine, but we do work throughout southern California. My own home is in San Diego County and I do much of my work from that base."

"Could we meet face-to-face, Mr. Richland? I'd be happy to see you at any of your company's locations."

"Certainly. I've got some calls to make this afternoon and evening, but we could meet at my home in the morning. First thing, if you wish. I'm an early riser."

"How about 8:30?"

"Perfect," he said. "I'll try to help in any way that I can. I look forward to seeing you."

He then gave me his address. It was on Torrey Pines Road, just below the university, a stone's throw from the Pacific. Business must have been good.

TWENTY-ONE

I figured I'd drive down early, dodge the worst of the rush hour traffic and have some coffee at one of the cafés in the village. The traffic in the upscale neighborhoods north of San Diego can be dense and I didn't want to be sitting in traffic while William Richland was staring out his front window, wondering when I planned to arrive.

I knocked on the door of Chris Dietrich's office and briefed him on what I had learned.

"Wine distributorships … " he said. "That's heavy industry, particularly these days. Big trucks. Big competition. Wine in bottles, cheap wine in boxes and jugs . . . it doesn't sound like something that Terry Randall would be doing. I'm thinking … teamsters … blue collar guys, not bank managers."

"Right," I said. "This is something more exotic, Chief. Companies commission special labels and use the wine for promotions or gifts. Individuals present themselves as winery owners, putting their own names on bottles. Mail order outfits sell hard-to-find wines. Companies sell fruit baskets with wine and olive oil … it's probably more like that kind of thing. A person like Terry Randall could speak comfortably with both individuals and companies. He could also manage the logistics that are involved in delivering the product."

"I suspect you're right," Chris said, "and something like that could lend itself to being a part-time kind of thing. This could be a high-touch business, with a lot of personal contact. You don't want to be working with robots and computers, getting a shipment with your name misspelled on all of the labels. It would also be pricey. This is all custom stuff. Maybe Terry was the Orange County guy or the Irvine guy, something like that. Whenever a prospect emerged there, he was called. He could have been working on commission."

"Exactly," I said. "His supervisor (who sounds more like somebody with a brandy snifter in his hand than a clipboard) said that Terry was a professional loss as well as a personal one. He may have had the perfect skill set for this kind of work."

"People skills, organizational skills, personal trustworthiness … " Chris said.

"Yes, all of the above."

"I hope this leads somewhere, Tom. I don't like to see a good man and his wife die under mysterious circumstances. At the same time I don't like to see you spinning your wheels, hoping against hope that there's a different explanation than the obvious one. The problem for me so far is that there's nothing really obvious here. Everybody who was close to them says that the two of them were saints. I guess you've got to keep digging, at least for now."

"I will," I said.

"I got the M.E.'s written report," he said. "Nothing new or surprising. When he dropped it off, Sally was with him. He said they were going out for lunch."

"Life goes on," I said. "The doc and the forensic anthropologist … it sounds like a TV show … coming this fall to ABC."

"With a May/December twist. Or maybe more like late July/early October."

"I wish them well," I said. "I like them both."

"Me too," he answered. "A little love would be nice. He's spending his days rooting around in dead bodies and she's spending hers mucking around with old bones and the remains of soft tissue. A little life and love in the mix would be nice all around."

William Richland's house was somewhere between upscale and baronial. A Spanish-revival with a series of balconies and towers, it was gated and guarded by a liberal sprinkling of security cameras, each of which appeared to be functional and not merely cosmetic. As I pulled up to the access control box I could feel the lens of the camera on the left pillar of the gate focusing on me. I turned to it and smiled. The control box had a keypad for regular users and a telephone button for visitors. When I hit it the gates opened. Either Richland was expecting me and being blasé about security or he was staring at me on a private television monitor.

I parked on the driveway made of inlaid brown pavers as he greeted me from the front door. It was old and dark and heavy and had gray, iron grillwork over a small Judas window. He was wearing beige wool slacks, a thin-striped shirt with French cuffs and a blue tie emblazoned with tiny gray medallions. Somewhere in a nearby closet was a blue blazer on a broad wooden hanger that would complete the set, but he wasn't yet wearing it. He looked like a TV anchorman who had come into serious money: $75 haircut, moderate tan, good muscle tone and a voice like those you hear in country club locker rooms and expensive restaurants.

"Lieutenant Deaton, William Richland," he said.

"How do you do," I answered. "I appreciate your seeing me."

"Can I get you some coffee?" he asked.

"Only if it's already made," I said.

"It is. I can also do an espresso or something more exotic, if you wish."

"Just black coffee," I said.

"Well, come in and have a seat," he said, directing me to a living room that was bathed in morning light. The far wall consisted of a set of sliding glass panels that opened onto a yard with a pool and tennis court. I'm always interested in how they can fit the two of them into limited space. There was also some abstract statuary on a series of offset plinths in the center of the lawn. The room itself had marble flooring, but the center of the room—where the sofas were located—was carpeted. The carpet was flush with the edge of the marble. The effect was that of a soft and welcoming island in the middle of a cold architectural space. On the side wall to the south was a long table that appeared to be a bona fide antique, maybe Moorish/Spanish, from some time between the middle ages and the renaissance. Above the table were two signed Miró lithographs. I recognized one as *The Sun Eater*, an image of a man with a lattice-work torso, trapping a large red disc.

"Here we are," he said, joining me and handing me a cup of coffee. I could see the translucence of the rim of the cup in the strong light. English bone china, probably. Light in weight, rich in color, fine in detail. Maybe Spode. For everyday use. Business *was* good.

"How long did Mr. Randall work for you, Mr. Richland?"

"Approximately three months," he said. "In some ways it seems much longer. Terry did a wonderful job for us; it was as if he had been here from the outset of the company's establishment. At other moments it seems as if he was never here at all, as if he was … I don't know … taken away from us before we could ever get to know him."

"But you *did* know him."

"I did, but not as well as I would have liked to. Much of the time we were transacting business, making arrangements for deliveries, discussing customers and their needs … we had the opportunity to talk about more personal things from time to time, but, again … not as often as I would have preferred. He was a fine young man, Lieutenant, and I still have no idea why he would have destroyed himself and his wife. I didn't delude myself that he would be with us forever. We all knew that he would only be with us for a relatively brief time. He was, after all, a former bank manager … I suppose you knew that … "

I nodded and he continued.

"I'm sure he would have eventually found an attractive executive position, but I do believe that he enjoyed his time with us. We certainly enjoyed having him."

"And did you ever meet his wife?" I asked.

"I met her once, but it was only in passing. She had come by our warehouse to pick him up. I believe that she was a nurse."

"Yes, she was," I said. "And you hired him how … ? Did he answer an ad in the newspaper?"

"Yes. We placed a notice in the *Register*. We had several applications, twenty five or thirty as I recall. He was the most qualified … and by a wide margin."

"You must forgive my ignorance, Mr. Richland, but just what is it that FirstGrowth does?"

He smiled and took a sip of his coffee before continuing.

TWENTY-TWO

"No problem, Lieutenant. No problem at all. I'd be surprised if you *were* familiar with our company. That's not a criticism in any way. We have a very small client base and they're spread across southern California. We don't really even advertise now. Individuals in the trade are aware of us and we get some business from word of mouth …

"We sell wine, Lieutenant. Our market is all high end, with prices that most would consider frighteningly high. The name of the company comes from the classifications of so-called 'first growth' red Bordeaux at the 1855 *Exposition Universelle de Paris*. There were four *premier cru* wines: Château Latour, Château Lafite Rothschild, Château Margaux and Château Haut-Brion. The world has changed since then and many more wines are of *first growth* quality. Even the French recognize that. They did, for example, finally relent and admit Mouton Rothschild to the *premier cru* ranks in 1973.

"Since the nineteenth century a number of the wines ranked as second or third growths have reached a level of quality that justifies astronomic prices and there are many household-name wines of first growth stature, such as Château d'Yquem (a Sauternes), Château Cheval Blanc, Château Pétrus and, of course, the whole array of top Burgundies. Some think the finest wine in the world is actually an Australian, Penfolds Grange, which was termed Grange Hermitage until 1989. It's a lovely Shiraz (as they term Syrah), and though it's delicious it's relatively inexpensive, *relatively* being the operative word. Pétrus commands excruciatingly high prices because of its relative scarcity. Ultimately, it's all a matter of supply and demand, of course. Individuals with means across the globe all want the same wines and even though the *premier cru* wineries make more than you might expect, they don't make enough to satisfy demand.

"It's an image thing to many of those who choose to purchase them. It's what's *done*. Like oil sheiks owning thoroughbred stables in the blue grass country, stables they've never actually visited … individuals become rich and they suddenly feel that they should collect and drink expensive wines, even if they don't possess trained palates. Often they're as interested in the name on the label as they are in the wine in the bottle.

"Each vintage varies in quality, of course. The French may enjoy the best *terroir*, but though the soil and growing conditions are generally exceptional they are still unable to control the weather in any given year. In general, the grower and winemaker seek the perfect level of acidity and sugar content. Sugar content is measured using the term Brix (it's named for a German inventor) and it's determined by the use of a device called a hydrometer. It's used right out in the vineyard. Between 55 and 60% of the sugar in the grape juice is converted into alcohol. The winemaker is seeking the perfect balance, you see. He has the records of the readings for the years which are considered the greatest and he seeks to harvest at that moment when all of the statistical stars (Brix, weather, acidity) come into alignment. Nature, of course, does not always cooperate and decisions must be made, decisions that inevitably involve compromises. In the case of a blended wine, there are usually different dates of harvest chosen for the different varietals that make up the final product. It's all very risky, needless to say. The greatest years command the greatest prices and the more distant we are in time from those years the smaller the remaining quantity. That part, at least, is simple.

"Let me give you some examples. The most recent releases of top first-growth Bordeaux are priced in the neighborhood of $700. They say $699.99, but that's $700."

"A bottle."

"Yes, but a standard bottle, not a magnum or larger-sized bottle.

Seven hundred and fifty milliliters or 25.4 ounces. Just about the same size as an American fifth (actually 4/5ths of a quart or 25.6 ounces). It may sound pedantic, but at these prices every milliliter matters. Some dealers will offer case discounts, depending on the wine. Many of the wine merchants are offering collections of 9 top bottles, one of them being a Pétrus. These are being priced at $7999.99 per set. It's interesting, isn't it? 'Eight thousand' sounds so crude and exorbitant. The Grange is much more modestly priced, say, $299 for a recent release. I always recommend it for people of more modest means.

"When you get into the great vintages the prices are far more steep. An imperial (that's eight regular bottles) of 1961 Pétrus nearly came on the market a few years ago. It was expected to command $150,000 at auction. Sotheby's sold a bottle of 1945 Mouton-Rothschild recently for $310,700."

"And those are the kinds of wine that you sell," I said.

"Those are the principal châteaux whose wines we sell," he said, "but I rarely see an imperial of Pétrus and I'm not an auctioneer. I'm a seller but, irreducibly, it's fair to say that I'm also something of a broker. Individuals sell their collections to me and I then sell them to others. I told you yesterday that I had some calls to make. I was visiting two individuals who wished to sell off parts of their collections.

"Ultimately I'm selling service and reputation. Purchasers at this level want to be certain that the wines that they buy have been properly stored. They want to be certain that the individual bottles have not become *corked* … that they're not *off*. Particularly with special vintages they will require certification with regard to the wines' provenance.

"Once I take possession of the wines—either from the châteaux, from another distributor or from a collector—I store the bottles in our warehouse, which provides appropriate racking, appropriate temperature controls and (you will understand) strict security."

"In short," I said, "the wine stays where it is safe, you travel throughout the region examining and purchasing collections and your company makes deliveries throughout the region, given the cost of the product and the small clientele."

"Precisely, Lieutenant. That is why the operation is decentralized. I could be located anywhere within the area, but it is most reasonable for me to be in one of the neighborhoods where I do the largest amount of business. I prefer La Jolla, as you see, but I could just as easily be in Bel Air, in Beverly Hills, Rancho Mirage, San Clemente, Newport Beach, Hope Ranch or Montecito."

"And Terry Randall was one of your drivers."

"I wouldn't quite put it like that, Lieutenant. He drove the vehicle, of course, but he was responsible for the security of the wine in the vehicle and for the proper temperature control within the vehicle. He was, as it were, the face of the company and he was expected to interact with our sometimes thorny and always demanding clientele and converse with them intelligently concerning our products. Your mental image should not be that of a driver sliding open a long, steel truck door, loading multiple cases onto a carefully-balanced dolly, restocking shelves and eventually handing a company invoice to an apron-wearing store manager. In most cases he would be delivering a case or two at the most, in some cases a single bottle. He wore a business suit, not a uniform, and he was generally delivering to gated mansions, though occasionally he might deliver to a corporate office."

"I see. That's very helpful," I said. "How many other individuals does the company employ?"

"Actually only one in addition to our deliverers," he said, "the director of security, Carlton Beauchamp."

"Is that B-e-e-c-h-a-m?" I asked, taking a note in my book.

"Actually it's spelled 'bo-champ'. B-e-a-u … "

"And he's at the warehouse?"

"Yes, in Irvine. It's right off of Jamboree. I can give you the precise address. I'm sure you'll want to speak with him at greater length. He's the one who actually answered your initial call."

"Thank you," I said. "And did any of the current deliverers overlap with Terry Randall?"

"Actually, no. We generally only have one at a time. I used the plural because there's been some turnover in that position. The previous person left approximately a month before we hired Terry. His name was Davidson--James Davidson. I just emailed the ad for Terry's replacement to the *Register* so we're without a deliverer at the moment. Either Carlton or I will make the deliveries in the meantime."

"And are there no other individuals? No investors, for example?"

"No, not really," he said. "I secured a personal loan to start the company, but that was paid off some time ago. In this business, Lieutenant, one or two serious sales can provide a secure base for future operations."

"I can understand that," I said, "given the prices … "

"Yes and they continue to go up. Often we'll purchase a collection or a portion of a collection and store the bottles in the warehouse, waiting for them to appreciate in value. We don't always have buyers ready to purchase them, but that's really not a problem. The later profits always far exceed the storage costs. The trick is to secure the inventory. There was a wonderful ad in *The New Yorker* several years ago . . . it was placed by one of the principal New York hotels on behalf of its dining room. The ad invited individuals to celebrate their birthdays there. It read, 'So what if you're a year older . . . so is the Château Margaux'."

"Very clever," I said.

"Hemingway's granddaughter was called Margaux. Her parents were drinking it the night she was conceived."

"I believe I'd heard that," I said. "She also died young, didn't she?"

"Yes, I think she did," he said.

TWENTY-THREE

The traffic on the **5** was heavy in both directions. San Diego is the new L.A. As we lurched forward, sometimes at 10-15 mph, I put on my earpiece and made calls. I briefed Chris Dietrich first. I gave him the names of both Beauchamp and Davidson. He asked me if I wanted him to set up a meeting with either. I told him I preferred to start with Beauchamp and then talk to Davidson afterwards.

"He knew Terry," I said. "Davidson didn't. That doesn't mean he couldn't be useful, but I'd rather talk to the security guy first."

"I agree," Chris said. "I'll have one of the sergeants call him. I don't want him bracing too much at this point. Better to keep him relaxed. You get more honest responses that way. Not that I think he'll lie to you. It's just that cases involving homicide put people on edge. I'll pitch it that you've spoken to Mr. Richland and that he suggested it might be helpful to also speak to him."

"Thanks, Chief," I said. "It would be interesting to know where Davidson went when he left FirstGrowth. And why he left."

"I'll see if Hector's available. I think he's ready to close that stolen vehicle case. I'll take him off the street, put him on his computer and have him check out Davidson. You know, when you think about it, it's an odd job. Sort of a gentleman's delivery boy job. Any way you slice it you're still sitting in traffic and dealing with demanding people. I can see why people between other sorts of jobs might only do it for awhile. And who knows, maybe every now and then the customers might invite you in to sit down and sample the product."

"Yes," I said, "a major fringe benefit. I figure there are some who are quirky collectors. They buy something enormously expensive, put it in their cellar, fondle it from time to time, show it off to their friends and neighbors but then never drink it. There are others who just want the best and are prepared to consume it. Then they buy more of the best and drink that. It's the kind of world that's filled with hype. They read what the wine gurus have to say about a certain vintage, look at the rating numbers, buy some and then want to try it. That's probably not the smartest thing to do with the recent releases. I've heard people say that you should 'lay the bottles down' for a couple of weeks after they've been in transit. Also, the kind of big wines that Richland sells could usually stand to age for a decade or two and some would have a life expectancy of 50 or even 100 years."

"Right. It's a question of human curiosity, isn't it? You know you should wait. You want to wait. You probably will wait … and then, hell, you want to taste it *now*. Besides, if you've got a couple of cases and enough money to buy a couple more, where's the harm?"

"Yes," I said. "And some want to keep charts—what did it taste like just after it was released? Then five years later … and ten … what do they say?—'It's drinking very nicely now.' It's a living thing and there's an arc. You want to drink it before it's over the hill. Some people like it when it's at its peak (or what *they* consider its peak). Some like it when it's just starting to open up. Plus, of course, they'll decant it, aerate it, tease it, talk to it, anything to be able to taste it."

"Did he offer you any?" Chris asked.

"Regrettably, no," I answered. "I thought maybe he'd have a little split or two of something, but that didn't happen. He offered me some coffee … in a nice cup … "

"Next time you should talk to him in the late afternoon," Chris said. "Up the odds that he'll crack open something special."

"Right," I said, "the problem is that in this price range that could be seen as a possible bribe. He was talking about inexpensive wines being a mere three hundred dollars a bottle."

"Interesting world, isn't it?" Chris said. "You buy a stripped sedan made in Korea and you pretty much know the difference between that and a Lexus or Mercedes. And some people will buy something they think is neat, like an old Jag, even though they know it won't be without its problems. We all sort of know about cars or at least we think we do. Food and wine are different. You buy a head of lettuce at Ralphs and you figure it will be OK. Maybe if you go to some tony grocer and pay thirty cents more or fifty cents more it will be a little better. And it's sometimes more fun to shop at a place like that. But wine ... that's a whole different ball game. You get some Two-buck Chuck or the stuff that Trader Joe buys on the spot market and it's drinkable. Sometimes it's actually very good. You go up to twenty or thirty bucks a bottle and there's a noticeable difference. But what about at seven hundred bucks a bottle? Is there really that much difference? Is it *that* much better?"

"A lot of it is supply and demand," I said. "That's what Richland stressed. The stuff is good, of course. It's very good, but it's also relatively rare and a whole lot of rich people want to buy it. Our problem, Chief, is that we look at the price from the point of view of the average person. If you're really rich the world looks very different. If you're making millions every year, that's ten thousand or twenty thousand a day. The average person thinks of things like car payments and utility bills. The millionaire pays cash for cars and often for houses. He pays off his water bill without even noticing the difference in his checkbook balance. He's still got thousands left every day. There's only so much you can spend for food. Everybody pays the same price for gas. To him an expensive bottle of wine with his dinner is a tiny part of his income."

"Right," Chris said. "I was at the mall the other day with a friend of mine. She needed a new purse. You can pay $100 or $125 and get a nice leather purse, a lot less at a discount store. You can also get something a little more upscale for, say, $300, if you've got that kind of money. We were at the mall in Costa Mesa and I said, 'what the heck, let's check out the high-priced spread'. There were purses there for $3,000-$4,000 and up. Is it worth it to pay ten times more? I don't know; what's it made of? How rare is it? Do you really want a purse made out of virgin ocelot or something? The point is that we shop based on the price as a percentage of our disposable income. To the multi-millionaire, $3,000-$4,000 for a purse is cheap."

Interesting, I thought. Dr. Barnes has a girl friend now; so, apparently, does Chief Dietrich. You don't go shopping for purses with a casual acquaintance. Nice to know that there's still some love in the air. It helps to balance out all the blood splattered on the ground.

TWENTY-FOUR

I passed through Oceanside and called Sarah. I got her voicemail but didn't leave a message. I didn't want her to think I was pressing her. A few miles into Camp Pendleton my head began to throb. I felt as if someone had put one of those tools they use to set finishing nails right in the center of my face--between my eyes--and then begun to tap it with a heavy steel hammer. It was something like a migraine, when the blood drains from your head and then re-enters, with each beat of your heart accentuating the pain.

I narrowed the benign causes to two—the late morning glare through the windshield and the fact that my sole sustenance so far had been four cups of black coffee. I pulled to the side of the road and opened my glove compartment, pulled out a granola bar that included some small chunks of chocolate and dark cherries, peeled away the foil wrap and ate it in four bites. I could sense the change in my blood chemistry after the second bite. I ate a second bar and the pain in my head began to dissipate. I put my sunglasses back on, pulled out onto the freeway and headed for Laguna.

Ten minutes later my cell phone rang. It was the desk sergeant, Glen Williams, informing me that Terry Randall's father was waiting for me in my office.

"Did he call first?" I asked.

"Yes," the sergeant said. "I told him you should be back by midday. He got here a little early."

"Did he say what he wanted?"

"No, Lieutenant, he said he'd wait to talk to you."

"OK, I'm passing through Pendleton. I should be there in fifty to sixty minutes. Ask him if he'd like some coffee."

"I already did, Lieutenant. He brought his own. You also got some calls from reporters … the usual suspects … I told them the investigation was ongoing and that you'd contact them at the appropriate time. I hope that was OK."

"Perfect," I said. "Thanks, Glen."

Walter Randall was sitting in the chair to the side of my desk when I arrived. He said that it was no emergency, that he just wanted to touch base with me and see if I had learned anything.

"I don't have anything major," I said. "The medical reports pretty much confirmed what we already knew. I spoke this morning with your son's employer at FirstGrowth. He filled me in on your son's responsibilities and gave me a feel for the company and its goods and services. I'm going to visit with the director of security for the company at their warehouse in Irvine. We're also tracking down the individual your son replaced at FirstGrowth. According to his supervisor the two of them never met. The first man was gone a month before they hired Terry.

"Still, you never know. Anyone connected with the company, particularly someone who specifically did what Terry did later might be able to shed a little light on the situation. It's a very small company, Mr. Randall, no more than three people at any one time, so we'll speak to all of them."

"Have you learned anything at all that might provide some reason why Terry might have done what the press is claiming he did?"

"No, I haven't," I said. "I've checked their phone, computer and financial records. They appear to have lived simple, orderly lives. There is nothing in the paper or electronic record that suggests anything that would raise questions."

"I appreciate your telling me that, Lieutenant. I understand the concerns that you would have with regard to confidentiality and I know that you're going the extra mile in telling me these things. I want to be of help as well—not to meddle in your case, but to assure you that something is very wrong here. If your gut tells you that, I want you to know that I believe you're on the right track. I have no idea what actually happened, but I'm certain that the press is wrong. Whenever you have a question … any question, no matter how personal or seemingly intrusive … feel free to ask it. At any time, day or night. We've already learned the worst news, Lieutenant. And we've already heard the worst possible interpretation of what happened. From here there's no way for the three of us to go but up."

"I understand," I said, "and I appreciate your driving down here to talk with me. I've spoken with Chief Dietrich and he believes we should continue the investigation, which I will certainly do. How is your wife holding up, Mr. Randall?"

"She's doing well under the circumstances," he said. "I spoke with Elise this morning. She was crying a little, but there was resolve in her voice. She's a good person, Lieutenant. She knows how much our son loved her daughter."

"I'll stay in touch," I said. "And I'll take you up on your offer … if I have any questions I'll be sure to call you."

"Do that," he said. "I've got to get back to JPL. It's funny … those of us at the lab … we're exploring outer space, directing vehicles across the surface of Mars, and you're exploring what happened to our son on a little patch of California desert. Somehow your job seems much more difficult than ours. I want you to know … to me … yours is the most important right now."

I saw him out, gave Chris a few more details on my meeting with Richland and asked Hector if he had eaten yet. He hadn't. He asked me what I had eaten so far and I told him two granola bars.

"You've got to eat more than that. Come with me," he said. "We'll fill you up and get you back on track."

He took me to a place called *Carmen's*. It looked like a remodeled shed. The colors were oranges and yellows with white trim. The menu appeared on a blackboard near the kitchen window. There were a few café tables inside, but we sat at a picnic bench outside.

"No microwave here," he said. "Everything is homemade and everything is good. The cook is an old compatriot of mine."

"From the Bboys?" I asked.

"Yes, but it's best not to remind him. He spent a little time as a guest of the state and he doesn't want to repeat the experience. He used to be known for his … more … physical skills. Now he's something of an artist. He uses simple, fresh ingredients. He said to me that even though the restaurant is modest, that's no excuse for the food not being beautiful. So much southwest cooking involves piles of food running together on a plate. He says that *presentation* is as important as the food."

"He *sounds like* an artist," I said, "somebody who makes beautiful things."

"He is and he does," Hector said. "His name is Ramón. Carmen is his daughter; she's four now. They named the restaurant after her. You want my advice?"

"Always," I said.

"Order the beef enchiladas or anything with the *mole poblano*. His wife Teresa makes it. In the kitchen … she works magic. And if he asks if you want rice or beans, tell him you want both."

"I will," I said.

"You won't regret it," Hector said.

TWENTY-FIVE

I asked Hector to go with me to FirstGrowth's warehouse. The best expert on security systems is the person with the most experience in breaching them. Hector was like his friend Ramón, the cook. He didn't like to talk about his past experiences, but he enjoyed demonstrating his expertise.

The warehouse carried a Jamboree address, but it actually sat at the rear of a strip mall that fronted on Jamboree, just below the **405**. From its positioning it looked as if it could have been a warehouse supplying the mall itself, but there was space between it and the mall for the parking of at least two vans. I hadn't seen a van at Richland's house, but I figured that he might be picking up consignments in one—particularly if he needed the refrigeration--while their deliveryman could be using another. I had trouble imagining someone as apparently fussy as Richland actually loading a van, but given the nature of the cargo it was easier imagining him doing it than trusting the job to someone else.

The building appeared to be exceptionally secure. Faced with slabs of stamped concrete it looked more like a fortress than a warehouse. There were lights with sensors at each corner of the building. The front door adjoined a vertical door for loading; each was made of hardened steel. The loading door could only be opened from the inside and the front door could only be accessed through the use of a keypad. The building was, in effect, a large safe.

I estimated it to contain approximately 3,000 square feet of floor space. Unless there was additional space below the ground level, the building consisted of a single floor with a high ceiling of perhaps 13'-14'. I figured it contained office space for the director of security and storage space for the wine. Hector noted the presence of generators at the rear of the building. "In case the power goes out … they've got to keep the wine at cellar temperature. Too much heat … and there goes the ball game."

"Right," I said. "It looks pretty secure, wouldn't you say?"

"Yes, but I don't see any external cameras. That doesn't mean that they don't have any, but if it was me I'd put up big ones. The little ones are designed to keep you from knowing that you're starring on Candid Camera. In this case I would think that they'd want to dissuade you from tampering with their building by assuring you that you're already on Candid Camera."

"Yes, I agree," I said. "And I suppose that no matter how formidable a structure looks, there's a saw made that will cut a hole in it."

"Right," Hector said, "but you'd have to mask the sound. That wouldn't be too hard. Paint up a van with a logo and some fancy lettering, make it look as if you're a pair of repairmen servicing their a/c or generator; park it in a way that blocks the view of the person with the saw; crank up the music on the van radio and hit the on-switch whenever the musicians hit the high notes. There's already a lot of street noise to help and since the structure's back in the rear of everything there wouldn't be too many curious bystanders."

"And you'd just knock first to make sure no one's there."

"Right. And call. It appears that their vehicles are parked outside rather than inside, so already you've got some indication of whether or not the building's occupied."

"But as a prospective burglar you'd also have to be aware that there's something inside worth stealing."

"Yes," Hector said. "That's their best security element—no logo or business name on the outside. Small-time thieves who are feeding drug habits will steal anything … the easier the better. They're not going to have the time or money for painting vans and renting saws that will cut stone or steel or cement. They'll throw a brick through a window and take whatever's not nailed down. Your professional thieves, on the other hand, will want to know what they're stealing. What's its worth? What's its worth on the street? What's its worth to a fence? Expensive collectibles are not usually very attractive to them. They're kept more securely and they appeal to a narrower market. Plus you have to have connections with the kind of individual who can reach that market for you. You can break out the jewels in a necklace and they're still valuable. You take apart an 18th-century chest and all you've got is kindling wood. They're far more likely to go for something like hard liquor or cigarettes, auto parts or electronics. If the theft is domestic they're looking for televisions and sound systems, jewelry or silverware. But expensive wine … most likely not."

"It would probably take more of a connoisseur thief," I said.

"Lots of them in the movies. Out on the streets … not so many. Now if I were the larcenous type," he said, this time smiling, "and somebody had expensive wine, I'd try for some sort of inside deal."

"Like what?" I asked.

"Well, let's say you're the buyer. You strike a deal with the deliveryman to give him a discount on a bottle here or a bottle there. You claim that the cork was shot and the deliveryman confirms that the customer was telling the truth. If you're talking about bottles costing $700 bucks apiece and up, you don't have to work the scam too often to show a profit."

"I checked," I said. "The top wineries aren't putting in plastic corks and they're certainly not putting on bottle caps, even though both of those technologies are more secure. They put in real cork, longer corks than usual, with pretty pictures of the châteaux on them, but corks that can still dry out and crumble and destroy the wine."

"You'd have to be very careful working a scam like that," Hector said, "because the boss would pride himself on presenting the wines in top condition. Any problems would be a direct reflection on him, so he'd be very skeptical about reports of damaged bottles. There are other things you could do, however, once you'd wired the inside guy. For example, you could have him switch the wine itself. You buy something expensive and good, but not something so rare that the price was artificially inflated. Grab a top wine for $100 bucks or so and exchange it for something that costs ten times that much."

"You mean decant each and simply exchange them in the bottles. The exotic bottles stay in the warehouse, but with cheaper wine. You get back your cheaper bottles, but filled with the A-list wine."

"Yes, but with a significant piece for the inside guy. You give the inside guy $100 worth of wine. He gives you $1,000 worth, but charges you a couple hundred per bottle for his trouble. The stock appears to remain unchanged; you get a deep discount and the inside guy pockets the cash. This would only work for a connoisseur, but a connoisseur would know the nuances of the various wines and their cheaper substitutes and, hence, the most plausible ways to work the scam. He could also have an empty bottle of the real stuff on hand for show, but serve his guests from a decanter. That way, if he still wants to play Wine King and impress his friends and neighbors he can. I still think it's a long shot, however. It's far too cumbersome and it's so much easier to simply steal other things. Plus, your connoisseur thief has a lot to lose reputation-wise. If he's developed a taste for the very best that means that at one time or another he's been able to afford the very best. Those kind of people don't like to be exposed as criminals, especially if their lives and businesses are built on appearance and bluff. That's not to say that you wouldn't find an occasional person who just couldn't stand to keep his fingers out of the till or cookie jar. All I'm saying is that it's a long shot."

"Why don't we go in and meet the director of security? See what he's up to."

"Let's do it," Hector said.

TWENTY-SIX

Carlton Beauchamp looked like the product of a marriage between an uptown debutante and an SEC offensive lineman. Relatively fine-featured and naturally blond (at least in appearance), he had an expensive haircut and one of those dress shirts like the lawyers wear, with solid colors on the collar and cuffs and stripes everywhere else. Hector said later that he had been wearing a Hugo Boss suit. It was black wool and had three buttons down the front. The watch was expensive but not gaudy. I only had a brief glimpse, but it appeared to be a Baume & Mercier. The shoes were heavy and leathery, with a lot of fine tooling, probably Italian, definitely not from Thom McCan's.

He introduced himself as 'Carlton Beauchamp', not Carl. His handshake was firm, but he didn't attempt to break any small bones. He offered us coffee and we accepted. His office was small, but well-appointed; we sat down in an adjoining conference area with a table and four chairs. The room was paneled in something that looked like cherry but might have been poplar. The chairs were upholstered in black leather. The coffee maker was on the sideboard; it looked like something that James Bond would be able to operate. Beauchamp pushed some buttons and beans began to grind. When they finished it started to gurgle politely.

"Terry was a terrible loss," he said. "The delivery job … it's not something that everyone can do. Actually, it's not something that people with the required personal skills would usually want to do. Terry was perfect at it. It's all about the *fit*. I guess that's true of all positions, but it's especially true with this one. I'm not optimistic that we'll ever find someone quite like him again."

"What about his predecessor?" I asked.

"Jimmy Davidson?"

"Yes."

"Too young. And a little unfocused. I'm not saying that he couldn't do the job, but his head was elsewhere. Why do you think he came to southern California? Three guesses but you'll only need one … "

"To become an actor," I answered.

"Like I said … when he'd have auditions and call-backs he was suddenly unavailable. I mean … we all understood that flexibility is one of the perks of the job, but flexibility within reason. I'm sure he took the job because it was easier than waiting tables and it definitely paid better. He'd tried that already and he had some significant experience with wine. He knew the language, the nature of the clientele … but, like I said, his heart was elsewhere and we're a little off the beaten track vis à vis the entertainment industry. Jimmy was a very nice young man but the *fit* was much better with Terry."

"Tell us about yourself, Mr. Beauchamp," Hector said. "What's your background?"

"Business," he said. "Not so much the security business per se as the security *dimensions* of high-end, contemporary business. I got out of Brown and went to work for a software company in Mountain View—a small place. It was later gobbled up by Microsoft. The usual story: they offered a deal we couldn't turn down and then made the software available free. We each got a nice payday (in my case practically enough to pay cash for a house) and started looking for other things to do. I had played some ball in college and I guess I'm able to look the part, so I transitioned from IT to security systems."

"What position did you play?" I asked.

"Offensive guard," he said, "but, you know, in the Ivy League. We're not talking Alabama- or Notre Dame-level."

"I understand," I said. "Which security system did you go to work for?"

"Brink's. Not the armored trucks. The home security division. You know those ads on television: 'Mrs. Johnson. I'm sending help now!'"

"Yes, I've seen them," I said.

"I was that guy's supervisor. Actually a lot of those guys. It wasn't as exciting as it looks. It's all about sensors and computers and phone lines and passwords … links with the local police … that sort of thing. I went from that to a freestanding company and from there to FirstGrowth. That was a pretty natural transition also. Living up there in the bay area … I'd go up to Napa and Sonoma on the weekends. There's also some serious wine being made in the Santa Cruz Mountains and some nice sparkling wine on the other side of the bay. I got interested in it. The FirstGrowth opportunity came along and I jumped at it. I've been here for well over three years now."

"And William Richland hired you?"

"Yes. I came in on the ground floor, as it were. It's been interesting."

"Does he ever let you taste the wine?" Hector asked.

"Not very often," he answered, smiling. "I know what you're thinking—there must be times when the two of us get a split of something special, sit down here, crack it open and give it a taste … "

"Yes, something like that," Hector said.

"It's happened once or twice, but the best wine is the wine in the larger bottles. It's related to the aging process … we don't open those; they're too costly."

Hector nodded. "I understand," I said. "What was the name of the company where you were working before Mr. Richland employed you?"

"Griffith Industries," he said. "We did a number of things—investments, consulting … "

"Were they in the bay area?" I asked.

"Actually they're in Los Angeles," he said.

TWENTY-SEVEN

"Would you like to see the *chai*?" Beauchamp asked.

"The place you store the wine?" I responded.

"Yes."

"Of course."

"I think it's pretty impressive," he said. "At the wineries they store the barrels in the *chai* while the wine ages. Some of the companies make a big deal of it. They put their reserve wines there ... the room is a kind of holy of holies ... even down to the mellow lighting and stained glass. It's as if you're looking at a cathedral filled with wine."

"Plus the great smell," I said. "Cool temperatures, mood lighting and the smell of the wine against the oak from when they topped off the barrels."

"So you know what I'm talking about," he said.

"I'm not a connoisseur," I said, "but the wine country makes a nice trip on the weekends. And there are some good wineries down here as well, in Temecula."

"Yes. They make some interesting things there. Italian varietals ... different sorts of dessert wines ... "

While he and I were making eye contact and small talk, Hector stood to the side, letting us pass and looking into nooks and crannies as quickly as he could.

"It's right through here," he said. We left the room by a different exit, walked down a short hallway and came to a steel door. It had both a keypad and a deadbolt lock. He opened the lock with a key—the only one on a keychain attached to his belt—and punched in a series of numbers on the keypad. The door opened automatically and he looked at us as if he expected us to stand in awe of his 'wow' room.

The room was large and cold; the temperature felt like the low 50's. I could hear the a/c system's works humming steadily in the background. The inside of the room was surrounded by steel grillwork that was bolted to both the cement floor and the ceiling, with no room for crawl space. "There's an additional precaution," he said, punching in a code on another keypad inside the room and then hitting the **open** button. "We have a security system with sensors inside the cage. We have to stay on the pathway that's painted on the floor."

"You're really protecting your product," I said.

"Absolutely," he said. "I designed the system. *Cool* space … in both senses of the word."

Inside the steel cage were a series of metal shelves containing wooden winery boxes. The names and pictures of the châteaux appeared on the boxes. A few of the boxes were without lids. They were incomplete cases and the bottles inside were visible. Each was individually wrapped in tissue paper, again with the name and picture of the château printed on the paper. Larger bottles, principally Magnums and Jeroboams, were boxed individually. Some of the boxes had rope handles attached to the ends. I did a quick count and saw approximately forty cases of wine, minimally $300,000-$400,000 worth.

"Is this a standard amount of inventory?" I asked.

"Hard to say," Beauchamp answered. "Sometimes a single wealthy buyer will deplete our supply and the shelves will be nearly empty. On the other hand, when we obtain a large consignment you can see more cases than this on the shelves, at least for a little while. The stock goes down during the holidays because some customers like to give gifts of wine to special customers and friends. Generally we specialize in red Bordeaux, but we had some nice Romanée Conti a few months ago. One of our clients prefers red Burgundy and purchased 4 cases for his wife's birthday party."

"And that's comparable to red Bordeaux in price?" I asked.

"It depends on the estate, but, yes, it can be very pricey. This was a 2001. We sold it for $12,000.00 a bottle."

"So … over $500,000 worth of wine for the party."

"Yes, around 575K and change," Beauchamp said. "The client was very generous. That's just under 300 glasses of wine and there were only 75 people at the party. They all had a good taste of it."

"Maybe he saved some for himself," Hector said.

"I certainly would have," Beauchamp said, smiling.

"This was very helpful," I said.

"My pleasure," Beauchamp responded.

"Do you have a contact number for James Davidson?"

"Actually, I don't," he said. "I did, but my understanding is that Jimmy moved to L.A. He was living in Huntington Beach when he worked for FirstGrowth, but then he moved … I think to somewhere in Culver City. There's still a lot of film industry activity there."

"And the rents are a lot cheaper," I said.

"Right. That would have to be a consideration for him," he said. "The Huntington Beach address was just off Beach Blvd. I can get that for you, if you'd like. I don't have the Culver City address. We gave Jimmy his last check on his last day of work, so we didn't have to forward anything to him."

"Not a problem," I said. "We should be able to locate him. I may call you if I need any further information."

"Feel free," he said. "I'll be here. And you've got the company number."

"Yes."

"That's me."

TWENTY-EIGHT

"What did you think?" I asked Hector, as we drove back to Laguna. "Impressive security," he said. "I've seen a lot of banks with less."

"Yes," I said, "I was thinking that as well. On the other hand, you want a bank to be welcoming. When I was in college I knew a guy who was studying in the UCI business school. He took a short-term course in something called 'business architecture'. He said that a business should think very carefully about what it wants to project to potential clients. Banks, for example, are often built with surface materials that project a feeling of security: marble, granite, steel … that sort of thing. At the same time they should never have a lot of steps at the establishment's front door. 'It should be easy to get in,' he said. 'It should say to the customer that he or she is welcome there, that you just can't wait to meet them and provide them services.'"

"Makes sense," Hector said. "FirstGrowth doesn't seem to want *any* visitors. You're *not* welcome there. They'll come to you. In the meantime, keep your hands off the product."

"Right," I said. "One thing did seem a little odd to me, but it's probably nothing."

"What's that?" Hector asked.

"Davidson's Culver City address. They gave him his last check, but they'd still have to forward his W-2 tax stuff after the first of the year. I don't know … I'm probably just being suspicious. Actors are like students. They move around a lot. Davidson probably told them that he'd be back in touch with them after the first of the year."

"Probably," Hector said. "Still … Tom … there's nothing wrong with being suspicious. It's what we do."

"That's right," I said. "We'll check him out. Ask him ourselves."

"I wonder who does their tax stuff for them," Hector said. "They probably use a service. It's not something that Richland or Beauchamp would want to monkey with."

"No. Richland wants to talk wine and Beauchamp wants to punch numbers on keypads. By the way, how hard do you think it would be to get past their security system?"

"It wouldn't be impossible," Hector said. "It looks pretty formidable, but only to a crackhead or a 15 year-old amateur. The tough thing would be to disable the electronic system. And that wouldn't be *very* tough. The rest would be easy. You could cut through the steel doors with a torch in a matter of minutes and saw through the steel cage even quicker. I'm not clear on why they painted the pathway on the floor in the *chai*. It's like a loud-and-clear warning that that's the best way to evade the sensors. Even so, once you disabled the electronic system you'd probably be good-to-go anyway. The whole thing was probably integrated and linked with a single security service. It was sure pretty though."

"Yes, and Beauchamp was anxious to show it off."

"Are you thinking that that was its purpose—to be shown off?"

"Maybe," I said, "but then again, I'm probably just being suspicious and, like you said, there are banks with less secure systems and a whole lot more to steal."

"Right," Hector said. "Cash on hand plus whatever goodies are in the safe-deposit boxes. And it would probably be a whole lot easier to carry out. Jewelry, currency, negotiable bonds … I'd rather throw things like that in a single sack than have to worry about how I'd transport all that wine. Besides, if you drop it, you're screwed. And if you don't refrigerate it properly and keep the corks moist, you're also screwed. Too *high maintenance* for my taste."

I had dinner with Sarah that evening. She was on a new crusade, believing that an Asian diet would keep me happy, healthy and wise. I told her that I could take fish oil in supplements and it would work just as well, but she refused to accept that. We were in a place in Mission Viejo that catered to the hot yoga/pilates/Omega 3/Curcumin crowd. I couldn't protest effectively, because she had actually studied diet and nutrition while I had studied history and literature.

We did agree on the wine, a good-value chardonnay; she had some kind of steamed salmon with lemon and asparagus; I had sea bass with a potato crust. She protested the latter briefly, but finally gave in when I had steamed vegetables on the side.

"I'm not trying to be preachy," she said, "but I know you, Tom, and I know that deep down you want to do everything you can to be healthy. I'm just trying to help."

"I know," I said, "and I appreciate it very much."

She smiled and ate a piece of her salmon.

"Still, it's not quite like a nice piece of veal with some pasta on the side, is it?" I asked.

"No, but it's much better for you," she said. "Drink your wine. It will help compensate … "

"Yes, ma'am," I said. "I most certainly will."

After I ordered coffee and Sarah ordered green tea she went to the ladies' room. I had felt my cell phone twitch a few minutes earlier and I was anxious to check it. Hector had sent a text message. It was short and to the point:

J. Davidson has disappeared.

TWENTY-NINE

When Sarah returned I went to the men's room and called Hector. "What do we know?" I asked.

"Less than we'd like to," he said. "I found an address for his L.A. apartment; it was just off Culver Blvd. There was a landline number; I called it and got a recorded message saying that the number was no longer in service. I checked the real estate records and found the owner of the apartment, a guy named Randy Tallette. He owns a lot of buildings in that area. His office was closed but I caught him at home. He had to call the guy who handles his rents. The rental agent then called me; fortunately, he had the information on his laptop. He said that Mr. Davidson had defaulted on his rent payments and that they were getting ready to list the apartment and hopefully lease it to a new tenant.

"At this point they're about to have his stuff hauled away so they can repaint and recarpet. I told him to lock down the apartment until we had a chance to check it out. He said no problem, but he wanted us to do it sooner rather than later because the clock is ticking on the vacancy. They can't just file an eviction notice and put somebody's property on the street. There's a grace period for the tenant in the event that he or she has claims against the landlord, so they've been waiting to do this. They've also probably been praying that Davidson would reappear and send them a check. In this buyer's market it's better for the landlord to give a good tenant a chance to get back on his feet if he's been sick or unemployed."

"Right, or called out of town unexpectedly. With actors it happens."

"Yes."

"Did you tell him we'd be there promptly?"

"First thing in the morning," he said. "I figured you'd want to finish your dinner and not have to run off tonight. Besides, we might be able to see something in daylight that's less apparent in darkness."

"Good. What time, Hector?"

"Eight o'clock."

"I'll see you in the office at 6:15."

"Did the rental guy say anything else about Davidson?" I asked. We were on the **405**, crawling in early morning traffic.

"I asked him about his rent payments," Hector said. "He said that the first two were right on time; then, suddenly, they stopped. He knew that Davidson was an actor and he said that their payments can be a little herky-jerky, but he said that Davidson seemed like an upstanding person, so why not take the risk in this market."

"And what's the guy's name, Hector?"

"Kevin Maris. He works for Tallette full time."

"Any information on other work for Davidson?"

"Yes," Hector said. "That was a little hard to come by after hours, but one California taxman at least was at his desk. After his time at FirstGrowth, Davidson was working for a restaurant on La Cienega. Here … "

He took his right hand off the wheel and handed me his notebook. "It's on the last page," he said.

"*Pinot Gris*," I said. "Sounds trendy enough."

"The paychecks varied in their amounts," Hector said. "He was either waiting tables or working part-time at odd hours. Probably both. I talked to the owner there right before they closed last night. He'll see us this morning after we're done at the apartment."

"Did you ask him about Davidson's whereabouts?"

"Yes," Hector said. "He told me the arrangement was informal, that he'd explain it when we met. He wasn't surprised by the fact that Davidson was no longer around."

"Right. Like I said before, actors get gigs out of town. They come and go. Davidson was probably an experienced waiter who could fill in as needed, but he couldn't promise a long-term commitment."

"That's what I figured," Hector said. "Restaurants maintain lists of guys like him. They need them for holidays, private parties, whatever."

Kevin Maris was waiting for us at the front of the apartment building. A vaguely-Spanish 16-unit from the 70's, it was beige stucco and a little tattered around the edges. The windows were covered with steel bars but some brave birds-of-paradise on either side of the entry walkway were surviving successfully.

We introduced ourselves. Maris pulled a set of keys from his jacket pocket and said, "It's Unit 8."

"We've got a good chance of renting this promptly," he said, as he unlocked the steel door to Davidson's apartment. "End units have slightly larger bedrooms and living rooms and they have windows on two sides in each of those rooms. They're another $85 a month, but people are willing to pay it. The inside units are harder to rent."

As we walked into the living room Maris told us that he'd be in his car, doing some paperwork. "If you need anything, just let me know," he said. "When you're finished I'll lock up."

We thanked him and started going through the apartment. It was sparsely furnished, but everything was of high quality. The living room contained a black leather couch and matching leather chair. The coffee table and side table were glass. "Makes the room look larger," Hector said. "You see through it. Good design choice."

"I didn't know you were an expert," I said.

"I have hidden talents," he answered.

The signed prints on the living room wall were the real thing, not cardboard reproductions. They weren't Picassos, but they were pleasant seascapes with a lot of ocean, sky and sun.

The bedroom consisted of a queen-size bed and matching chest of drawers, each made of upscale hardwoods. This time the prints on the wall were more muted with darker colors. They consisted of vague portraits of attractive human figures. Nothing edgy or erotic, just warm and restful. There was a nightstand with shelving below for bedtime reading materials. There was one book there and a few dozen on the table and shelving in the living room—some novels, popular history, five or six books on acting and the theatre.

The kitchen included an expensive coffee maker, a small food processor and a toaster oven. The china was expensive, but from another era, probably inherited. The stainless was more modern in design. In one cupboard was a champagne bucket and some cookware. In another were English bar towels and napkins.

There was some Diet Coke and German beer in the refrigerator, a plastic container of curdled milk, some shriveled lemons, butter, catsup, mustard, Worcestershire sauce, soy sauce, blue cheese salad dressing, carrots, wilted lettuce, expensive parmesan cheese and an open box of baking soda.

In the freezer was a 12 ounce package of center-cut bacon, some frozen vegetables and two casserole dishes of leftovers, each with a post-it note and a month-and-a-half-old date. One contained carbonnade of beef, the other chicken à la King.

"Interesting," Hector said. "Here's a guy who has good taste, but limited money. When he has a good payday he buys nice things, but he can't afford too many of them. He's a good citizen. Everything smells nice. He's got the baking soda in the refrigerator to keep it that way. He entertains from time to time but nothing on a grand scale. He sticks to himself. He's trying to make it, but it's an uphill climb. Meanwhile he doesn't overextend himself. He keeps it simple but decent. Probably a standup guy."

"I agree," I said. "Where's his computer?"

THIRTY

"And I wonder if his car's here," I added.

"Maybe the rental agent will know," Hector said. "I can do the fine tuning stuff if you want to talk to him."

"I will," I said, leaving Hector to check the dark corners—the spaces under the kitchen sink and mattress, the bathtub drain and the back of the utility closet. He would spray a little luminol here and there, see if anything turned blue. He'd look for multi-colored hair in the drains and any recent patchwork in the walls or flooring that might cover up something that a perp would prefer that we not see.

I asked Maris about internet service. He told me that there was no wi-fi provided by the management for the building. Each tenant would contract separately for it and he didn't know whether or not Davidson had done so. I asked him about Davidson's car and he indicated the parking space reserved for his unit; there was an **8** spray-painted in front, on the edge of the curb. The space was empty. I asked him for the name of the tenant in the adjoining apartment and he said that the unit was vacant. "It's been vacant for two months," he said. "Like I told you, the end units are easier to rent."

I was hoping to be able to talk to the neighbor about Davidson's activities. After Maris left we knocked on the remaining doors at Davidson's end of the building, but no one answered except for an elderly woman who told us she had never seen the occupant of Unit 8. When I prompted her with a rough description she reiterated the fact that she had not seen him. "I usually work days," she said, "and once I'm in for the night, I'm in. I don't pay any attention to the neighbors unless they're making noise or blocking the hallway."

Hector told me that he was unable to find anything interesting and that the only color hair he could find in the tub drain was light brown. We gave the owner/manager of *Pinot Gris* a call and drove to La Cienega. The restaurant was halfway between the freeway and Beverly Hills, just above the section with all of the nail parlors with fluorescent paint ads covering the windows.

The restaurant had a small parking lot to the south with multiple signs promising significant retribution to anyone parking there who was not a *Pinot Gris* customer. The owner was sitting at a table in the window when we arrived. His name was Morris Lowen. When we introduced ourselves he shook our hands and said, "Everybody calls me Murray."

He asked us if either of us would like some coffee. We thanked him, but declined.

"I guess you want me to tell you about Jimmy," he said. "What's happened to him?"

"We don't know that anything's happened to him," I said. "We'd just like to talk to him, but we haven't been able to locate him."

"He's an actor; they come and go, you know. I'm not saying that they're irresponsible. It's just that they … you know … get jobs all over the place. One day they're here in town doing bit parts or commercials. The next day they're doing a play at some dinner theatre up on the central coast. The usual thing to do would be to call his agent, but I don't think Jimmy had an agent yet. You've got to build up some work credit … you know, make it worth the agent's while to take you on. This town is filled with kids who want to act and the agents can't just spin their wheels. They've got to have some assurance that the kid is actually … *employable.* You know what I mean."

"Are you sure that he didn't have an agent?" Hector asked.

"I'm not *sure* sure," Lowen said. "All I know is that Jimmy would talk about parts that he was reading for and sometimes he'd say that if he got one of them … you know, *this* one or *that* one, that that would help him get an agent. He didn't say it like that. He said it would 'help him find appropriate representation'. That was sweet, I thought, and maybe a little sad. *I* would have hired him. What am I saying? I *did* hire him. He was a very nice young man. Listen to me; all of a sudden I'm talking about him in the past tense. He *is* a very nice young man. He's good looking. He's well-spoken. The customers loved him."

"How long did he work for you, Mr. Lowen?" I asked.

"Off and on for about seven weeks. I knew when I hired him that he'd be coming and going. Still, it takes a long time to break into the entertainment business. People come here with high hopes … sometimes it takes years, if it happens at all. In the meantime … any time I can hire an experienced, able person, I'll do it. There's a lot of turnover in wait staff anyway. And people like Jimmy are a rarity … "

"In what way, Mr. Lowen?" Hector asked.

"Well, for one thing, he was always on time. If we had a special party or a holiday event and he was scheduled to work at, say, 6:00, he'd be here at 5:45 and ask if there was anything he could do to help us get ready. Other people … they come in at 6:05 or 6:15 and talk about how they got caught in traffic. He was also very personable with the customers. It was like he *had time* for them, like he really cared about whether or not they enjoyed their dinner. People would come in and ask for him. They'd ask if he was working that night. They remembered his name. You know, waiters come up to your table and they say, 'Good evening, my name is Brian and I'll be your waiter this evening.' Five minutes later the wife is turning to the husband and asking, 'What was that guy's name again?' They never did that with Jimmy. He made an *impression*. I'm surprised he didn't find acting work right away. That's what it's all about, isn't it?"

"What's that, Mr. Lowen?" I asked.

"Making an impression. The face on the screen. You remember it. You want to see it again."

"We've put together a rough description," I said, "and we have his driver's license photo, but it would be helpful to us if you could describe him a little more precisely."

"Like I said, he was a nice looking man. I'm 5'11" and he was just a little taller … maybe 6'1" say. He had light brown hair, not blond, not like one of those surfer types like Troy Donahue or something. I guess I'm dating myself there … anyway, he had … he *has* light brown hair and wonderful blue eyes. Clear … bright … eyes like a movie star's. Like a Paul Newman. He was trim. I wouldn't say *thin*, because he wasn't scrawny or anything. He looked strong, but he was … well … *trim*. They have to be, I guess. What do they say? The camera adds ten pounds? Or is it more than that? Anyway, he's trim."

"Any noticeable marks?" Hector asked.

"You mean like scars or tattoos?"

"Right, anything that would be noticeable."

"Nothing that I remember. Certainly no facial marks or anything like that. Jimmy was very classy. No tattoos (at least none that I could see). No piercings. No earrings. None of those diamonds on the side of the nose or studs coming out of the tongue. None of that stuff. Not that I'm criticizing people who do. I understand that times change and fashions change and all that, but Jimmy wasn't one of those trendy types. He was more … I don't know … *classic*. He looked like an old-time movie actor. Not *old* old-time. I mean like from the fifties or something. You know what I mean. Like Bill Holden or Bob Mitchum or somebody like that. Back before they all became so … *cute*. I'm not saying gay; I don't mean it like that. I mean, they just all look like they haven't grown up yet, if you know what I mean."

"I know exactly what you mean, Mr. Lowen," I said. "When was the last time that you saw Mr. Davidson?"

"Just a second … " he said, removing a small book from his coat pocket. "I use this as well as the big book at the front door … it was just about six weeks ago. We had a birthday party in the room upstairs that Jimmy worked. Very nice evening. Special wines … signature desserts … "

"Did he say anything to you about going away for awhile?" I asked.

"No, nothing specific like that. I remember patting him on the shoulder, telling him that he had done a wonderful job. He just smiled, said 'Thanks, Murray' and left for the evening. I haven't heard from him since. I called once or twice, but no one answered. I figured something had come up, that he had gotten a job somewhere. I thought I'd be hearing from him again, but … well … I haven't."

We thanked him for his help. When we left he gave us miniature menus for his restaurant. "We don't do carry-out; this is just for advertising. Sometimes people take them as souvenirs. Take one. Come back and see us sometime."

I drove back to Laguna and let Hector read the menu. "This sounds great," he said. "He gets a lot of his food from around Petaluma. Everything's fresh … simple … high quality … classy … not way over-priced."

"I think he may have found a new customer," I said.

"I don't know," Hector answered. "That's a long drive for dinner. Maybe if Jimmy Davidson was waiting on me … "

THIRTY-ONE

The next step was to check in with other jurisdictions on unidentified decedents. There was no criminal record for Jimmy Davidson and no service record, so it was unlikely that his fingerprints or DNA were on file. I checked back with Carlton Beauchamp and asked him about FirstGrowth's health insurance, hoping to find Davidson's doctor. He told me that they were very explicit about their benefits package, but that they didn't provide health insurance *per se*. "People buy their own," he said. "The benefits package is generous. We make it very clear at the outset … here's the salary … here are the benefits … there's money for the 401K, money for insurance … the whole deal."

"And do you recommend any provider in particular?" I asked.

"No, that's up to them. They like it that way. For example, if the employee gets health coverage through his spouse, the money in the benefits package is all gravy."

"I understand," I said, "So you don't have a provider as part of a small-business consortium or anything like that."

"No," he said. "I get mine from Mutual of Omaha."

I thanked him and hung up, thinking that I might check in with local hospitals and see if he had had any treatment there. I could then backtrack to his provider and check with them to find out who his primary care physician was. I made some other notes to myself, worrying that I might be spending too much time on the possible help we might receive from Davidson on the Randall case. I knew that Chris would pull me off the case if I didn't make progress, but I also knew that I didn't have anything else at this point and that any information that I could develop might ultimately prove helpful. I looked at my watch and then started to make calls.

Hector came in a few minutes later and told me he had to leave for a few minutes to talk to the DA about his stolen vehicle case. "I'll get back on Davidson later this afternoon."

I sat at my desk, eating a take-out turkey-and-cheese sandwich between calls. My notebook was filled with possible things to do, but it was short on fresh information. I checked with hospitals and emergency rooms in Orange and L.A. counties, asking if they had had a patient named James Davidson. Many had, but the majority of the Davidsons were infants or elderly; one was a woman named Jamey. There was no James Davidson in the last year who was of the age, height and weight of ours.

Later that afternoon Hector returned and said that he would check with the major insurers. "I'm not very optimistic," he said, "but I'll do the best I can. There's always the possibility that he didn't carry any insurance at all. There are millions who don't. A young, healthy guy ... he figures he might get by without it."

I called some of my counterparts in other PD's and told them we hoped to talk to Davidson in regard to another case, but had come up dry in trying to locate him. An hour later Hector was standing at my door.

"I've got good news and bad news," he said. "Jimmy Davidson had health insurance through State Farm. He bought the policy through an agent in Irvine named Bill Burdette. He also had his auto policy there and a small policy on his household goods. Now the bad news: he never had a burglary, he never had a car accident and he never got sick. Check that; if he did have a burglary or a car accident and if he did get seriously sick he never filed a claim for it with his insurer."

"Did the insurance agent have any information concerning his doctor?"

"More good news and bad news," Hector said. "Davidson actually asked Burdette to recommend a doctor, said he was new in town, wondered if Burdette had any ideas. He told him about his own internist, a man named Eisenman, in Newport Beach. I called Eisenman's office; they said that Jimmy Davidson *is* one of his patients, but that he had only been in once, to get an allergy shot. His policy has a fairly large deductible and the cost of the shot was minimal, so Davidson simply covered the cost out of pocket and that was it. He hasn't been back and they haven't been asked to forward his records—such as they are—to a new doc. They told me that Eisenman himself hasn't even seen him. One of the nurses gave him the allergy shot. He was back on the street in five minutes. The nurse *did* remember him, though. She said he was a nice young man, very 'good looking'."

"Thanks," I said. I must have been staring into space for a second, because Hector asked me if there was anything wrong.

"Not really," I said. "I've been thinking about something, something that's been bothering me. It may be nothing … "

"What's that?" Hector asked.

"When I was talking to Beauchamp about FirstGrowth's fringe benefits, about their lack of a health plan, but the fact that they provide a total package that includes money for health insurance … "

"Yes … ?"

"In and of itself it's not a big deal. A lot of companies offer what they call *cafeteria* plans. There's a fixed amount for fringe benefits on top of the salary, say 30% or 35%. They tell you 'this is what you have in the pot; now pick what you want'. Some people want care that includes eye exams and eyeglasses. Some people want a dental plan. Some want a big life insurance policy or a long-term disability policy. Some people have health coverage through their spouse and want that portion of their fringe benefits washed into their 401K instead … "

"Yes … ?"

"Like I said, in and of itself it's no biggie; this is a common practice.

What keeps nagging at me is the way that Beauchamp described it. It was almost as if he was an H.R. vice president at some large corporation. He kept talking about *the employee* as if the person was some kind of abstract presence. He said that *they* like it this way."

"Yes … ?"

"FirstGrowth only has three employees, Hector: the boss, Richland, the security guy, Beauchamp, and the delivery man. And the company's only been in business a short time. There's been Terry Randall and Jimmy Davidson and … who else? Anybody?"

"What are you saying, Tom?"

"I'm not sure, Hector. It's as if the answer was somehow out of synch with the question."

"Like it was canned."

"Yes. If I ask you where your girlfriend is tonight, you're supposed to say something like, 'at the movies' or 'over at her parents' house', but if you say something like 'all of the women in my girlfriend's family have long had an interest in sewing' and then give a complete answer to a question that called for a shorter answer … "

"It's suspicious," Hector said. "It's like there's something that the person doesn't want you to know, but has an answer ready instead, something that's plausible but—I don't know—a little off the mark."

"Exactly," I said. "Maybe I'm just grasping for something … for anything. I don't know; somehow it just bothers me."

"You think he's dirty."

"Yes. Or at least that he's hiding something."

"That's not a lot to sell to the chief."

"I know, Hector. I know."

THIRTY-TWO

Before I could put together a case to take to Chris Dietrich my phone rang. It was Frank White, a robbery/homicide lieutenant in the LAPD. "I don't know if this will be of help to you," he said, "but we've got one John Doe who might fit your parameters."

"Tell me more, Frank," I said.

"He was found at a dump site. About four weeks ago. The best guess is that he was put in a dumpster. There's always the remote possibility that he was specifically taken to the dump site, but it's much more likely that he was thrown in the dumpster first. The guy operating the bulldozer that day saw a human limb standing out amid the muck. He stopped, called us, and we recovered the remains."

"But no ID."

"No. The soft tissue was still intact, but there were no prints on file and no DNA."

"And no wallet ID."

"No, no wallet and no watch or rings. We figured it for a robbery that turned into a homicide."

"And the body's still in the morgue."

"Yes. The case is still open; we've been waiting for something to break. Maybe you're it, Tom."

"What would you think of my bringing in a forensic anthropologist, Frank?"

"You got one? Bring him along. The more the merrier. We'd just like to complete the information on the case, empty the drawer, and let the family give the vic a decent burial."

"It's actually a she, Frank—a friend of our ME's. She works with him on cases."

"Bring him too if you want. He can recheck our work. Not that there's much of it. A guy gets robbed, gets shot, gets tossed in a dumpster. This is not a new story for us."

"You know that he was shot, though."

"That's what the report says." I could hear the movement of paper in the background.

"Height, weight, hair and eye color?"

"A little over six feet, 180 pounds, brown and blue."

"Age?"

"Just a guesstimate—late twenties."

"This is very helpful, Frank. Let me call around down here and then get back to you."

"We'll be here," he said. "So will he."

Chris made the call to Leonard Barnes. "She's his person," he said. "We should go through him. Maybe he wants to come along too."

It turned out that she was available, but he was not. He was at a conference in Baltimore, not scheduled to return for two days. She was just getting out of class and had to call Chris back an hour later.

"I had a student," she said. "What's up?"

"John Doe in L.A.," he said. "Possibly of interest in the Randall case. If you could, we'd like you to have a look at the remains."

"Tomorrow afternoon would work," she said. "I've got a student coming in in the morning to talk about his dissertation. He's coming in from out of town and I'd prefer not to make him reschedule. We'll be done by mid-morning. I could be in Laguna by noon."

"That would be great," Chris said. "Tom and I will drive you to L.A. and we'll see what we can see. We'll even buy lunch, if you don't mind eating in the car."

"Anything with cheese on whole wheat," she said. "And maybe a piece of fruit."

"So you're skipping the Happy Meal," Chris said.

"Yes, this time," she said.

"We'll see you around noon," he said. "Park in my space."

He turned off the speaker phone. "That was quick," he said.

"I'll call Frank back right away," I said. "Tell him we've scheduled our road trip."

The principal L.A. morgue is on North Mission, right by the county medical center. A former hospital building, the marble, tile, iron work and coffered ceilings combine to create an odd effect, as if the building were a hotel for the dead rather than a storage facility for their remains. It must be one of the few, if not the only morgue that includes a gift shop. You arrive, identify the remains of your loved one, pick up a tote bag with a chalk outline of a body and you're back on the **10** or the **5** in a matter of minutes.

The coroner was at the same meeting in Baltimore as Leonard Barnes, but a representative of the Director's office was there to meet us. She gave us a photocopy of the coroner's report for our files and introduced us to a technician who escorted us to the examining room.

Sally was reading the report as we walked down the corridor. "There's a note on clothing," she said. "The clothes were badly soiled, of course, but they appeared to have been those of a tourist rather than those of a homeless person or derelict. He was wearing a Ralph Lauren polo shirt and a pair of beige, cotton slacks with a Nordstrom label. Nice. Not part of the glitterati set, but nice."

"The sort of thing an aspiring actor might wear on his day off," I said.

"Yes," she said.

The remains were already on the examining table when we entered the room. "Tight ship," Chris whispered to me. "If we ever end up here it's reassuring to know that they'll take good care of us."

Sally opened the small bag of implements she carried inside her purse, pulled back the sheet and we took in the full sight. One of the legs had been damaged badly, probably by the bulldozer at the dump site. The chest cavity was open, but the rest of the body was reasonably intact.

"Large entry wound," she said. By now she was wearing thin rubber gloves and wielding what looked like a large dental pick and a pair of tweezers. "The dozer missed the torso, but the gunshot did more than enough damage already."

"A shotgun, you think?" I asked.

"Definitely," she said. "Look here—multiple marks on the rib cage. You can see some scatter as well as a large, central wound. I'd like to think about this a little more, but my initial guess is that there was a shot from a slight distance and then a second shot—up close and personal. An individual using a shotgun usually goes for the upper center of the torso. You get the heart, the lungs and other things in the neighborhood. It's a guaranteed kill."

There were ruler numbers on the side of the examining table, but Sally did her own measurements. "I make him about six foot, one and a half inches," she said. "Light brown hair, almost blond." She peeled back one of the eyelids. "Bright blue," she said. "At least they were once."

She puttered with the scalp for awhile. "Notice," she said, "no wisps of hair. Everything laying very nicely, even after the indignities visited upon it. Probably a razor cut. Not a quickie at the walk-in discount shop. Appearance was important.

"Ditto the nails," she said. "At first I thought there was some clear polish there, but no. Just very nicely trimmed and filed. Probably a professional job."

She flipped through the coroner's report. "No evidence of recent sexual activity, no suspicious marks on the body in that regard."

"No tattoos," I said. "And no piercings … "

"No," she said.

"That squares with what his employer told us," I said to Chris.

"The guy who owns the restaurant on La Cienega."

"Yes," I said. "If this isn't Jimmy Davidson, it's someone doing a perfect imitation."

"We can track him down," Chris said, "find some parents somewhere, get some dental records. What about the teeth, Sally?"

"Picture perfect," she said, "but not capped. Nature was kind. Everything well-aligned. I doubt that he even needed orthodonture." She took out a pocket flashlight and looked more closely. "Almost no plaque," she said. "Good dental health. A flosser."

"An actor's smile," I said.

"What a waste," she said. "He should have been on the silver screen instead of the stainless steel table."

THIRTY-THREE

I called Hector as soon as we got back in the car so that he could begin to work his way through Jimmy Davidson's social security and federal tax records. By the time we returned to Laguna he had some information for us.

"It was actually very easy," he said. "The IRS and Social Security Administration came through instantly. Well ... they came through after I established my bona fides and talked to them on a secure line. Davidson was from a small town in Nebraska, just above the Kansas border. He had summer jobs there while he was in high school. I checked and found that there were only three dentists in his town—all still in business--and one of them, a Dr. Charles Mullin, looked after all of the Davidsons and still had all of their records. In fact, Jimmy was still going to Dr. Mullin when he was in college, so we have more than his records as a child or adolescent. They're overnighting them to us. The college jobs were in Lincoln. I checked with the registrar's office (talked to the assistant registrar, a man named Bentsen) and he verified that Jimmy Davidson was indeed a Cornhusker."

"A drama major," I suggested.

"Communications, actually," Hector said, "but he minored in Theatre--in what is now the Johnny Carson School of Theatre and Film, to be specific. This was almost like one-stop shopping for me. The Registrar's office had a home address and the names of his parents. The alumni association even had Jimmy's address in Culver City. (How do they do that? They're better than Homeland Security.) Anyway, the parents' address in Jimmy's records is no longer current, and, unfortunately, the father—John R. Davidson—is no longer with us. The mother, Laura, is alive but in poor health. I assume that, at least, because she's now in an assisted-living facility just outside of Omaha."

"She would be very young for that," I said. "What—mid-50's?"

"Yes," Hector said, "but I'm thinking that their son was born a little later in life than usual. If his mother were in her late 30's then, she'd be around 65 now. Unless she was much younger than her husband, who would have been just under forty when his son was born … "

"Did you contact anyone at the assisted-living facility?" Chris asked.

"I spoke to the associate director. She said that Mrs. Davidson's health was delicate but that she was resting comfortably. I asked her if she knew whether or not she was in contact with her son and she said that she was, since she has cards from him displayed on her nightstand. I didn't ask whether or not the cards were dated. I figured we'd check the dental records before we cause her any unnecessary grief. I'm thinking she hasn't heard from him in weeks, so she's probably already concerned."

"No doubt," I said.

"I made some notes on the teeth," Sally said, "and I took some pictures. They're not as good as X-rays, but the victim had some work done on one of his bicuspids that would be considered relatively rare. When you get the records I can give you a quick read."

"I really appreciate this," Chris said.

"It's no problem; I'm happy to do it. I think I'll stay over tonight, check the dental records in the morning, and then drive back to La Jolla."

"The Department can put you up in a hotel," Chris said. "Not the Ritz-Carlton, but someplace nice."

"Thanks," she said. "I've got a key to Len's condo; I'll just stay there."

After she left, Chris invited both Hector and me into his office. "Good work on this," he said. "Two guys in the same three-person company … each was young … each is dead … each died from a shotgun blast. It reeks."

"What are we being told, Chief," I asked, "that Jimmy Davidson was killed by Terry Randall?"

"Maybe, but where's the motive? Terry kills Jimmy for what … a deliveryman's job? And even there, the dates don't work. Jimmy was already gone; Terry didn't have to kill him to get the job; he already had it. And if there was something funny about the FirstGrowth operation Jimmy wouldn't be pressuring the new deliveryman; he'd be pressuring the owner."

"So maybe Jimmy's telling tales out of school," I said, "and Richland and Beauchamp send Terry to silence him? They want to keep their own hands clean and instead scapegoat the soldier. It makes a little bit of sense, but I don't buy it. There's no reason for Terry to sign on for capital murder. He knows the price attached to that. Besides, why would they entrust him with a task that's that important? It's *their* company, not his. It's *their* investment at stake. He's not going to kill a complete stranger just to help out old Bill and Carl. He barely knows *them*. The only other possibility is … "

"That they threatened to hurt his wife," Chris said.

"Right," I said.

"Doesn't work for me," Hector said. "The guy was a soldier. You threaten his wife and family … he doesn't roll over; he brings the army."

"If he could," I said. "Maybe he couldn't. Still, I agree with you, Hector. This is a guy for whom personal sacrifices were part of the job, a guy who had lived and worked in uncertain environments. He wouldn't just cave to save his wife or do the job to save her but risk everything else … he'd examine his options first and try to find some other way. In the end he'd sacrifice himself rather than her, but first he'd try to buy time. He'd create some misdirection. He wouldn't just say, 'OK, whatever you want me to do'. Now if *Davidson* was somehow threatening him or his wife and family, that'd be altogether different, but there's no reason for Davidson to have been doing that."

"Let's first make sure that the vic in L.A. was Davidson," Chris said. "Then we'll plan next steps."

I slept fitfully that night. I never knew Terry Randall, but I had trouble even beginning to contemplate the possibility that he had killed another individual in addition to himself and his wife. If he did, however, need a reason to destroy himself and his family the commission of capital murder would be as good a reason as any, but that was my head talking, not my gut. My gut said that this was a standup guy, a soldier, an *orderly* person, the kind you'd entrust your life savings to, the kind you'd hire to run your bank, the kind a wife could count on and parents be proud of. They all knew him; I didn't. They couldn't believe he was capable of such actions and even though there were a hundred reasons why they might *want* to delude themselves, I couldn't believe that they had.

No one in our line of work trusts coincidences. Not coincidences like these. Maybe you walk into a local restaurant and your favorite soup is the evening special. That's a bona fide coincidence. Maybe you've been thinking about buying a new hand tool and the next Saturday you walk into Sears and you see that tool on a point-of-purchase sale display. That's a coincidence. *This wasn't* a coincidence. Too few people. Too many deaths. Too much blood. The same kind of weapon. This wasn't an accidental thing, a tangential thing, the kind of thing you notice and then walk past as you're working a case. This was a neon sign, a sign blasting a message with an accompanying soundtrack. The only problem was that we weren't yet capable of actually reading it.

THIRTY-FOUR

"It's Jimmy Davidson," Sally said. "It's not just the unique work on the bicuspid; it's the fact that the rest of his mouth is nearly perfect. Even with fluoride in the water and in the toothpaste, kids still get cavities. They have crooked teeth. They need braces. They get hit by the fists and shoulders of defensive linemen or the elbows of power forwards. They get in playground fights. They fall off their skateboards. They don't have mouths like this. This is a gift from the gods; it's why he could be an actor and others couldn't, at least not without significant work."

"I'll forward the records to Frank White," I said. "The LAPD can then formally identify the body. I'll also brief him on what we've learned so far."

"He's a good guy," Chris said. "If we keep the lines of communication open, he'll be there for us later."

"Right," I said.

"Now … next steps," Chris said.

"I figure we tighten the screws a little on FirstGrowth," I said. "Make some calls; ask some questions; let them know we're not going away."

"Do it," Chris said.

I called William Richland and caught his answering machine. I told him that I needed to speak with him as soon as possible. Three hours later he called back. "I was making a call," he said, "in Santa Barbara. What can I do for you, Lieutenant?"

"The LAPD has found James Davidson," I said. "He was murdered."

"Murdered?" Richland said. "That's horrible. When?"

"I'm not at liberty to discuss the time line," I said.

"Do the police know who killed him?"

"They're still pursuing their investigation," I said. "He was killed with a shotgun."

"What are you saying, Lieutenant—that Terry killed him? To my knowledge the two of them never even met."

"I realize that, Mr. Richland, but you must also see that his death and the weapon used in the commission of the murder raise some questions."

"I see what you're saying, Lieutenant. It's too suspicious to be a simple coincidence."

"Yes, and the obvious connection between the two men is their employment by FirstGrowth."

"Well, we'll certainly cooperate in any way that we can. This is simply terrible. *Terrible*. I hoped that we'd see Jimmy in films or on television. I never expected to hear this. He was so young. He had so much personality, so much promise ... "

"I appreciate your willingness to cooperate," I said. "We'd like to speak with your clients, the ones with whom Mr. Davidson and Mr. Randall came in contact."

"Our clients ... " There was noticeable hesitation in his voice. "I am sure that you understand, Lieutenant ... these are individuals who value their privacy."

"We will certainly respect that privacy, Mr. Richland."

"Forgive me for my hesitation, Lieutenant. Do you believe that one of them might have had something to do with Jimmy's death?"

"We have no way of knowing that at this time, Mr. Richland. Both men are dead. Both men worked for your company. Both men made deliveries to your clients."

"I see what you're saying, Lieutenant. Let me compile a list for you. Would you prefer that I send you a fax or an email?"

"Either one would be fine," I said. I gave him my department email address as well as a fax number.

"I appreciate your willingness to keep these inquiries as lowkey as possible, Lieutenant. It's very difficult for me to imagine that anyone in our client base would kill someone. It's just as difficult to conceive of Terry or Jimmy doing something that would lead to their being killed."

"Thank you. You can understand our thinking here."

"Certainly. It would be possible (though highly, highly unlikely, I believe) that Jimmy and Terry could have somehow cheated one of our clients or done something else to provoke a violent response from them."

"Yes. You do see that the sorts of individuals who purchase your products are people of great means, people who are accustomed to having their way—people who would have the resources to employ individuals capable of achieving ... significant retribution."

"I see your line of thinking, Lieutenant, but I feel very comfortable in saying that our clients are above reproach. I have met them all and I consider a number of them to be friends. They are individuals of means, of course, but they are cultured ... they are people of taste and discernment ... they enjoy fine things and move in a world of ... gentlemen and gentility."

"It may well lead nowhere, Mr. Richland. We *do* have to pursue every possible lead, however."

"I understand. I'll get that list to you as soon as I can."

It took nearly four hours for him to send it, though each name, address and phone number looked as if it had been copied from a previously-existing list, a list that had been checked and refined over a period of time. All of the abbreviations had been standardized. The names and addresses appeared to be free of misspellings and each name, address and phone number was in the same type face and the same font size—as if the list had been used to print mailing labels. Actually it looked like my mother's old Christmas card list—the product of several iterations of attentive work. I wondered if he had simply transferred it from a previously-existing file hours ago, printed it out, set it aside and then called each of them to warn them that they would be hearing from me.

The most striking thing was that the list was so brief. I didn't expect a cast of thousands; there are only so many individuals who are willing and able to pay $700 for a bottle of wine. He had told us that he had clients from San Diego to Santa Barbara. The list was beautiful in its clarity and accuracy; I expected it to contain more than nine names.

THIRTY-FIVE

"Where will you start?" Chris asked.

"Close to home," I said, "then work my way north."

"Looking for something that smells . . . *off?*"

"Exactly," I said. "Unfortunately, at this point I can't be much more specific than that."

"You don't need to," Chris answered. "Just start turning over some rocks and see if anything slithers out."

Charles Davies (pronounced *Davis*, in the English mode, as he promptly informed me) lived at the beach in Newport. Developers had taken a small stretch of industrial space and converted it for residential use, throwing up a set of three-story structures that they considered bargains in the low 8-figures. In Baltimore they would be called row- or townhouses. Here they were more like townmansions. All frame and glass, sea and sky, they weighed in at six thousand square feet and up, with private docks and a set of public rooms in a common facility that were a heavy mix of marble and walnut.

Davies was dressed for formal relaxation—a tattersall shirt with knit tie, dark brown wool slacks with a knife-edge crease, narrow Gucci loafers that looked as if they had just been removed from their box and a set of Burberry horn-rims that went nicely with the English bone china cup and saucer in his left hand.

"Lieutenant Deaton," he said. "Please come in. Would you like some coffee?"

"No, thank you," I said.

He pointed to what looked like the most comfortable chair in his living room, invited me to sit down, and put his cup and saucer on a glass table that ran the length of his couch.

"Beautiful weather," he said. "Calm seas ... clouds off against the horizon ... it's why we settle here. Simply lovely ... but you didn't come to discuss the weather ... "

"No," I said. "I appreciate your seeing me on short notice."

He nodded, turning his head to the side modestly.

"You are a client of a wine dealership named FirstGrowth."

"Yes, William Richland's company. I'm not what one might term an avid collector. I have a small cellar, with no more than thirty-five or forty cases at a time, all for my personal use. You see, I *do* drink the wine, unlike some collectors."

"I've never quite understood that," I said. "It *is* an investment, of course, but eventually even the greatest wines deterioriate, so it's an investment with ... what would you say ... an identifiable *arc* and *horizon?*"

"I think you've put it very well," he said. "Of course, for the great wines that could be a century or more in duration. It outlives *us,* Lieutenant."

"But not our heirs, as land does, for example."

"True. I suspect the answer is that those who collect *seriously,* which I do not, already have land and antiques and art. They are able to purchase other things as well and while wine has its limits as an investment (as you noted), it has other advantages. It is both food and art. It connects us with nature, with the *terroir,* and it is associated with fellowship and celebration. It is very beautiful and it nourishes us. One might almost say that it is *sacramental* in ways that other commodities are not."

"How long have you purchased wines from FirstGrowth, Mr. Davies?" (As I questioned him he crossed his leg and straightened the kiltie on his right loafer.)

"I think from their beginning, several years ago. Prior to that I had been purchasing through several wine merchants--principally in New York, sometimes in London--and one day I learned of Richland's venture. I'm sure you know that he has an exceptional storage facility, not far from here, and the quality of the storage is an absolute in that business."

"And you chiefly purchase red Bordeaux?" (Now he was searching for an elusive piece of lint on his pants cuff.)

"Principally. I have white Burgundy on hand for my guests and a few cases of red Burgundy, which I like with specific foods, but, yes, I largely purchase red Bordeaux. Latour nearly every vintage, Pétrus if I have confidence that I'm not being extorted, Margaux always, sometimes Palmer in certain years … "

"And it is delivered to you here."

"Yes."

"And you deal directly with the deliveryman."

"When I'm here," he said, "but I'm often elsewhere, unfortunately. My work takes me to a number of places, principally foreign capitals. I do economic consulting. When I'm away I have a man who looks after the property and takes deliveries."

"Did you know Terrence Randall?"

"He was one of their deliverymen, I believe."

"Yes, the most recent one."

"I think I met him once. He called himself Terry. I also remember his predecessor; his name was James. I may have seen James twice. I don't make frequent purchases, Lieutenant. When I do purchase, I do so in quantity."

"Ten cases?"

"More like twenty. Enough to last nine months or more. I like the wine when it's young. Richland teases me about that. If it's properly decanted it's not a problem. I like it with strong cheeses and other foods. For me it needs to have *spine*."

"Do you know Richland well?"

"No, not really. He calls me three or four times a year, informing me about what he has on hand. We had lunch once, several years ago. I'm probably not one of his more important clients, Lieutenant, the type who are in the hunt for a Balthazar or Nebuchadnezzar of something excrutiatingly rare. I've even been known to purchase wines from California from time to time. A special *Ridge* Montebello or *Dunn* Howell Mountain ... I also like the *Diamond Creek* wines. I have a special fondness for the Gravelly Meadow, though the Volcanic Hill is the longest-lived, as a rule. It all comes down to taste, doesn't it? And the taste is what's important to me, Lieutenant, far more than the collectability."

"Did you know that Terrence Randall was dead, Mr. Davies?"

"Dead? No, I didn't."

"James Davidson as well."

"Really?"

"Yes."

"Why? Do you know who killed them?"

"I'm not at liberty to discuss the investigations, Mr. Davies, but I'm sure that you can appreciate the fact that the coincidence of their respective deaths is striking."

"You find it suspicious. Well, of course you would. And why not? It *is* suspicious."

"Yes, it is," I said. "Can I ask you another question?"

"Certainly."

"Do you know any of FirstGrowth's other clients?"

"No, as a matter of fact I don't. One would think that such a business would be built by word of mouth, but I responded to an ad when Richland began the operation. Actually, I doubt that he would want us to know one another. Not that he's ever said anything ... "

"He might want to offer certain wines to certain clients, high bidders first, for example."

"Yes, exactly. Our understanding is that he knows my tastes and he will contact me whenever he believes that he is capable of satisfying them. I wouldn't be one of the higher bidders anyway because, as I told you, I prefer *drinking* the wine to collecting it."

"Could I see your cellar before I go?"

"Of course," Davies said, "but I must warn you. It's nothing on the grand scale. And it's actually not in the cellar. It's just here … "

He led me down the hallway from the living room to what looked like a large utility closet. Inside the space was a storage facility that was actually a room within the room. It looked like an oversized sauna. I could hear the sound of a motor in the background. He opened the door; we entered and he turned on the light. The room was cool, probably a little over fifty degrees. He closed the door behind us and I could hear a slight swoosh of air as it closed against the jamb. There were shelves on each side of the room, most containing wooden boxes with the images of the châteaux stamped into the grain. There were a few loose bottles laying on simple pine racks.

"As you see, Lieutenant … purely functional. I don't have an elaborate tasting table and furnishings crafted of grape vines. We simply assemble around the kitchen island. Why would one want to stand in a cold room anyway?"

"Exactly," I said. "I've never quite understood that concept."

As we walked back toward the living room he opened the swinging doors to the kitchen. "Nicer than a cellar," he said, "don't you think?"

It was square, approximately thirty-five feet on each side, with light cherry cabinetry, professional appliances, a kidney-shaped granite island in the center, leather furniture, a gas fireplace and views of the Pacific on two sides.

"Yes," I said. "It certainly is."

THIRTY-SIX

The next FirstGrowth client on my list was a man named Faber. He lived in Rancho Santa Fe in a mansion that made Oprah's digs in Montecito look like a genteel outbuilding. In the midst of the pillars, stucco, slate, granite and marble splendor I expected a latter-day conquistador, but Al Faber looked like the kind of secondhand car salesman who did his own commercials. Dressed in a monogrammed bathrobe and the kind of house slippers worn by Winston Churchill (Al's had gold lion heads on each instep), his spindly ankles contrasted with his bare, chubby calves. He was smoking a cigar and running his free hand through the tufts of red hair that curled above his brow.

I introduced myself and he offered me a pudgy hand with short pink fingers. "Bill Richland gave me a headsup," he said, "told me that each of his deliverymen has turned up dead. Helluva mess for him and for you too, I expect. I met 'em both once; usually one of my people takes deliveries, but it just so happened that I was out in front the day they arrived. Jimmy was an actor type. Probably would have made a nice leading man in a perfect world. Out here? He'd have been lucky to do some commercials. Terry was special. A soldier, I understand. I chatted with both of them for awhile. My business is people and I like to get to know everybody I meet."

"What is your particular line of business, Mr. Faber?"

"Call me Al, Lieutenant. I'm in the jewelry business. The bigger and gawdier the better. I was the same with wine. Exactly the same. I sold jewelry that I never wore and I bought wine that I never drank. For me it was always an investment, nothing more. Large stones come on the market now and again. When they do I snap them up. Put them in the right setting, surround them with smaller stones, mark them up several hundred percent and unload them on Beverly Hills and Bel Air. I've even sold diamonds to people in Holmby Hills. Hef was in Holmby Hills, I think. Geography wasn't my best subject, Lieutenant. Anyway, they call it the platinum triangle, and I like to cover that platinum with diamonds and emeralds."

"And you bought wine, held it, and then sold it."

"Sometimes I'd flip it; mostly I'd hold it awhile. Always the large bottles. Fires the imagination. That's the trick. You can go to any major wine dealer in the world and they'll have cases of famous wines in 750 ml bottles. Mags are pretty common too, especially early on after the release. The big bottles are rarer. Some people have never even seen them. You tell somebody you've got a Salmanazar of something big and famous and their eyes light up. 'How big is that?' they ask. 'I don't believe I've ever seen one of those,' they say. Then you tell them that the bigger bottles are better for aging purposes and that that makes them rarer and more valuable. You watch their eyes open wider. Before you know it they're reaching for their checkbooks. The largest consignment of bottles I've ever purchased from old Bill is two, Lieutenant. Usually I just buy one, because he seldom gets any more than that."

"But you never drink it."

"Can't. Allergic to the sulfites. Hell, isn't it? One of nature's great gifts and I can't share it. Gives me an asthmatic reaction. Severe, too. Whites are worse than the reds usually, but it doesn't make too much difference to me. They'll each lay me low. So no, Lieutenant, I can't drink it. What you see standing before you is nothing more than a simple middleman. Successful, though."

"When did you last see the decedents, Mr. Faber? Al."

"Saw Jimmy a year ago or so. Saw Terry . . . what . . . maybe two months ago?"

"And how long have you been purchasing wine from Mr. Richland?"

"I think from when he got started in the business. What was that, three, four years ago? I buy from various suppliers, Lieutenant. Still. Mostly from New York, but sometimes from London and sometimes from Brown Derby."

"Brown Derby?"

"Not the old restaurant. They're long gone, Lieutenant. Brown Derby is a wine dealer in Springfield, Missouri." (He pronounced it *Missourah*, as if he was a native.) "Big deal. They used to have a place in St. Louis. Used to go there regularly for business. Nice jewelry outlet in Frontenac. Use to peddle my wares there. I'd stop at Brown Derby on the way; check out the goods. Gone now, unfortunately. Things change; we move on; that's business, Lieutenant."

"Do you usually buy red Bordeaux, Al?"

"Exclusively, Lieutenant. Biggest bang for the investment buck. Pétrus, when I can get it. Astronomical prices. Stratospheric, even."

"Did you ever meet any of Mr. Richland's other clients?"

"No, and wouldn't want to. Some of them are my competition. What does the godfather say about keeping your enemies closer than your friends? Doesn't work in this case. I like to have a sense of the market … a sense of what people will pay for what … but this isn't like an average business. You take the California wine industry … the so-called *fighting varietals*. It's more like your usual business. There's a few labels that are all trying to rule the market. They're making the same kinds of wine, from the same kinds of grapes, that is. There may be a little difference in style from winery to winery, but essentially they're selling you your basic chardonnay, your basic cabernet, your basic merlot. And they want to sell oceans of the stuff. It's all about branding and advertising. It's about distribution and the picture on the label. They hire consultants to tell them what to put on there. Bob Mondavi called old sauvignon blanc *fumé blanc* and made a fortune. That's not my business, Lieutenant. I'm much more like an antique dealer. I sell the object but I also sell the story behind it. I find a big old bottle of Pétrus and dangle it in front of the eyes of the hungriest of the collectors and see how high they'll jump for it. They'll jump pretty high, Lieutenant. Pretty high indeed."

"Did you learn about Richland through an advertisement?"

"No, I think one of my people did. Somebody up in Newport saw the ad and said something to one of my people here. Said 'your boss might want to get to know this guy.' That was years ago, like I said."

"Any idea who or what could have caused the deaths of the deliverymen?"

"None whatsoever," he said. "I guess you just start working your way down the usual list, Lieutenant. What have you got? Greed … Lust … Anger … the old seven deadlies. You'd know that much better than I."

"I appreciate your taking the time to talk with me," I said.

"Doesn't cost a thing. If you're ever in the market for a big jug of fermented grape juice or a diamond as big as a midget's fist, you just let me know."

"I'll do that," I said, "but I suspect your prices are a little too rich for my blood."

"Probably so," he said. "Tell you what … when you're ready to pop the question or get something special for an anniversary … "

"Yes?"

"Go to an individual you trust. Get yourself a personal jeweler. Don't go to one of those places at the mall. Develop a relationship. It's a people business, Lieutenant. I hate to see it turn into something crude and cold."

"I understand. Thanks very much."

"My pleasure. Now you be careful on those freeways."

THIRTY-SEVEN

I drew to an inside straight on the third interview. The FirstGrowth client was a woman named Julia Tucker. Her company was in Century City; my plan was to interview her the following morning, but she was in Laguna for the day and she invited me to join her for drinks at the Ritz-Carlton in Laguna Niguel.

She was easily recognized. She was the one with the Cartier watch, the Prada purse and what I guessed might be a Vera Wang jacket over black slacks. She was making notes in a small leather book when I arrived. There was no drink on the table. I introduced myself. She shook my hand (more firmly than Al Faber had) and invited me to sit down. As soon as I did a waiter appeared.

She ordered a Bombay Sapphire martini, up and very dry. I asked for a glass of white wine. That turned out to be a Sonoma Chardonnay at $16 a pop. Though we were sitting at a table in the corner next to the window, she never looked out at the coast below.

"So how can I help you, Lieutenant?"

"You are a client of FirstGrowth," I said.

"The wine distributor."

"Yes."

"Yes, I am. I wouldn't characterize myself as a significant client, but we have a corporate account with them."

"Not a personal one."

"No, I'm not a great wine aficianado, Lieutenant. My company is an export firm whose clients are almost exclusively Japanese. The Japanese love fine wines. Twice a year we host a dinner for special clients, one in Tokyo, one in Los Angeles. The Japanese are particularly taken with *prominent* wines. I wouldn't say that they lack cultured palates, but I *would* say that they enjoy the *experience* of fine wine. You know how important the tea ceremony is to them; the wine ceremony can be equally attractive—the elaborate decantings, the varietal-specific glassware … they *do* have an eye for the label (sometimes more than for the wine itself, I find). They know its cost and they feel that a dinner with wines of that order is a great act of respect. The bottom line is that they buy our products and this is a nice way for us to thank them for their business."

"So you order specifically for these events."

"Not exactly, Lieutenant. Because of the market we must purchase well in advance of our events. This after all is FirstGrowth's comparative advantage—their counsel and their storage services. They help us buy at the optimum moment. Sometimes we buy futures. Sometimes we buy end lots. FirstGrowth then stores the wine for us until such time as we need it. As you probably already know, they have an exceptional facility for that purpose."

"And then they deliver to your event site or they ship to Asia."

"Exactly. They recommend that the wine have an opportunity to rest after it's been moved. Give it time to get over the so-called *bottle shock*. They make these arrangements with the hotels. There are additional fees, of course, but to us it's all part of the ceremony. We inform our guests that the wine that is being served has been resting comfortably for several weeks, awaiting their arrival … etc. They enjoy this little bit of drama."

"Did you personally know either of their deliverymen?"

"No. The only deliveries at this end would have been to Los Angeles hotels and Richland's people work directly with the hotel people. I only see the wine when it is served and all of our payments to FirstGrowth are by electronic transfer. There is a good bit of trust involved in the operation, of course, but that is one of the things for which we are paying."

"Each of their deliverymen has been murdered," I said, watching for her reaction.

Her reaction was to take a slow sip of her martini, pause, and say, "That's perfectly horrid. Do you have a suspect?"

"I can't discuss that," I said, "but we're talking to all of FirstGrowth's clients to see if they can add anything to our investigation. Do you know any of the other people who purchase wine from FirstGrowth?"

"No, I don't," she said. "I had a discussion with Richland when we initiated the arrangement. That would have been about three years ago. Perhaps three and a half. Since then it's all been done at a distance. He calls us with regard to price and availability of product. We purchase and he stores. We then give him a location, a date, and an estimate of the number of individuals who will attend our events. Then, as I said, I see the wine when it's served."

"How did you first come to learn about FirstGrowth?" I asked.

"I asked one of my assistants to check with local distributors. He's interested in wine; he told me about an ad that Richland had placed. I called him and we struck up this rather modest relationship."

"Certainly not modest in price."

"Do you have any idea what the Japanese are prepared to pay for certain fish, Lieutenant? Even for certain types of melon?"

"I know the prices are very high," I said.

She nodded and took another sip of her drink.

A few minutes later, after some small talk, she asked me if I wanted another glass of wine. I said no, thanked her, and told her I needed to be going. She said that if she thought of anything that might be useful to the investigation she would call, but she said, candidly, that she doubted there would be anything additional. She did say that she would check with her assistant who had initially called FirstGrowth to her attention. "If he has any thoughts, I'll pass them along. And if you want to speak to either of us, we'll be available … in Century City."

When I got to the valet parking stand I ticked off her name in my notebook, put the book back in my jacket pocket, tipped the attendant and got in my car. "Have a nice day," he said.

"Thanks," I said. There's not a great deal of it left, I thought to myself.

THIRTY-EIGHT

The next six clients were similar to the first three. David Lonis was a speculator in Malibu, a younger, thinner, more finely-wired version of Al Faber. He showed me the computer files he kept on release prices and later auction prices. He showed me some graphs that charted the appreciation rates of different labels. "The vintage is key, of course, but that doesn't mean that some wines don't perform better over time than others."

While I was sorting out the double negative he showed me a photograph of an auction in which a bidder had paid $57,000 for a magnum of a certain wine. "I had to pay the auction house fees, of course, but I still made a tidy profit," he said.

Michael Campbell was a drinker, like Davies. He lived in Hope Ranch in Santa Barbara. The home was palatial but the lawn was brown because of the city's recent ban on watering. "We may lack water," he said, "but I don't lack wine." His cellar contained 375 cases. The hardwood racking had been installed by a cabinetmaker who specialized in creating such facilities. At the center was a dark oak bas relief featuring two fat monks sampling wine from two large, oval barrels. The thermometer on the wall read 54 degrees.

"Lafite is my principal passion," he said, "but I must confess to a host of others as well. White burgundy is always a bargain; I prefer Puligny Montrachet. I've also been known to drink an occasional Australian. Grange, of course, but they do some other things well from time to time.

Richland's specialty is red Bordeaux, but I have other distributors besides him. They find it and I drink it."

Clarice Mahin was Julia Tucker's buttoned-down *haute couture* twin. Her gray, beehive hair looked as if it could sustain wind gusts from a Category 4 hurricane. The managing partner of a corporate law firm in Los Angeles, she invited me to lunch at the Jonathan Club. We each had iced tea and club sandwiches. "I don't drink wine," she said, "but I give away a lot of it."

Like Julia Tucker, she gave Richland a general sense of their annual need. He purchased things for them as they became available and then stored them in his Irvine facility. Her firm gave tasting flights as corporate gifts at Christmas. "We represent a number of prominent companies in southern California," she said. "The retainers are ... substantial. We give each of their CEO's a thank-you at Christmas. And, I must confess, we send a nice bottle or two to their CFO's as well."

"To keep them comfortable with the size of the retainer?" I asked.

"A crude gesture, I admit," she said, "but no one has jumped ship yet. The firm used to give food baskets from Fortnum and Mason's, but I thought a little upgrade was in order."

None of the three were able to provide information that was of use in the case. Each had a modest relationship with Richland and except for Campbell, who had a faint recollection of meeting both Davidson and Randall, none had any specific knowledge of the deliverymen that materially contributed to the investigation. I stayed overnight in Pasadena, meeting with Darryl Culbert the next morning at his estate in San Marino. He and his wife Betsy were wine lovers and had a substantial cellar, but she had died the previous spring and she had been the principal connection with FirstGrowth. "I'm sure she met the deliverymen," he said, "but I did not. She made the original connection with . . . what was his name--Richland?"

Karl Pfeifer lived in a Greek mansion in Calabasas. He commented on its square footage and on the astronomical differences in price between his home and comparable properties in Beverly Hills and Bel Air. An investment banker, he fiddled with his iPhone while I questioned him. He himself drank cheap wine, he said, *cheap* being defined as $100-150 a bottle. The expensive wines were purchased as investments. He had done correlations between the speed with which they matured and the speed with which they appreciated in value. He explained these to me in some detail, all the while focusing on his phone screen.

Clement Byrne was a CFO for an engineering firm just north of Studio City. He lived in Coldwater Canyon. The engineering concern did things that he mentioned elliptically but *preferred* not to discuss directly. I gathered that these concerned such things as missile guidance systems and electromagnetic pulse technology. He purchased wine from Richland for gifts to those in Washington who awarded federal contracts to his firm. "It's very complex," he said. "There are many rules which must be observed. We work through our lobbyists, who understand these things. We are scrupulous about observing the law ... *scrupulous*, Lieutenant."

I asked him about his own interests in wine and he said that he mostly drank spirits, with a special love of cognac (but only on his birthday and during the holiday season). He had learned of FirstGrowth from Richland's initial ad, but had communicated with him only by phone. There were no deliveries made to his company. The wine was shipped directly to their lobbying firm, whether to their K Street address in Washington or the senior partner's home address in McLean, Virginia he couldn't remember. "Some jurisdictions are sticky about out of state deliveries. I can't remember how they worked it out, but I know that they did. We weren't involved; we only pay for it."

When I returned home that evening I had a carry-out sandwich and a glass of refrigerator white wine. I thought about what I had learned and as I tried to determine what, if anything, was of any significance I remembered a scene from an old movie. A woman who fancied herself a photographer had been taking pictures while on safari in Africa. However, the animals she thought she was photographing were all obscured by the shade from the trees under which they were resting. As she enumerated the animals and flipped through her glossy 8x10 black-and-white photographs, her boyfriend commented that she wasn't taking pictures of animals at all; she was actually taking pictures of *trees*. "You only thought you were taking pictures of animals," he said.

I thought about what *I* had learned and then wondered if I had learned something quite different than I had intended. I thought I was learning about clients of a wine distributor, about a distributorship with a small staff, limited clientele and a pair of deliverymen who had met violent and completely unexpected and seemingly unrelated deaths. Perhaps I was learning about something else entirely.

THIRTY-NINE

My freshman philosophy teacher was an Aristotelian who urged us to 'learn through all of our senses'. I didn't have any wine and murder music, but I did have a large tablet on which I could jot words, draw pictures, make asterisks and mark lines of connection between names, numbers and other data. I said the names aloud when I wrote them down and visualized the people they represented. I sketched a map of southern California and located Hope Ranch, Calabasas, San Marino, Bunker Hill, Malibu, Coldwater Canyon, Century City, La Jolla, Irvine, Rancho Santa Fe and Newport Beach.

I made a simple chart, putting individual clients into common boxes. Getting nowhere very quickly I began to sketch wine bottles … Bordeaux … Burgundy … Riesling. Then I drew a very amateurish version of a double-barreled shotgun, two bodies on a dusty hill above Lake Elsinore and one in a dumpster in a Los Angeles alley.

The long and the short of it was that I had a little more than nothing. FirstGrowth's clients fell into one of three categories: drinkers, givers and investors. They (and in some cases, the firms that they represented) were obviously prosperous/bordering on filthy rich. They lived in the nicest, most expensive areas of southern California. They had nothing of any great interest to tell me about the two deliverymen who had played a very small role in their lives but a very large role in my investigation. They knew Richland (or knew of him), but to them he was little more than a tradesman who touched their lives in tangential ways once or twice a year.

They did not know one another and they had not expected to. Moreover, they had no motive to kill Terry Randall or Jimmy Davidson. If they had been cheated or deceived in some modest way they would simply have severed their relationship with FirstGrowth. If they had been cheated in a significant way they would have held Richland responsible and it was far more likely that they would have contacted the local police than a professional killer. For that matter, a professional killer would have used a .22 to the brainpan rather than a set of shotgun shells to the gut (or, in Susan Randall's case, to the hand as well).

Computer searches on FirstGrowth had come up dry. *If* Richland was scamming his clients at least one of them should have found out and exposed him. No one had. Or if they did, it had gone unnoticed and that was improbable in the extreme. The story of a winebroker ripping off the glitterati would have been a tale dear to every newsman's heart: lifestyles of the rich and famous, how the rich and famous get royally screwed, the justice in that, the vengeance for that, the confirmation that high-priced commodities are a disgusting indulgence that has brought some form of divine retribution in a turning of Fortune's wheel … I could have written the story myself. The only problem was that no one else had. There was no scent of mortal sin, genteel larceny or bloody revenge, not even a whiff of suspicion. All there was was a set of dead bodies, the bodies of, by all accounts, decent people playing a minor or even unrelated role in a set of business transactions that were interesting because of the positioning of the decimal points, but otherwise unremarkable.

The next morning I talked to Hector. "I'm just free-associating here," he said. "I'm just guessing. But think about a possible scam … Richland needs four things—a bottle, a label, a cork and a foil wrap. The bottle he can get anywhere. The label he can get from any decent forger. Ditto the cork and the foil wrap. Maybe a European forger. He finds the companies that make things for the primo wineries, finds a disgruntled former worker, puts him on that part of the FirstGrowth payroll that doesn't carry fringe benefits. Then all he has to do is put good wine in the expensive wine's bottle. Put in a $100 wine and then charge $700 for it. Sure, he's got expenses. Maybe the disgruntled guy takes $50 a bottle at first. So Richland's investment is $150 a bottle. Hell, make it $200 a bottle. That $500 a bottle's worth of profit is still looking pretty good. Then, one day, it all turns to shit. Jimmy D hears Billy and Carl talking about the scam; suddenly Jimmy's got to go. Later, Terry discovers the scam; he's got to go … and with him, his wife, because he might have mentioned the fact to her. The clients are all legit. They literally do not know jack shit and couldn't help you. The crimes were all discovered in house, so Billy and Carl cleaned house."

I thought about it a little. "Maybe he was cutting corners," I said, "slapping on labels at the last minute. Maybe he got sloppy with the glue … Jimmy noticed … no, wait a minute. The upscale bottles were usually wrapped in printed tissue paper. They'd be all twisted up tight. The deliverymen wouldn't unwrap them."

"Maybe the ink smeared or something," Hector said.

"Maybe," I said. "Any way you slice it we have to investigate further. That means tipping our hand, getting warrants, conducting the full shakedown inspection of their storage facility … but what else do we have?"

"Nada," Hector said. "What we have is absolutely … nada."

"Let's talk to Chris."

"Works for me," Hector said. "I've got to believe these guys are dirty. We just haven't figured out the how yet."

FORTY

"If we go in, we have to go full-tilt," I said. "We can't make nice any-more. We have to acknowledge that they're our prime suspects and that we plan to turn them upside down and shake them until something interesting falls on the floor."

"What if nothing interesting does?" Chris Dietrich asked.

"Then we go back to the client list," I said. "Two guys die in a three-person company? I'm not buying that, Chief. It's something inside, something circumscribed by the FirstGrowth orbit. The notion that Terry Randall and Jimmy Davidson had unrelated problems, problems that intersected outside of the FirstGrowth operation, problems that were solved by a shotgun ... it reeks, Chief. You know it does; you said yourself that it did."

"Especially within the tight time frame," he said. "If the Randalls turn up dead in twenty years and Davidson in thirty on the other side of the country ... OK ... life stinks and bad things happen to good people. Or at least to people who were once good. This is too immediate, too coincidental. There has to be a reason. What do you need from me?"

"Warrants, some uniforms to help with the search, some techs ... "

"How soon?"

"Tomorrow morning, if possible. Early."

"I'll call a sympathetic judge and prepare the way," Chris said. "You or Hector can pick up the warrants."

The next morning we were assembling the team at 6:15. Chris had assigned four uniforms to help us with the search. Since Beauchamp had been forthcoming in showing us their storage facility, we decided to begin at Richland's house. "It's big enough to hold a lot of secrets," I said. "If we don't find anything there we can proceed to Irvine. In the meantime we'll bring Richland in for questioning so he can't tip off Beauchamp that we're coming."

As we ran through our final equipment check and made sure our documents were in order, Bill Brighton came into the conference room. "Dan Foley's on the phone, Tom—the Sheriff's Department captain in Encinitas."

"Thanks," I said, and hit the flashing button.

"This is Tom Deaton, Captain," I said.

"Tom, Dan Foley. Just heard something from La Jolla that might interest you. The case you're working ... the one involving the wine guy ... "

"Yes, sir?"

"They just arrested somebody trying to break into his house. When the locals went in they found somebody there."

"Dead, Captain?"

"As dead as a cat in a cheap Chinese restaurant," he said.

"So the guy was trying to break in, but the occupant was already dead."

"That's what they're saying. I thought you'd want to know."

"That's two we owe you, Captain."

"We're here to serve and protect," he said, "and keep the lines of communication open here in paradise."

III

RICHMOND

FORTY-ONE

As Hector, the uniforms and I drove south, Chris made the calls that would open the proper doors. One of Richland's neighbors had seen a man futzing with the keypad for Richland's gate. At first he didn't think anything of it, figuring that the guy had forgotten the code and had to call up to the house to be let in. After awhile, however, he got suspicious. The guy was trying to break into the box, short-circuit the system. He called the Northern Division of the SDPD.

A cruiser pulled up a few minutes later; the guy ran to his car, but was stopped before he could escape. They put him in plastic restraints and locked him in the cruiser. Nobody responded when they called the house on the squawk box. They got the unlisted landline number of the house and tried to call. When no one answered they managed to get one of the officers over the fence. He went up to the house, gained entry and found a body. The helpful neighbor identified the decedent as William Richland.

The guy trying to get in identified himself as Carlton Beauchamp. He told the SDPD that he was Richland's business partner and that he had simply forgotten the entry code. He also said that Richland could identify him and would assure the officers that he was legit.

"Under the circumstances this was not possible," Chris said.

"Very interesting," I said. "Beauchamp's trying to break in, but Richland's already dead. I wonder what he knew that he was trying to tell Richland."

"Good question," Chris said. "Was he trying to warn him or had he already been there? Maybe he was trying to establish some sort of alibi, persuading the cops that he was on the outside looking in when all of this went down."

"Possible," I said.

"Anyway, the officer on the scene is a lieutenant named Cary Watson. He's expecting you, Tom."

"Thanks, Chief. I'll let you know what I learn. Have they taken Beauchamp to the station?"

"I figured you'd want him out of there; no reason to clue him in on our interest. Watson said they took him in a few minutes ago. He's cooling his heels."

"He'll understand the concept," I said. "He likes cooling systems."

Cary Watson met us at the open gate of Richland's mansion. Hector was with me but the uniforms stayed in their cruiser. He told me that Hector and I were welcome to explore the scene. "I'd prefer it if your uniforms would stay put," he said. "I've already got two uniforms, a couple of techs and an ME working the scene."

"Not a problem," I said. "We appreciate all of your help."

"This has something to do with your murder/suicide case, doesn't it?" he asked.

"Yes, we think it does."

"Well, make yourselves at home but watch where you walk. If you see anything that catches your attention we'd be pleased to hear about it."

"You too," I said.

Their ME was standing over Richland's bed, where his remains rested in state. State was a heavy terry-cloth bathrobe, silk boxers and some thin slippers. Part of his body was covered with a thick cotton comforter; part was exposed.

"It's as if he was starting to cover himself, but conked out halfway through the process," the ME said. Then he introduced himself. "Dr. Bill Harris."

I introduced myself and asked him if he had any thoughts on the cause of death.

"Looks pretty clear to me," he said. "There are no marks on the body. No wounds … no bruises … no pinpricks … no nothing. Just a little drool." He held up a plastic evidence bag with a small plastic vial inside. "Looks as if he took enough Ativan to calm the 82nd Airborne and enable them to sleep for a week. Only one thing out of the ordinary … "

"What's that, Dr. Harris?" I asked.

"It's in the bathroom, on the granite counter. He washed the pills down with bottled water, not tap water, and he drank it from a Riedel crystal wine glass. He went out in style."

I told him briefly about Richland's business.

"Icelandic Glacial," he said, "in the bottle with the sculpted top. He drank most all of it. It would have fit in that tasting glass. Big boy. The kind you can swirl with to your heart's content. I wonder why he didn't go out on top though … maybe a little something special from Bordeaux … "

I asked him if there was any other reaction besides the drool.

"You mean like his bladder giving out … something like that?"

"Yes," I said. "Or any indication that he might have been … induced to swallow the pills."

"Nope. Looks like a quiet evening at home, a nice warm bath, the mega-medication and then the endless nap."

"Were there any obvious prints on the vial?" Hector asked.

"One, I think, probably a thumbprint. It's going to the lab. Sorry I don't have anything else. Give me your card and I'll see to it that you get a copy of the autopsy report."

"This place looks like the Clue House," Hector said. "I keep expecting to see Miss Scarlet and Colonel Mustard come around the corner, armed with lead pipes and candlesticks."

"Everybody *should have* a billiard room and ballroom and conservatory," I said. "The problem is that we can't all afford them. Old

Bill seems to have done it *his way*. You've got your big bedroom, your bigger bedroom, your biggest bedroom, your tile bathroom, your granite bathroom, your marble bathroom, a living room, dining room, den, library, tasting room … all the comforts of home."

"The kitchen is bigger than my apartment," Hector said, "but I bet the food wasn't as good."

"The wine was though," I said. "I'm surprised he only had, what, 40 or 50 bottles in his wine frig?"

"He probably repacked the shelves every week."

"I'll talk to Watson about his computer," I said. "I want to know what's there that we don't know about yet. I didn't see a cellphone anywhere. Watson may already have it."

"Let's go downstairs," Hector said. He opened a door that led to the garage. "Oh, wrong door," he said. "And only enough space for four cars."

"Another wrong door," he said, finding an 8' x 8' closet that was filled with brooms, mops and cleaning equipment.

"The maid's domain. Here we go," I said, opening a door that led to a landing and a set of steps that curved below. Everything below the landing was dark.

FORTY-TWO

The largest of the cellar rooms contained the two furnaces that heated and cooled the mansion. Each was fitted with an electronic filter and a humidifier. The hot water heater held 80 gallons. "Enough for at least three teenagers," Hector said. There was a subsidiary refrigerator there that contained soft drinks and beer and a matched washer/dryer and adjoining folding table. "Long way to carry the laundry," Hector said. "Not a problem for him, though. Somebody named Maria or Consuela had to worry about that."

The rest of the rooms were small. One contained a matched set of leather luggage. "For the man who has everything," I said, "and a room to store each part of it in." A second had built-in shelving that was filled with wine glasses of various sizes and shapes.

"So far no miscellaneous storage closet," Hector said. "I'm not seeing Christmas ornaments or window screens, a set of old dishes or seasonal furniture. I guess we shouldn't have expected old concert posters or a concert tee-shirt collection. They don't sell them when they're playing Vivaldi."

"No family," I said. "This is a hypertrophied bachelor pad, not a home. And he probably spent all of his time in California. No set of winter coats and jackets here and none of the mementoes from the family home back in Massachusetts or Michigan or wherever it was. His life started and stopped here. At least that's what the basement is telling us."

The third room contained some dated computer hardware and a set of old telephones. "Maybe he was thinking about giving them away," I said, "but they sat around so long that nobody would want them now. Not that Richland seemed like the kind of guy who would make a lot of runs to Goodwill or the St. Vincent de Paul Society."

Hector commented on the absence of tools. "I wouldn't expect a lot of them," he said. "This guy wasn't a home craftsman making fancy doorstops and kids' toy chests. I guess I wouldn't expect a lot of gardening tools either. All of that was hired out. I would expect some basics, though. A small tool kit … some screwdrivers, a hammer, a flashlight … "

"Maybe it was in the cupboard with the mops and brooms. I'll take a look when we go back upstairs. I haven't seen any generator system either. If I had tens of thousands of dollars worth of wine I'd want some kind of backup system in the case of a power loss."

"One room left," Hector said, opening a door that had tight insulation around the jamb. "Empty. I was thinking a darkroom at first, but only a real hobbyist would do anything other than digital these days. This is actually a pretty good-sized room. It's wasted. If we lived here we'd have filled this room up first."

"Maybe this is the room he used to dummy up the wine bottles, assuming that he *did* do that."

"Incriminating evidence," Hector said. "Maybe that's the kind of thing you rent temporary space for, temporary space far away from where you live and work."

"Quite possibly," I said. "But you wouldn't need to clean up after that. All you'd need would be some basics—a table, a glue pot, a stack of labels, a stack of foil, a stack of tissue paper, some boxes full of bottles … "

"What do you mean 'clean up'?" Hector asked.

"Don't you smell it?" I asked.

"What's that?"

"Bleach."

"I thought that was from the washer/dryer," he said.

"Not with the seal around the door," I said. "Somebody's been sprucing up in here."

"What's to spruce up?" Hector asked. "Four walls, a cement floor, an exposed ceiling and a bare light bulb."

"But what *was* here?" I asked.

FORTY-THREE

Hector swabbed the room at various points and put each of the swabs in a separate, marked evidence case. We walked back to the large utility room and checked the materials on the folding table next to the washer/dryer: a large bottle of concentrated, liquid detergent, a small bottle of Clorox and a box of Softener sheets. The Clorox bottle was almost full. When we went back upstairs we checked the cleaning closet and found a small, canvas bag of tools at the rear, on the floor. It contained an adjustable wrench, a flashlight, a small set of Craftsman screwdrivers, a rubber hammer, claw hammer and a can of 3-in-1 oil.

We went into the garage and checked the recycling bins. The paper/cardboard bin was half-full of newspapers and cardboard cartons. The metal can bin was also half-full: lots of tomato cans and large tins of olive oil. "He was on the Mediterranean diet," Hector said. "Didn't increase his longevity." The plastic/bottle bin was empty. "Maybe he made a separate run," I said. "Somebody from the forces of truth and justice might raise an eyebrow if he found a half-dozen empty jugs of bleach there."

We checked back with Watson, thanking him for letting us have a look around. "How soon will you kick Beauchamp loose?" I asked.

"We'll hold him overnight," he said. "You want to check him out too?"

"His place of business," I said. "And his home as well." I paused a second before proceeding. I don't want to interfere with your investigation, but … "

"What is it?"

"It might not be a bad idea to keep him on suicide watch. This is a three-person company. One's dead (along with his predecessor); the second just committed suicide, it appears; Beauchamp's all that's left."

"Good idea," Watson said. "Thanks. If we find anything interesting on Beauchamp's person or in his car, we'll let you know. I've got Richland's phone and computer also. We'll let you know what's there, if anything."

I sent the uniforms ahead, dispatching one team to watch the storage facility in Irvine. "The moment anybody appears, call me," I said. "Follow them in and don't let anyone touch anything."

Then I called Chris, briefed him on what we'd found, and told him that we'd check on Beauchamp's property and the storage facility next. I asked him to have someone check on Beauchamp's home address; we could stop there first before going to the FirstGrowth building.

Beauchamp's condo was in Newport Beach—a modest two-bedroom that would have been a steal at 1.2-1.5M. It was all surface—travertine, cherry, stainless steel, granite and glass—with views of the water and the beautiful people sailing there.

His favorite color was black. He had black silk shirts, black wool coats and slacks, black cotton underwear, black rayon leisure shirts, even some black handkerchiefs. "So 90's," Hector said.

"I wonder what happened to that lawyer's shirt that he was wearing when we first talked to him," I said. "Maybe it's at the cleaner's." The furniture was mostly black leather, though there was a single white leather chair. "Affirmative action," Hector said.

No wine. A lot of expensive scotch from islands like Islay, Jura, and Mull. Some Absolut, some Tanqueray Gin, some single cask bourbon, B&B, Drambuie, Cointreau, some exotic tequila.

No weapons. "Odd for somebody in security," I said. "Maybe they're kept somewhere else."

"An armory," Hector said. "He doesn't want to scare off his dates."

"Another bachelor's pad," I said. "These guys worked and they played. No pets. No paintings, photographs, or mementoes of any kind that would link them with a family--nuclear or otherwise."

"No history," Hector said. "They lived (and probably sinned) in the present. You go to my relatives' houses ... you see the whole genealogy on the walls. There's no room on any of the tables; they're covered with photographs. Baptisms ... first communions ... confirmations ... weddings ... family dinners ... they're all there. The houses are museums ... shrines. Not like this. This is a playpen."

"Not that there's anything illegal about that," I said. "There's no *wealth* either. No expensive jewelry. No antique furniture or Persian carpets. No sterling silver or crystal glassware. No rare clocks or crystal decanters. No keepsakes. I didn't expect afghans, samplers or crocheted doilies, but there might have been something more manly: pictures from a fishing trip, sports memorabilia or some knockaround tennis shoes."

We checked out his storage bin in the basement. It was empty. "And no tools," Hector said. "What's up with that? I figure the condo fees are exorbitant, enough to cover the visits from a plumber or handyman, but every man I know has tools, even if they're just for ... what ... reassurance?"

"These guys each traveled light, even if they had fancy digs. No roots. No pasts. No obvious plans for the future."

"Maybe they had pasts they wanted to forget," Hector said, "or pasts they wanted us to overlook. The bulk of their ill-gotten gains are probably in the Caymans. This may be little more than a movie set or sound stage."

"Dave Hendrix is checking them out," I said. "We'll see what he turns."

Each of the occupants of Beauchamp's condo had an assigned parking space in a gated, underground garage. "No oil stain," Hector said. "At first I was curious. Then I became suspicious. Now I'm mystified. This guy … he's inside my head … "

"Probably hoping you don't get inside his."

FORTY-FOUR

We needed a locksmith to help us gain access to the FirstGrowth storage facility. "Better that than foot the bill for damages," Chris had said. We also needed to touch base with the company's security provider and the local police, so that they would ignore the bells, buzzers, whistles and flashing lights on their monitor boards when we went in.

I told the locksmith that the facility was a set of Chinese boxes, that he'd need to open the exterior door, all the interior doors, the cage surrounding the *chai* and anything else with a lock on it. "Not a problem," he said. "If it's made by man we can open it."

I searched Beauchamp's office; it was as empty as his house. There was a six-pack of bottled water in a miniature refrigerator, a drawer with paperclips, spare staples, a highlighter, two ballpoints and some No. 2 pencils. I handed off the computer (a laptop, surprisingly) to one of the uniforms. "We'll take that with us," I said.

Hector returned a few minutes later. "I'm the suspicious type," he said, "so I checked the tanks of the toilets, the paper towel *and* the soap dispensers. Nothing. I also checked the cupboard in the hallway. Just a rack for coats, a shelf for hats and a collection of cleaning supplies. I *did* find some tools, however, but there was nothing out of the ordinary. Standard, generic, you-see-one-you've-seen-them-all office stuff."

"At least they had some tools," I said.

Ten minutes later Hector said, "I'm starting to feel weird, checking underneath tables and chairs. I'd feel better if I at least found some chewing gum there. This place has been swept clean. And I didn't smell any bleach."

"The action's in the *chai*," I said, "if there *is* any. My guess is that if they were doing anything illegitimate on a significant scale they did it someplace else, someplace very private. Here they could have visitors. Not many, but … still … several sets of prying eyes beyond ours … this is the showroom, not the workroom. Remember how proud Beauchamp was of it? You could see the glimmer in his eyes. He was *moved* or at least he wanted us to think that he was. He wanted to show it off. If he showed it off to us he probably showed it off to others. Told them about the security system, told them that he designed it all himself. Some of the clients would have wanted to see it, particularly if FirstGrowth was marketing it as their principal comparative advantage."

There was half as much wine in the chai as there was during our previous tour. "Either somebody just made a delivery or somebody wanted to sequester something," Hector said.

"Let's take a closer look," I said. We inspected several cases of wine at random. They all looked legitimate. I lifted some prints from several of the larger bottles—ones not wrapped in tissue—but they appeared to match. "Pudgy," I said. "My money's on Beauchamp."

We checked out the nooks and crannies with a flashlight, but didn't find anything beyond a little dust. "Again … I don't smell any bleach," Hector said. "All I smell is the wood from the pine wine cases. And maybe just a splash of insecticide or strong detergent."

An hour later one of the uniforms returned with a police dog, a dark German Shepherd female. "I don't know if she'll smell anything, Lieutenant, but it's nice to give them a little work from time to time. They enjoy it. They want to be here with us, feel like cops." His name was Bradford; her name was Sophie.

"Come on, girl," he said. "If it's here you'll find it. Check it out."

Her nostrils flared and she went to work, smelling everything, including Officer Bradford's shoes. "I'm innocent," he said. "Keep checking."

Twenty minutes later she had finished sniffing the perimeter of the room and was concentrating on the shelving and the wine cases. Suddenly she stopped, got up on her hind legs and braced her front paws against one of the middle shelves. Then she started barking loudly.

"Good girl," Bradford said, "good girl."

"What is it? Hector asked.

"Drugs," I said. "She's not trained to smell Cabernet Sauvignon."

"Game on," Hector answered, walking toward the box that had piqued Sophie's interest.

FORTY-FIVE

We each put on fresh rubber gloves and opened the lid of the box. Sophie was in between us, sniffing feverishly and continuing to bark. There were bottles of wine inside, each wrapped in tissue. I removed them carefully and put them on a shelf eight feet away. At first she started to follow me but then lost interest immediately. As I returned to the box, she was already there, fixated, sniffing and barking, even though the box was now empty.

"I'm not seeing eight kilos of blow," Hector said. "I don't even see any major powder residue."

"So what are we thinking," I asked, "that they were transporting drugs along with the wine, that Terry Randall found out and was murdered?"

"Maybe," Hector said.

"With this little residue there could have been some transfer from the hands of whoever packed it, or from whoever unloaded it, but that would mean that the boxes were reused, which doesn't seem plausible. Whoever unloaded it would have kept it."

"I'm thinking about cost ... " Hector said. "Cocaine's more expensive than wine, but it's come down in price lately. The recent bust near San Diego State ... "

"Yes?"

"They were selling half-ounces for as little as $400. That's about 14 grams. Admittedly, it had been seriously cut, but what is that, 25, 30 bucks a gram? In the 80's a gram of coke would run you somewhere between

100 and 125 dollars. The price has really plummeted. If you inflated the cost from the 1980's you'd expect to see a gram run somewhere between 250 and 300 dollars today. It doesn't."

"It's still illegal and it's still being sold," I said. "A person who buys wine for $700 a bottle might buy by the kilo. Still, I see your point. The illegality is key. If you're selling old master paintings or diamonds or rhodium or whatever, you can do so across the counter. There are no coke stores, at least not yet."

"But if you're selling stolen paintings, stolen diamonds or stolen rhodium … " Hector said, "it can make a huge difference. There for awhile a kilo of rhodium was worth about 400K. The value fluctuates, just like with coke. With diamonds now … the cartel destroys a lot of them just to keep the price high. You could put a lot of diamonds in and around a dozen bottles of wine. And if the wine was phony to begin with … "

"Right," I said. "We've got to figure out what he was selling. It's like the old joke about the smuggler taking things across the border in wheelbarrows. Eventually they figure out that what he's actually smuggling is wheelbarrows. Let's first take this box to the lab and check it out. In the meantime," I said, turning to Bradford, "let's let Sophie keep doing her thing. Maybe she'll come up with another hit for us."

She didn't, but the lab confirmed that the dust residue in the box was cocaine, nearly 90% pure. "Two bucks a gram in Colombia," the lab tech said. "About 350x that in New Zealand. It's all about supply and demand, proximity to the source and the degree of purity. It's also about the reputation of the seller. In a one-off buy you could get ripped off royally. If you're a steady customer on the other hand, you'll want assurances of quality control."

"Tell me about that Italian baby laxative," Hector said. "Does it give you the runs along with the coke high?"

"Why do you think they call it laxative?" the lab tech answered. "Of course, if you're only doing a teeny bit of it, you'd be OK. Are you having a problem, Detective?"

Hector laughed. "Young man, on my diet, you'd ... wait, I'm not going to go there."

"Just as well," the tech said. "Anyway, Lieutenant, what you've got here is some very high quality product. This is distribution center quality, not street quality. A person who would buy this (assuming it's not for personal use) would expect to see the product diluted several times before it reached the final user. The only problem is ... "

"What's that?" I asked.

"Well, the problem is that a box like this ... it's empty. It's like you found the barn where the thoroughbreds were all staying, but they're all gone now. It's all about the quantity, Lieutenant. It's about the intent to distribute. The quality here is high, but the quantity undercuts your case. Unless there's more where this came from ... "

"I take your point," I said.

Hector and I left the lab. "There's another possibility," I said.

"What are you thinking?" Hector asked.

"Somebody may have salted the mine."

"You mean dropped in a little dust to implicate someone else ... maybe Beauchamp?"

"Possibly. Think about it. Richland and Beauchamp may have been playing Spy vs. Spy. This could have been a little insurance policy, in case the one wanted to take the other off of the field."

"So much money at stake ... things get tempting. Each of them figures, why split the profit when I could have it all?"

"It's a thought," I said. "Anyway, the only one left at this point is Beauchamp. Check that. The only one left *that we know of* is Beauchamp."

As we walked toward my office Dave Hendrix met us in the hallway. He greeted us briefly and then said, "That Richland guy, Lieutenant ... the one you wanted me to check on ... I've got something."

FORTY-SIX

"What have you got, Dave?"

We were sitting in the evidence room. Dave Hendrix had a computer station near the caged window, so he could work there and still be available if someone needed to talk to him or request evidence.

"I've been trying to track him down for you," he said, "whenever I had some time. I've turned a couple of things that I think you'll find interesting."

"Go ahead, Dave," I said. He was obviously proud of what he had found and wanted to take a second to enjoy the moment.

"Well, first off, his name wasn't Richland. I mean, it *was*, for awhile, but he *changed it* to *Richland*. His actual name was Richmond. It's the long arm of the government, Lieutenant. We can always find you because there's one thing you always have to do if you want to operate a business … "

"Pay taxes," Hector said.

"And social security," Hendrix added. "And for that you need a number. And William Richland's number was also William Richmond's number. He had to keep those records in order. And he did. And now he's not going to be collecting any monthly payments, but he's helped us find out who he really was."

"That's great, Dave," I said. "When and where did he change his name?"

"In Fairfax, Virginia," Hendrix said. "Five years ago."

"And he did it all legally?"

"Oh yes," Hendrix said. "Some people just start using a different name and eventually it catches on. That's called 'common usage'. Usually people are making a minor change. For years they were *Katharine*; suddenly they want to be called *Kate*. Or Kat or Katie or Kathy or Katya or whatever … people use the more formal court process when they want to make a more significant change. Somebody named Larry has a sex-change operation and wants to become Lorraine. Some people change their names when they get married. Some do it when they get divorced. Some have been tagged with weird names. A boy named Sue wants to become a man named Sam, for example. Some people are reconnecting with their pasts. The Moscowitzes came through Ellis Island and became the Moscoves. A couple generations later, when they've become the Mosses, one of the kids decides that he wants to become a Moscowitz again.

"There are rules, of course. You can't change your name to avoid paying your debts, for example. You can't infringe on somebody else's trademark. For example, you can't change your name to *Trader Joe* and then set up your own grocery store. And you can't change your name to *Arnold Schwarzenegger* in hopes of getting some acting gigs or better tables at upscale restaurants. You can't use violent words and words involving racial slurs. You can't use numbers or symbols, call yourself '911' or 1000%. You *can* add Roman numerals behind your name. I could be David Hendrix XII, for example. Porn stars sometimes have weird names, but those are considered 'stage names'; they're treated like nicknames.

"When you come up with your new name of choice it has to be approved by a judge. If everything's kosher and non-threatening it's pretty much a formality. You file your papers and you pay your fee. If you want to change your name to something a little more 'out there' the judge has to decide whether or not to approve it."

"But you can't get into the specific court records on this case over the internet."

"No, you'd have to talk directly to the people in Virginia."

"The change seems innocuous enough," I said. "He was going nationwide; instead of being associated with a town in Virginia he was going to be an all-American. Rich*land*."

"At least six feet by three feet plus however-long-his-casket-is of it," Hector said.

"Anything else, Dave?"

"Yes, as a matter of fact. Prior to the time at which he changed his name … there was an arrest in Virginia."

"Conviction?"

"No."

"For what?"

"Fraud."

"Very interesting. Anything else?"

"Not yet, but I'm still working on it."

"Keep us posted," I said. "And thanks."

"You're very welcome," he said.

Five minutes later I was in Chris's office. Ten minutes after that I was booked on a flight to Dulles in the morning.

FORTY-SEVEN

Cary Watson called early the next day; we hadn't even had our coffee yet. There was nothing of interest on Richland's computer, but Beauchamp was demanding the opportunity to have access to it. He said that he wanted to try to keep the business alive, but he couldn't do that without having Richland's list of contacts. Actually, as Lieutenant Watson explained, there was no list of contacts. There was only a list of clients (which squared with the list that Richland/Richmond had sent to me), no list of the collectors, vendors or speculators who sold the wine to him before he sold it to his clients.

"How plausible does he sound?" I asked, testing Watson's bullshit alarm.

"Not very, at least not to me," he answered. "It's *what he'd say*, right? Suddenly he's the victim and we're the bastards, keeping him from pursuing his livelihood. We pressed him on why he was trying to get in to see Richland. He had a couple different versions of the story. At first he said he had to touch base with him about some business issues. A couple hours later he said that somebody had come to the company's storage facility and wanted to buy some wine. He said he couldn't sell it without Richland's OK, because he didn't know what Richland had promised to other clients. There was a lot of money involved, he said, and he wanted to clinch the deal, but he had to talk to Richland first. The story got more urgent every time he told it. The one thing on which he was consistent was his claim that when he got to La Jolla he had forgotten the code to open Richland's gate."

"Maybe Richland changed the code," I said. "Maybe things weren't so copacetic between the two of them."

"We like that possibility too," Watson said. "There *is* a problem, however. We make the time of death at least six hours before Beauchamp got there. Maybe even seven or eight. Bottom line: we don't think Beauchamp forced him to take the pills. From all that we can see there was something fishy between them, but we don't like Beauchamp for the actual murder, assuming it was a murder and not a simple suicide."

"And he wouldn't have obscured the time of death by putting him in a refrigerated space back at the storage facility," I said. "That'd be too convoluted and too difficult logistically. Plus, you've got to figure he *was* unable to get into Richland's house. Otherwise, why expose himself like that on the street? Especially in a neighborhood where burglars might find interesting pickings and the neighbors are more jumpy than most."

"Exactly," Watson said. "If it was a murder and not a suicide we're figuring there was some third party involved. If so, however, the person was a pro. The only fingerprints in the house were Richland's and his maid's—a very nice woman, by the way, though her green card looks more than a little suspicious. We talked to her at length. She hadn't been in the house for five days and she had an alibi for the full night of Richland's death."

"Did she have the code to get through Richland's gate?"

"Nope. He always let her in when she came to work."

"How about his cellphone? You said, that you had it, right?"

"Yes, but there was nothing on it except some innocuous stuff—Richland liked to check the weather all the time. I don't know why; it never changes that much in La Jolla. He also had some calls to restaurants, probably to make reservations or order carry-out. We're checking on that and will get back to you if we turn anything. What's interesting about the cellphone is that it was so uninteresting. No calls to clients, for example. We figure he used a throwaway for his business dealings and that the one we found was just there to generate smoke."

Watson had been very forthcoming with me. I told him about Richland's change of name and about his arrest for fraud. I also told him that I was going to Virginia to check on the details. He thanked me and promised to stay in touch, asking me to do the same.

With the stop in Dallas and the time difference between the coasts I didn't arrive at Dulles until 6:30 that evening. The hotel was off of route 50, near the Fair Oaks Shopping Center, a short distance from downtown Fairfax, assuming you weren't killed en route by a commuter hurtling out of Washington toward Manassas or Front Royal on **66**. Even by California standards the traffic was fast and heavy, the principal difference being the number of trucks scattered among the sedans, vans and SUV's.

That night I had a light dinner at a chain restaurant and drove into Fairfax, checking on the parking for the Circuit Court facilities on Chain Bridge Road. Then I returned to the Hilton Garden Inn, checked my email, set the alarm on my cellphone and thought about William Richland, né Richmond.

FORTY-EIGHT

The clerk was helpful; my lieutenant's shield was helpful; the fact that we had called ahead and warned them that I was coming was helpful and the file was as helpful as I might have expected. There was even a written document which Richmond's attorney had filed as part of the name change process. Basically, it argued that Mr. Richmond had been accused of a crime which he had not committed, a crime for which he was neither indicted nor convicted. However, the fact that he had been accused of the crime had created a great hardship for him in seeking new employment. Mr. Richmond (the attorney continued) had held a series of significant positions and hoped to compete for positions of increased responsibility, but this blemish on his record (an unfair, unfounded, undeserved blemish) was precluding him from receiving offers of such positions.

The attorney acknowledged that names could not be changed for criminal purposes, but argued that Mr. Richmond's name should be changed so that he was no longer discriminated against on unfair grounds. He was *being considered a criminal* when, in law and in fact, he was not. The name change would be modest and the good that would be done by it would be considerable, advancing the career of an upstanding citizen and taxpayer. I could almost hear voiceovers from a bit-part actor reading passages from a Horatio Alger novel.

So Rich*mond* would become Rich*land* and no one in the future would be tempted to believe that the presence of smoke inferred the presence of fire, that a person arrested for fraud might actually have been guilty of fraud and, as a result, discriminate against him. In the eyes of the law, a man arrested for fraud should now be seen as what he actually *was*--a victim, throwing himself on the mercy of a reasonable, righteous, liberty-loving-and-protecting judge.

The judge (one Willis Hudson) approved the request and William Richmond duly became William Richland. The hearing appeared to have been little more than a formality. More to the point, there was nothing further in the court documents concerning the **arrest**, so I returned the file, thanked the clerk and found a coffee shop with wi-fi where I woke up my laptop.

The arrest had actually been reported in the *Washingtonian* magazine, two years before the name-change action. The account was part of a larger story on land development in Arlington, Fairfax, Loudoun and Prince William Counties. As the population of the D.C. area multiplied and the land available for development shrank, individuals turned to edgy strategies for capitalizing upon the supply/demand crunch.

Since the Richmond story was little more than a sidebar in a long report, it was short on details. Richmond had been trying to put together the funding for a fly-by-night deal and he had been less than fully forthcoming with his co-investors. First he secured their trust, then he secured their money. The uses to which the money would be put were a little cloudy, but the blue-sky talk about profits beyond the dreams of avarice came through loudly and clearly.

Essentially, Richmond was putting together a down payment on 7/8ths of an acre of land within five minutes of Tysons Corner, a parcel worth a little more than a million that had stumbled onto the market for an asking price of a little over 700 thousand. Two of the investors had been happy with the result of the eventual flip, but the third had cried foul, expecting a larger return on his money. He charged fraud and made a lot of calls to people who made a lot of other calls. The forces of justice eventually decided that the investor was more guilty of greed than Richmond was of fraud. Richmond might not be the sort of person you'd want to sit next to at a family reunion, but his efforts did not merit an extended stay in government housing with more serious criminals.

My own take was that while Richmond was probably not guilty of a felony he was also something less than the paragon of integrity, business acumen and good breeding that he was projecting in his role at FirstGrowth. Call me a traditionalist, but my father was a traditionalist and so was my grandfather. One of their strongest beliefs was that a man who will cheat in small things will cheat in big things. The Tysons land deal may have been more a matter of hedging and exaggerating and obfuscating rather than cheating, but it was enough to get him into *Washingtonian* magazine, an enterprise with libel lawyers who would have checked out the story and, quite possibly, toned it down from the original version, a version that might have had more point and bite with regard to the actual facts.

I decided to make a few more stops before I returned to Laguna. I began by calling the office of Richmond/Richland's lawyer and asked his secretary if I could see him today. She got my professional details, put me on hold and then returned after a minute and a half.

"He's fully booked this morning and afternoon, but he could see you for lunch if that would be convenient."

"That would be fine," I said. "Where should I meet him?"

"He has an appointment in McLean at 1:30. You'll have the most time together if you eat there." She gave me the name of the restaurant, a little place on Chain Bridge Road. She also gave me directions. "It's very easy to become confused," she said, "because everyone wants to be on Chain Bridge Road. It ... meanders ... and sometimes it's called Dolly Madison Boulevard, sometimes route 123."

The restaurant was little more than a storefront in a strip mall near Old Dominion Drive, but the food was French and there were quiet corners in which to talk, plot and plan. The lawyer's name was McCartland. Dudley McCartland. He had an expensive haircut, another one of those hand-tailored shirts with a solid-colored collar and cuffs but stripes down the front, a heavy gold watch, Italian silk tie and knotted cufflinks that matched the color of the stripes in the shirt.

We introduced ourselves; he had a firm handshake and mint-scented breath. "The service can be a little slow here," he said, "but everything's fresh and made to order." He ordered a salad and broiled fish; I asked for a cup of soup and a small steak sautéed with pepper.

"Now," he said, "you want to talk about one of my clients."

"Yes," I said. "William Richmond. You helped him change his name to *Richland*. He just turned up dead. Apparent suicide."

"But you have doubts?"

"We really don't know," I said. "We know that his body was filled with an overdose of prescription medication … "

"But you don't know why."

"We're still investigating."

"Well, there's not much that I can tell you. He was not a long-term client. There was no retainer; it was a one-off deal."

"No offense, but … a hired-gun deal."

"Exactly. That's what I would call it too, Lieutenant. He wanted representation … just to be sure. Name changes are no big event unless you're trying to pull something slippery. Judges figure that out very quickly. He probably hired me because … well … this is Washington and … "

"Yes … ?"

"There are six million people in the area, Lieutenant, give or take. It's still a small town and a town that's very … *person-specific*. It's a town full of lobbyists and power brokers, some who are in, some who are temporarily out. They all know one another and it raises their comfort level when they have the opportunity to work together … "

"You're a prominent lawyer. Seeing you sitting next to Mr. Richmond was reassuring all around. It … oiled the wheels of justice."

"Yes. *Greased the skids* may be closer," he said. "Some places … you are what you wear. Other places … maybe where you come from … you are what you drive. Here, everybody dresses more or less the same. They *are* ... who their lawyers are."

"Do you mind my asking your fee for representing him in such an action?"

"I billed $575 an hour then," he said. "but in this case I had to do up a document for the judge ... we had a preliminary meeting ... lunch after the hearing ... I'd have to check my records, but I probably billed somewhere around $5,000."

"I'm sure you're worth it," I said, "but it seems like a lot of money ... "

"It *is* a lot of money, Lieutenant, but, like I said, when you want to be sure ... "

"The name change was important to him."

"Apparently, yes."

We passed on the desserts, but had some coffee.

"Did he ever talk to you about his arrest for fraud?" I asked.

"Yes," McArtland said. "That was the reason he wanted his name changed. Whenever he proposed a deal or applied for a job people would google his name and the screen would light up."

"Did he talk about the case specifically?"

"Yes, we had to discuss it. I didn't want to get blindsided in court."

"Did you think there was any substance to it?"

"No. Cases like that are a dime a dozen, Lieutenant. This is ground zero for lawyers. Hell, this *country* is run by lawyers. The Soviet Union was run by engineers; that didn't work very well either. People sue here over everything. The architecture's quaint. You see all those Palladian windows, all those brick walkways, pineapple sculptures, restaurants with pictures of fox hunts on the walls and brass candelabras hanging from the ceilings ... you'd almost think you were in Colonial Williamsburg. Not so, Lieutenant. You're in a shark tank governed by regulatory agencies. They'll bite you too."

"The story I read suggested that the investor who went to the police was disappointed because he didn't make more on the deal."

"Sure. He wanted more ... figured he'd threaten Richmond, that Richmond would cave and the investor'd take back a larger chunk of the pie from him in an out-of-court settlement. He didn't think Richmond would stand up to him. Still raises a question though, doesn't it, Lieutenant?"

"Why would Richmond do business with somebody like that in the first place?"

"Exactly. Unfortunately, the answer may be that that's the only kind that was available. They're thick on the ground here, Lieutenant."

We each paid for our own lunch. "More comfortable that way," McCartland said. "People around here are always looking for ... behavioral irregularities."

"High crimes and misdemeanors," I said.

"You wouldn't think sharks would hold grudges," he said. "They're just eating machines after all, but around here ... well ... we have some exotic species."

FORTY-NINE

I had a final stop to make, but sitting in the parking lot in my rental car, watching McCartland drive off to his 1:30 appointment, I thought about Richmond/Richland and what had happened to Terry and Susan Randall. Killing with a shotgun is a messy way of dispatching someone. There is a rage and a violence attached to it … a level of brutality … which I had difficulty associating with a person like Richmond. A man who would kill himself with nerve pills is not the sort of man who would blow apart his victims with a 12 gauge shotgun. If he didn't have the courage to put a pistol under his chin or into his mouth or the affection for tradition that would have placed him in a warm bathtub with razor blades in the soap tray, he was unlikely to stare into peoples' eyes and dismember them with a scattershot firearm.

Beauchamp maybe, but not *Richmond*, as I was beginning to think of him. He was *sales and marketing*, not *security*. Beauchamp may have been the evil servant, the extension of the master who did his bidding and kept the blood far from his door. Richmond was the guy with the clean fingernails and the friendly smile, the accountant with the private client list. He wasn't the enforcer. When he was ready to check out he did it the way he lived—softly.

Beauchamp I wasn't so sure of. Who was he? What did he know? What was driving him besides greed? Why was he pounding at the gates of Richmond's castle, begging to be let in from the cold? And if Richmond had his own dark places, why had he not shared them with his underling? What *was* their relationship and how did Terry Randall,

Susan Randall and Jimmy Davidson find their way into the killing room which someone was operating?

I made a series of notes to myself—nothing definitive, nothing even grounded in particular fact or a clear chain of evidence. Just notes. Thoughts. Questions that were still unanswered. In the meantime there was something else I had intended to do. I drove to a coffeeshop on Old Dominion Drive, got a 12 ounce cup and went to work on my laptop.

Richmond's home at the time of his change-of-name action was in McLean. I mapquested the address; it was just off route 193, the Georgetown Pike, the long road that snaked above the edge of the Potomac, from McLean through Great Falls to the edge of Loudoun County. Richmond didn't live far from Chain Bridge Road/route 123 (there called Dolley Madison Boulevard). His street was called Turkey Run Lane and it was surprisingly close to the CIA, though there was no reason to believe that there was any connection between a triple-A league grifter like Richmond and the Company.

I checked the local ads for wine stores and the reviews which those stores got from area consumers. One jumped out: *MacArthur Beverages* on MacArthur Boulevard in the District. MacArthur was also called *Bassin's*, the founding owner being a man named Addy Bassin. With *Calvert Woodley Wines and Spirits*, on Connecticut Avenue, *Bassin's* ruled the local wine trade. More to the point, *Bassin's* was on the major migration route from the Palisades section of the District to the sumptuous suburbs of Northern Virginia; its site was about a mile from Arizona Avenue, which led to Canal Road, which led to the Chain Bridge, which took the tired and by-now thirsty commuter into the upscale neighborhoods of North Arlington, McLean and Great Falls. On a lucky day with light traffic, if there ever was such a thing, *MacArthur Beverages* was a tad more than twelve to fifteen minutes from William Richmond's front door.

When I got there the store was packed with people, with dusty wine racks, with beer fridges and high liquor shelves. Business was brisk, voices were loud, package goods were being bagged and wine was being purchased in quantity, with cardboard cartons at the edge of each register for customers buying by the case. There were northeast and mid-Atlantic accents but the ethos of a Middle East bazaar. Questions and answers were shouted across the floor. Wine snobs investigated the labels of individual bottles; amateurs sought advice from the sales staff. Occasionally an interloper made his way to the refrigerated cases to grab a six-pack of domestic beer.

There was a sign on the wall that designated the wine *consultants*, which is to say, the sales staff, all of whom seemed expert at what they did. I heard one commenting to a customer that he hadn't tasted a particular wine since its release a few years earlier, but that the château in question had enjoyed an increase in reputation with the acquisition of their new winemaker and that the tannin level of the wine upon release was such that it should be 'rounding out' nicely by now. Of course, the consultant added, that particular wine was known for its backbone more than its nose and finish and that its long suit was its ability to 'stand up' to food rather than fade into the background. When the customer asked how that vintage would compare with that of a previous year (2008) with which he was familiar, the consultant answered that 2008 was an average year at best, that many would describe it as somewhere between undistinguished and poor, depending on the growing region, the microclimate and the château. "I, myself found the 2008 of that wine pleasant enough, but far less interesting than the vintage you're considering."

They went back and forth like that for several minutes. When they were finished and the customer had made his selection (something else entirely) I approached the *consultant*. His name tag read **Tim Kelly**. I showed him my shield and then I showed him the picture I had printed from the story on Richmond in the *Register*.

"He doesn't look familiar," he said. "Is he one of our customers?"

"That's what I'm trying to determine," I said. "He lived in the area a few years ago."

"Well, *Bassin's* has been here since 1957 and I've been here since

1988. He doesn't look familiar to me. That doesn't mean he didn't shop here. We get a lot of customers, as you can see. Just a second … "

He walked to the back of the store, looked around, walked to the other side of the store, looked around, and then opened a door at the rear of the store and disappeared for a second. A short time later he reappeared with another man, one slightly older. The two of them approached me. The older man's name tag read **Don Allen**. "Don's been here a little longer than I have," Kelly said. "Maybe he'll recognize the person you're interested in."

I showed him the picture. "Bill Richmond," he said immediately. "This is a little more recent than when I knew him. He's put on some weight. I guess we all have."

"He was a customer?" I asked.

"Actually, no. What I mean is, that's not how I knew him. He was a student in one of my wine classes. I used to do these tasting courses. Sort of like *Wine 101*. I'd do an 8-week introductory course and then what we called the 12-week master class. You really didn't come out a master or anything like that, but you learned something about wines, about the principal growing regions and the principal varietals."

"And he enrolled in one of your classes."

"Two, actually. He stood out a little because of his age. I had a lot of MBA-types … you know, from the local Business schools. I think they figured that knowing something about wine would impress their bosses and their clients. I'd also get a lot of older people, people looking for a hobby, people with a little time on their hands. Bill was somewhere in between."

"Was he a good student?"

"He took a lot of notes," Allen said. "He always had questions about terminology, I guess you'd say wine *lore*. I think he wanted to be an instant expert. It's a big problem, of course … "

"What's that?" I asked.

"The lingo. Wine is food after all. It's expensive sometimes, but it's basically fermented grape juice. I'm into it and I think it's important to be an educated consumer, but the language is sometimes an impediment. People want to sound knowledgeable but they end up just sounding pretentious. It's off-putting. Here at *Bassin's* we're not about creating cults and wine snobs who want to impress their neighbors and intimidate their assistants. We just try to give clear, helpful information on a complex subject."

"What you're saying is that Richmond was trying to be able to pass himself off as somebody who knew much more than he actually did."

"I don't want to be judgmental," Allen said. "Besides ... he was a student of mine ... "

"William Richmond is dead," I said. "I'm investigating his death."

"Really?" Allen said. "I had no idea ... "

"He was running a wine business, selling top wines to high end consumers and speculators."

"Bill Richmond?"

"Yes," I said.

"That's really interesting."

"In what way?" I asked.

"In the sense that ... I don't think Bill Richmond even liked wine. When we'd taste it ... well, some people would always drink it all, no matter whether it was good wine, average wine or plonk ... you know, garbage ... crap. They'd have trouble spitting it out or dumping the remainder from the tasting glass. Bill was different. He would taste it, but it was always as if his doing so was purely for educational purposes. Like back in my high school Chemistry class ... we had this teacher who was sort of ... flamboyant, I'd guess you'd say. When we studied substances, something like acids for example, he'd come around the room with a beaker and a stir rod and ask us to taste it. It was all showmanship. People were freaking out, thinking, '*Acid!* Omigod, if I try to taste that my tongue will burn up and fumes will come out of my mouth.' It didn't happen, of course. There's a lot of acid in soft drinks ... anyway, Bill

Richmond would taste the wine the way that some of my classmates would taste the acid."

"So he never bought any of it from you."

"Oh, he'd come into the store," Allen said, "but he'd never buy wine. He always bought Scotch."

FIFTY

I had some remaining time and decided to check Richmond's tax records. I was hoping to find a former employer or place of business that might shed some light on his actions at FirstGrowth, but he consistently listed his position as 'self-employed'. The *Washingtonian* story had referred to him as a consultant/entrepreneur, but that characterization covered a significant portion of the D.C. demographic. His tax records *did* record significant income in the mid six figures from a client list of private companies and government agencies whose acronyms spanned the alphabet and rivaled a beltway bandit's files for obscurantism, opaqueness and the judicious use of euphemism. A Catskill comic would have said that he was a *schlepper* who became a *macher*, but never quite made it to being a *mensch*.

The next morning I checked out of the Hilton, drove to Dulles, dropped off my rental car, took one of the remaining 'mobile lounges' to the D Concourse and called Chris Dietrich. It was still early in Laguna. He had just gotten to his office and I could hear him sip his coffee between sentences. I brought him up to date on what I had learned.

"Interesting," he said. "Your notion about a guy who drops pills not being able to use a shotgun makes sense to me. The more we learn the more he comes across as a glorified con artist. Con men don't like violence. A gun or a knife isn't one of their props. It hurts their image … disrupts their act."

"Security guys on the other hand … " I said.

"Yes. From what you've told me about him, I can see Beauchamp as the enforcer. He would have been the guy to take out Davidson and Randall. And Randall's wife for that matter. That would have been his gig. Richland or Richmond would have brought in the business, maintained the cash flow, dreamed up the scams, while Beauchamp would have been the muscle."

"But that still doesn't explain how or why Richmond was killed," I said. "If Beauchamp wanted Richmond to disappear and he wanted it to look as if Richmond had killed himself, the last thing he would have wanted was to be seen on the street in front of Richmond's house at the time of his death, trying to jimmy the electronic system on his gate and jumping up and down, threatening to hold his breath."

"I agree," Chris said. "Either Richmond did himself in or somebody else helped the process along. Of course, the person didn't have to actually be inside the house. He could have let him know that something much worse than a bottle of pills was in his future. The problem is that there's nothing in the phone records of any interest at that time and there's no evidence that someone else was in the house that night."

"They still haven't found his real cellphone?"

"No, unfortunately. Of course, he could have gotten a call a few days earlier, then disposed of the phone. It's also possible that someone was in his house that night, somebody he was comfortable enough with to let in. Then things went south ... if so, the guy was a pro. He didn't leave any marks on the body and he didn't leave any prints in the house. Maybe he came in wearing plastic baggies on his shoes; does that sound too much like the movies?"

"I don't know, Chief," I said. "If I was expecting a social call and a guy showed up dressed in a way to hide his identity and protect himself from blood splatter ... that would get my attention ... "

"We're grasping," Chris said. "One thing I *would* like to know—what was Beauchamp doing there? What was so urgent? Why did he need to get into that house?"

"It's altogether possible that he didn't know that Richmond was dead," I said. "If Beauchamp was the muscle and nothing more, then there could have been somebody else, maybe a group of people involved."

"The money people, maybe," Chris said, "the people who funded the scam … maybe they didn't like the direction that things were going. They had agreed to a huge investment. That storage facility is like a Hollywood set, but maybe it would be worth it … and for awhile it was. Everything was copacetic; the money was flowing like the Nile … suddenly there's a shit storm; the frogs are falling from the sky; bodies are turning up in the desert and the landfills. They didn't want the attention … decided to cut their losses. Beauchamp and Richmond were nothing more than the hired help."

"And not up to the job," I added.

"It's a possibility," he said. "What's next?"

"I think we bring in some experts to check out their wine *chai*, see what's what. If we turn anything we use it to sweat Beauchamp. We've already got the cocaine residue. Let's see what else we can find."

"The dog couldn't find anything else, but the dog wouldn't be able to tell the difference between Château Margaux and Château Rotgut."

"Pity I can't bring the guys from Washington I was talking to yesterday. You ask them about a specific wine and they can tell you what the weather was like the day that they harvested the grapes and whether or not anybody had been picking up the grape leaves that had fallen on the ground beneath the vines."

"We've got guys like that in our neighborhood," Chris said. "We're talking serious decadence here. We're talking real self-indulgence. We're talking big money, big appetites, rarefied tastes and brand-name commodities. This is ground zero for that, Tom. Out here … we've got the A Team."

"If you've got a big gun, shoot it," I said.

"I'll make some calls," Chris said. "Meanwhile, travel safely. I'll see you this afternoon."

FIFTY-ONE

I briefed Hector on what I had learned, talked to Chris about the list of local wine experts he had compiled, agreed with him on a small panel and worked my way through some accumulated correspondence and phone messages, 80% of which were from the press.

The next day we met with our group of consultants, thanked them for their willingness to help us and introduced them to one another. "This is Clarence Woodson," Chris said. "Mr. Woodson directs the *Lycée*, a private secondary school in Ojai."

"Thank you, Chief Dietrich," he said. "As the Chief noted, I direct an independent school in Ojai. The school was established by my grandfather. I have directed it for the last fourteen years. My own training is in Greek history and civilization. Regrettably, I am unable to teach as frequently as I once did. I became interested in wine many years ago when I read Greats at Pembroke. The college cellar was rather distinguished. Not quite like All Souls, of course, but one does what one can. I have continued my interest over the years and am happy to be of help today."

"This is Robert Warling," Chris said. "Mr. Warling is a businessman in Glendale."

"Thanks, Chief. Bob Warling. I own and operate Mainline Beverages in Glendale. I see Mr. Woodson from time to time in the store. We specialize in high end wines, mostly from France and California, though we have a nice line of vintage ports and a few items from Italy, Spain and Australia. My own taste runs to red Bordeaux. I guess that's why I'm here."

Chris nodded and introduced the third man. "This is W. R. Breeling. Mr. Breeling is an attorney. His offices are in Century City. He represents two winegrowing associations and was hired by them, in part, because of his personal knowledge of the industry." Breeling remained silent and simply nodded. Chris then introduced me and I explained the task at hand.

"Gentlemen," I said, "we are conducting an investigation into the deaths of several individuals associated with an enterprise named FirstGrowth. Perhaps you've heard of it … "

Blank stares all around.

"FirstGrowth markets wine. It specializes in highly-rated red Bordeaux and sells to a small list of southern California clients. The client base is in inverse proportion to the cost of the wine."

More blank stares.

"We suspect that FirstGrowth may have been selling wine that was … *misrepresented*. The labels may have been switched. Less expensive wine may have been substituted for more expensive. What we would like you to do is inspect the bottles, sample some of their wine, at random, and tell us whether or not you believe their products to be authentic."

Still the stares, but with a hint of recognition behind them.

"Their warehouse is in Irvine. We'll drive you there in a few minutes. As per Mr. Woodson's suggestion, we have secured appropriate glassware, clear white paper, wine biscuits and a jar for discarding residue. We also have some bottled water and some magnifying glasses for inspecting the labels, the foil, the corks and tissue wrapping. What we need, gentlemen, is your experience and your palates."

Stares, with the slightest hint of smiles.

Forty minutes later we were in the conference room at FirstGrowth. The panel spread the white paper beneath their glasses so that they could assess the color of the wine against it. We had begun by choosing a number of bottles at random. We planned to open one at a time and taste it as a group. The first was a 1989 Mouton-Rothschild.

The panel seemed to focus on color as much as taste, though they swirled and gargled and spat very carefully. They nodded to one another, without speaking, swirled, gargled and spat again, nodded some more and eventually set down their glasses. "Should I open the discussion?" Woodson asked. The other tasters simply nodded.

"Well," he said, "this is most definitely not a 1989 Mouton. The 1989 was a nice wine in its youth, long on nose but very unimpressive on the finish. It lacked weight and depth in the mouth. I would describe it as *flashy* but it reached its maturity far earlier than a great Mouton and is now quite over the hill. The color of *this* wine is all wrong and the taste is too young and ripe. This is a nice California wine, perhaps a relatively recent Caymus."

"Perhaps a Caymus Special Selection," Warling said. "It's a very nice wine, but it's definitely not a Mouton. This tastes like pure Cabernet to me. The Mouton would have had some Cab Franc and Merlot, not a whole lot, but some … "

"Eighty-five percent Cabernet," Breeling added, laconically.

"Right," Warling said.

"Quite," Woodson added.

The second wine was a 1982 Latour. Their eyes seemed to open slightly more widely as the wine was decanted. They repeated the inspection and tasting ritual, but there was less spitting this time. "How about if I try this one?" Warling asked. The other two cocked their heads slightly as they nodded.

"This is whatchacall your basic great wine. The '82 was a gem, one of the two best Latours since the monster '61. Big and deep and as intense as a suspicious wife. All ruby and purple lushness. Lots of tannin. Structure galore. I'd say this one has another 20 years left to go. Minimally."

"I can't disagree with that," Woodson said.

"Nor I," Breeling added.

"I didn't ask about the labeling, on this wine or on the previous one," I said.

"Looked kosher to me," Warling said.

"Yes, quite in order," Woodson said. "On both."

"Agreed," Breeling said.

The third wine was a 1986 Margaux. The panel tasted it with a sense of anticipation, but the anticipation appeared to wane quickly. "You're up," Warling said to Breeling, who seemed noticeably shy about speaking. "Every word is a potential lawsuit," Chris whispered in my ear.

"Well," he said, first clearing his throat, "this is most definitely not a 1986 Margaux. That wine was mammoth in its proportions, an extraordinary wine in every way—color, fruit, structure, depth and a finish that was … definitive. No, *remarkable*. This is a modest, recent wine from the southern Médoc. Perhaps a du Tertre. A pleasant little table wine. Soft, medium-bodied … "

"Yes," Woodson said.

"I can't disagree with you on that," Warling said.

"One more," I said. "This is a 1975 Pétrus."

"Let's *hope* that it is," Warling said.

They tasted it carefully. "I believe it's your turn, Mr. Woodson," Breeling said.

"Well … " Woodson said, "he's certainly consistent. He lies, then he tells the truth. This *is* a '75 Pétrus, one of the great wines of the 1970's. A giant. Opulent … massive. The blackcurrant fruit is delightful and the finish is … well … unforgettable. It has another 50 years, at least."

"It's a winner, that's for sure," Warling said. "I've always kind of preferred the '71. I like the chocolate along with the silky fruit, but the '71 didn't have the staying power of this one. Great pity."

"It's a 1975 Pétrus," Breeling added. "You might be lucky enough to find a bottle at $1500 these days." Suddenly Breeling had become talkative.

"I'll tell you what, Lieutenant," Warling said. "Whoever is running this company has two kinds of clients, the kind that like great wine and are willing to pay for it and the kind that don't know diddly squat and are prepared to be ripped off big-time."

"Yes," Woodson said. "The great wine *could* be put to other uses as well. For example, if a potential client wanted a sample … or (more to the point) if a policeman did. The authentic wine would be a kind of insurance policy. The person would pick the bottle he wanted you to try and steer you away from the fraudulent bottles. You must also remember that some individuals collect wines with no intention of ever drinking them. You offer them the real wine as bait and then sell them something else entirely."

"You can make money selling expensive wine," Warling said. "That could have been a nice little *side business*. The main business was something else … ripping people off, at least … maybe something else entirely."

"But it was done with a slight attention to plausibility," Breeling said. "It was actually decent or at least drinkable wine that he put in those bottles. The layman could tell that it wasn't simply plonk."

"But the true *layman* couldn't tell that it wasn't what it was represented to be," Chris said.

"No," Woodson said. "This is something of a complicated affair, as you must realize. We just tasted the '75 Pétrus. The '73 Pétrus was one of the best of that vintage, but the yield was huge and the wines were thin as a result. That Pétrus peaked in the early 90's. It would be priced now at … say … one-third the price of the 1975. A layman tasting it would be struck by the difference between its quality and its price. He might even say that it was … well … *bad*. What I'm saying is that whoever sold the wines appeared to be selling real wine that would command respect along with the price. This was not a … a *mindless* ripoff."

"But it was still a ripoff," Warling said. "He wasn't pouring wine from a box into those bottles, but he was still perpetrating some serious felonies."

"Well, he's dead now," Chris said. "That's one of the reasons for the investigation."

"Dead?" Warling said.

"Rough justice, perhaps," Woodson said.

"We take it where we can find it," Warling said. "No one likes to have his pocket picked. When the prices are stratospheric one might expect the rage and desire for revenge to be as well. You might want to have a look at that client list, Chief, see if anyone has any … anger issues."

FIFTY-TWO

We thanked them for their help and drove them back to Laguna to pick up their cars. We also received their promise to testify in court, should that be necessary. "That was certainly worthwhile," Chris said.

"Yes," I said. "It's always nice to have your suspicions confirmed, even if the full picture is still unclear."

"Some things *are* clear though," Chris said. "We've got a case of fraud along with some murders and suspicious deaths. We don't know how the pieces fit together, but we know that the puzzle is real and so are the crimes."

"We would have to show that the fraudulent wine was actually sold," I said. "It's not a crime to have some boxes of new wine in old bottles. It's suspicious as all hell and we've got more probable cause than we can shake a wine pipette at, but none of the clients gave any indication that they suspected FirstGrowth of selling bogus wine. None complained of the services they received; none reported any complaints from the individuals to whom they had given or served wine as gifts."

"We do have one thing though," Chris said.

"Something to rub Carlton Beauchamp's nose in."

"Exactly. He'll plead ignorance, claim that he was the security guy, that the wine was Richmond's business. He'll hold out his hands, tell us they're as clean as freshly-fallen snow, and say that he wouldn't have gone to Richmond's house to press him to release some wine for sale if he thought it was in any way tainted."

"Yes, he *will*," I said, "but we can watch his eyes as he lies. Even if we don't have something we can use to convict him, we'll have some further knowledge on the case."

Which is exactly what he did when the SDPD handed him off to us and we interrogated him. We knew that he was lying because he stopped his eyes from blinking for a moment, stared at us without expression and pled his own ignorance and innocence. I took another tack.

"I still don't understand why you were at Richmond's house that early in the morning," I said. "If you had business to transact with him, why not just call or send an email?"

"You mean Mr. *Richland*," he said.

"His real name was Richmond. He changed it because he had been arrested for fraud in Virginia and the case popped up every time someone googled his name."

"I don't know anything about that," Beauchamp answered. "To me he was always Richland. And I don't know anything about an arrest for fraud."

"The question still stands," I said. "Why were you so desperate to see him? Why were you out in the street at that time of the morning, making a spectacle of yourself like that?"

"He didn't answer his phone and he didn't respond to my emails," Beauchamp said.

"We've checked the phone records and his email," I said. "You didn't try to contact him. You're lying, Mr. Beauchamp. *Why* are you lying?"

"I called the number he gave me and I used the email address he asked me to use. People use different cellphones, you know. And they receive email with those phones."

"So you're saying that the cellphone and computer we found were just props, that he was doing all his real business on other machines?"

"How would I know? I used the phone number and email address that he gave me."

"Why would a businessman go through all that cloak and dagger?" I asked. "Wasn't he a regular businessman?"

"What's a *regular* businessman?" Beauchamp answered.

"Someone who's not a criminal, someone who wants to attract business, someone who has the front door of his establishment open to customers so that they can walk in and purchase his goods."

"His business was special," Beauchamp said. "He worked with people very confidentially. He was trying to buy low and sell high, right? You try to keep the prices … quiet."

"You'll have to excuse me," I said, "but that is utter and complete bullshit. You can go on the internet and find a range of prices for any wine in the world. The prices vary, of course, but the range is clear. It comes down to provenance, the state of the individual bottle and the trustworthiness of the dealer. You went to Brown, Carlton. You know what the word *provenance* means."

"Yes," he said.

"Richmond told us that his reputation was everything, that his personal integrity, his company's storage facility, his guarantees with regard to provenance were his comparative advantages. That's why he was successful. That's why he could charge what he charged."

Beauchamp turned to his lawyer for help. The lawyer's name was Pinkard. Stanley Pinkard. He was wearing $5,000 worth of clothes, $10,000 worth of wristwatch and an expression of absolute boredom.

"Lieutenant Deaton," he said, forcing the words out one at a time, "my client has answered your question. By my count he has answered your question seven times. He was attempting to apprise his superior of a business opportunity. He communicated with him in the ways specified by his superior. When those ways proved unsuccessful he attempted to communicate with him directly. He did not wish to lose the potential sale. He was a responsible employee attempting to do his job in the most expeditious manner possible."

"His job was security, not sales, Mr. Pinkard. He claims that the individual who wished to purchase the wine was a Mr. Madison, a Mr. Wayne Madison. He gave us the phone number that Mr. Madison asked him to use. There is no record of such a number, Mr. Pinkard, and the Wayne Madisons in southern California are infants, incapacitated elderly, and individuals prepared to swear that they have no knowledge whatsoever of FirstGrowth, William Richland, William Richmond or Carlton Beauchamp. The description which your client provided of Wayne Madison is ... shall we say ... *generic* in the extreme and he clings to the claim that he actually met this individual despite the fact that there is absolutely no evidence to substantiate that individual's existence."

"Individuals often give false names, Lieutenant. They don't want to be harried by salesmen. They also give false numbers for the same reason."

"May I remind you that FirstGrowth is not a normal retail outlet, Mr. Pinkard. An individual does not go to the trouble to seek out an individual, go to a warehouse, get past its security systems, inquire concerning rare and expensive commodities, express an interest in purchasing such commodities and then give a false name and number."

"*This* individual appears to have done just that, Lieutenant. It may be that my client overestimated his level of interest. As you noted, his role is security, not sales. He was trying to be helpful to his employer. For that he should be thanked, not badgered. At any rate, your questions have been asked and answered. I see no purpose in continuing. If you have further questions my client will be happy to address them, but his patience and mine are now frayed, Lieutenant."

"Well," I said, "I expect that Mr. Beauchamp has other concerns at this time. If I were him, I certainly would. He has been employed by an individual arrested for fraud who has been operating a business that gives every indication of itself being fraudulent. Every individual associated with that business is now dead. I can understand why that might give Mr. Beauchamp pause."

Beauchamp stared at his lawyer; the lawyer maintained his bored look, pressed his lips together in a forced smile of the purest insincerity and rose from his chair. "I believe we're finished here," he said.

"Quite possibly," I said, my eyes focusing on Beauchamp's.

FIFTY-THREE

"Not a very good liar," Chris said. "Richmond may have been the brains and Beauchamp the muscle, but most of that muscle is between his ears."

"What do you think Pinkard bills an hour?" I asked.

"I heard $1,500," Chris said.

"That's a lot to cough up if you know that you're innocent."

"If that's the face of innocence I'd hate to see the face of guilt," Chris said.

"Right," I answered. "I just wonder who's paying Pinkard's retainer."

Before we could continue, Hector was at the door of Chris's office. "A little news from Virginia," he said. Chris waved him in.

"I talked to the guy who wrote the piece on Richmond for *Washingtonian* magazine. He said that when he wrote the story he was really holding back. Richmond was innocent on a technicality, but as dirty as a coal bin by any reasonable moral or ethical standard. (The *coal bin* was the guy's expression. He's older and remembers them I guess.) Basically, he said that Richmond was a cheat soliciting other cheats for a chance to turn a quick profit at some other guy's expense. All of the investors were shady. It just turned out that one was greedier than the others and tried to squeeze a few pennies more out of Richmond.

"He also said that he decided to do the story because he had investigated Richmond in the past but was never able to make anything stick. He called him a *gonef*. I liked the guy, Chief. You and the lieutenant would enjoy talking to him. He's like an old-school reporter type, you know, with the typewriter with keys that stick and the bottle of rye in the lower drawer of a beat up desk … "

"Did he say anything about Richmond doing regular work?" I asked.

"No, he just said that he was a guy who skated around the edges all the time, sniffing out the fast dollar, looking for a weak member of the herd to take down."

"Anything else?" I asked.

"I talked to the guy who arrested him, a Sergeant … Hathaway. Very disappointed that the DA wouldn't prosecute. I asked him if he had any knowledge of other near arrests or convictions. He talked to a number of people in the department there, called me and said that Billy Richmond (that's what they called him in Virginia) was on a lot of suspect lists, but never took the fall for anything. Hathaway described him as a guy who was always on the lookout for something sweet and easy."

"He must have found *some* things like that," I said, "because the house he was living in would sell now in the low seven figures."

"Maybe he also lowered himself and did some honest work from time to time," Chris said, "playing against type."

"I've got to hand it to him," I said. "He went from being a street hustler to a high end con man in a very short period of time. It must have also been a profitable time, because his place in La Jolla would have set him back four or five times what he would have gotten for his split-foyer in Virginia, maybe more. He took wine classes from that guy at *Bassin's*, Don Allen. They didn't do him any harm, because he was able to fake it pretty well. He came across as a rich and connected businessman with a strong taste for self-indulgence and the savvy to satisfy it regularly. He knew how to talk; he knew how to dress and he knew all about wine, even though Allen said that he wasn't really a wine drinker. Where did he learn all of that so quickly?"

"Maybe the street guy was an interim personality," Chris said. "Maybe he came from money but lacked a taste for work. He reinvented himself as a middlebrow huckster. When he started to see some success he fell back on his old ways. He knew all about the high life; he just hadn't been able to afford it."

"Hector … " I said.

"I've already been there," he said. "I didn't want to interrupt. He was from Philly. Main Line type. His father was a banker. Went to Yale. His mother was a junior leaguer. Went to Bryn Mawr. No other kids. Billy was groomed, coddled, pampered, spoiled and finally turned loose on the world. He went to a tony prep school in Massachusetts. Ready for the best?"

"What's that?" I asked.

"He went to Brown. Want to know what he majored in?"

"Yes, but I also want to know whether or not Carlton Beauchamp was one of his classmates."

"He majored in Theatre."

"That may answer our question," I said.

"And Carlton Beauchamp was not his classmate. He was a junior when Billy enrolled as a freshman."

"And what was *his* major?"

"Sociology."

"That may explain why he's such a poor actor as well as a poor liar," Chris said. "He told us that Rich*mond* was always Rich*land* to him."

"So Richmond may have recruited Beauchamp to FirstGrowth because they went back a long way together," Hector said.

"Or maybe the other way around," I said. "The muscle guy was looking for somebody who wasn't averse to cutting corners, a guy who could play a part convincingly."

"Works for me," Chris said. "Good work, Hector."

"I live to serve, Chief," he said, "and I love to turn over rocks."

FIFTY-FOUR

I told Chris that I wanted to put surveillance on Beauchamp 24/7. "One unit on the warehouse, one on his condo, minimally. If somebody turns up with a shotgun, hoping to take him out, I want to find out before Beauchamp does."

"Good idea," Chris said. "I wouldn't want to write any insurance policies on his life these days, not after what's happened so far."

"I figure we've got three possibilities. This is an internal dispute between the principals or FirstGrowth has a disgruntled customer or set of customers who decided to settle things their own way. The third possibility is that there's someone else involved, someone we don't know about yet."

"I agree," Chris said.

"The problem," I said, "is that it's unlikely (at least to me) that a disgruntled customer would also take out the deliverymen. It's possible, of course, that he could figure that the deliverymen were behind the scam, but that's really a long shot. Possible, though. Let's say he figures that the deliverymen were scamming him, but then thought better of it and decided to start working his way through the rest of the company, one at a time. Maybe Richmond saw it coming and decided to bow out. Maybe somebody greeted him with a shotgun and a bottle of pills and told him to take his choice. It's all possible, but it's not … it's not gelling for me. There are too many things that don't quite fit … "

"I know what you mean," Chris said. "I figure that Richmond and Beauchamp were the masterminds and Davidson and Randall were the innocent bystanders who stepped into the line of fire. Maybe Randall found out about the scam and they killed his wife because they figured he might have said something to her. Then they decided to kill Davidson just to close the loop."

"They figured that when Randall got suspicious he might have contacted Davidson, asked him if he smelled anything funny when he worked for the company. Then they killed Davidson just for insurance purposes."

"It's plausible," Chris said, "but like you said, it doesn't fit as tightly as you'd like."

"Yes," I said, "and why would they turn on one another or start eliminating deliverymen if there was no heat on them? Why would the deliverymen have suspicions if none of the clients did? It's also hard to imagine white collar guys being ripped off in a wine scam and turning vigilante rather than picking up the phone and calling the police. For that matter, I'd imagine them calling the Better Business Bureau or some agency like that the moment they had any suspicions. They didn't. And they all presented a united front to us. Not one of them said a discouraging word. Everything was fine as far as they were concerned. So if *they* weren't suspicious, why would Richmond and Beauchamp get panicky and start taking out deliverymen? Maybe one of the deliverymen said something? Another possibility is that some of their customers might have been legit, but others dirty. The legit ones got legitimate product. The others were like some of Billy Richmond's old friends, on the lookout for an easy dollar. Maybe they used company money to buy the phony wine and then got kickbacks from Richmond."

"Possible," Chris said.

"Yes," I said, "it's possible, but it's a very circuitous route to take if you're trying to make a fast buck. These bucks came in very slowly and they didn't start to come in until Richmond, Beauchamp or someone else had fronted the operation, big time. Building a storage facility like the one they've got is a major investment. Millions, at least. Richmond's home was a major investment. We would have to believe that they created some huge sets and sound stages for the scheme. I understand that we're talking serious money for the wine, but it still seems like ... what ... an elaborate superstructure to erect in order to generate some illegal cash flow. Let's say for the sake of argument that the initial investment was five to ten million dollars. How many shady land deals could you launch with money like that?"

"Plus they had to get the phony wine into the authentic bottles," Chris said. "That presented logistical difficulties also. Significant logistical difficulties."

"We've got to learn more about their customers," I said. "On the face of it they look more or less straight arrow, but I'd like to look behind the surfaces ... see if there's anything interesting there."

"I wonder if any of *them* went to Brown," Chris said.

"Yes, poor Brown. The public relations people there probably wouldn't be very happy to see the direction of our investigation. I'll do some more checking and see what I can turn."

The next day I checked with the officers watching Beauchamp. He was sitting tight. He had registered another request, through his lawyer this time, to gain access to Richmond's computer, but that could have just been smoke. If he and Richmond *were* the scam and if his dramatic skills were as weak as Chris Dietrich and I judged them to be, his best course would be to steer clear of the law, sell off the legitimate wine that he had on hand to another dealer, liquidate assets like the FirstGrowth delivery van and put the storage facility on the market. Cut his losses, cash out and move on to another enterprise. For the moment, however, he was sitting on his hands.

Then, that evening, the officer watching Beauchamp's condo called in. "He's moving," he said.

"Where?" I asked.

"He's on the 405, heading toward Los Angeles."

"I'll send somebody to join you, Jim (the officer's name was Jim Daley). I don't want to pull Gary Grote from the FirstGrowth facility, because this could just be smoke. They might want to divert our attention so they can do something in Irvine. Dave Gable is available. I'll send him after you, so that the two of you can leapfrog and follow Beauchamp more easily when he gets to L.A."

"Thanks, Lieutenant. I'd appreciate it if you'd hurry, because Beauchamp is now driving between 75 and 80 and weaving between cars. He's acting as if he's on some sort of mission."

FIFTY-FIVE

"Are you and Dave within contact, Jim?"

"Yes, Lieutenant. Dave is closing fast. He used the siren for the first twenty miles. Fortunately, there are lots of sirens out here, so there's no indication that Beauchamp heard it and got spooked. He's still driving very fast, when he has the opportunity. The good news is that the farther north we drive, the slower the traffic is."

"Dave is here now, Lieutenant. We've been bracketing Beauchamp and switching off. Traffic is slow. We just passed Century Boulevard and LAX. We're staying behind him in case he pulls off on the **10**."

"He passed the **10**, Lieutenant, but he's getting off on Wilshire."

"Heading east or west?"

"East."

"He's driving into UCLA. I don't like that. Too much traffic control. Too many parking ramps … we'll be too easy to spot."

"Keep bracketing him, but keep a good distance."

"He's left the campus, Lieutenant. I don't like this. I think he was suspicious. He was driving aimlessly, checking his flanks."

"As long as he keeps moving he has to be headed somewhere," I said. "He left his comfort zone in Newport for a reason."

"Right. We'll stay on him."

"He's back on the **405** again."

"North or south?"

"North. He's heading through the Sepulveda Pass."

"Have you seen him talking on a cellphone?"

"No, Lieutenant, but he may have an earpiece. We're not close enough to see whether or not he does."

"Stay on him."

"We're in the Valley now, Lieutenant. He's turning onto the freeway. I can never remember where it's the **101** and where it's the **134**."

"Which direction is he headed?"

"East."

"It's the **101** there. It becomes the **134** above Universal City. Watch him very carefully. If he's headed toward Pasadena and beyond, he'll continue to move into the left lanes. The other major migration routes peel off to the south."

"It's not Pasadena, Lieutenant. He's getting off in Glendale."

"On the Glendale freeway?"

"No, we're not that far, Lieutenant."

"He's going into the shopping mall, Lieutenant."

"The Glendale Galleria."

"Yes, sir."

"Be very careful," I said. It's a maze. Unfortunately, that might be his plan."

"He seems to be looking for a parking place. It's really crowded."

"Stay in touch with Dave. One of you park as close as possible to him and the other stay in visual contact."

"Bad luck, Lieutenant. After driving around he suddenly pulled over for the valet parking service and headed into the mall."

"One of you has to follow him as quickly as possible, the other stay near the valet service in case he's just heading in and out in order to lose you."

"Dave's got a place, Lieutenant. He's heading into the mall. I'll stay here and watch the valet stand."

"Keep me posted."

"Yes, sir."

"We've lost him, Lieutenant, at least temporarily."

"Stay by the valet stand."

"I will. Dave's checking public spaces and restaurants, the kinds of places where you might meet up with somebody. I know that's a long shot, but it's the best way to start. It would have helped if he was wearing something that would draw attention in a crowd. Unfortunately, he was wearing dark slacks and a dark jacket. I couldn't see the shirt he was wearing."

"No fluorescent hunter's hat though."

"No, Lieutenant."

"He knows security, Jim. He knows how to follow and how to avoid being followed. He could be wearing a reversible jacket, pop into the toilet and turn it inside out or even just discard the thing. He's in a mall; he could buy a new one … add some accessories. He won't be easy to find. If he's got any brains and if he really is trying to link up with somebody he'll probably do it way off the beaten track. That's what I would do. He'll be right where you don't expect him to be … near a women's restroom or the gift wrapping desk, somewhere in the bowels of a large store. He won't be anywhere where there are good lines of sight, like a candy store or a sporting goods store. He'll be back behind racks of clothes in one of the anchor stores, some place where he could see somebody searching for him but not easily be seen himself."

"Yes, thanks Lieutenant."

"It's not hopeless, Jim. The stores have surveillance cameras; we'll have the time of his entrance and exit bracketed and we can run through whatever they've recorded later. It's one thing to dodge a man on foot, quite another to do that without looking up in the air all the time, trying to determine whether or not you're starring on Candid Camera."

"He's coming out, Lieutenant. He was in there for . . . forty-seven minutes."

"He probably did meet with someone. I'll have someone check with the mall staff. Meanwhile, you and Dave get back on him and see where he goes."

"He's been working his way south, Lieutenant."

"Toward the 5?"

"Yes, sir."

"He's coming home, Jim. His work is over for the night. And he *did* go there for a reason. You don't drive a hundred miles in traffic and spend four hours or so just to charge up your car battery. Nor would you do it just to see if someone is following you. He knows he's a person of interest in the case. He went there for a reason. Now we'll see if anybody was able to take his picture inside the Galleria."

FIFTY-SIX

Hector called me at 2:00 the next afternoon. He had spent much of the night and all of the next morning in Glendale, studying videotape from the mall's stores and common areas. I got there at 3:45 and we went to a conference room in Bloomingdale's, where Hector had assembled a set of discs for my review.

"Very suspicious, Tom, *very* suspicious. Somebody should have told this guy that the first thing you do when you think you're being followed is resist the urge to look over your right shoulder. For awhile there I thought he had some sort of tic.

"Now, here he is, just walking through the mall. Look, he's practically breaking his neck and dislocating his shoulder. The average guy … he walks … how? He just goes from point A to point B. He wants a flatscreen TV; he knows who sells flatscreen TV's; he goes directly to the store that sells TV's; he buys a TV. Then there's the average guy who's killing time. He's waiting for his girl friend or he's waiting for a job interview or … whatever. That guy, he looks at his watch a lot. He checks his iPhone. Sometimes he lights somewhere and checks his iPhone again. He studies the mall map because there's nothing else there to read; then he looks at his watch some more. He looks in store windows, but he's not really shopping because he's not really interested. He's just killing time.

"Then there's the serious shopper. He goes from store to store, looking at merchandise, comparing prices. He's buying himself a pair of gloves, so he goes and checks out Penney's, then he tries Macy's; finally he ends up at Nordstrom's. The *average* guy, Lieutenant … he sees a pair of gloves that he likes, a pair that fits him, a pair that doesn't cost him a fortune … he buys them on the spot. He's not a comparison shopper. The average guy *isn't* a serious shopper; he's just a shopper. He needs something; he buys it.

"Then you've got your lost soul. He goes to the mall and actually has dinner. He stares into space. He treats himself to a single scoop of ice cream. Maybe he goes to the movies while everybody else is at work. He doesn't have anything else to do; he doesn't have anybody to go with him. It's sad. A hundred years ago he would have gone to the town square, sat on a bench and fed the squirrels. These days he goes to the mall.

"If he had a girlfriend, she'd be doing the serious shopping and he'd be tagging along, trying to find a place to sit down while she tried on clothes, trying to look interested while she asked his opinion on spoons or napkin rings.

"Our guy, on the other hand … he's been mostly looking over his shoulder. Here he is … by the food court." Hector popped in the disc and showed a 15-second segment. "Here he comes … and there he goes … "

He popped in another disc. "Here he is walking past a jewelry store with a well-endowed sales clerk. He doesn't even look at her."

"But he's looking over his shoulder again," I said. "Urgently."

"If you think of him as a bad actor in a bad movie, that's his one expression."

"Do we have any video of him making contact with somebody?"

"We do. It's brief, but we do. It's on two different discs."

Hector popped in another disc. "This is the entrance to Bloomingdale's. That's Beauchamp there, on the left. Instead of looking over his shoulder he's looking straight at the door. Picking at his ear. Nervous habit. Maybe that means he wants to hear something from somebody. And here comes … somebody … there, on the right. The guy in the hat."

"That's almost like a fedora. Mr. Formal."

"Yes and the rest of the outfit is pretty spiffy also. The picture's a little grainy, but I'd say that the suit came from a tailor's shop. It didn't come off the rack. And ... here. Look at the shoes." Hector froze the frame. "Those aren't Thom McAn's. Those little bumps there ... they could be ostrich. Watch carefully, they're about to disappear."

"Is that the only shot of the other guy?"

"No, he returns in a few minutes. Right here ... "

Hector removed the previous disc and inserted the last disc from his stack. "They're all palsy walsy now. The guy with the hat has his hand on Beauchamp's shoulder. The therapy session's over."

"Where do you think they were?"

"We know where they were. They were getting their shoes shined."

"Really?"

"Yes, I'll show you out on the floor. It's a new service for Bloomingdale's, probably copying Nordstrom's. (They left the Galleria a few years back.) You can see from the entrance and exit discs the directions in which the two of them were heading. The logical end point and origination point is the shoe shine booth. Plus, I cheated. I talked to the shoe shine guy. I showed him the images; he remembered them."

"Did he hear what they said to one another?"

"Unfortunately, no. He had his earpods in. He was listening to music. He said that the guys seemed to be talking very quietly, like it was something real important. They turned to each other and seemed to be whispering. No loud jokes or knee slaps. Nothing like that. Then they tipped him, went in the men's room for a second, came out, said good bye to him, and left."

"Do you think the shoe shine guy could identify Beauchamp's playmate?"

"I doubt it. His attention was focused more on his shoes than on his face. He said that they were very nice shoes ... on both men, but especially on the guy in the hat. He sees everything at ankle-level, unfortunately. He *was* able to confirm that they were together. He commented on the hat too. That was a mistake, drawing attention to himself like that. On the other hand, it shaded his eyes and covered his hair. He should have worn a baseball hat, but that wouldn't have gone with the suit."

"What's the best picture of his face, do you think?"

"This one ... here." He put in the disc of the man entering the store. "We've mostly only got the left profile, but that's more than we had twenty-four hours ago. I'll have it blown up and we'll start circulating it."

"Good work, Hector. I want to get that guy in a small room without windows ... start asking him a whole *lot* of questions."

FIFTY-SEVEN

An enhanced photograph of the man meeting Beauchamp at Bloomingdale's had been circulating for two days. So far a Pasadena sergeant had tentatively identified the man as his brother-in-law, a California highway patrolman had identified him as a fry cook at a Denny's in Santa Ana and a police cadet in L.A. thought he looked a lot like his old political science professor at Cal State, Fullerton, minus the nice clothes. All three of those individuals had alibis for the time of the meeting.

A San Diego beat cop who had worked as a clerk for a haberdasher before joining the department identified the manufacturer of the hat that the man was wearing, noting that a fur felt from that company goes for a minimum of $300, but also pointing out that they're sold over the internet and rarely carried by men's clothing stores. "I was just trying to be helpful," he said.

After lunch I began tracking down some other leads when the desk sergeant buzzed me. "There's a guy here to see you, Lieutenant; he says you're looking for him."

"Send him in," I said. A minute later the man appeared at my door; this time he was wearing a brown hat rather than the black one he had on at Bloomingdale's. He entered, introduced himself as Victor Donnelly, and shook my hand.

"I'm the man in your picture," he said, "the one meeting with Carl Beauchamp in Bloomingdale's."

"Thank you for coming in," I said. "How did you know I was looking for you?"

"One of my security men has a friend in the LAPD. The friend told my man and the man told me."

"I'm surprised that the officer in the LAPD didn't tell me first," I said, trying not to sound defensive, but trolling for Donnelly's answer.

"He said it's always better to volunteer than to be sought out," Donnelly said. "Besides, I had business in Irvine and I thought I'd come by and save you the trip to Los Angeles."

"I appreciate that," I said.

"I know about the problems at FirstGrowth," he said. "Carl called me, briefed me on what had happened and said that he wanted to meet with me. Carl used to work for me, at Griffith."

"Griffith Industries," I said.

"Yes, I'm the CEO. I wasn't sure how I could be of help to Carl, since I know next to nothing about wine. It's a specialized business, as I'm sure you know, Lieutenant. It requires expert knowledge. Carl wanted to pick up after his former partner and try to continue the operation. He wanted my advice on how to do that."

"What did you advise him?" I asked.

"I advised him to punt," he said. "Carl doesn't have the expertise to either purchase the wine or market it. He doesn't even like wine. I told him that if I were in his position I would sell the existing stock to a dealer, liquidate any other assets that the company might possess and put their warehouse on the market. I gave him the name of a broker who handles commercial property."

"I wasn't aware that he and William Richland (his actual name was Richmond, by the way) were partners. I thought Beauchamp was Richmond's employee."

"Legally they were partners," Donnelly said, "but I gather that Carl deferred to him because of the fact that he fronted the operation while Carl provided security. He's a good security man, by the way. I'd hire him back if he wanted to come back. Of course, I couldn't pay him the kind of money he was making at FirstGrowth, but that source has now dried up. No pun intended."

"I understand," I said. "You appreciate the fact, Mr. Donnelly, that it's my job to be suspicious, so you'll forgive me if I ask you if you would normally meet business acquaintances in a clothing store rather than in your office."

"Perfectly legitimate question," he said. "My office is in the west Valley and my home is in San Marino. Carl said he wanted to meet, I asked him when, he gave me a time, and I suggested the Galleria. It was on my route home and I thought it would save Carl a longer trip. There's also a little restaurant nearby that I've been wanting to try, so I didn't mind coming down from the freeway to see him. I also needed a shoeshine and Bloomingdale's now offers them free, so I took the opportunity."

"It sounds as if you're a very efficient man, Mr. Donnelly."

"I try to be," he said, "but it's not what keeps our company afloat. We're like the late Mr. Richland or Richmond. We sell expertise, principally with regard to international business."

"Finance?"

"Yes, some. And engineering. And some risk analysis. One-stop shopping, Lieutenant," he said, smiling. "Manufacturers decide to seek global markets. We advise them."

"Do you advise with regard to security?"

"To a limited degree. There are other companies who specialize in that. Our expertise tends to be in money, finance, software systems and international law. We have individuals on retainer to us who advise on local customs … banking … markets … political systems … that sort of thing. These individuals are largely in-country; they are fluent in the local languages and attuned to questions of cultural nuance."

"How long have you known Mr. Beauchamp?" I asked.

"Four, five years, no more than that."

"Then you didn't attend Brown with Mr. Beauchamp and Mr. Richmond."

"Did they both go to Brown? That's interesting. No, I attended Princeton and studied international affairs at Columbia."

"Were you surprised when Beauchamp told you that the two deliverymen who had worked at FirstGrowth were murdered?"

"I thought that the second killed himself. I assumed he was disturbed by his experience in the Middle East."

"His wife was killed as well."

"Hemingway says that we all kill the thing we most love," he answered. "I still don't understand it. Perhaps he didn't want to … go alone."

"Perhaps," I said. "Don't you think it's a strange coincidence that the other deliveryman is dead as well?"

"Of course, but I don't know the circumstances of his death. Carl said he was an aspiring actor. That's really all I know."

"Do you consider Carlton Beauchamp an honest man, Mr. Donnelly?"

"Honest? Of course. We entrusted our company's security to him and he never gave us a reason to regret it."

"Do you consider him capable of criminal activity?"

"I consider anyone capable of criminal activity, Lieutenant, but I deal in possibility and likelihood. I do not consider it *likely* that Carl was involved in criminal activity. Do you?"

"I don't know yet, Mr. Donnelly. We're still sorting through the pile of dead bodies."

FIFTY-EIGHT

I hadn't mentioned the fact to Donnelly that when we began our conversation and I reached into my desk drawer to retrieve a pencil, I also hit the **record** switch on the tape machine there. I played the tape for Chris rather than briefing him on the interview.

"Preemptive strike," he said. "He thinks it will dispel suspicion if he acts cooperative and forthcoming, but he's a smart guy and he should see all of the holes in Beauchamp's story. He's clearly lying. He's involved somehow; I'd bet serious money on it. Maybe he's the cash behind the operation."

"Possibly a little subsidiary enterprise," I said, "sort of like Enron. A rogue executive or two decide to make some cash on the side. International consulting is fine as a specialty, but a little wine scam or cocaine distribution operation could throw some cash to the bottom line on that *other* set of books, the one the authorities never get to see."

"And he'd probably be able to afford the investment, particularly if he thought it was a gift that would keep on giving."

"And he's misrepresenting his relationship with Beauchamp. He's not giving advice to an old pal or compadre; he's giving orders to one of his street soldiers. Told him it's time to shut down this scam and think about ways to start up another, once the temperature cools a little and the police write off Richmond and Randall as suicides and Davidson as a victim of random violence."

"How can you ever trust a guy who wears hats like that?" Chris asked. "What is he going for, some kind of Bogart vibe? It's not a smart move. Guys as dirty as he probably is … they should be trying to draw less attention to themselves, not more."

"Maybe it's an Indiana Jones thing," I said. "He's the scholar adventurer, but then Indy's hats were usually drawing dust in the cupboard while he worked his day job. This guy gets decked out that way *for* his day job."

"I'd like to know a lot more about Griffith Industries," Chris said, "but then you've probably already got Hector working on that."

I smiled and nodded my head. "I called him on his cell before I came in here with the tape."

"And this Donnelly guy … I want to see his tax forms and his resumé. Where's he been? What's he done? Whose back has he scratched? Whose pocket has he picked?"

"Who's he killed?"

"Yes," Chris said. "Especially that."

"Hector's on it," I said.

"Good. Keep me posted. What are you going to do?"

"I've got one of the uniforms making calls to cellphone providers. It's a long shot, of course. I'm sure Richmond was using a throwaway, but we can't afford not to check. Maybe we can find a record of the real calls he was making, not just the smoke and mirrors stuff he left for us to find.

"I want to start working my way through Richmond's client list. I don't like the odor there. Maybe some were buying real wine and some were buying fake. No one complained. No one made any calls. Why not? Were they actually fooled? Or were they part of the scam? I want to see some genealogy, see which of these characters knew one another in the past, maybe worked together, maybe spent some time lying, cheating and stealing together. Or killing."

"Sounds good."

"There's something else, Chief." I tried not to put too much apprehension in my voice, but Chris picked up on it immediately.

"What's that, Tom?" He looked at me carefully, staring at my eyes. "Are you OK?"

"I'm fine. The headaches are all earned at this point."

He smiled. "What is it?"

"This is going to sound a little 'new age', Chief … "

"Yes … ?"

"I think we've been investigating all the right things. I don't think we've been sidetracked or been focusing on things that were trivial or tangential …"

"Yes … "

"But I think that we've … I know that *I* … have been looking at this as a case of grand theft with some murders attached. Instead, I think we should be looking at it as a case of murder with some theft attached."

"That's not 'new age', Tom. It makes perfect sense. We've got both murder and theft and the two are related. Solving one will help solve the other … "

"I know, Chief, but that's not exactly my point. The point is that these sleazebags killed a soldier and his wife, a guy trying to support his family with a bridge job during tough times. They also killed a decent kid who was trying to make it as an actor. *I* think they did, at least. They saw them as disposable. They used them. Then suddenly they didn't need them any longer or they worried that they knew something that could help convict them. When they became a liability they blew them away. And they did it in an ugly way. Now we speak for *them*, for the victims. And we've got to hear what they're telling us. What would they say to us if they were here? What *did* they say to us, if anything?"

"What are you thinking in particular, Tom?"

"I'm thinking that when Terry Randall was killed … when he was blown apart by the shotgun … probably after his wife had already been killed before his eyes … he was shot through the cheek. Nobody commits suicide that way and nobody kills his wife and then has second thoughts about killing himself and jerks his head just as he's pulling the trigger.

I think he was fighting for his life. I think they rammed the shotgun in his mouth and he kept struggling until they pulled the trigger. I think he ... he ... wanted somebody to know that. That somebody turns out to be us. Now we have to investigate Victor Donnelly and Griffith Industries and we have to continue to investigate Carlton Beauchamp and we have to learn all that we can about the client list that William Richmond left us--most of it probably smoke--and we have to continue to try to find Richmond's cellphone and we have to find out what he and Beauchamp were trying to sell in addition to phony wine, but first and foremost ... **first and foremost** ... we have to find out who killed the would-be actor and who killed the soldier and his wife."

"And *prove* that they did it."

"Yes ... absolutely *prove* that they did it ... so we can put them in the small room with the glass walls, the one with the gurney with the leather straps and the big needle with the sodium thiopental. Square this with the victims' families. Put things right. Put the final numbers down on the balance sheet."

"Let's do it," he said.

IV

BOX CANYON

FIFTY-NINE

"I can tell you a little bit," Hector said. "These guys move in their own world. It runs parallel to ours, but the fees are higher in theirs and there's a lot more white wine in their hands and diplomas on their walls. It's like an axis, from the Fletcher School at Tufts, through Columbia and down to D.C. with Georgetown and SAIS."

"SAIS?"

"Hopkins' School of Advanced International Studies. Right across from Brookings in D.C."

"And they do … what … ?"

"Well, it's sort of like an MBA for people who want to work in the international community, except that they don't study business. They *can*, but it's more economics, history, political science, that kind of thing."

"Like the London School of Economics."

"Yes, that would be the British equivalent. It's like … all things international. Some do go into business; some do international law; some work for the State Department. Think of it this way: you're young, you're rich enough to afford this kind of tuition; you're not exactly sure what it is you want to do, but you want to do it in fancy places around the world. This is how you start. This is how you enter their world. And then you drink a lot of white wine. And you wear dark business suits with chalk stripes and pocket handkerchiefs."

"And the intellectuals end up at think tanks and they get interviewed on the evening news. And some end up in middle management in government agencies."

"Yes, and some become international consultants," Hector said. "They tell people to buy low and sell high, only they say it in French."

"Or they tell people to be sure to bribe the local dictator before they try to sell things in his country."

"That's the long and the short of it," Hector said. "Donnelly also had a little business training and he developed some expertise in a specialty area—Latin America."

"As in Colombia. As in Medellin."

"Possibly," Hector said, "but he didn't start there. He started out in Ecuador. This was after he passed the foreign service exam (which is, apparently, not very easy). He was posted to the consulate in Guayaquil and then to the embassy in Quito. Guayaquil is a rough port town; the Quito gig was cushy. From there he went to the embassy in Santiago, Chile. Then, suddenly and abruptly, he left the foreign service."

"Next stop?"

"The World Bank, briefly, then the International Monetary Fund, also briefly. Eventually he decided to cash in on his experience and went to work for a New York consulting firm called GlobalNet Partners. Bought a tidy little manse on the upper east side. Got his picture taken a lot, usually while he was wearing a tuxedo and smoking a cigar."

"But no fedora?"

"Not yet. He picked that up in L.A. Part of his softer image, I guess. He came to Griffith about ten years ago. Old man Griffith was essentially an engineer. He started out digging wells in poor countries when he was in the Peace Corps. Later he built bridges and highway systems. When he died, the company diversified. They did more consulting than building. Eventually they hired Donnelly. Except for their personal bank accounts and 401K's they don't build anything anymore."

"So L.A. has been kind to Victor."

"Very. He's got a large house in San Marino--just off Oxford Road, by the Huntington Library. Probably worth between seven and ten mil. Also a tidy little villa in Montecito. That one's worth between five and seven mil. Just a little weekend getaway place, when he has to see the ocean and feel the sun on his face."

"How about a personal life?"

"None, so far as I can see. He was married when he was in New York, but that ended in divorce. Her name is … (checking his notebook) Mary Alice Radil. Radil was her maiden name; she's remarried … to a guy named Glissten. A lawyer."

"Is her nickname 'Muffy'?"

"No, 'Missy'."

"Close enough for government work," I said. "So now he's playing the field."

"Or hiring it," Hector said.

"He's got a sheet?"

"He was initially charged, but the charges were eventually dropped. Probably a dispute over price. He was thinking $200; she was thinking $2,000. Probably ended up costing him $10,000, plus fees for his lawyer."

"Anything else?"

"There were allegations of some sharp dollar deals in New York, but nothing ever resulted in an arrest or indictment. He claimed that he was the victim of professional jealousy, that his competition was trying to besmirch his reputation. That was the word he used, *besmirch*."

"Where did you see that?"

"Story in the *Post* (Washington-, not New York-). Reporting on the rumors, which Donnelly immediately moved to squelch."

"Any more details?"

"The deal was financial. It had to do with currency trading. The opposition was charging that he had consulted with the country in question and had some insider information that he was exploiting for personal profit."

"Scuzzballs at play."

"Yes."

"Tell me about Griffith, Hector. Where are they?"

"Near Calabasas. Just above the freeway. A small building in an industrial park. Relatively nondescript."

"That's a long way from LAX. If I'm an international consultant I'd want to be closer. It's also a long way from San Marino. Has Griffith always been there?"

"Actually they started in La Cañada-Flintridge. They acquired the present site … (checking his notebook again) … about four years ago."

"After Donnelly took over the company."

"Yes."

"But he lives all the way over in the San Gabriel Valley."

"Maybe he got a good price on the place in Calabasas. Or maybe he likes to keep a lot of distance between where he works and where he lives."

"Who's in the other buildings in the industrial park in Calabasas?"

"I haven't been able to find out yet," Hector said.

"Maybe that's where they run some of their subsidiary enterprises."

"Here's an aerial shot I got from the internet," Hector said.

"Only one way in and one way out," I said, "and the buildings form a circle."

"For arranging the wagons?" Hector asked.

"Maybe. Maybe for luring others into your basic box canyon."

SIXTY

I wanted to see Griffith Industries with my own eyes. I didn't know what I expected to find, but seeing people and things in their chosen habitat sometimes sparks ideas. If Donnelly's company was in D.C. it would have been located near 17th and K Streets. Its building would be relatively uninteresting but its location would say, loudly and clearly, 'we're important; we're running with the large dogs, paying the big rent, spreading the influence, charging the fees with the multiple zeros at the end'. There might be a corporate logo above the door of the building, something in stainless steel. It would say, 'we rent enough of this building to call it our own. We're as important as a branch of the government and our logo cost more'. I wondered what the facility in Calabasas would say.

I stopped in Pasadena to visit with Terry Randall's father. The Jet Propulsion Lab is managed by CalTech for NASA; it's located above the **210**, beyond the Rose Bowl. It was mid-morning when I arrived and we met in a coffee shop in the building where Walter Randall worked. He thanked me for bringing him up to date on the investigation.

"I can't go into a lot of detail," I said, "but I wanted you to know that the case is progressing. I'm personally certain that what happened to your son was not an isolated event, separable from his work at FirstGrowth."

"Go on, Lieutenant," he said. He wasn't drinking his coffee. He wasn't even touching the cup handle.

"There was another deliveryman who worked for FirstGrowth; he was there before your son. He died as well."

"How? If you can tell me."

"He was also killed with a shotgun, but he was clearly murdered. No one was attempting to hide that fact. His body was found in a landfill, not in an isolated location with a shotgun at his feet."

"Terry never mentioned another deliveryman," Walter Randall said.

"There was only one deliveryman at a time," I said. "This young man had left and moved to Los Angeles by the time your son was working for the company."

"Perhaps he knew something and they wanted to silence him. Or perhaps Terry learned something and they were afraid that he had discussed it with the other man … and with Susan."

"Yes," I said. "We're considering that possibility. We've also discovered some … irregularities within the company."

"Something worth killing for?"

"Potentially," I said. "The chief officer in the company is also dead."

"What was his name?" Randall asked.

"Richland, recently. His actual name was Richmond."

"I didn't see anything in the paper about it," Randall said.

"It was in the OC Register but not the Times. It appeared to be a suicide. That's the way it was reported. There was a brief obituary and a picture."

"Did he die violently?"

"No, he died from an overdose of prescription medication."

"Do you believe it was a suicide?"

"We can't be certain at this point," I said, "and I'm not at liberty to share any other details."

"Quite a company," he said. "Everyone it touches dies."

"Yes," I said.

"So the bottom line is that the investigation is proceeding, perhaps with some increased momentum now."

"Yes."

"I appreciate your letting me know, Lieutenant. I know that you don't need to do that. I'll mention it to my wife and to Susan's mother.

Nothing in detail. I'll simply say that we had a brief discussion and that you're continuing to investigate Terry and Susan's deaths, that they're not being forgotten."

"I'd appreciate it if you'd keep it at that," I said.

"I will," he answered.

It took me nearly thirty-five minutes to cross the Valley and reach the Griffith Industries facility. That part of southern California is strange. There are large, bare hills but scattered, dense enclaves of homes and businesses. The Griffith building sat above and beyond the freeway in a small valley surrounded by foothills. The hills served as a natural fortification. They were barren except for some small metal buildings along the ridgeline.

There were four buildings within the industrial park. One appeared to be a utility building serving the other three. The largest building was Griffith Industries' headquarters. The others were numbered. There was no logo or signage on any of the buildings. There was a small parking area in front of the headquarters building, but no parking area for the company's employees. It was either beneath one of the buildings or behind it, between the building and the hill beyond. There was a single black van parked in front of the headquarters building, but no other vehicles in sight.

I assumed that some of the meetings with clients would have been held in other locations--the more confidential the clients the more confidential the locales. The firm would have a set of analysts along with the senior leadership and a group of writers and designers who would prepare reports, reports whose graphics and bindings would seem to justify their costs.

I had been to enough Washington meetings to see the edges of the consultancy culture—bright young people with pens and pads, overnighting reports to the participants, summarizing discussions, printing and binding ephemeral material with a degree of seriousness out of all proportion to the quality of the material itself--huge, expensive exercises whose central purpose seemed to be to confirm the self-importance of those involved.

The headquarters building was five stories high and perhaps twelve offices wide and three deep. More than enough space in which to do their work. There would be some cubicles, some functional conference space, some workrooms, some ceremonial conference space and some outsized executive space.

I had driven to the edge of the facilities and observed the physical outline from a distance, choosing not to drive into the center of things, lest I be observed by someone with a camera with a long lens. I was glad that I did because suddenly I saw something much more interesting.

SIXTY-ONE

Some people say that you should buy binoculars that provide greater breadth of vision rather than greater depth of field and magnification. The reason is that the distance binoculars (say, a 10 power, or so pair) require a very steady hand to keep the images from moving and that the narrow width of field makes it difficult for the eye to track lateral movement. Now you see things; suddenly you don't.

A tripod would have provided more stability than the window of my unmarked sedan, but I was grateful for the 10 power glasses. Without them I wouldn't have seen the tear tattoos on the man exiting the black van and entering the headquarters building of Griffith Industries.

Tear tattoos can mean a lot of different things. In Australia, for example, such tattoos are sometimes forcibly drawn on the faces of convicted child molesters. In American prisons a tear tattoo can represent the death of a brother. If the tattoo is empty or filled or partly filled, another range of meanings becomes possible. A tear with an empty top and full bottom, for example, usually means that the wearer has avenged the murder of someone he loved. (Or, Hector might have added, that the person ran out of ballpoint ink at an inopportune moment.)

This man had three and each was slightly different in its degree of shading. The binoculars weren't so powerful that I could see each of them in detail. I knew several things, however. The three tears did *not* represent a bachelor's degree from Georgetown, a master's degree from Johns Hopkins' School of Advanced International Studies and a Ph.D.

from the Fletcher School at Tufts. What they *did* represent was the fact that someone with a highly questionable past had access to a van either owned by Griffith Industries or by an organization doing business with them.

This was not a good thing (for Griffith Industries), but it was a very good thing for our investigation, confirming the fact that the stench issuing from the building was real and not some figment of our overactive imaginations. Unfortunately, the man had turned his face and entered the building before I could reach for my camera and take his picture. I *did* photograph the license plate of the van and called the number into headquarters.

Officer Jim Tunney called back with the i.d. a few minutes later. "It's registered to a company called Griffith Industries, Lieutenant," he said.

"Thanks, Jim," I said.

"Anything else I can do for you?" he asked.

"Not just now," I answered.

I waited another half hour, finishing my now-tepid cup of coffee, but the man did not reemerge from the building. Nor did anyone else. I didn't want to stay there so long that I might draw attention and have them photographing me rather than me photographing them, so I secured my binoculars and camera, left the area and got on the freeway to return home.

As I came up on the exchange for the **405** I started thinking about something that I had briefly suppressed, lest it distract me from discovering the identity of the man at the Griffith van. Did the three tears represent Jimmy Davidson, Sue and Terry Randall? Was this the company's real enforcer and Carlton Beauchamp little more than window dressing for their FirstGrowth operation?

The obvious problem, of course, was that I had no evidence whatsoever to support my suspicions. There is no law prohibiting the wearing of tear tattoos by employees of a corporate organization. In fact, there have been several government directives encouraging the employment of individuals who required a second chance, individuals who had paid their debt to the society they had wronged and were now prepared to walk the straight and narrow and never again fail in their responsibilities as upstanding citizens.

All I had was my gut instinct and gut instinct counts for less than nothing in a court of law. One of our old desk sergeants, a crusty veteran of a thousand street events named Ralph Marshall, used to say that 'if you want *sympathy* you can find it in the dictionary between *shit* and *syphilis*'. Though it would have been expressed in more polite terms, that was likely to be the exact response that I would receive from a judge if I went into criminal court armed only with suspicions and second guesses.

The traffic on the **405** slowed to a crawl just east of LAX, though it was moving briskly on the other side. Then, when I was above Long Beach the northbound traffic was at a dead stop, while we were moving at a brisk 65. Years ago I had stopped wondering why such things happened. It was simply freeway karma.

Hector was out of the office when I returned. "He's checking on Richmond's FirstGrowth clients," Chris Dietrich said. "He wanted to go root around in some unusual and unfamiliar places and I told him to go for it. What have you got, Tom?"

"How about a guy getting out of a Griffith Industries van and going into their headquarters building, a guy with a shaved head and three tear tattoos beneath his right eye?"

"I would say that that would be very interesting," he said. "The international elite meet the head of the welcoming committee from San Quentin. Maybe they're not so elite after all. Maybe they're street scum in three-piece suits."

"And fedoras," I said.

"Pictures?" he asked.

"Unfortunately, no. It was like the roach motel, Chief. He checked in very quickly, but he didn't check out. I waited as long as I thought I could. I didn't want to draw attention."

"I understand," he said. "I saw Hector's aerial photograph. You can't see the height of the hills around it without estimating the length of the shadows, the time of day, etc., but it looks like a classic box canyon."

"That it is," I said.

"What are the rectangular boxes on top of the hills, utility facilities?"

"Probably," I said. "There were locks on the sides. Those that I could see looked more like access ports than doors."

"See any satellite dishes?"

"No."

"Some of the old systems required large-scale computer technology to track the satellite. You'd have a dish attached to a box with the computer system inside. French technology, I think. You'd need it if you wanted to watch Russian television, for example."

"You mean if Griffith Industries was *seriously* involved in international consulting and had State Department-level facilities."

"Right. Or maybe CIA-level facilities. They still could, of course. At this point I'm thinking that they've got above-board operations and off-the-books operations. We've got to figure out which are which. I know what you're thinking, Tom."

"Yes, sir?"

"You're thinking that the guy with the tattoos is more likely to be involved with the latter than the former."

"Exactly."

"Pretty brash, wouldn't you say? Letting a guy like that walk around in broad daylight ... using a company van ... entering a company building."

"Want to know what my gut is telling me, Chief?"

"Always."

"I'm thinking that this is their weak point--their *arrogance*. They think they're smarter than everybody else. Their basic plan is so damned clever that they don't have to worry about incidental details, particularly when they're operating against small-town cops. They think we don't have any substantive evidence and they're right, but they think that gives them permission to operate with impunity."

"You're right, Tom."

"Chief … "

"Yes … ?"

"Let's make them sorry they did."

SIXTY-TWO

The next morning I met with Hector. His eyes looked like black stones set within concentric red rings.

"Late night with the files?" I asked.

"Yes, but not without some results."

"Lay it out for me."

"OK, I think that some of Richmond's clients were legitimate. Al Faber really is a wine investor and there's nothing in his past to link him with Griffith Industries, Richmond or Beauchamp. He's a blusterer, but very serious when it comes to business. Ditto David Lonis, a wiry little bantam rooster who loves his money dearly. No suspicious past ties. Karl Pfeifer looks kosher also. These guys would all know if they were being bilked. Their sole goal in life is profit and they each have a successful track record of meeting their goal. You don't get that by being a pushover for scam artists."

"They would also be wary of scams," I said, "skeptical … suspicious."

"Yes. I also thought that the drinkers would be clean, since they would know the difference between top-of-the-line wine and merely very good wine. Culbert probably is clean … and Campbell … but I have some doubts about Davies. Not serious doubts, but doubts."

"Why, Hector?"

"Because he sat on a commission with Donnelly, a few years back, when Donnelly was in Washington. They're old buds."

"Davies does economic consulting. How many people do that?"

"I don't know," Hector said, "probably too many."

"I'm thinking that in that small world a lot of peoples' paths would cross."

"I don't see what he could do for Donnelly, though," Hector said. "He's a lone wolf, a self-employed guy with no assets beyond his professional expertise."

"I understand," I said, "and we'll certainly keep an eye on him. What about Tucker and Byrne?" And the lawyer … Mahin."

"They reek," he said. "Tucker's firm employed Donnelly's company on at least three occasions. I know that fact from public records of events that made it to internet sites. From the frequency of the events I suspect that he may well be on retainer to them. Mahin's tight with him as well. She was an associate in a Washington law firm that worked closely with GlobalNet Partners, Donnelly's firm in New York. My guess is that she did all the work and generated the billable hours for the grayhairs in charge of the firm."

"So she was GlobalNet's D.C. lawyer."

"Her firm was," Hector answered, "but I think she was the lead attorney. Guess what … she and Donnelly are also Princeton classmates. L'il tigers, one and all."

"Isn't that special?" I said. "What about Clement Byrne?"

"Now it gets even more interesting," he said. "Byrne works for an engineering company called *Diatom*. Just above Studio City, by the **101**. Little building; big profits. *Diatom* doesn't refer to the algae-type diatom or to molecules with two atoms. I went down that road already. The name comes from the founders, two guys named Diamond and Thomasson. They do defense work. Highly-classified defense work. Make that über-classified defense work."

"But Byrne's a fiscal guy."

"Right. That's what he was when he worked for Griffith Industries four years ago."

"Their CFO?"

"Number 2 fiscal guy. The gig at *Diatom* was a promotion. I'm wondering if the appointment was engineered by Donnelly. Byrne could be a plant."

"So he and Donnelly have a relationship."

"Yes, probably a very cozy one."

"He would have beaucoup access to information that Griffith Industries could use. If Donnelly knew what kind of weaponry or defensive systems we were acquiring he could make that information available to foreign governments for a tidy sum."

"Yes," Hector said. "I'm not sure that Byrne would have the savvy to figure out what the engineers were actually doing, but he'd know enough to be dangerous."

"Of course," I said. "He'd know the government sources of *Diatom's* contracts and it wouldn't take a genius to figure out which agencies were likely to be most interested in which technologies. He'd know what kind of money was involved. He'd know the length of the contracts and how far along the research was. He'd know if contracts were suspended abruptly or extended for a noteworthy period of time. He'd know which engineers were working on which contracts because he'd see the allocation of effort numbers in the contract and the ways in which the agencies were being billed."

"He'd know enough to be *very* dangerous."

"Yes."

"I've got some other stuff."

"Go ahead," I said.

"Here's the original ad," Hector said, "the one placed by Richmond to drum up business." He handed me a xerox of a page from the morgues at the Orange County Register. "It also ran in the L.A. Times and the San Diego Union-Tribune. If you've got a good magnifying glass you can almost read it."

"I can see now why he had only nine clients, only five or six of whom may have been legitimate."

"It *does* get him on the record though," Hector said. "He could claim, truthfully, that he had advertised in the major southern California papers. Hard to believe that anyone would have actually read the ad, but they might have googled for *fine wine dealers* or something like that and gotten a hit."

"What about phone books or the parallel yellow-page books for which people sell advertising?"

"Just a listing in the white pages for Irvine. The number listed is the phone at the storage facility."

"How about Richmond or Richland?"

"Unlisted," Hector said.

"Yes, I think Chris mentioned that. And Beauchamp?"

"His condo's unlisted. You'd reach him through the FirstGrowth number only. Terry Randall had a personal number—the unlisted one that was one number different from the company 800 number."

"Like we've been saying all along … their front door was hardly locked in an open position, inviting business."

"Right, but it supports Richmond's story. Everything was somewhat hush-hush because of the limited market, the costs involved, the fact that individuals might have actually been bidding against one another unknowingly … "

"Yes. What about commercial wine dealers? Did any of them know about FirstGrowth?"

"Not that I could tell," Hector said, "and I talked to several dozen of the biggest ones, dealers located close to Richmond's alleged clients. The dealers also tended to agree on some key issues."

"Such as … ?"

"For one thing, the market is not that tiny. Sure, there are a lot of people trying to buy a limited amount of wine, but it's not like there are a million people trying to buy a thousand bottles of wine. Château Margaux, for example, has … (checking his notebook) … 210 acres that can legitimately use that name. Annual production of their lead wine is

150,000 bottles and they make another 200,000 bottles of their second-label wine. Plus some white wine ... around 35,000 bottles.

"When they release a wine, it's not a closely-held secret. And the price is set by the international markets ... and the price is high. If you want some, chances are you can buy some ... if you've got deep enough pockets. There are plenty of wine dealers around the country ... in New York ... in D.C. ... even in places like Springfield, Missouri ... who will be happy to take your money and sell you the wine.

"Things get trickier with the older wines, of course. The older and better they are, the scarcer they are ... no big surprise there ... and the prices will vary based on availability, condition and provenance ... but, again, if you've got the bucks you can usually get the wine ... assuming that there's any of it left to get. Each of the dealers said the same thing ... "

"What's that?" I asked.

"They said that there would have been a nice little business niche for FirstGrowth to carve out ... *once upon a time.*"

"And that time was ... ?"

"Before Vice-President Gore invented the internet."

SIXTY-THREE

"So with that information (very well done, by the way) I think our path is clear."

"What's your pleasure?" Hector asked.

"When we pressed Richmond he suddenly turned up dead and Beauchamp went running to Donnelly."

"They showed their hand."

"Yes. It worked once; let's do it again."

"Press one of the clients?"

"Yes," I said. "Pick one."

"Which of them is the most likely to crack?"

"Not the lawyer. She's used to being yelled at and having her genetic inheritance called into question. It's what lawyers do. She'll respond in a cool, measured fashion, weighing words and options. She won't panic and when she *does* communicate with Donnelly it will be in some secure way."

"I agree," Hector said. "Combat ... it's what she does."

"Byrne is our potential star, but let's keep him in reserve. If we're right and he *is* the dirtiest of the three, Donnelly will know that also. If we go right for him, Donnelly will infer that we know more than he thought we knew. Better to tinker a little around the edges. Make him think that we're still nibbling, but that we're starting to get warm."

"Go for Tucker."

"Yes," I said. "This time we'll meet on her turf."

"Century City, wasn't it?"

"Yes. I'll call and see if she's in."

Her male secretary asked if I wished to make an appointment. I told him it was urgent that I see her immediately and that I would be there at 10:00. He said that she had an appointment at 10:00 and that she would be unable to meet then. I told him to cancel it. "We can also meet at our headquarters instead of her's," I added. He said that he'd see what he could do. Hector and I grabbed a cup of coffee and got in an unmarked, heading north.

She was noticeably perturbed when we entered her office, a single-windowed space which seemed smaller than her position and personality would have demanded. She was still dressed like the head of a major couture house, ready to prepare for a show in which she would boss skinny models around and stare daggers at laggards through her hornrims, but her office was no more than 15'x15' with a small walnut desk, laptop computer, credenza and two client chairs.

The suite contained a few work stations and three or four enclosed offices, but though I heard some background noise I didn't see any other employees except for her 'personal assistant' Geoff, a fussy twentysomething who looked as if someone had seriously upset his biorhythms. The sign on the hallway door said *Western Export* and there were no names or further information there, except for the suite number.

"I hope we can do this quickly, Lieutenant," she said. "I've postponed a very important meeting in order to see you."

I didn't respond to that. Hector and I sat down in the client chairs; she hadn't acknowledged his presence, a fact which seemed to amuse him.

"The last time we met we discussed your relationship with a company called FirstGrowth," I said.

"Yes," she said.

"The CEO was a man named Richmond."

"His name was *Richland*, I believe," she responded.

"He changed it to Richland," I said. "His actual name was Richmond."

"And how is that important?" she asked.

"It must have been important to him; most people wouldn't go to the trouble," I said, waiting for a further response from her. She remained silent, repressing her anger.

"Actually he changed his name because he had been accused of fraud and found that his name—the name associated with that charge—was limiting his business opportunities."

"Was he *convicted* of fraud?" she asked.

"Actually, no," I said, surprised that she would pursue the matter. "I should say that he hasn't been convicted of fraud so far and won't be convicted in the future. William Richmond is dead."

"I'm sorry to hear that," she said.

"It appears that he took his own life," I said.

She didn't respond to that.

"In the history of FirstGrowth there have been four employees. Three of the four are now dead."

"As I told you, Lieutenant, my connections with them were quite distant. They made wine available for our meetings. The dealings were always through intermediaries."

"I wasn't suggesting that you needed an alibi, Ms. Tucker."

She started to come out of her seat at that, but then thought better of it, adjusted her chair and sat back.

"After Mr. Richmond's body was found, the sole surviving member of the company--their security officer--a Mr. Carlton Beauchamp, sought advice on the company's next steps."

"That was prudent," she said.

"He sought the advice of a man who had employed him in the past, a man named Victor Donnelly," I said.

She didn't respond to that, so I continued. "You have done a great deal of work with Victor Donnelly," I said.

"He runs a consulting firm called Griffith Industries," she said. "They have particular expertise in international matters. We have sought their advice from time to time."

"Donnelly's own expertise is in Latin America, not Asia," I said.

"There are members of his firm who specialize in Asian affairs," she said.

"Do you have his company on retainer?" I asked.

"We have a contractual relationship, but we are billed for specific services only."

"And how long have you had this relationship?"

"For approximately two years. What are you getting at, Lieutenant?"

"I'm not getting at anything, Ms. Tucker. I'm simply attempting to determine the nature of your relationship with these individuals. Carlton Beauchamp was employed by Griffith Industries, Mr. Donnelly's firm. He is now a part of a company in which every other employee has died, some under mysterious circumstances, one at least under criminal circumstances. When Beauchamp was under stress he ran to Donnelly. You have had a relationship both with FirstGrowth and with Griffith Industries. A suspicious person would find that triangle of connections interesting."

"A naïve person might," she answered. "Anyone doing global import/export needs advice with regard to local laws and customs. Griffith provides that. And they're the best. They're also *here*, so that we don't need to pay the costs for them to shuttle between L.A. and New York or L.A. and Washington. It's *interesting* that Mr. Beauchamp provided security for both FirstGrowth and for Griffith Industries, but that's none of *my* concern."

"I didn't say that he provided security for Griffith Industries," I responded.

"Well what else would he have provided? That's his area of expertise."

"True," I said. "I wasn't implying anything … "

"Of course you weren't, Lieutenant," she said, her tone contradicting her statement.

I just smiled.

"I believe we're through here," she said.

"For now," I said, turning to Hector, who rose from his chair without breaking his expression. He had been staring through Julia Tucker, like a bemused but detached god who had become accustomed to human lies.

"I don't think she enjoyed that very much," Hector said, as we got into our unmarked. "She shouldn't have made it so obvious."

"I think we picked the right person to squeeze first," I said. "Now we wait and see what happens. I doubt that we'll have to wait very long."

SIXTY-FOUR

I shared with Hector my concern that we were overstretching the department. With one team watching FirstGrowth's storage facility and a second watching Beauchamp, I now had a third team watching Griffith Industries and was considering putting a fourth on Julia Tucker.

"We're a small department," Hector said, "but this is capital murder, times 3, at least. Possibly times 4."

"And counting," I said. "I wish we could have officers on each of Richmond's clients."

"Before we go back … " Hector said.

"Yes?"

"I'd like to have a look at Griffith Industries' headquarters, see if I could get a look at the guy with the tear tattoos."

"That won't take long," I said. "Who knows? We might be back there before long anyway. It would help if you knew the territory in advance."

The traffic was slow through the pass and slow at the interchanges in the Valley. A trip that should have taken twenty-five or thirty minutes took nearly an hour. There was no sign of a police unmarked near the entrance to Griffith's facilities.

"So far so good," I said. "Not that I expected to see an LBPD officer with a set of binoculars, but I know one is supposed to be here. If I'm looking for him and don't see him, it means he's done a good job of sequestering himself."

I called him (his name was Jim Jeffords) on his cell. There was no ring sound in the area, but he came on immediately.

"Jeffords," he said.

"Jim, it's Tom Deaton. Hector and I are in the area and we wanted to touch base."

"I can see your vehicle, Lieutenant," he said. "Look to your right. I'm just below the crest of the hill."

He emerged from a crevice in the hill; he was wearing beige slacks and a light brown shirt, as close as he could get to desert fatigues without making his mission explicit. "Nothing major to report," he said. "Minimal vehicular traffic. Donnelly came in in his Mercedes at 8:15 this morning. Another seven cars came in between 8:45 and 9:00. No one's left yet for lunch. I expect them to do so soon."

"How about the van?"

"The one they park in front?"

"Yes."

"It was here when I arrived and no one's gone near it since."

"I'm going to send Hector up to join you for awhile, Jim. Show him around, give him a sense of the place. He'd like to have a look at the guy with the tear tattoos, if possible."

"No problem, Lieutenant. I could use the company. No sign of the tattooed guy yet this morning, but maybe we'll get lucky."

While I was talking to Jeffords Hector was covering his street clothes with a set of brown coveralls that he kept in the trunk. He also took off his leather shoes and put on a pair of old tennis shoes.

"I'm going to move the car out of sight and make some phone calls," I said. "Call me on my cell when you want me to return."

"It'll probably take at least an hour," he said. "Why don't you go get some coffee?"

"I'll get some sandwiches," I said. "We can eat them on the way back. I'll return at 1:15."

"Good," he said, taking a pair of binoculars from a box that was stored in the rear of the trunk. He slipped them inside the top of his coveralls, looked around and then climbed the hill to join Jeffords in the notch between the hills above Griffith's headquarters.

I found a small restaurant on Calabasas Road that looked as if it had been there before the mini-mansions, chain stores and apartment sprawl. They had a set of tables outside, where I drank a couple cups of coffee and made calls to Chris Dietrich, my dad and my friend Sarah. My personal and family life had been on hold and I wanted to assure them that I planned to surface before long and see them both again. My dad and I made tentative plans for a late dinner that evening. Sarah told me that she had been busy as well, working long shifts at Saddleback and running errands whenever possible in an attempt to hold her own life together. We arranged a time to get back in touch by phone, after which we would attempt to get back in touch in person.

I briefed Chris on the meeting with Julia Tucker and he authorized an officer to follow her. "I can't do it around the clock," he said, "but we can keep an eye on her during her workday and early evening. If she's a cog in Donnelly's machine she'll have to meet with him on his terms. We'll give Jeffords the information on her car, in case she comes there. Unfortunately, we can't cover all of southern California."

"Understood, Chief," I said. "The good news is that I think they'll move quickly. They're on notice now that we're investigating them and with a rising body count they'll want to consolidate their operations and cut their losses before they go to ground. Maybe even try for one big score before they scatter or hibernate."

"Right. Whatever the scam, they can't go on with business as usual, not with us looking over their shoulders. They'll have to make some adjustments, particularly if we're having an effect on their cash flow. Then again, we could get lucky. They might clutch and do something stupid."

"Always a distinct possibility with arrogant people," I said. "Just a sec, Chief; I've got a call coming in from Hector. He's at their facility … "

"Take it," he said. "I'll talk to you later."

"I'm ready," Hector said. "I saw what I needed to see and it isn't pretty."

"Got a sandwich choice?" I asked.

"Something that will take the bad taste out of my mouth," he said.

SIXTY-FIVE

I called Hector back when I was a few minutes away from their observation site. "Interesting development, Lieutenant," he said. "There's a car here that circled through their facilities, paused, and then circled a second time. He's just leaving. Jim is trying to get a photo of him, but there's a lot of glare on his windshield."

"What kind of car?" I asked.

"Avalon," Hector answered. "New. Maroon."

I pulled to the side of the road, positioning myself for a look at the driver. When he came by we looked at one another. Then he pulled over, just beyond where I was parked, got out and crossed the roadway to my car.

"Lieutenant Deaton," he said.

"Mr. Randall," I answered. "I can't say that I expected to see you here."

"Likewise," he said. "It looks as if we're walking the same path."

"What brings you here?" I asked.

"Beauchamp," he said. "I have a friend in Washington who has access to government contract information. He did some checking for me. It seems that Beauchamp was previously employed by Griffith Industries. His name turned up on one of their contracts with a government agency. I was about to call you. Now it appears that that's unnecessary."

"He did security work for Griffith," I said, "before he took the job with FirstGrowth."

"FirstGrowth is a very small operation, Lieutenant, but one that required significant capital for its startup."

"So you were checking out the next layer. The *possible* next layer."

"Yes, if that's what it is," he said. "Interesting facility, don't you think?"

"In what way?" I asked.

"Remote. Enclosed. Not completely secure, of course; nothing is, but it's very close to being so. Can I ask you a question, Lieutenant?"

"Of course," I said, wondering what that question would be.

"I walked into something, didn't I?"

"I don't know yet," I said. "I think it's best that we not find out the hard way."

"You would like me to keep some distance between myself and your operation."

"I didn't characterize it as an operation," I said. "We're investigating all possibilities. If this turns out to be a *significant* possibility, I wouldn't want you to be caught in the middle of it. We don't need the complications and we don't want to see you … hurt."

"You mean that literally, don't you?"

"It's always a possibility," I said. "We have four dead bodies already … not that I have to remind you of that fact."

He looked me in the eye before responding, aware that I had escalated the rhetoric.

"I'm not a stranger to violence, Lieutenant. And I know how to keep an appropriate distance between it and myself."

"I understand," I said, "but you have some special *motivation* in this case."

"You think I'd do something foolhardy to avenge my son's and daughter-in-law's death."

"The thought crossed my mind," I said.

I wouldn't," he said.

"Try to avenge their deaths?"

"No. I wouldn't do anything foolhardy."

"We need to stay in closer touch, Mr. Randall," I said.

"Like I said," he responded, "I was just about to call you. When the time comes … I hope you'll do the same."

"I'll stay in touch," I said.

"You know, Lieutenant," he said, "I'm glad you're here. I never doubted the fact that you'd stay on the case, but you're … what … eighty miles from home? And I'm here and then, suddenly, you're here. I'm an engineer, you know. I deal in facts, not fanciful coincidences. I *did* walk into something … something … *likely*."

"Let's hope that it is," I said. "In the meantime … "

"I'll be on my way back to Altadena," he said.

A few minutes later I briefed Hector and Jim Jeffords.

"Great minds traveling the same road?" Hector asked.

"Maybe minds with good computers traveling the *obvious* road," I said.

Hector wanted to drive. "I can eat at the same time," he said, "particularly when the freeway is an extended parking lot."

"I've got roast beef and cheese and roast beef and cheese," I said. "Your choice."

"Whichever one you don't want," he said. "They both sound good to me."

"I got some cold drinks too," I said.

"So Walter Randall wants to join us for the closing scene."

"Yes, I think he does, assuming that we're approaching it."

"I'm not sure that that would be a very good idea," Hector said. "So far I've been thinking that the FirstGrowth operation was a little too sloppy around the edges."

"And you've changed your mind?" I asked.

"I've changed my perspective a little," he said. "The guy with the tear tattoos … "

"You know him?"

"Yes, I do. From what Jeffords could see he was here all night. The other people who drove in this morning were all in suits with ties. The guy with the tears was wearing a mock turtle neck and what looked like cotton pants. He was also wearing dark tennis shoes."

"Dressed for action."

"Yes. Of course, he could have come in and then changed his clothes. You can't see faces very clearly from Jeffords' observation post. But if his job is security … "

"He would have been here all night."

"Yes."

"Who is he, Hector?"

"His actual name is Luis Alvarez. On the streets they call him San Luis."

"As in *Obispo*?"

"As in the Uptown Saints."

"Orange County gang."

"The nastiest."

"They locked horns with the Bboys from time to time, didn't they, Hector?"

"Yes," Hector said.

"And he's a notable member."

"Was. Before his sabbatical with the state."

"High up?"

"The leader," Hector said.

"I didn't think they let you … *detach* … that easily."

"As a rule they don't, but someone had to take his place while he was away."

"Someone equally unpleasant."

"Yes. A man named Carlos. He doesn't have a last name. At least he never uses it."

"A one-named star. Like Madonna … or Tyra."

"Something like that. He likes the anonymity but he also likes the celebrity, though he's not as fond of photographers as Madonna and Tyra are."

"And he took over when Luis was in prison, so he's happy to have him otherwise-employed now. Better that than to have somebody looking over his shoulder, waiting in line for his job."

"That's probably close to the official story," Hector said. "I didn't know where Luis was after his parole, but I knew that the Saints were comfortable keeping Carlos at the top of their organization."

"Tell me about Luis," I said.

"There isn't a great deal to tell," Hector said. "He's very intelligent. He's very violent. He's very ruthless."

"And he has the blood of many of your friends on his hands."

"As a matter of fact, yes, he does," Hector said. "I hope that doesn't mean that you'll remove me from the case."

"On the contrary," I said. "I wouldn't want you anywhere else."

SIXTY-SIX

Hector held his soft drink can between his legs and nibbled at his sandwich as I briefed Chris on what we had learned. He told me he'd check some records and get back to me. We were at the interchange for the **110** when my cellphone rang.

"Alvarez was convicted of some minor offenses; the heavy stuff didn't stick. He had a three-piece suit with alligator shoes and a silver tongue representing him. Kept it to a three-year bounce. He was out after twenty-one months. There's no record of employment since his release. These guys don't worry about collecting social security. That means that Donnelly is paying him off-the-books, which is a major no-no, especially in the case of a convicted felon. He can't hide behind the claim that he's trying to contribute to his rehabilitation if he's clearly trying to hide the fact that Alvarez is part of the Griffith team."

"Alvarez is too far gone to have his tattoos removed, let his hair grow out and change his name," I said. "He's not going to give up his street cred, even if a change in appearance would help keep him out of San Quentin."

"It may be that Donnelly needs his street cred," Chris said. "If Alvarez is his enforcer he'll want to keep the enforcees on notice."

"I can't imagine any other role for him in a consulting firm that specializes in international business and economics. By the way, what's his educational record look like, Chief?"

I could hear some papers shuffling. "He dropped out of high school … took a class at a community college … that's about it."

"I'm thinking he didn't take Art Appreciation," I said.

"No. It was something to do with auto mechanics."

"Probably pressured by a parole officer. Let me guess … he dropped out."

"He got an **NR**. I think that means 'no report'. No surprise there. By the way, I've got a guy en route to Century City in an unmarked. He'll keep an eye on Julia Tucker."

"Thanks, Chief, I appreciate it."

"What's next, Tom? Pressure on the fiscal guy?"

"Yes, but I'd like to wait a day or so, see if anything develops on the Tucker front. I want Donnelly to know that we're probing but I don't want him to think we're about to tighten the noose. I'd like to apply just enough pressure to force him to make a move. I don't want him to feel comfortable and I don't want him to feel like his world is about to blow up. I want to give him just enough space to encourage him to make a move … show us what he's really up to … give us the chance to take him off the street permanently."

"Makes sense," Chris said. "We're still not waist-deep in evidence, even though our leads and hunches are good. I wish we could bug his office … catch him in the act of being himself. He'll be too guarded for that right now. Maybe if this becomes a long-term deal … "

"Yes. He has answers for everything now. He's on the edge and thinks he's at the height of his game. Maybe if he thought the heat was off and he was in the clear … maybe then he'd let his guard down."

"It's a future option," Chris said. "Let's hope for a quicker strike. Raise the pressure incrementally but give him enough room to do something stupid."

When I got back to Laguna I familiarized myself with the records that Chief Dietrich had assembled. I checked in with the officer watching Julia Tucker (so far nothing of note to report) and met my dad for a late dinner.

We went to a steak place in Irvine, part of a chain, at the Fashion Island. It was very manly, with dark wood booths, thick white napkins and a special martini list. We each ordered soup and salads. Dad was old and I was tired. We weren't ready to assault a Kansas City Strip, even if the steak knives they gave us looked as if they'd cut through steel pipe.

"Look at us," he said, "we're a step away from Geritol and Depends."

"I know," I said. "Big case. Long hours. Too many freeway miles."

"Well, they never last forever. Either you catch them and convict them or you don't and you move on. Have you heard from Sarah lately?"

"I talked to her today. I'm supposed to call her back; we're going to try to get together this weekend."

"She working the ER again?"

"Yes. Long shifts."

"Too much business. Too many people trying to drive and medicate at the same time. Mind you, I'm trying to be sensitive and politically correct. Too many people attacking other people with barbecue forks. Here I thought those video games would dispel peoples' violent impulses, but all they seem to do is give people carpal tunnel problems. Your grandmother used to say, 'it's a great life if you don't weaken'. I guess she was right. The good news is that a police lieutenant is never short of work."

"That's right," I said. "If I had studied more psychology and anthropology I still wouldn't have gotten the lessons in human nature that I've learned on the job. I'm always amazed at the steps people will take to turn an illegal dollar. I feel like I'm becoming one of those nuns that used to grab us by the shoulders, shake us back and forth, and then tell us that if we applied ourselves directly to our tasks we'd be much more successful than we were in taking all of those elaborate steps to avoid them."

"Except that *you* can't tell them. You've got to let them go their merry way. Then when they screw up big-time you can arrest them. They'd never listen to the warning anyway. That's what makes them criminals.

They think they're taking shortcuts. They don't see that 'easy money' is hard to get and carries with it unpleasant side effects."

"You're right, Dad. All you can do is be patient, build your evidence and eventually make your arrest. By the time I enter the scene the preachers and counselors have all failed."

"Well, at least it's worth it. Somebody has to stand up for the people they've killed or stolen from. You get to balance the scales, at least for once … at least for a little while."

"Good job description," I said.

"Me, I was always into beauty … order … that kind of thing. Lovely boats, the Pacific on a sunny day under a blue sky, the harbor all in order. People enjoying themselves. Having some harmless fun. We tried to keep it *harmless* anyway. I especially like the marina at Christmas time, with the colored lights on the masts, reflecting off the water. It's beautiful. Not that we don't have problems from time to time. Pilferage, some petty vandalism, public drunkenness, the occasional angry husband or wife … a shout here, a curse there … but by and large it's a good place. Good things happen there. Expensive things, but good."

The waiter asked if we wanted dessert. We passed, but ordered coffee. "High test, not decaf," my dad said. "What the hell, let's live dangerously," he added. I smiled, but in the back of my mind I thought that that was exactly what we were getting ready to do.

SIXTY-SEVEN

At 8:15 the next morning I got a call from Bill Crawford, the officer tailing Julia Tucker. "They're on the move, Lieutenant. I just talked to Officer Jeffords; he was in San Marino this morning. Donnelly didn't go to work. He just passed through downtown; he's on the **10**, heading west. Tucker is on the **405**, heading south. She's already gone past the interchange for the **10**; she's not going to Century City."

"She lives in Beverly Hills, right?"

"In a condo on Doheny. Seven figures easily; very nice."

"Did she go anywhere else this morning?"

"No, sir. The lights went on in her condo around 6:30. She pulled out around 7:45. I thought she was going to work, but then she just kept on driving. Donnelly should have been heading west through the Valley instead of taking the **110** toward downtown. They're heading in the same general direction, assuming that he follows her on the **405**."

"They're going toward LAX," I said. "If his destination is farther south there are easier ways to get there than driving through the four stack at rush hour and then going west on the **10**."

"I understand, Lieutenant. You think they're flying out?"

"Possibly. You and Jim will have to tag-team them very carefully, Bill, particularly if they park in different lots and take different airlines."

"Yes, sir," he said. I could hear the apprehension in his voice.

"I'll check in with Jeffords," I said, "and tell him what I just told you."

"He got off the **10**, Lieutenant," Jeffords said.

"At La Cienega?"

"Yes, sir, how did you know?"

"He's going to LAX."

"Easier, I guess, than taking the **405**."

"Yes," I said. "Stay with him, Jim, and stay in touch with Bill Crawford. Unless they're parking in the same lot, taking the same courtesy bus and flying the same airline, it's going to be very difficult to stay with them."

"I understand, Lieutenant. We'll do the best we can."

"I know you will, Jim. Did Donnelly go anywhere else this morning?"

"No, sir. He got up at the usual time. I saw him in the kitchen window with his robe on and a cup of coffee in his hand and a little while later I saw the light go on in his upstairs bathroom. Thirty minutes after that he was dressed and pulling out of his driveway."

"She's not flying out, Lieutenant," Crawford said.

"Where is she, Bill?"

"At the airport Marriott."

"Breakfast meeting," I said.

Ten minutes later I heard from Jim Jeffords, confirming the meeting. "Go in from a side or back door," I said. "Have you got a laptop with you?"

"Yes, sir."

"If they're meeting in the lobby they'll be looking around to see if anyone's watching them. You need a prop, something to make you less conspicuous."

I checked back with Crawford. "I've got an attaché case, Lieutenant. I'll futz with some papers and a calculator."

"With both of you there you can switch off," I said. "One of you can go get some coffee and then return. Another can go to the men's room, etc. Look preoccupied. Check your watch a lot, as if you're waiting for someone who's late or worried about the courtesy shuttle to the airport. Don't try to be invisible."

"Got it, Lieutenant. Thanks."

Forty-five minutes later they both checked back in. We linked for a conference call. "Talk to me about the atmosphere," I said.

"Intense, Lieutenant," Crawford said. "She was flustered. Visibly upset. He stared at her and started whispering. His lips got narrow and he stopped blinking. It was like he was giving her orders."

"Yes," Jeffords said. "She got the two of them coffee, but neither of them touched it. He looked at his cup as if it was contaminated. Some kind of power trip thing … he was trying to keep her in her place, tell her they were there to do something besides drink coffee. After a sentence or two they were each on the edges of their seats. This wasn't social. This was serious business. He was the boss and she was the frightened employee. He was trying to calm her down and tighten her up at the same time. It was like he was saying, 'listen to me and listen closely … '"

"Did either of them give the other one anything—an object or something in writing?"

"No," Crawford said. "Not that I could see. Jim … ?"

"No, I couldn't see anything pass between them. I *did* see him gesturing a lot with his finger. It was as if … as if he wanted to put his finger between her eyes and start poking her, but couldn't. He knew somebody could see that. Instead, he was, like, poking at the table or poking at the floor between them. He was really wired tight, Lieutenant- -seriously upset, as if something's really gotten to him … "

"Good," I said, "perfect. Where are they headed now?"

"Both are on the **405**," Jeffords said.

"She pulled off for Century City," Crawford said.

"OK, they've had their meeting. Now they're going to work. Stay on them. They're off balance. They're going to either circle the wagons or take another step. Whatever they do next … it could be very interesting. This is not the time to let up. Understood, gentlemen?"

"Yes, sir," they each said.

I clicked off my cellphone and briefed Chris.

"Trouble in paradise," he said. "Good."

SIXTY-EIGHT

Two days later, early in the morning, the call came in from Will Andress, who was watching Beauchamp. "Something's up, Lieutenant. Beauchamp came in early this morning, at first light. He went inside the storage facility at Irvine and stayed there. A little while later--it wasn't any more than ten minutes--a van pulled up. The driver backed it against the door, so I couldn't see what he was unloading … "

"Did you run the plate number, Will?"

"Yes, sir. I'd seen it before. The van is registered to FirstGrowth. Usually it's parked out front and to the side, but it wasn't there this morning when Beauchamp arrived."

"Go ahead," I said.

"OK, anyway, the guy driving the van is the guy you told us about, the one with the tattoos that look like tears. The guy with the shaved head."

"Yes … "

"Anyway, he unloaded something from the back of the van and then closed it up, got back in the driver's seat and parked it. He then went back to the front door, punched in a code and went inside."

"So the door was locked for the few seconds that it took him to close up the back of the van and drive it a few yards away from the door."

"Yes, Lieutenant."

"OK, go on, Will."

"I waited another thirty minutes and Beauchamp came back out. This time he was carrying a box."

"What kind of box?"

"One of those crates they pack the wine in."

"Just one box?"

"Yes, sir, just the one. Beauchamp put it in the truck and started driving."

"And the guy with the tattoos stayed inside the facility?"

"Yes, sir."

"And you're following Beauchamp."

"Yes, sir. He's on the **405**, heading north towards L.A."

"Stay with him."

"Do you want me to pull him over, Lieutenant?"

"No, just let him drive, Will."

"I was just thinking, Lieutenant … "

"Yes?"

"Well, the guy with the tattoos is gang-related. He just brought something to Beauchamp and Beauchamp probably put it in the wine crate."

"Yes … "

"Well, it's a little obvious, don't you think?"

"Yes, I do," I said.

"I mean, it's almost as if they're tempting us … inviting us to arrest them."

"Yes," I said. "They know we're watching them closely, Will. They know that we've consciously decided to turn up the heat. If we arrest them they'll claim that we're disrupting their business, that we're harassing them … "

"Right. I was watching Beauchamp pretty carefully, Lieutenant, and … "

"Yes?"

"Well, he's a pretty goodsized guy and all, but the crate he was carrying didn't seem to really stretch him or anything … "

"What are you saying, Will?"

"I've got a computer here in the car, Lieutenant, and I was doing some calculations … "

"Yes?"

"Well, a case of wine weighs around thirty or thirty-five pounds. The wood box would be heavier than a cardboard carton, but not a whole lot heavier. If he loaded it up with other stuff, you know, sort of filled in the space between the bottles, there's only so much that he could carry. He didn't look bent over when he was carrying it. There was no sweat or strain or anything like that, so he couldn't have added too much of anything to the box. Gold is something like sixty thousand dollars a kilo. Coke is about half that, but the price is down lately. We've seen coke on the street for as little as a quarter of the price of gold. It can run twice that, depending on location, but there's a lot of risk involved for a comparatively small gain. I mean, if we arrest Beauchamp and the guy with the tattoos and whoever he's delivering it to, and anybody else standing on the sidelines when the deal goes down … "

"Yes, Will … "

"Well, unless he was really trying to herniate himself, he could probably only carry a few extra pounds comfortably and if he tried to carry much more than that it would be obvious that he was doing so. Even if you figure he's carrying heroin at something like fifty to sixty thousand a kilo, he's got to have some expenses up front. How much would you have to make in order to make the deal worth the risk? I know they're not rational, Lieutenant. I know what you always say about criminals being stupid, but these guys are hiding whatever it is that they're doing under some very expensive cover. Even if there's a hundred or even two hundred thousand dollars worth of profit in that box that Beauchamp's carrying … would he risk a big prison bounce for a number of people, plus the loss of all of their business assets to do it?

"I'm thinking that if their facilities get tied up in a court case and if Donnelly and the Tucker woman and some others suddenly see their reputations go down the tubes, they're in a world of hurt. They can't make money legally or illegally and it looks as if they've been doing pretty well making it legally … "

"Right, Will."

"I know that the dog found some drugs in one of the boxes, but that could have come off of somebody's fingers. Gang guys deal it; they also use it, especially the kind of guy who could get stuck with the job of loading cases. Not the brightest bulb on the tree, right, Lieutenant? Maybe he's bored. Maybe he's doing some product while he's on the job. It could happen. Gang guys that we pull in … a lot of them are tweakers, Lieutenant. It's like a Happy Meal to a kid—a standard part of the diet."

"Where are you now, Will?"

"On the **405**, Lieutenant, about a half mile farther than we were before. It's a parking lot."

"Stay on him and stay in touch."

I checked in with Chris and shared Will Andress' thoughts. "I think he's right, Chief. They may be as stupid as dirt in the way that they choose to lead their lives, but they're not stupid when it comes to economic calculations. They've made a huge investment and they're not likely to blow it all for what would be, for them, a relatively small short-term gain."

"Maybe they're dealing in something more valuable," Chris said.

"Yes, I think they actually may be dealing in a number of things. There's no evidence to that effect, but it makes perfect sense. They *would* diversify, wouldn't they? However, there's a major disconnect between them and the homeboys. A hundred K of something is a lot of money to the gangs, even if they have to divide it several ways. And they don't give a damn about the risk. On the other hand, *risk analysis* is what the suits do. It's their bread and butter. They can still work with the homeboys, but on, what would you say, *different terms*. They're not equal partners. Their relationship is symbiotic."

"What do you mean, Tom?"

"Well, think about it from the point of view of the gangs. Their biggest problem is exchanging money for product. They meet in a vacant lot, an abandoned warehouse, some place in the desert … whatever. They all worry that somebody will get greedy. Take the money and keep the product or take the product and keep the money. Either way, they'd leave a lot of bodies behind. It complicates things unnecessarily. But think about this … what if the deals were brokered by a commercial operation, a commercial operation with secure facilities … a commercial operation with professional dealmakers, whose job it was to provide assurances all around … most of all, a commercial operation with an inside guy who was one of their homeboys, somebody they trusted, somebody they knew would look out for their interests, somebody who knew the terms of the game, who knew what was on their minds."

"Go on, Tom … "

"Let's assume that the suits' legit businesses are turning a profit. A tidy profit. But they decide to throw some big numbers to the bottom line with a subsidiary enterprise or two. These people are natural go-betweens. Why not be the go-betweens in some street rackets, where the money is good and the transactions are swift and relatively uncomplicated? They'd need international suppliers to take care of the local bribes and the initial transportation costs, but Donnelly wouldn't lack for contacts, particularly in Latin America. They could then use the wine business as cover to transfer product. Maybe only every third or fourth run was dirty. Besides, the deliveryman would carry the risk, not the suits. If one was caught, the suits would plead that he was lone-wolfing it, that he was … what … *besmirching* their perfectly legitimate, upscale business. The product could be assembled and stored at one of their commercial locations and then exchanged there. But they could use multiple locations and the street guys would never know where the deal was actually going to be struck. They *would*, however, know that if they got greedy they could all go down. At the same time, they had their guy inside the organization to build their confidence. Ultimately it would be in everybody's best interest to just play it straight. Exchange money for product and get rich slowly and deliberately, instead of being greedy and risk losing everything."

"Right, and with their profit margins they'd always be ready to make their next purchase and keep the process rolling forward. If, say, two mil's worth of coke turns into thirteen or fourteen mil's worth on the street, their only issue is to keep a close eye on their distributors, track their revenue and be ready to reinvest it at the optimum time."

"Exactly, Chief. They've even got economic consultants on hand to run calculations for them on supply/demand issues. Ultimately the suits and the street gangs have the exact same desire--to buy low and sell high. And in the meantime maybe their little Orange County wine business just pays for itself. Or maybe it's a loss leader. Either way, they can pursue all of their dirty operations and still hold onto its assets. If they decide to do so, they can always sell their van and storage facility, dump whatever's left of the wine on the local market and recoup the bulk of their initial investment. And the FirstGrowth organization provides them with all kinds of cover. At the same time, from the perspective of people and risk, it's small. If things get hot or the employees start to fidget … "

"You just eliminate them."

SIXTY-NINE

Carlton Beauchamp delivered a case of something or other to Western Export at 10:17 a.m. He was inside Julia Tucker's office for approximately six minutes before returning to the FirstGrowth van, checking his mirrors, putting on his seatbelt and driving directly to the storage facility in Irvine, where he stayed the remainder of the day.

This was very odd, as I explained to Chris Dietrich, because the Tucker gospel had been that she never made direct contact with FirstGrowth; they delivered directly to the sites which managed the functions for her clients, sites in the U.S. as well as sites in Japan. The delivery today brought her into physical contact with Beauchamp, something that she did not need, something that undercut her prior claims that her relationship with the company was tangential at best.

I argued to Chris that Donnelly was probably just propping her up, convincing her that she need not be concerned about us, that we were more bluster than bite, that we had little or no evidence and that she should be prepared to conduct business as usual in the near future. He probably told her that we were intruding in affairs beyond our own jurisdiction and that we would have difficulty securing the warrants necessary to investigate the multiple premises that Donnelly was using for his operations.

She had probably responded that this was the first time that there would be a record of a deliveryman from FirstGrowth being on her premises and he had promptly brushed away her concerns in an effort to convince her that we were powerless to intervene in his affairs anyway.

He might have threatened her as well. At this point, I said, I believed him capable of doing anything in order to be able to sustain his organization and continue his activities. There was also the obvious fact of his pride and arrogance. The other members of his network were at best employees, at worst, simple pawns. I could hear his voice in the back of my head, telling her that she would just have to tough it out … then narrowing his eyes and telling her that she had no choice.

Chris compared their actions to a chess match in which one player sacrifices one or more of his pieces to gain later advantage. He thought that Donnelly was luring us into an obvious move. If we took it we would be embarrassed, our motives would be challenged and our credibility threatened, thus providing him the latitude for more ambitious moves later. I liked the analogy.

Two days later Beauchamp made a delivery to Diatom, Clement Byrne's engineering company. This undercut Byrne's story that FirstGrowth only delivered to Diatom's lobbying firm in Washington. The interesting fact for us was that we had ranked Tucker's and Byrne's firms high on the list of FirstGrowth's clients that were most likely to be involved with Donnelly in criminal activities.

The lawyer Clarice Mahin was third on our short list. FirstGrowth delivered to her law firm four days later. Mahin had claimed that her firm used FirstGrowth's wine for Chrtistmas gifts, but given the fact that the holidays were three and a half months away, her story was undercut as well. Clearly, this was of no significance to Donnelly.

Chris and I worked our way through several scenarios. Donnelly was testing his people. Donnelly was testing us. Donnelly was giving Beauchamp some busy work to do. Donnelly was communicating through Luis, via Beauchamp. Luis was his real security man; Beauchamp was a stooge. Luis gave materials or messages to Beauchamp to give to these other elements within the organization. The least likely explanation was that Beauchamp was carrying payoffs of some sort, encoded numbers of offshore accounts, for example, something that he could convey but not understand or utilize. This explanation was the least likely. The one thing on which we both agreed was that Donnelly was buying time in anticipation of a major move. He wasn't packing it in. His arrogance wouldn't permit that.

A week after the delivery to Mahin's law firm Hector called me first thing in the morning on his cell.

"That hunch I wanted to run down … " he said.

"Yes?"

"Something may be happening."

"Go on … "

"Well, last night I was following this guy named Alberto. One of the Saints. More than a street soldier, but not one of the anointed ones at the top. Jumpy kind of guy. Unsteady. The kind that makes mistakes … anyway, Alberto went to this building in Santa Ana. Industrial, past its prime. Broken windows. Peeled paint. Lots of mold and rust … *surprise*: Carlos was there. *Hello*, I thought. I'll trade Alberto for Carlos and see what the head homeboy is up to these days. Alberto hands something to Carlos just as Carlos is leaving. Probably cash. Carlos takes it without saying anything and gets in his Range Rover. He drives south on 55, gets on the **405** and turns off onto Jamboree in Irvine.

"He drives for several blocks and then turns off into a parking lot behind a restaurant. He sits there for about ten minutes, making phone calls on his cell. A little while later a Hummer pulls in and parks next to him; they're facing in opposite directions, so it's driver to driver at their windows. And guess who it is … "

"Luis Alvarez."

"Bingo," Hector answered. "They talk for about fifteen minutes. I'm writing down license plate numbers, but for obvious reasons I can't get too close to them. Neither of these gentlemen would be very … welcoming … to me."

"I understand," I said.

"Anyway, the Hummer is registered to Luis' mother and the Range Rover is registered to Carlos' father."

"So they don't have to give their own addresses … "

"Right. And we could probably make something of it, since Carlos' father is blind and doesn't have a driver's license, but I figure we're hoping for something bigger this time out."

"Did they exchange any objects? Notes … instructions … money?"

"No, but Luis was gesturing a lot, as if he was explaining something in detail to Carlos."

"Which one seemed to be in charge?"

"Luis, hands down, but Carlos was playing it as cool as he could under the circumstances. He's used to having people genuflect when they come to meet with him. He let's them kiss his ring, flick dust off his shoes, that kind of thing. I'm thinking maybe Luis misses that. He's working for somebody else now, but here he has a chance to give the orders, just like in the old days. Anyway, Carlos listens attentively and nods every now and then … "

"They're both going for the money," I said. "They can't afford to play too many who's-on-top games. That would be distracting."

"Right, but you can tell … they each want to play Generalissimo and order the peons around them to fall at their feet. There's a certain tension there. Anyway, they talk. Luis gestures. Carlos nods. They finish. Each closes his window and they drive off."

"Which one did you follow?"

"Carlos. I figure if Luis is giving the orders he's doing so for Donnelly. His part is done. So I follow Carlos, see if he's going to start putting Luis' orders into operation. He drives back to Santa Ana, to the same building. Alberto's not there, but a guy named Joaquin is. I'm thinking that Carlos may have called him after he talked to Luis. I didn't see any cellphone when he was driving, but he was probably using a Bluetooth. An upstanding citizen like that, he wouldn't want to drive recklessly and jeopardize the lives of any potential customers who might want to buy his dope. Anyway, Joaquin is actually Carlos' brother-in-law. He's married to Carlos' sister, Graciela. Joaquin is Carlos' number two. He's his operations officer."

"Something's going down."

"That would be my assumption," Hector said.

"I'll be in in less than fifteen minutes," I said. "I'll meet you at the arms room."

SEVENTY

"There's something we're missing," I said to Chris. "We've run through multiple scenarios. Some of them are plausible, some less so. None of them are … clean."

"You mean none of them are *simple*. None of them are *elegant*."

"Yes. Assuming that Donnelly and his people are proceeding rationally, they have a coherent plan. Jerking us around may be part of the plan, but it's only that … a part."

"Go on," Chris said.

"I talked to Will Andress again, the uniform who's been watching Beauchamp. He said that each time Beauchamp made one of his runs—to Tucker, to Byrne and then to Mahin—he did the same thing. He drove from Irvine to their offices and then he drove back to the storage facility. Alvarez was there waiting, when he returned. When Beauchamp arrived, Alvarez left. Andress is watching this and he concludes … what? He concludes that Alvarez was watching the facility in his absence. When Beauchamp returned, Alvarez could leave."

"Right."

"What threw us off was the fact that Alvarez began the process by bringing something to Beauchamp, something he unloaded at the door of the storage facility, while he blocked Andress' view. Maybe it was nothing. Probably it *was* nothing. We were led to believe that Alvarez brought something valuable, something to be traded or distributed, something to be hidden among the wine bottles. Meanwhile they were waiting to see if we would take the bait and take Beauchamp down."

"Yes."

"But what if we've missed the fundamental concept? Beauchamp *was* dropping something off, but that could have all been mystification. What if he was driving to Tucker, Byrne and Mahin's firms to pick something up?"

"Like the old joke about the smuggler. The customs agents were watching the goods and finally discovered he was smuggling wheelbarrows."

"Yes. And maybe he didn't receive anything from one of them, or even from two of them. He's making three stops to establish a pattern and we're buying it. Maybe he only received material from one of his three contacts. Maybe he just received some *information*, some documents."

"From Byrne in particular," Chris said.

"Yes. That would be his most lucrative source. And we've been thinking something heavy … something thick. A kilo of Mexican heroin. Five kilos of cocaine. Precious metals. Precious stones. Something in … *quantity*."

"Alvarez was opening up the back doors of the van for our benefit … so we wouldn't pay attention to the fact that what was really important was actually inside his shirt."

"That could all be part of the fairy tale they were constructing for us. Something that needed to be *unloaded*, not simply transferred. We're looking for a lump of platinum or a box of emeralds and they're passing miniature envelopes. Simple misdirection—the magician's mainstay. The documents could be on a piece of microfiche. A whole library of documents could be on a flash drive. Andress saw Alvarez open the doors of the van—a nice, grand gesture--but he wouldn't have seen anything that Alvarez might have passed to Beauchamp in the hallway and he wouldn't have seen anything on Beauchamp's person when Beauchamp returned from his drop-offs. Whatever it was it was small. At the most it was a folder that Beauchamp could have slipped inside his shirt. Beauchamp handed it off to Alvarez in a second and he did it out of Andress' line of sight. Then Alvarez left with it. Even if we had stopped him we might not have found it. Think of the possibilities of miniaturization; think of the places the material could have been hidden … in his Hummer … or in his body."

"But Hector says that Alvarez's former gang is being mobilized. What's their role in this?"

"Remember earlier, Chief, when I said that their relationship was symbiotic?"

"Yes."

"Maybe the roles change, depending on the contraband involved. If Donnelly is selling drugs, drugs that are being distributed by the Uptown Saints … "

"Yes?"

"You don't need the whole team. In fact, you don't want any of the team. Somebody might be tempted by greed. All you really need is Carlos--Carlos and maybe one or two other people. They meet with one or more of Donnelly's people at one of the corporate sites; money and drugs exchange hands. Alvarez stands in the background, smiling approvingly. The deal is done. Carlos' people take the drugs to the street and start accumulating profits. Donnelly makes a deposit in an offshore account. And drugs are something the Saints understand. They understand its economy; they understand its profit margins; they understand the supply and they understand the demand."

"But what if they're dealing in something that Donnelly understands … "

"Exactly. International security, international geopolitics, state secrets, cutting-edge security and weapons technology … these are not things that Carlos and his people know how to sell, at least not for maximum profit. These are not things that laymen might even understand. But if they were to be sold … and if they were … *consequential* in their importance, the buyers would understand that importance because they would be paying the price that Donnelly would demand."

"And it would not necessarily entail the kind of relationship that he had developed with the Saints … one refined over time … one in which there was a certain level of trust."

"No," I said. "And there would be the potential for great risk. The danger would be in proportion to the value of the documents being sold. Donnelly would require *security*. Significant security."

"So instead of buying goods, the Uptown Saints provide the security surrounding the transaction. And you're probably talking tens of millions of dollars rather than hundreds of thousands."

"Enough to pay the Saints a nice fee for a simple day's work, assuming that everything goes according to plan. Of course, if the other side brings their own people, things could get … *testy*."

"And you think the deal would go down at Griffith Industries' headquarters."

"It's the easiest to defend," I said, "and in many ways the easiest to control. That would be important to Donnelly. If this is to be his last big score, at least for awhile, he'll want to keep his risks to a minimum."

"It's *simple* enough," Chris said, "at least in the conception if not in the execution. So we've got fraud, drug dealing, murder and now … what … treason?"

"Possibly. All of which he would simply see as different types of business transactions."

"He's a ruthless son-of-a-bitch."

"And not stupid," I said. "There's one thing we have to remember … "

"What's that?" Chris asked.

"When we take him down … we take him down for all of the crimes, including the murders."

SEVENTY-ONE

With all of the surveillance teams in place we hit enough of a lull for me to talk again with Beauchamp. I wanted to do so on my terms. After checking with Will Andress I went directly to Beauchamp's condo. The sun had not yet risen. He appeared at the door in his bathrobe.

"Good morning, Carl," I said, "not to worry, I brought coffee."

"What do you want?"

"I want to talk to you. I want you to start thinking about some things."

"I want my lawyer present."

"You can always call your lawyer if you think it necessary, Carl. Stan is always up for the billable hours, especially at his rates, but I'm not sure you need him at this point. And I'm not sure that you'd want Victor Donnelly or Luis Alvarez to know that you've called him in. You're not under arrest. I'm not holding any warrants. All I've got is a bag with two cups of coffee. It's not an interrogation, Carl. It's just two guys talking."

"It's never just two guys talking when one is a police lieutenant," he said.

"No, Carl, this time that's all it is."

He stared at me some more, looking into my eyes for clues of one kind or another and then invited me in. "Don't worry about Alvarez, Carl. I've got a man outside. If Alvarez shows up he'll let me know. You can then go through an elaborate theatrical routine, yelling at me … throwing me out of your condo … whatever it is that you think might convince him that we're not cozy."

He didn't bite at Alvarez' name. "What do you want?" he asked, peeling back the lid on his cup of coffee and taking a short sip.

"I want to talk about your position in all this, Carl. And I want to talk about some … inevitabilities."

"So talk," he said.

"I will," I said. "How's the coffee?"

"It's OK," he said, his tone noncommittal. He pointed to the chair and couch and we each sat down.

"Good. I hope you enjoy it. Anyway, here's how it is, Carl. Luis Alvarez is a convicted felon, the former head of the Uptown Saints, an OC gang that specializes in drug distribution and general mayhem. He works for Griffith Industries and he's serving as a go-between between you and Victor Donnelly. He's also in direct contact with the current head of the Saints, a man by the name of Carlos. No last name. Both Carlos and Luis have reputations for violence and ruthlessness that are grounded in hard fact. They're not nice people, Carl. They didn't go to eastern colleges."

Beauchamp interrupted me. "Donnelly hired Alvarez to give him a second chance. He had made some mistakes, serious mistakes, but he's smart and he's a good learner. There's no law against hiring someone who's taken a fall. There are organizations that encourage it … "

"Carl," I said, "with all due respect … I think this will be a much more productive meeting if you resist the temptation to counter facts with bullshit. On a good day Luis Alvarez is a vicious piece of slime; we both know that. May I continue?"

"Go ahead," he said, sipping his coffee.

"Good. When we searched the FirstGrowth storage facility in Irvine we brought in a large team, including a police dog trained to sniff out contraband. The dog was a female German Shepherd named Sophie. I know, Carl … that's a Greek name for a German dog, but we both went to college and we both know that the name Sophia means *wisdom*. We call her Sophie for short, but Carl, this dog is very sweet and very loving but one thing that she is most definitely not is stupid. She worked her way through your facility, checking every nook and every cranny very carefully. Then she found a residue of cocaine in one of the wine boxes, Carl."

"Maybe some cokehead packed the box … back in Bordeaux."

"Carl, remember what I said before … about the bullshit … "

He stared at me and sipped his coffee.

"I'm trying to be helpful to you here, Carl. You're going to have to make some serious decisions and I'm giving you a … context … in which to make those decisions. I'm telling you some of the things that we've learned, Carl. You don't have to comment on them. We both know that they're true."

He continued to stare and sip.

"This coffee is pretty good, isn't it?" I said. "It's not Starbucks. I got it from a Mom-and-Pop just down the street. Some people think that Starbucks over roasts the beans. I knew somebody who used to call them *Charbucks*. Anyway, Carl, we've had the wine at the storage facility tested by experts. Some is legit; some is bogus. It's phony, Carl. The wine in the bottle … it isn't the wine on the label. Just a reminder, Carl … the break point between a misdemeanor and a felony in California is less than a thousand dollars. Every phony bottle there would have been priced much higher than $1,000, Carl. That means that the storage facility over which you exercised control is filled with cases of wine, each bottle of which would represent a felony count. And some of those cases were spiked with cocaine."

He started to speak but I held up a finger, stopping him. "I know, I know, Carl. We would have to prove a number of things in order to convict you. That's not my point, Carl. I'm not here to talk about convicting you. I'm here to talk about protecting you. At this point I am sure that it has not escaped your notice that you are the only employee of FirstGrowth who remains among the living. And Carl, you went to Brown. You studied sociology, Carl. Now you're a part of a social group that kills people it no longer needs. This group kills people who know things that could incriminate them. They killed Bill Richmond, Carl. Bill was a drama student, wasn't he? He couldn't act his way out of this one, Carl. And I think we both know that you won't be able to either.

"We're aware of your recent trips to the offices of Julia Tucker, Clarice Mahin and Clement Byrne. We're also aware of the business connections between those three and Victor Donnelly. They all go back a long way, Carl. They've been connected longer than you have, Carl. Their liability is also greater than yours, Carl. And they're students of *risk*. They do *risk analysis*. People pay Victor Donnelly a great deal of money to advise them with regard to risk. I'm not a student of risk, Carl. I'm a student of guilt. But I know one thing ... you pose a risk to all four of them. You were the runner, Carl. You were the point of contact. You were the person in the center of the lenses used by the surveillance teams. And we both know what that means. You pose a risk to the gang of four, Carl and me ... well ... let's not forget the fact that I saw Terry Randall's body and I saw his wife Susan's body, what was left of it. I saw Jimmy Davidson's body on the coroner's table, Carl. Think of it this way. You're the bridge between the gang of four. These people *burn* their bridges, Carl.

"They were a little gentler with Bill. They probably figured they had drawn enough unfavorable publicity already. They wanted it to look as if Bill was masterminding things and finally decided to pack it in. Doesn't look like Luis' work to me, Carl. Cutting people in half with a shotgun ... that's more Luis' thing, don't you think? I won't insult your intelligence by talking about the possible methods he might use in your case. Let's just say that Luis won't hold anything back."

"What do you want from me?" he asked.

"I want to continue this discussion," I said. "It's nice talking to an intelligent person. I don't have to explain the whole *scapegoat* concept to you, Carl. You already understand it. The society symbolically loads up the goat with their collective sin and guilt. Then they turn it loose in the wilderness. You're an educated man, Carl. You know that the fact that the goat is innocent doesn't mean a thing. You also know what life is like in the wilderness for a goat. What would Hobbes say, Carl? *Nasty, brutish and short?* Except that he wasn't talking about goats. They had it much worse. He was talking about men, men without government or restraint, men dedicated to taking all for themselves at any costs. Men like the ones you've been involved with, Carl--the kind who wouldn't hesitate to slide their knives across the goat's throat."

"What do you want to talk about?"

"For starters?" I said, taking a long drink of my coffee, "I want to know what you and Bill were using that room in his basement for. You know the one, Carl. The one that's stark and empty. The one that you cleaned up so carefully with the oceans of bleach."

SEVENTY-TWO

The call from Chris came in twenty-five minutes later. "It's all coming down," he said. "We've got to roll."

I called Jim Jeffords and warned him. "Half of the evil in Orange County is headed your way, Jim," I said. "If they're coming to Griffith Industries (which I think they are) they'll want to secure the perimeter. That means that if they find you they'll take whatever action they need to clear the area."

"I understand, Lieutenant. These are the gang people?"

"Yes. I was out of the office when Chief Dietrich called. All of the OC principals are heading north. There's no reason to expect that the muscle elements would be there to conduct the transaction. Their purpose will be to provide security."

"Do you have an ETA, Lieutenant?"

"Less than an hour, Jim. There could also be some advance elements from L.A."

"I'll make myself scarce … from the immediate area anyway. I'll station myself so that I can see how many are coming and where they're positioning themselves. Any guesstimates on the total number?"

"Probably twenty security people, hopefully fewer. Probably five or fewer of the executive types."

"But the security types will be heavily armed," he said. "They *do* like their guns."

"Yes, they do," I said. "And Jim … "

"Yes, sir?"

"Choose your position very carefully. You'll be our prime source of intelligence when we arrive."

"Will do, sir."

"I've called the LAPD," Chris said. "I've told them as much as I could. They're providing backup support."

"How many are we, Chief?"

"Ten, counting you and Jim Jeffords. The LAPD is sending ten initially. They'll also have another twenty in reserve. I'll check back with them as soon as we see the dimensions of the situation."

"Jeffords will give us a count of the vehicles at least. You never know how many they might have inside. The numbers should tell us how important they consider this operation to be."

"Right," Chris said, "and as we've been discussing, Tom, I don't think this is about drugs. They wouldn't mobilize the Saints for a drug deal. Adds too many imponderables to the mix … "

"Yes. This is about something else. Where are you now, Chief?"

"On the **405**, near Torrance."

"I'm right behind you, just above Long Beach."

"Good. Mahin and Tucker have each gone in to work. Usual time, nothing suspicious. Bill Kenner is on Byrne. Check with him. I spoke to him about fifteen minutes ago and he said that Byrne had gone out earlier than usual. I've got to stay on the horn with the LAPD. Let me know what Bill says."

"Will do, Chief," I said, and pulled up Bill's number on my cell.

"Good morning, Lieutenant," Bill said.

"Hi, Bill, the Chief says you're on Byrne this morning."

"That I am, sir. I'm not sure what he's up to, but he's broken his usual pattern."

"How so, Bill?"

"Well, usually, he goes straight into work in Studio City. Sometimes he'll stop at a coffee shop on the way. This morning he was up earlier than usual. You've seen his house, haven't you, Lieutenant?"

"Yes. Leans out over the canyon. Boxy but pricey."

"Right. Well, I don't think there are too many interior walls, since one light seems to brighten the whole space. He was up before 6:00 this morning, more like 5:30. He got all dressed up and I eventually saw him on his deck, drinking some coffee. Well, I figured it was coffee. He was drinking out of a coffee mug."

"What time was that, Bill?"

"Around 6:15. A few minutes later he got in his car, drove down from the canyon and went into Westwood, just below UCLA."

"And … ?"

"He went into a coffee shop and got some more coffee. He bought a bag of beans—a large one--as well as a cup of already-brewed."

"Did anybody join him there?"

"No, not that I could see. He was also working on his laptop. He'd sip for awhile and then he'd type. Then he'd sip some more and then he'd type some more … "

"And by then it was what … 7:00?"

"He was there until 7:30, Lieutenant. I'm thinking that he ran out of coffee and drove to his favorite supplier to restock. However, the guy is surgically attached to his laptop, so when he went into the coffee shop he couldn't resist sitting down for a second and checking his mail. Once the screen lit up his addiction kicked in. That's what I'm figuring at least. When he finished blogging and surfing and downloading and emailing he drove back home. Maybe he was just expending nervous energy; maybe he had some last-minute arrangements to make on a major operation. I have no way of knowing which."

"Was he looking around, trying to see if he was being followed?"

"Not that I could tell."

"Did he make any calls on his cellphone?"

"No, and he didn't receive any."

"Any suspicious moves?"

"No more so than usual, Lieutenant. He's sort of a jumpy guy to begin with. Finicky. He clicks his pen a lot, straightens his tie … "

"Did he take a circuitous route to Westwood?"

"No, not really. Sometimes when a guy thinks he's being followed … he'll drive into mall lots or other places where it's hard to follow him … he didn't do anything like that. The interesting thing is that he still hasn't gone to work. He's at home, out on his deck again, drinking more coffee. Maybe he's drinking up what he just bought. I hope it's decaf, Lieutenant. Otherwise, his heart'll be jumping out of his shirt by now from all the caffeine."

"Keep an eye on him, Bill. Call me the moment he moves again."

"Will do, Lieutenant. Wait a sec … no, false alarm."

"He's still there?"

"Yes. In the bathroom."

"I'm surprised he's not living in there, from all that coffee."

"He's back out. Putting on his jacket … he just set his security alarm … got into his car … heading out."

"East or west?"

"That'll take me a minute or two, Lieutenant. OK … he's headed … west. He's not headed for work, Lieutenant."

"That depends on what his real job is, Bill."

SEVENTY-THREE

Jim Jeffords called in twenty-five minutes later. "Three Ford Explorers, Lieutenant. All black, all with tinted windows. A mini-convoy."

"Pretty maids all in a row," I said. "How about Donnelly?"

"He came in earlier; at least his car did. He drove directly behind the facility, so I couldn't get a look at him."

"How about plate numbers on the Explorers?"

"Already called them in, Lieutenant. All registered to women in Orange County. Latina surnames."

"Did they park in front or back?"

"All in back, Lieutenant. There are no vehicles in front of the building at all, not even the usual van."

"Clearer lines of sight," I said. "Whoever's coming to visit is coming in with no place to hide."

"Did the people in the SUV's position themselves yet?"

"Yes, sir. There are six around the perimeter of the facilities. They're all in dark jackets ... almost like uniforms. They're basically lining the roadway. They didn't climb to the top of the hills. I was able to move back into my regular position."

"What are they doing, Jim--milling around? Standing at attention?"

"They're standing at something like port arms, except they don't have any obvious arms. The jackets are loose, though. I'm sure they have weapons inside them. They're talking to each other on cellphones, standing in place, looking around like doormen or bouncers."

"Lights on in the main building?"

"Throughout the building, Lieutenant. They're open for business. The only difference from the average day is the absence of the van and the presence of the gang of six on the sidewalk, along the roadway."

"Let me know if there are any changes, Jim. Any at all."

"Will do, Lieutenant."

He called back fifteen minutes later and told me that Clement Byrne's car had arrived as well. Bill Kenner had followed him from Coldwater Canyon and asked Jim to tell me that he would wait nearby in case he was needed.

I briefed Chris Dietrich on the arrival of Byrne and the vehicles containing the Saints; he told me that the LAPD was being very helpful. "They may have another six inside the building, but I doubt that they'd have many more than twelve total in the three SUV's. We'll have more than enough officers to contain them."

"We're not dealing with choirboys here, Chief, but they should have a normal fight-or-flight response. They like to hurt people but they also like to stay alive and stay out of prison, whenever possible. If we show preponderance of numbers we should be OK."

"And seriousness of purpose," he added. "That's what they understand, first and foremost."

"Right."

He arrived at the site with the LBPD officers a few minutes before I did. The convoy of LAPD vehicles was on-call, less than forty seconds from the entrance to Griffith Industries. Our principal problem was to position our vehicles so that they would be available for rapid deployment but not obvious to anyone incoming. Whoever the guests of honor at Donnelly's party were, we didn't want them to bolt before we could welcome them appropriately. Jeffords was instrumental in handling the logistics of the vehicles. He was by now so familiar with the terrain and the volume of vehicular traffic that it sustained that he was able to advise the chief and his LAPD liaison effectively.

Once the cars were sequestered and the men staged for various assault scenarios, Chris and I joined Jim at his favored observation post. "Now we wait," Chris said. "It shouldn't be too long. The Uptown Saints aren't in the habit of donating their services for free. Donnelly's mobilized them for a purpose … for what he sees as an *important* purpose … and if it's important it's been timed precisely. This isn't some farmer's fruit stand, open for business, and now waiting for the occasional tourist to drive by."

Fifteen minutes later a vehicle approached. "This looks promising," I said. It was a black stretch limo, a modified Cadillac Escalade. There were no accompanying vehicles. It drove slowly into the Griffith Industries industrial space.

"Hello," Chris said, looking through his binoculars.

"What is it, Chief?"

"Diplomatic plates."

Jeffords took out his cell.

"From a Consulate," Chief Dietrich said. "Initial letters: KV."

Jeffords executed a few touches and keystrokes. "KV, Chief … that's Saudi Arabia." He brought up another screen. "They didn't have to drive very far, Chief. The consulate is just off the 405, just below Santa Monica Boulevard."

"So what do you think?" Chris asked. "Mid-morning tea and cookies or something more interesting?"

"Definitely something more interesting," I said.

"Only one problem," he said. "They're going to have an inkpad and a big rubber stamp and each of their foreheads is going to be stamped with the same word."

"*Immunity*," I said.

"That's the one," he answered.

SEVENTY-FOUR

"That one is the one in charge," Chris said, "the one in the black suit."

Jeffords was snapping pictures as the men got out of the car. "The boss rides in the back," he said. "The other two are just spear carriers."

"Young," I said. "Probably not the chief official. More like a cultural attaché or whatever the Saudi equivalent is."

"Lone wolf?" Chris responded. "A guy with his own agenda? Not that the Saudis haven't played footsie with the terrorists on a regular basis … "

"Probably," I said. "It's just not likely that some ambassadorial type would take the risk of being seen in public with the likes of Donnelly, particularly if the purpose of the meeting was the exchange of cash for government secrets. The studmobile is also a little out of character. I'm thinking the Saudis would go for a more conventional sedan-type limo. Maybe a Cadillac or Mercedes."

"They've got the bucks," Chris said. "Maybe they've got the hearsemobile for the old guys and the studmobile for the youngsters."

"Have you got enough, Jim?" I asked.

"Good side shots, one face-on when he turned to give the other guys orders."

"Download them and we'll shoot them over to the Bureau," Chris said. "I'll call the AD's office and give him a headsup."

"That was a pretty big briefcase he was carrying," I said.

"Filled with cash probably," Chris said, as he checked for the FBI office number in his cellphone.

He was patched through to the Assistant Director's office promptly and given an email address for the photos, which he read to Jeffords. Four minutes later we got a return call from the AD's personal assistant. "He's in a meeting again," she said, "but we've got your i.d. Last name, **Rafik**; first name **Moammar**. At the Saudi Consulate. Honorific title. Literal translation, something like *servant of the honorable House*, etc. etc. Actual translation, *glorified gofer*. On a scale of one-to-five in importance, probably a low 3 on a good day."

"Many thanks," Chris said.

"He *will* be interested in learning how the story ends … " she added.

"I'll stay in touch," Chris said. "We may have further need of your services."

"We live to serve," she said.

"We've got a problem," Chris said.

"The attaché case," I answered. "Rafik will claim that it's a diplomatic pouch."

"Yes. We won't see the money going in or the documents coming out. It's like a little bit of sovereign Saudi turf."

"They're always more grandiose in the movies," I said. "Special wax seals. Hand-tooled leather with silver-plated handcuffs attached to the diplomat's wrist … that sort of thing. We had a lecture about it once in an IR class at UCI. Technically, it's all about the seals and the stamps and the magic marks. It's not about the form of the case or the so-called *pouch* itself. The Russians have claimed tractor trailers to be diplomatic pouches. And as you know, Chief, governments have shipped drugs in them and, for that matter, bodies."

"We're still in a bind, Tom," Chris responded. "Donnelly isn't stupid. The moment Rafik enters the building he'll be spirited into some secure space. It will only take a moment or two for Rafik to show him the money and he and Byrne to show Rafik the documents. The attaché case will be opened and closed and instantly off-limits. If we charge in now they'll stuff a copy of the Vienna Convention down our throats and laugh as we leave the building. Donnelly will say that he has prepared a report for the Saudi government, that no laws have been broken, and that we should all have a nice day. We won't be able to prove him right or wrong."

"Give me a second or two, Chief," I said. "We may not be able to take him down for this offense, but we can complicate his life a little and maybe buy some time."

"How?" he asked.

"Just let me make a couple of calls."

SEVENTY-FIVE

Twenty-five minutes later the doors of the Griffith Industries' head-quarters building opened and two aides stood at the sides as Moam-mar Rafik emerged. Donnelly was walking behind him. Rafik turned, the two shook hands, exchanged pleasantries, bowed ceremonially and parted. Donnelly went back in the building. Jeffords said that he could see Byrne standing in the shadows along with a Latino man—Luis Alvarez.

"The party's over," Chris said.

"Hopefully it's just beginning," I said, as the KABC News van drove into the complex, along with a satellite truck and a brightly-marked sedan. They blocked the roadway and Melanie Patterson got out of the sedan. She was carrying a hand mike and giving directions to two cameramen and some tech support people.

"The Fourth Estate," Chris said. "Someone must have called in a tip."

"The public has a right to know," I said, "especially if their government's secrets are being sold to a foreign power."

"Bad guys skulking in corners probably fear *them* more than they fear us."

"They'll at least be hesitant to shoot," I said, "especially with the cameras rolling."

"Let's go down and have a look," Chris said. "Don't flash your shield until we have to."

The sky was overcast, but Melanie Patterson was ready for any eventuality, blasting the Saudi Consulate limo with bright lights. The driver's window rolled down and the man began yelling, "You must move those vehicles. This is an official consulate limousine. You may not obstruct us!"

To Melanie Patterson this was the same as saying 'this way to a good story'; she approached the driver's window and looked into the backseat. "Mr. Rafik, I must speak with you. Now."

He spoke to her in quieter tones than the driver had; fortunately we were close enough by now to hear him. He saw us approach but turned back toward her and continued speaking. "This is a diplomatic vehicle on an official mission," he said. "You may not obstruct us in this way!"

She moved slightly to the side so that her cameraman could come in for a closeup of Rafik's face.

"We have received a report that your party is in grave danger," she said. "You should exit the vehicle now."

"That is preposterous," he said. "We are in no grave danger, as you call it. We are conducting official business and you are concocting false reports to create false stories!"

"Mr. Rafik," she said, "Griffith Industries is under suspicion of conducting fraudulent enterprises. A number of their associates have been murdered. This information has been verified with the authorities."

She then put the microphone two inches from his lips.

"I have no idea what you're talking about," he said. "We take full responsibility for our own affairs. Please move your vehicles immediately!"

At that point Chris and I stepped forward and showed him our shields. "Mr. Rafik," Chris said, "I must ask you and the members of your party to step out of your vehicle now. This is for your own safety, sir."

He got out of the limo, visibly upset but trying to control his emotions as the KABC cameras focused on him. "Can't you do something about them?" he said to Chris.

Classic good cop/bad cop, I thought to myself. Except that the press is the bad cop. What's not to like here?

"Please," Chris said, holding up his hand in the general direction of Melanie Patterson and her crew. He then put his hand on Rafik's shoulder and walked him a few yards away from the car. "I don't know who has been communicating with her," he said, "but what she says is essentially correct. Griffith Industries is under suspicion of criminal activity and individuals connected with them have been the victims of violent death. I will be very blunt with you, sir … "

"Yes … I appreciate that," Rafik said.

"Our belief is that whenever Mr. Donnelly's organization conducts its business, they protect themselves from all possible adverse effects."

"What are you saying?"

"What I am saying is that they will protect themselves against any testimony that you might give and any evidence that you might adduce."

"Speak plainly," Rafik said. He was now visibly rattled.

"Whatever Mr. Donnelly has given you may contain an explosive that would eliminate both you and whatever evidence might remain."

"I saw the materials," he said. "They were placed in a small envelope. There *is* no explosive."

"Mr. Rafik, we do not have a great deal of time here. All of our lives are currently at risk. A bomb made of Semtex with a detonating cap can be placed in a space the size of a greeting card. A few pounds of it will destroy a multi-storied building. It would take very, very little to destroy an automobile and the individuals inside it."

"What do you propose to do?" he said.

"We will remove the attaché case from your vehicle and check it for explosive devices. When we are satisfied that it is safe we will return it to you and let you be on your way."

"That is out of the question," he said. "That is a diplomatic bag, a *valise diplomatique.* You may not touch it and you may not obstruct the individual carrying it!"

SEVENTY-SIX

While Chris was talking to Rafik, I hurried over and spoke with the LAPD liaison. When I returned Rafik was still raving about the diplomatic bag and the fact that we could not touch it.

"Mr. Rafik," I said, "with all due respect, sir. I have spoken with the LAPD liaison officer and he concurs with me. Under normal circumstances the diplomatic bag would be sacrosanct. These, however, are not normal circumstances, sir. The law enforcement agencies carry the responsibility for public safety. That includes your safety, sir. It also includes the safety of the Griffith Industries employees you see behind you. It includes the safety of the press corps, the police officials and the residents of this area. It also includes the safety of the individuals traveling the streets and freeways of the city. We have no intention of disturbing your property. We *must*, however, insure that it is free of explosive devices."

Rafik was still sputtering, but I could see in the corner of his eyes a glimmer of suspicion that Donnelly might actually have betrayed him, or at least, planted some insurance in the brief case that would enable him to cut his losses in the case of unanticipated difficulties.

"What do you propose to do?" Rafik asked. "The case cannot leave my possession."

"The bomb squad has already been called," I said. "They will inspect the case to insure that it does not contain any explosive devices."

"They absolutely cannot open it."

"They will use a dog trained to smell explosives."

That seemed to quiet him, at least for the moment.

"In the meantime, we must move the vehicle and the case to a position that does not jeopardize your party, the Griffith Industries employees, the press corps and the police."

"What do you mean?" he asked.

"The hill to the northwest, sir. The land is vacant beyond it. The hill will serve as an appropriate barrier in the event of an explosion. We will simply drive the vehicle, with the case, around to the other side of the hill, park it, and wait for the bomb squad."

"It cannot leave my sight."

"Sir, I prefer that you remain here."

"I repeat; it **cannot** leave my sight."

"Very well, but you will have to position yourself at a safe distance from the vehicle. I cannot be responsible for your unnecessary injury or death. Officer ... "

I signaled to Hector, but did not call him by name. "Drive this vehicle to the other side of the hill to the northwest of us. Park it; open the rear door and leave immediately. The bomb squad will then come and inspect the case."

Hector drove off and I walked a few feet with Rafik. "I very much appreciate your understanding of our responsibilities in this regard, sir."

"Yes. Now let us hurry to the observation point, so that I may insure that the vehicle is not disturbed."

"Of course. "It is very dusty, sir, and we will need to have some concealment in the event of an explosion." I called over one of the uniforms, who secured two sets of coveralls from the trunk of his cruiser. "I believe that these will work well, sir," I said.

He handed his suit jacket to one of his aides and put on the coveralls. I handed my jacket to the uniformed officer and put on my set. "It is a somewhat arduous climb, sir, but it will only take us a few minutes."

By the time we got to the top of the adjoining hill and positioned ourselves in a crevice that still afforded a line of sight to the vehicle, more than ten minutes had elapsed. The rear door on the far side of the vehicle was open; Hector was nowhere to be seen.

"He left the door open on the far side in case of an explosion," I said.

"Yes, yes, I understand," he replied.

"It shouldn't take long for the bomb squad to get here," I said. "Hopefully there will be no explosives present and you will be able to secure your property and return to the Consulate."

I called Hector on my cellphone. "Yes, officer. Mr. Rafik and I will be observing the vehicle, waiting for the bomb squad. Would you please bring us some bottled water?"

"That is unnecessary," he said.

"A mild precaution, sir," I responded. "It is warm, particularly with the coveralls, and a small amount of refreshment will be appreciated."

"Very well," he said.

I met Hector a few yards from the crest of the hill. We spoke briefly as he handed me the bottles of water. Rafik took the bottle from me, grunted something in appreciation, and then turned to continue observing the car. Eight minutes later the bomb squad vehicle appeared. "There they are, " I said, "over there, to the east."

Their arrival seemed to comfort him. "There are actually two training sites for the bomb squad," I said. "The team receives constant reports of suspicious activities, many of them, of course, unfounded. Los Angeles is a large city and people are always finding things that look like bombs or sticks of dynamite. Often they're just flares. Sometimes they find things like grenades, most inert, of course. The bomb squad is highly trained, as is their K9 unit."

"Dogs, you mean."

"Yes, sir," I said. "They also have a whole host of robotic devices, in the event that the presence of explosives is detected … "

The members of the bomb squad pulled up in their modified bus. They exited the vehicle and put on protective gear. I could see Hector speaking with them. One of them brought out a large German Shepherd on a thick leash. He was the dog's trainer. While I watched I unscrewed the cap of the water bottle Hector had given me. I wasn't thirsty, but I wanted to draw some of Rafik's attention and take his mind off of the proceedings below. I took a drink and said, "that tastes good," then replaced the cap. He left his unopened bottle beside him in the grit, perhaps to impress me with his manliness.

He scooted forward as the trainer and dog approached the vehicle. The leash was long, at least fifteen feet, and the trainer kept at a distance from the vehicle, while the dog jumped right into the back seat and began to sniff the attaché case.

Then he barked, loudly and insistently.

"What does that mean?"

"I don't know," I said. I took out my cellphone and called Hector.

"Yes, officer … " I said, "the dog's barking … what does that indicate? … Yes, I see … I see … "

"*What* do you see?" Rafik yelled at me.

"The dog has detected the presence of explosives," I said.

"What?"

"That's what he said," I answered.

"This is preposterous!"

"Just a second," I said. I continued to listen to the voice at the other end of my cellphone, as Rafik's small amount of patience continued to fray.

"I've been speaking with my junior officer," I said. "The members of the bomb squad understand the nature of the case—the fact that it is a diplomatic bag … "

"Yes?"

"They propose that they remove it from the car, using a robotic device. They will then use another robotic device to open it for further inspection (in your presence, should you so desire) or simply detonate it."

"I must be there and see it," he said.

"They will ask you to sign a waiver concerning your personal safety," I said. "Their standard procedure would be to detonate the case."

"No, I will not permit that."

"You could always just ask Mr. Donnelly for another copy of the documents he provided you."

"I prefer not to do that," he said. "I do not believe that there are any explosives in the case."

"Your choice," I said. "We wish to be as cooperative as possible, Mr. Rafik."

"Yes," he said, standing up and leaving the bottle of water behind him as if it was somehow unclean or beneath his dignity to retrieve it.

Then came the flash and the shock wave, as the roof of the car rose ten feet in the air in a cloud of fiery smoke and the doors blew off their hinges as the windows shattered, spraying the surrounding earth with shards of glass and steel.

SEVENTY-SEVEN

For a moment he stood still, waves of emotion passing over his cheeks and eyes and forehead. First fear, then shock and finally realization. Perhaps even a bit of relief. Then he began hurrying down the hill.

"We can't approach it immediately," I said.

"And why not? Our property has already been destroyed."

"Because it's common practice to have multiple bombs," I said. "The first detonation draws a crowd of gawkers and onlookers. The second inflicts additional damage."

"That's preposterous," he said.

"Mr. Rafik, that's reality, as you should well know."

He started to respond, but then stopped. When he reached the bottom of the hill he was met by Chris Dietrich. "We'll wait to see if there is a secondary explosion," Chris said. "The bomb squad is responsible for everything at this point."

Chris then proceeded to tell him that full reports would be provided to the Saudi Consulate and that he would be available to speak to Rafik's superiors. Rafik seemed to back off from this, probably because he was aware that he had acted alone or that he had acted ineptly. Eventually he became cooperative, if not actually contrite.

They were standing at a considerable distance from the remains of the car, but they could see the members of the bomb squad gesturing and talking among themselves. The dog who had been trained to smell explosives was sitting at the right heel of its trainer, patiently waiting for directions.

I asked Rafik if I could get him any water. He said no and I dissolved into the crowd, looking for Hector. Meanwhile, the Saints who had functioned as guards for Donnelly had moved to the front of the headquarters building and were standing there, arrayed like a picket line. Melanie Patterson was on a live feed to her studio, pointing, gesturing, and chattering away for the home audience. By now some other press vehicles had arrived. She intermittently stared at the remains of the Saudi limo, waiting, perhaps, for a second detonation as the cameras panned between the closeup of her and the activities of the bomb squad in the distance.

Hector found me a few moments later. We moved behind one of the cruisers, out of the line of sight of Rafik.

"Excellent work," I said. "Perfection."

"Thanks," he said.

"What have we got?"

"Very strange," he said.

"How so?"

"There was a flash drive and, with it, a set of passwords and codes for gaining access to the data inside."

"You're thinking that Rafik should have been given the passwords and codes separately."

"Yes, but he must have been counting on the diplomatic immunity bit, figuring that no one would possibly be able to see the two together. The codes are also complex, not the sort of thing that could be easily memorized. He probably thought that he would simply be driven back to the consulate, where he would pocket the codes and the flash drive. So long as either one was secure, he would be fine. In the meantime, he didn't want to open up the attaché case in front of his gofers."

"So were you able to download the data?"

"Oh yeah. No problem. It's all on my laptop. I had to force open the attaché case to remove the drive and the card with the codes, but since the whole thing was going to go up in a cloud of flame anyway, that was no problem. One of the advance men from the bomb squad put a nice lump of C-4 in the case. I doubt that there's a single square inch of leather still intact."

"Did you have a chance to look at any of the material that was on the flash drive?"

"Very briefly. It was highly technical, of course—lots of numbers, lots of arcs and angles. Most important, there was Diatom's name and a contract number at the bottom of one of the photographed pages. Byrne must have overlooked that. Dumbass. Thank God for stupid opponents. I'm just guessing, but from what I was able to see in a matter of a minute or two it looks as if the documents had to do with a missile intercept system. You want another guess?"

"Sure."

"The Israelis are anxious to protect themselves from anything incoming ... so are we and we're willing to share the technology with them. The other side would like to breach the system."

"Trying to stay a step ahead," I said. "So Rafik's either operating on behalf of the Saudis, who are operating on behalf of another organization or country or he's simply an entrepreneur, taking some goodies home with him to auction off to the highest bidder."

"Right," Hector said. "He *was*, at least. Now he's personally expendable and he has to explain the loss of a pretty pricey set of wheels."

"I love it," I said, "I love every bit of it," but then paused before saying anything else. Behind the column of press vehicles further clogging the road was a Toyota Avalon. It was new and maroon. It was Walter Randall's car.

He got out and approached us. I walked toward him, stopped him and told him that he really shouldn't be here now. "It's obvious that something important is happening," he said. "I wanted to be here . . . to see the resolution."

"How did you know about this?" I asked.

"We have technology to observe the movement of vehicles on

Mars, Lieutenant," he said. "It wasn't very difficult to see a flurry of activity … including an explosion … in Calabasas."

"So you've been observing Griffith Industries as closely as we have."

"Twenty four hours a day, seven days a week," he said.

"I really don't think you should be here," I said.

"Don't worry, I won't interfere," he said. "I'm just here for Terry and Susan. Just a set of eyes and ears … witnessing. I have a feeling that you have a lot of things to report to me, but that this is not a good time. Don't worry. I'll be patient. I'll stay out of everyone's way."

"I think that that would be a very good idea, for your own safety also," I said.

"I understand," he said. "I'll pull my car off the road."

As he walked away Hector put his hand on my shoulder for a moment and we walked toward Chris.

"Chief," I said, so that Rafik could hear me, "the bomb squad believes that it is safe to proceed with the inspection."

Chris allowed Rafik to accompany him, but they stood more than a hundred yards from the remains of the vehicle. The trainer brought the German Shepherd forward and inspected the vehicle. This time the dog did not bark. Then the rest of the team moved in. A few minutes later one of them approached the Chief and Rafik. "It's available for your inspection, sir," he said.

Chris was deferential to Rafik. "Why don't you accompany me?" he said.

"Certainly," Rafik answered.

When they got there, of course, there was nothing left of the attaché case and nothing left of the seat on which it had been resting. "Plastic," the bomb tech said. "A small amount can bring a world of hurt."

Chris and Rafik walked away from the car. "It's up to you, sir," he said, "but it would be my advice to you to consult with your head of mission before proceeding further with any dealings with Griffith Industries."

"Uh … yes," he said.

"We can make a vehicle and driver available to take you and your associates back to the Consulate," he said. "It would help minimize publicity … "

"I … appreciate that," he said.

Five minutes later they were driving out of the compound. I briefed Chris on what I had learned from Hector, who was standing a few feet away. "Well," he said, "we've got the army here. Let's not stop now."

SEVENTY-EIGHT

"First let's clear out the civilians," Chief Dietrich said. "The press won't really leave, but let's move them at least a hundred yards from the perimeter. In some ways I like having them here; it keeps the Saints honest. At the edge of the perimeter I want a line of LAPD officers blocking the road. The rest of them will accompany us when we approach the building. Their job will be to dissuade the Saints from taking any action against us and to keep them on the outside of the building. The LBPD will enter with us. However, I want a small team led by Hector to enter the building from the rear. They can pick up any stragglers and block the exit in case some of Donnelly's people decide to make a run for it.

"My guess is that Donnelly's on the horn to an army of lawyers, preparing himself for his next steps. He's received reports from the Saints on the outside and he's probably talked to Rafik, disavowing any knowledge of the explosives and blaming the whole thing on us, calling it a stunt. Tom and I both believe he'll try to bluff his way out of this, but if he has other plans … if he wants a shooting war … let's not be shy about giving him one. He's outmanned and outgunned and if he tries to make a stand rather than let his lawyers fight for him … well … it has a simplicity to it that might ultimately be preferable. Let's be careful … but let's not be afraid to be … *definitive.*"

When the Saints saw the LAPD officers with automatic rifles they held their ground but didn't reach inside their jackets. Then they stood silently as they were disarmed and moved to a holding area. Chris and I led the remaining group into the building, where we were greeted by a very tense receptionist. "They're in the conference room," she said. "It's just up the open staircase … on the landing … on the right."

The conference room had a wall of glass overlooking the rest of the industrial park. The table had seating for at least twenty, but there were only three individuals there: Donnelly, Byrne and Luis Alvarez. The room was calm, momentarily, but there were ugly things on the horizon. Donnelly was coiled in his seat; Byrne was twitching; Alvarez's eyes were sucking in the darkness. Chris entered the room first and called Byrne outside.

"You do *not* have to go with him," Donnelly said, his voice rising with each word. Byrne hesitated for a moment, but then got up from his seat and walked outside into the hallway. Chris closed the door behind him, took Byrne toward the stairwell, out of hearing range of those in the conference room, and braced him. "Clement Byrne," he said, "you are under arrest. You have the right to remain silent … "

After he read him his rights Byrne asked what he was being charged with. "Treason," Chris responded. "Get him out of here," he said to Jim Jeffords, who cuffed him and took him to one of the cruisers that had been brought up to the parking area in front of the building. We watched as the cruiser drove away, then reentered the conference room.

Donnelly spoke first. "You seem to have a great capacity to waste peoples' time," he said. "And the money of your sleepy little town. And your personal reputation. If you took anything from Mr. Rafik's diplomatic pouch it will not only be inadmissible as evidence in any case against him or Mr. Byrne; it will also be evidence of a serious crime perpetrated by yourself. I hope you are prepared to spend many years of your life in prison, for that is precisely what awaits you if you proceed with this."

"Wrong answer," Chris said. "You must be more frightened than I thought. If you *were* innocent, or calm enough to *pretend* that you were innocent, you would be protesting that all you did was give Rafik a report and that Byrne was here as a consultant, providing financial or other advice. If I then contradicted you, you would say that I couldn't possibly know what was in the attaché case because anything contained therein would be privileged. You might even flatter me, saying that you know that I would not breach diplomatic immunity, all the while thinking that the information would be inadmissible anyway. What you *did* say, instead, is tantamount to an admission of guilt. I find that very reassuring. Despicable, of course, but nonetheless reassuring. You're too tired to bluff and you've run out of lies."

"You can comfort yourself with the memory of this little moment of melodrama," Donnelly said. "You will have a great deal of time to fill when you're sitting in your prison cell or walking in the yard, dodging the knives of the men you helped put there earlier."

Chris just smiled. I looked at Alvarez, who was sitting impassively, staring through us. Then Chris ordered Donnelly to stand up. "Victor Donnelly," he said, "you are under arrest. You have the right to remain silent … "

"You didn't mention the crimes for which you are arresting me," he responded.

"Conspiracy to commit murder. Three counts. Conspiracy to commit treason. Conspiracy to perpetrate fraud. Arrogance. Pretentiousness. Poor fashion sense … "

"You'll lose that sense of humor," he said, "when my attorneys have finished with you."

"Cuff him," Chris said to Sergeant Dave Hendrix, "and get him out of here."

Again, I was watching Alvarez. He was seething, but trying not to show it. He knew that he would be next.

Just as Hendrix put the first cuff on Donnelly, Alvarez slid his right hand beneath the table top and pulled out an automatic pistol that had been hidden there. He aimed it at Chris's eyes as he stood up. "Remove the cuff," he said, "and all of you sit down. Mr. Donnelly and I will be exiting the building. Anyone who attempts to stop us will be killed."

"You were going to be next, Luis," Chris said. "Do you really want to prolong this? I can promise you that *you* will not leave this area alive unless you put down that weapon and surrender."

"You believe you know this area?" he said. "You believe that you have this area blocked? We shall soon see whether you do or not."

Chris directed Dave Hendrix to remove the cuff and Donnelly joined Alvarez. He was smiling broadly as Alvarez opened a panel on the wall behind them and began to back his way through it, his gun still aimed at Chris Dietrich.

Just as Alvarez stood at the panel's frame there was a blur of motion and a spray of bullets as Alvarez' weapon discharged into the ceiling. Donnelly was startled and blocking most of my view, but I could see a hand on Alvarez' forearm and a second hand near his neck. A second or two later Donnelly stumbled back into the room as if he had been kicked. He was groaning in pain when he fell to the floor. "Don't move," I said. All of us had our weapons out and aimed at him. Then we heard a thumping sound as Alvarez' body hit the frame of the panel on the other side of the wall. A few seconds later he staggered back into the room. There was no gun in his hand but the large handle of a weapon that looked like a tool of some kind protruded from the center of his throat. He was making gurgling sounds and blood was bubbling from his mouth and nose. When he fell face-first across the table the point of the weapon punctured the back of his neck and stood out, glistening with blood in the dusty light coming through the conference room windows.

Hector emerged from the shadows and entered the room. Officer Vic Morales was standing next to him. Vic was in riot gear, with heavy boots, at least one of which had found its way to Donnelly's back and kidney. Chris looked down at Donnelly who, by now, was convulsing on the conference room floor. "I told him he wouldn't be permitted to leave the area alive," he said. Then, leaning down, he said to Donnelly specifically, "None of you appear to be very good listeners. Sergeant … "

Dave Hendrix pulled Donnelly to his feet and cuffed him tightly. There was dust on Donnelly's jacket and tie and a rug burn across the edge of his forehead. He was still laboring to catch his breath. "Now where were we?" Chris said. "Oh yes … your arrest."

SEVENTY-NINE

Walter Randall's car was parked behind the press vans and sedans. Chris was being besieged by the members of the press corps as I approached Mr. Randall. "The chief has asked me to brief you," I said.

"Is it all over?"

"Yes," I said.

"If you can, I'd like you to come with me," he said. "I know a place. It's not close by, but I would prefer to do it this way."

"Of course," I said.

"It will take awhile."

"I have plenty of time now," I said.

He drove me to the Church of Our Savior in San Gabriel and the adjoining cemetery. "The church is Episcopal," he said, "the Patton family church, actually, but the cemetery is nondenominational. It's just here, Lieutenant ... "

He walked me to an estate lot that was demarcated by granite benches. "Terry and Susan are here," he said. "Just beneath us. Let's sit and you can tell me what happened. And please don't spare me the details, Lieutenant."

After a few moments I began. "The wine operation was largely fraudulent; the authentic wine all came from Donnelly's own cellar. The legitimate bottles were used as window dressing at the storage facility and for sale to a small number of actual buyers whose testimony could be used later to authenticate the operation. The fraudulent wine cases were used to transport contraband--drugs, in most instances--usually for sale on the streets by a local youth gang. Several of Donnelly's former associates were involved in the operation, using corporate headquarters or offices as secure transaction points. In some instances the material exchanged was of a much more sensitive nature—classified government documents that were sold to foreign powers or terrorist organizations."

"And Terry found out."

"I don't believe he would have known all of the details, but he expressed his suspicions and objections. His wife was seized … are you certain you want to hear the details of this, Mr. Randall?"

"Yes, I am certain, Lieutenant."

"She was seized and held in a room in Richmond's house, where she was subjected to … violent treatment. Pictures were sent to Terry's cellphone in an attempt to force him to comply with their requests. When he resisted further, both he and his wife were murdered."

"And they took off her hand to conceal the fact that they had been torturing her there."

"Yes," I said.

"And you have evidence of this."

"Yes. Richmond was a reluctant dupe, anxious to make money but not realizing the enormity of the situation in which he had become involved. Beauchamp was hired to keep an eye on Richmond and report back to Donnelly, but he didn't have the stomach for the … for the violence."

"And one of them retained the evidence that will enable you to convict Donnelly."

"Yes, Beauchamp. Richmond helped him do this, before he himself committed suicide."

"So he actually did kill himself."

"Yes, he did."

"And what of the diplomats, the Saudis?"

"We're not yet certain if the Consulate was involved, Mr. Randall. It may be that the one individual there—the one at Griffith Industries this morning—was the person involved."

"And surely they'll plead that you can't use the evidence because it was held in a diplomatic pouch."

"Yes, they'll plead that, but Byrne (the supplier) has no way of knowing what actually happened. He doesn't know whether, in fact, the pouch *did* contain an explosive in case that the operation failed or whether the explosive came from ... the authorities in law enforcement."

"All he knows then is that you have evidence linking him with treasonous activities."

"Yes."

"And the Saudi might have actually turned on him and Donnelly. He might have surrendered the documents to you."

"Yes."

"Or the documents might have actually fallen from the case without your making an effort to take them."

"Yes."

"Or that the courts might actually find in your favor and rule that you had justifiable cause in breaching the diplomatic immunity."

"Yes, that would be a long shot, of course, but in any case, he did not know. All that he knows is that there is evidence available to convict him of treason. Officers are now in the process of seizing his computers and files, both at home and at his office at the engineering firm. There may be incriminating material there, which makes it unnecessary to use the material found this morning. In any case, he knows that he is guilty; he knows that we know that he is guilty and he knows the penalty for his crimes. He is positioned to cooperate with us."

"And his testimony will help cement your case against Donnelly."

"Yes, but we already have enough from Beauchamp to convict. Donnelly will be executed. It happens very rarely in California and it will take time as he exhausts his appeals but he *will* go down. I'm sure of that.

Byrne will be in prison for life; whether or not he will be executed I can't say at this point."

"And the killer, Lieutenant, the person who actually murdered my son and his wife?"

"A former gang leader, Mr. Randall, a man named Alvarez. We have that on Beauchamp's testimony."

"And did he also kill the other deliveryman and torture Susan?"

"Yes, sir; he did."

"I saw a body taken out from the building this morning … "

"Yes, sir. That was Alvarez."

"And he is dead."

"Yes, sir. He is dead."

"And how did he die, may I ask?"

"He resisted arrest. He had a loaded weapon. In his attempt to escape he was overcome by one of my officers."

"And he himself was shot?"

"No, sir, he was not shot."

"Lieutenant … ?"

"He was stabbed through the throat with a sharpened screwdriver."

"Your officer was carrying a sharpened screwdriver?"

"It's not something we would wish to see made public," I said.

"Of course not. The handle would have provided a great deal of leverage, would it not? Knives are made to cut, but screwdrivers are made to grip. I can see the advantages … and in any case there would have been time before he actually expired … time in which to realize that he had been captured and that there would be no … further… alternatives. It's crucial, I think … "

"Sir … ?"

"For the justice … the realization of the nature of the crime, of the resulting guilt and of the just punishment."

"In his case there was a history of violent acts, sir. This settled many debts."

He rose and took me by the hand and put his left hand on top. "I will tell my wife," he said, "and Susan's mother. I won't speak of the details, but I will assure them that our children died in an important cause, that they kept faith with the values to which they had always adhered and that those who did this to them were dealt with professionally and … appropriately."

"Thank you, sir," I said.

Then he did something unexpected, something that touched my heart, before he walked to his car and drove away.

EIGHTY

Two weeks had passed and, with them, much of the press interest in Griffith Industries. Two actresses had emerged unrepentant from forced rehab, gasoline prices had spiked and then ebbed and there had been a 4.8 quake in Palm Springs—more than enough to seize the attention of the members of the fourth estate. Clement Byrne and Victor Donnelly were now in the hands of federal authorities who promised to interrogate them 'for some period of time'. Carlton Beauchamp was being held without bail in California, but he remained the most likely of the three to see the outside world again before he would need a cane or walker in order to do so. Luis Alvarez had been cremated but no one as yet had stepped forward to receive the remaining ashes and bone fragments in the simple metal canister.

Chris, Hector and I had had a celebratory dinner with the leaders of the LAPD units which had helped us with the case. This included a surprise visit from Bo, the German Shepherd whose trainer had directed him to bark, once the explosives were present and remain silent after the detonation. He was trained to do that, of course, but he also responded to voice commands, just in case. Bo received the same steak that the rest of us ate and seemed to enjoy it a great deal, even though it disappeared a few seconds after the separate pieces of it were put on the plate in front of him. He was too disciplined to beg for scraps, but he received many of them nonetheless.

A few days later the three of us gathered again. We had been busy with other casework, work which had been temporarily set aside while we were focusing on FirstGrowth and Griffith Industries. Beauchamp had urged us to secure some of Donnelly's wine from FirstGrowth, arguing that we wouldn't need all of it as evidence and that the wine was innocent, even if its owner had not been. Chris passed on the offer. "There's still a moral taint," he said, "if only by association and I don't want to be touched by it."

Instead, we had some premium tequila in a handsome decanter, which Hector had furnished, and some food provided by Ramón, his old friend, fellow Bboy and now chef. Ramón refused any reimbursement. He had lost a younger brother to Luis Alvarez a decade earlier and wished to contribute to our efforts in his own way. He prepared some beef for us which he had marinated in a special sauce and then cooked to order. The ingredients were simple and fresh and the meal was delicious. His sister had provided sopapillas with cinnamon sugar and honey. Hector insisted that I have more tequila than I would normally have consumed. "Sometimes a headache is only a headache," he said. "We have all earned a good one."

"I spoke to Mr. Randall today," Chris said. "He has met with the members of the family and they have had a second service at the cemetery. They are still distraught, of course, but they are moving toward a growing sense of peace. They told me to thank both of you, especially Hector. He promised to say nothing about the specific nature of … Alvarez's … demise."

"I wanted to say something to you about that, Chief," Hector said. "I know that my methods are sometimes … unconventional … "

"No need," Chris said. "Mr. Randall described it as an *on-the-spot correction* and an ingenious use of a *field expedient*. That works for me."

"He's a good man," I said, "Mr. Randall … Hector also, of course."

"He was controlling himself very carefully," Chris said. "I knew of his military background. I thought that he had been in the Corps of Engineers. He was, but he was also assigned to the Special Forces for a time. He didn't just come to Griffith Industries to observe. He came to help. I asked him—off the record, of course—what he had been carrying in the trunk of his Toyota and he said that it would probably be better if he didn't comment on that."

"Something far worse than that ... implement ... that I happened to ... *find*," Hector said.

"I think so," Chris said. "Probably something capable of blowing up the better part of the west Valley."

"So he was like an angel," I said, "looking over us and looking after us."

"A quite lethal one, I think," Chris answered. "He said that his son was the bravest member of their family. From what I know of the father's record the son was being judged against a very high standard."

"Interesting, isn't it," Hector said, as he refilled all of our glasses. "We sit here in this comfortable room, in these comfortable chairs, with this wonderful food, and all around us there are monsters and there are angels. We go out every morning trying to find out which is which. Still ... " he said, smiling, "it is better than being a roofer, no?"

Chris and I were forced to laugh. "You're right, Hector," I said. "I didn't tell either of you this yet ... but after it was over ... when I sat down with Mr. Randall ... Colonel Randall, I suppose I should say ... in the cemetery, where his son and his son's wife were buried ... we talked and then finished. He thanked me ... and when we rose ... he stepped back and he saluted me. I returned his salute. I didn't know what else to do or say. Then he put his hand on my shoulder, squeezed it, smiled faintly ... and left."

"Solidarity," Hector said. "The army of the good. They hear the whispers of the dead and their prayers for justice."

"I don't believe I've ever heard you be so philosophic before, Hector," Chris said.

"It's Ramón's *carne asada*," he said, "and perhaps--I admit it--the tequila. It always makes me sad and happy in a special way."

"I felt a little guilty," I said, "implicating the dog in our ... *plan.*

He seemed so ... honest ... so simple in his feelings ... ready to obey ... ready to please ... regardless of what was asked of him."

"He's a soldier too," Hector said. "Did you see him with that steak? He would have made fast work of Alvarez's throat. We should be thankful that he was on *our* side."

He refilled our glasses again. "Let's drink to that," I said, "to *our side*, the side of the angels, the side with the hopes, the dreams, the prayers for the innocent ... and the *field expedients* for those who hurt them."

"Indeed," Chris said, and clinked our glasses with his, being careful not to spill any of Hector's tequila.

www.ingramcontent.com/pod-product-compliance
Lightning Source LLC
Chambersburg PA
CBHW061304190726
48288CB00002B/342